HAPPY

PEOPLE

IN

TEARS

PORTUGUESE IN THE AMERICAS SERIES

Portuguese-Americans and Contemporary Civic Culture in Massachusetts
Edited by Clyde W. Barrow

Through a Portagee Gate
Charles Reis Felix

In Pursuit of Their Dreams: A History of Azorean Immigration to the United States Jerry R. Williams

Sixty Acres and a Barn Alfred Lewis

Da Gama, Cary Grant, and the Election of 1934 Charles Reis Felix

Distant Music Julian Silva

Representations of the Portuguese in American Literature Reinaldo Silva

The Holyoke Frank X. Gaspar

Two Portuguese-American Plays
Paulo A. Pereira and Patricia A. Thomas
Edited by Patricia A. Thomas

Tony: A New England Boyhood
Charles Reis Felix

Community, Culture and the Makings of Identity: Portuguese-Americans Along the Eastern Seaboard
Edited by Kimberly DaCosta Holton and Andrea Klimt

The Undiscovered Island
Darrell Kastin [Out of Print]

So Ends This Day: The Portuguese in American Whaling 1765–1927
Donald Warrin

Azorean Identity in Brazil and the United States: Arguments about History, Culture, and Transnational Connections João Leal
Translated by Wendy Graça

Move Over, Scopes and Other Writings Julian Silva

The Marriage of the Portuguese (Expanded Edition) Sam Pereira

Home Is an Island Alfred Lewis

Land of Milk and Money
Anthony Barcellos

The Conjurer and Other Azorean Tales Darrell Kastin

Almost Gone Brian Sousa

Land, As Far As the Eye Can See: Portuguese in the Old West
Donald Warrin and Geoffrey L. Gomes

Another City upon a Hill: A New England Memoir Joseph A. Conforti

Happy People in Tears João de Melo
Preface by Onésimo T. Almeida
Translated by Elizabeth Lowe with Deolinda Adão

HAPPY PEOPLE IN TEARS

a novel

JOÃO DE MELO

Preface by Onésimo T. Almeida

Translated by Elizabeth Lowe

with Deolinda Adão

Tagus Press · UMass Dartmouth · Dartmouth, Massachusetts

PORTUGUESE IN THE AMERICAS SERIES 23

Tagus Press at UMass Dartmouth
www.portstudies.umassd.edu
© 1988 João de Melo; translation © 2015
Elizabeth Lowe
Published by arrangement
with Publicações Dom Quixote
All rights reserved
Manufactured in the United States of America
General Editor: Frank F. Sousa
Series Editor: Antonio Luciano Tosta
Managing Editor: Mario Pereira
Copyedited by Deborah Heimann
Designed by Mindy Basinger Hill
Typeset in Adobe Jenson Pro

This book was published with the support
of the Government of the Azores

REGIÃO AUTÓNOMA DOS AÇORES
SECRETARIA REGIONAL DA EDUCAÇÃO E CULTURA
Direção Regional da Cultura

For all inquiries, please contact:
Tagus Press at UMass Dartmouth
Center for Portuguese Studies and Culture
285 Old Westport Road
North Dartmouth, MA 02747-2300
Tel. 508-999-8255
Fax 508-999-9272
www.portstudies.umassd.edu

Library of Congress Cataloging-
in-Publication Data

Melo, João de.
 [Gente feliz com lágrimas. English]
 Happy people in tears : a novel / João de Melo ;
preface by Onésimo T. Almeida ; translated by
Elizabeth Lowe with Deolinda Adão.
  pages   cm. — (Portuguese in the
   Americas series ; 23)
 Originally published in Portuguese
 (Lisboa : Publicações Dom Quixote :
  Círculo de Leitores, 1988).
 Summary: "This is perhaps the most important
Portuguese Language novel written on the theme
of Immigration. It follows the joys and pains,
triumphs, and tragedies of an Azorean family's
search for a better life in Canada and their
changing relationship to the place of their birth
and those left behind" — Provided by publisher.
 ISBN 978-1-933227-64-1 (pbk. : alk. paper)
 1. Azoreans—Fiction. 2. Portuguese—Canada—
Fiction. 3. Immigrant families—Fiction.
4. Canada—Fiction. 5. Domestic fiction.
 I. Almeida, Onésimo Teotónio, writer of preface.
   II. Lowe, Elizabeth, 1947– translator.
   III. Adão, Deolinda, translator. IV. Title.
 PQ9275.E448G4613 2015
 869.3'42—dc23   2014042365

5 4 3 2 1

CONTENTS

Preface, or a Short Introduction to an Unknown World
ONÉSIMO T. ALMEIDA · ix

Translating Diaspora: The Polyphonic Novel of João de Melo
ELIZABETH LOWE · xiii

BOOK ONE · The Time When We Were All Together · 1

BOOK TWO · Third Person Singular · 185

BOOK THREE · Mama's Last Breath · 233

BOOK FOUR · The Other Version of Marta · 293

BOOK FIVE · The Invisible Return · 337

BOOK ZERO · Wise Happiness · 371

PREFACE, OR A SHORT INTRODUCTION
TO AN UNKNOWN WORLD

If this preface is meant to be of any relevance to the reader's enjoyment of this powerful novel by João de Melo, I am in trouble, because my words, whatever they may be, will not suffice to accomplish such a goal. How does one call a reader's attention to a world geographically so close to the United States yet so removed from it? Indeed, in spite of being relatively near the U.S. Northeast, and despite a two-hundred-year presence of Azorean communities in southeastern New England and in California, and, moreover, in spite of an important American military base on Terceira, one of its islands, the archipelago falls systematically out of range of the American radar. The Azores is a seemingly remote place, lost in the middle of the Atlantic, between New York and Lisbon. Not even the Americans traveling to and from Europe notice its existence. On their way to Europe, usually at night, everybody either sleeps or tries to find ways to entertain themselves. On the way back, following the direction of the sun, the proverbial clouds of the anticyclone hanging over the archipelago cover and blind our view of the islands. Once in a while, the very tip of the imposing Pico Mountain cuts across the thick layers of cotton-looking clouds. But the scenery goes mostly unnoticed. Actually, its majesty, like many beauties of that unique archipelago, can only be appreciated from below.

Yet so much lies underneath those clouds. A lot of it has actually been put in writing, yet it remains hidden in the Portuguese language, which, according to the writer Aquilino Ribeiro, is the mausoleum of a great literature. The Azoreans lived more than five hundred years of isolation from the rest of the world, tormented by storms, volcanoes, and earthquakes. Inevitably, all of that had to leave a mark on those islanders almost lost, or half-abandoned, in the middle of the wide and wild Atlantic Ocean. Some of their history has been depicted by fiction writers and great poets. Pedro da Silveira, one of those poets, and one who, like others, saw emigration to America as the only possible exit, captured the archipelago's isolation in five lines in an attempt to define "islandness." The poem is called simply "Island."

> Only this:
> Closed sky, hovering heron.
> Open sea. A distant boat's
> hungering prow eyeing forever
> those bountiful Californias.1

Not many Azorean writers have succeeded in breaking the sea barriers that separate them from their mainland readers. Not for lack of literary quality, but because for so long the islands were practically forgotten by Portugal, after they ceased to be a mandatory stop on the way back from Africa, Asia, and Brazil, during the centuries that the Portuguese were crossing and controlling the seas. Yet a sizeable number of writers have had their voices heard in the Portuguese mainland, where they can get a much wider readership as well as critical acceptance. Some of them have been duly recognized and their works celebrated and embraced by the mainstream Portuguese literature. This was, for instance, the case of the Azorean classic Vitorino Nemésio with his novel *Mau Tempo no Canal*,2 considered by many critics one of the best novels of twentieth-century Portuguese literature. Another example is *O Meu Mundo Não É Deste Reino* (*My World Is Not of This Kingdom*), by João de Melo, translated into English by Gregory Rabassa,3 the well-known translator of García Marquez's *One Hundred Years of Solitude*. (Rabassa deemed Melo's novel the greatest work of fiction he has read since Marquez's masterpiece.)

The English-speaking readers who are already familiar with João de Melo's writings and his discovery of magical realism in his native island, where the Government and the Church were for centuries a united front in the control of the hearts and minds of the inhabitants of that almost mythical archipelago, are in for a surprise. In *Gente Feliz com Lágrimas*, Melo's creativity brings him to a wider universe, one that follows the routes of the Azorean diaspora. There, the children of a poor Azorean family of nine get away from each other. Some go to mainland Portugal, but most move West in search of the bountiful Californias of Pedro da Silveira's poem. Even the parents emigrate to Canada, thus emptying completely their island nest and participating in the breaking up of the rigid norms and values of their safe old world, thus also contributing to the splitting and disintegration of a family. So much so that not even Nuno, the main character and narrator who travels to Vancouver to make a last visit to his dying mother, can any longer anymore identify with his kin, almost completely transformed, as he is, by the diasporic experience in the Anglo-American world. He is present at his mother's funeral, thus witnessing for himself the symbolic end of a family built within a bygone universe.

While Nuno Miguel is the key narrator, there are two others, his brother Luís Miguel, and his sister Maria Amélia, who tell their stories in their own voices. Through them, one reenters the world of *My World Is Not of This Kingdom* where the sociopolitical as well as deeply religious oppressive environment is now shown as experienced in the bones of a large family ruled by a dictatorial father, one who often resorts to violence to keep his house under control. It is not only the women in the family that are victimized. The only power there lies in the blind way in which the father vents his frustrations through the use of abusive force on everybody at home.

Then, the break-up unfolds. One by one, the children leave, the first ones to the mainland, searching for freedom, ironically, in the prisons of a seminary (Nuno Miguel) and of a convent (Maria Amélia), where their humiliation is the same, only the oppressing figures change. A fourth voice emerges in the final part of the novel and in the life of Nuno Miguel. It speaks harshly and is brutally realistic, as Nuno faces the outside world after the closed walls of the seminary. Love, gender conflicts, real-life dilemmas combine as a tsunami that the opening of the door to the modern world dumps on the face and shoulders of Nuno Miguel. Used to hardships since childhood, he manages to survive, thanks to his resilience and his ever-evolving desire to make sense of life, as well as to his eagerness to search for its meaning in the midst of so much adversity.

Gente Feliz com Lágrimas was widely read in Portugal when it appeared in 1988, and it won the four most important literary prizes awarded in the country. It won also a fifth prize, the Latin Union, which the author went to receive in Lima, Peru. Before this version in English, the novel has been translated into Spanish, Italian, French, Dutch, Romanian, Bulgarian, and, in part, into German.

Onésimo T. Almeida
BROWN UNIVERSITY

NOTES

1. Translation by George Monteiro in *The Sea Within: A Selection of Azorean Poetry*, edited by Onésimo T. Almeida (Providence, RI: Gávea-Brown, 1983).

2. Published in 1944 in Lisbon and translated by Francisco Cota Fagundes with the title *Stormy Isles: An Azorean tale* (Providence, RI: Gávea-Brown, 1994).

3. Minneapolis, MN: Aliform, 2003.

TRANSLATING DIASPORA:
THE POLYPHONIC NOVEL OF JOÃO DE MELO

Translating João de Melo's magnificent diaspora novel, *Gente Feliz com Lágrimas*, was one of the most challenging translation tasks I have undertaken, primarily because of the unique nature of the Azorean dialect, the terminology particular to the islands, and the historical context of the Salazar dictatorship: the colonial wars that Portugal was waging in its African colonies from 1961 to 1974 in the theaters of Angola, Portuguese Guinea, and Mozambique. As Onésimo T. Almeida has remarked, the islands have remained remote from the mainland and the rest of the world and few Azorean writers have been read by mainland Portuguese or in translation. While not officially considered to be separate languages, the differences between Portuguese dialects, of which Azorean Portuguese is one, are mostly in phonology, the frequency of usage of certain grammatical forms, and between formal and informal registers of speech. Lexical differences are numerous, however. There is a stark contrast between Brazilian Portuguese and the Portuguese of the Azores (considered a southern dialect of Portugal). These differences show up most clearly in lexicography and syntax.

The project required a good amount of research of the terms associated with the botany, ecology, economy, geography, geology, history, politics, and the culture and cuisine of the archipelago. The Autonomous Region of the Azores is composed of nine volcanic islands situated in the North Atlantic Ocean, 850 miles west of continental Portugal and about 1,196 miles southeast of Newfoundland. The main industries are agriculture, dairy farming, livestock ranching, fishing, and tourism. The islands are volcanic in origin, some active and some that have not been active since the islands were settled. Monte Pico, referenced often in the narrative, is the highest point with an altitude of 7,713 feet. Because the islands were settled sporadically over a period of two centuries, their culture, dialect, cuisine, and traditions vary considerably.

The grip of the Catholic Church on the islands and the constant merging of secular and sacred in the lives of Azoreans — the seminary was one of the only routes to social and economic mobility for Azorean youth — has had a deep influence on the evolution of the language and its cultural referents.

Adelaide Monteiro Batista, author of a study of the works of João de Melo, observes that time and space in the islands are not just physical phenomena but markers of an existential condition of intense suffering and the struggle between preserving the island identity and a desire to belong to the larger world. Thus time and space are elevated to the dimension of myth, and this tradition is a strong one in Azorean literature, culminating in João de Melo's *Gente Feliz com Lágrimas*. She notes that the idea of movement, as a human condition, takes on notable proportions in this literature. The mythical and emotional elements of the novel are important aspects that must be captured in any attempt to translate this work.

In addition to these considerations, the novel is polyphonic in structure. As described by Onésimo T. Almeida, the voices of the novel include those of Nuno Miguel, the main character, his brother Luís Miguel, and his sister Maria Amélia. Their voices are very different, reflecting their separate life journeys, levels of education, and gender perspective. Nuno Miguel is the family "poet" and intellectual; Maria Amélia is a nurse; Luís Miguel has done manual labor all his life. The last section of the novel consists of a duet between Nuno Miguel and his estranged wife, who launches the narrative into the present time and alters the register of the novel once again. The polyphony comes not only from the mix of narrative voices but from the rhythms and cadences of João de Melo's highly poetic and metaphorical literary style. Adelaide Monteiro Batista notes that language in the novel is a fusion of "varied and opposing voices that develop and illuminate each other, renew each other and silence each other in a process of mutuality and exclusion."[1]

Gente Feliz com Lágrimas has been widely recognized as an important modern Portuguese work, not only in Portugal, but around the world, with six extant translations into languages other than English. I hope that this English version will do honor not only to the masterful work of Gregory Rabassa, who translated *My World Is Not of This Kingdom* (2003), but also to the haunting "music" of the original. The title in English has prompted much discussion between the translator and the author. By way of explanation, "Gente Feliz com Lágrimas" refers to the Azorean immigrants who left the island in tears, sad to leave their homeland, but eager to find long-desired prosperity in their adopted countries. Their hard-won happiness is baptized in tears; indeed they will never return. The sense of the title also comes from an observation that one of Nuno's aunts makes about him: "What you have is a great wound in your eyes, son of my soul." This wound, those tears, are the expression of the Azorean soul.

I wish to dedicate this translation to my dear friend and fellow classmate at the Graduate Center of the City University of New York, Adelaide Monteiro Batista, who first introduced me to the work of João de Melo. Tragically, she was struck with Alzheimer's disease at a very young age. I am grateful to my collaborator, Deolinda Adão, director of Portuguese Studies at the UC Berkeley Institute of European Studies, lecturer at San José State University, and a specialist on Azorean culture and literature, for her assistance with validating terminological choices and cultural references. Finally, I appreciate the opportunity from Tagus Press for this assignment that has opened the door to João de Melo's world and allowed me to partner with him in this new interpretation of the work.

Elizabeth Lowe
CENTER FOR TRANSLATION STUDIES
UNIVERSITY OF ILLINOIS AT URBANA-CHAMPAIGN

NOTE

1. Adelaide Monteiro Batista, *João de Melo e a Literatura Açoriana* (Lisboa: Publicações Dom Quixote, 1993), 48 [my translation].

BOOK ONE

The Time

When

We Were

All Together

CHAPTER ONE

Any One of Us

I

With the exception of their names and colors, which had faded with time, the boats remained — the same ones that Papa had decided to take her to see close up for the first time on that happy day. There they were still, beached, hulls propped on the sand, the canvas partially covering their decks. There were the wheelhouses, the round portholes like fish eyes, and the same dried-out life preservers hanging from rusty hooks. When they left the dock — and the prow cut through the blue cloth of the Atlantic, heading for Lisbon — the same acidic rain was falling as it did in the evenings... Likewise, the very same cows were being herded at the loading docks, all destined for the slaughterhouses on the Continent. And the wailing of the crowd of people who stood there waving hankies in gestures of good-bye soon turned into a howl that ended up mingling with the sound of the wind on the high sea.

Then, one after the other, they saw the Island receding in the distance, the cloud-shrouded lights extinguishing little by little, wrapped in the veils of gray that fell from the sky. As the rolls of sea foam flowed in their wake, in a swath that blanketed the receding Island, the volcanic range slowly sank into the horizon. On the lee side of the wind and in the electric static surging through the maritime night the last view of the Island is the image of a frightened mare's head, thrashing on the crest of the ridge they call Pico da Vara. Everyone knows that it is drowning and it does so with a noble and superior bellow; at last the indomitable blade of the ocean sinks into the creature, and its ears, suddenly still, submerge...

And now that the years have confused the order and intensity of the emotions of that voyage to Lisbon, the difficulty is in reconstructing the names, the shapes, the shadows of the dark forms of the boats of long ago. Even the ones that gave way to the majestic cruise ships leave no trace. Nuno and Amélia recall the flags embroidered with nautical symbols and the enormous masts, with spreaders with steel shrouds attached to the topsails. Maria Amélia, unlike her brother, especially remembers the blue and yellow smokestacks. She can still hear the sound of the boilers and feel the salt on the sticky handrails that encircled the deck, but little else comes to her. Of the bucking quarterdecks she retains only a diffuse recollection, still and always clouded by the curse of seasickness. Whether blue, yellow, or muddy ochre eaten by rust, the colors are of little importance to her. She restricts herself to describing them disinterestedly. She doesn't want to recover that useless time, nor infect the memories that she might still retain, of these or of all the other boats, with bitterness. She harbors a mix of tenderness and terror for the boats. Nevertheless, she can't forget the sight of those living monuments, lying in ruins — with their coiled ropes, different decks, and enormous anchors forgotten next to the small outboard engines. The guillotine-style windows of the first-class cabin bring back these memories. She peered out of them so many times in vain, in the hope that someone would come to rescue her. The nuns had abandoned her in an airless cabin without portholes. A tomblike light shone over her headrest, there were little plastic bags for seasickness arranged neatly in an abandon-ship box, there was a narrow bunk and the particular mélange of smells that you only find on boats — saltpeter, hot tar, and the suffocating ammonia stench of the nearby latrines. Feeling intense vertigo, she heard the cries of the cows and goats, the guttural belch of vomiting, and the continuous lament of other women coming up from the hold. Then she felt the sea humming in the vibration of the cabin walls. And like an earthquake with no beginning and no end, the Atlantic storms lifted the vessel into the air and then dropped it like an empty trunk into the valleys between the giant, colliding waves. The sea did this with the same ease that long ago any one of us might be lifted by the wind to fly, not birdlike, but transformed into little winged creatures, blinded by the dust, only to land in the muddy ravines that cut through the trails of our childhood. The next minute, the convulsing seas again lifted and dropped this second ark. Terrifying craters appeared in the water, and the sea's jaws yawned to swallow the keel: an indescribable roar deafened the stone-gray night — never had God been so distant as on those days of infinite loneliness.

Relief came on a night at anchor in the Funchal Bay, with its Nativity-scene houses cradled at the top of the cliffs; she was lying half dead in a deck chair recently abandoned by someone who had disembarked and left it unoccupied on the deck. In the morning the boat departed at sunrise. Again Amélia found herself curled up into a ball in her bunk, head between her knees, and thank God that on the fifth day of her first and last death at sea, someone finally came to tell her that the luminous, magnificent city of Lisbon awaited them. Only then did she start to revive.

Nuno Miguel remembers perfectly the letters engraved on the pitch-black hulls, and also painted on the side of the large smokestacks. He remembers asking about those words, since it seemed to him that the names of the boats were bigger than the vessels themselves and whatever experiences he'd have at sea — the five coming voyages between Lisbon and Ponta Delgada would take so much out of him. On all the docks there were always piles of planks, mountains of logs, lead shipping containers, and sacks of wheat and sugar. There was always a little man up in the air, sitting in the cabin of each crane, in front of a panel of illuminated levers, keys, and buttons. This was another secret of the boats: for hours and hours, even if he was on the other side of the city, he could hear the grinding of pulleys, chains uncoiling to lift containers and to open holds, the teeth in their ratchets sounding like bones being crushed.

Sitting with Papa on the sea wall on Avenida Marginal, waiting for the boat to depart, on the incredibly long afternoon of that first November at sea with the pulsing of metal in the distance, the shifting of the stubborn gears on board, and his voice — he never really had a knack for tenderness, and because of this he used the same domineering tone as ever to demand that I eat something and stop sobbing:

"Psst, listen you! Stop blubbering, man. And blow your damn nose."

He'd like to know how to cry too, to be able to embrace his little boy, suddenly terrified at the proximity of the boat. But he wouldn't know how to do it without seeming ridiculous or scaring his children even more by suddenly acting like someone else. The most sensitive nerve in Papa's psyche was his decision that very morning to see him off, and Nuno kept applying pressure to it. When Nuno went to say his good-bye in the barn, Papa had stood for a moment looking him up and down. His head inclined till it was oblique on his neck, and Nuno saw how Papa's lips tightened and his eyes became almost sweet. He was almost certainly going to hug him tightly to his chest, without a word, or perhaps just limit himself to repeating some formulaic fatherly blessing, when suddenly Papa straightened his head, took Nuno by the hand and brought him into the kitchen. There Papa faced Mama's tearful eyes and took in the clamor of the sadness of the entire family and barked:

"Bring me my Sunday boots, my jacket, and some clean pants. I am going to take the little one to the boat, so he won't get lost there in the city."

Besides this, Amélia added, one had the impression that the boats weren't just machines, but living, voracious creatures whose hunger could devour everything, like an ancient plague. The steel-hook claws of a crane closed over trunks, crates, cartons with pineapples and bananas; all of this it threw on board. Far below, minuscule men took refuge under the hatches covering the hold. They disengaged the hook from the crane, accommodated the cargo in the bottom of the ship's crustacean stomach. Their faces smeared with the metallic oil of the boats, their hoarse voices and especially their intensely blue eyes shining from their masked faces belonged to a downtrodden people. Nuno imagined their emaciating, melancholy poverty, buried alive in those tombs...

At that point the crowd, standing on the docks, started to wave in the direction of the boat, their hankies damp with tears. Someone shouted a last message to a man leaning over the rail, his hand behind his ear, in the vain attempt to capture it far above. The person shouting did so with increasing desperation, cupping his hands around his mouth. But since the wind continued to drag his message far from its destination, the shouter opted to express himself through mime: please forgive him, he had arrived late, all he wanted was to embrace his departing friend and wish him a good journey...

But before this, interrupted Nuno, there is the story of the loading of the animals. As they were hoisted aboard, the bulls bellowed in panic, spreading their legs, and swimming in the air above our heads. Never in his life had he seen such a perfect image of terror, over the abyss. The bulls stretched out their legs, threatening to loosen themselves as they bucked. And their eyes, already so bulbous, glistened with a metallic sheen, even colder than before. The goats and sheep curled themselves up, like skeins of wool or giant fur balls, inside the wire nets, completely off balance — they wrapped themselves into bales of fear, wobbling, stumbling clumsily on their own hooves, disoriented by the smell of the holds. As for the horses, they stared at us with the same malignant look, albeit petrified to death. They tried to free themselves, straining against their bonds, foam flecking their flanks; they reared and kicked out, striking sparks from the sheet metal. So that, posted on the deck, Nuno himself arrived at the sensation of that maritime death, overcome by guilt and wishing they would calm down. His father's angry voice and the overcast sky over Rozário loomed behind the way he felt. Above all, he remembers the longing in Mama's blue eyes, in his younger brothers and sisters, as having been unbearable. His brain filled with the echoes of their tenderness and replayed the cries, the words, and the sight of that morning's good-byes. He didn't deserve Mama's presence or that of his siblings at the dock, only Papa, who accompanied him to the boat, his voice repeating year after year:

"Psst, listen you! Don't cry, man!"

After hours of waiting, when the hurrying crowd ran down the dock, and the boat, starting to move, bellowed with its horn, Amélia was surrounded by the cries, the handkerchiefs waving good-bye and the din of names called into the air. She never liked to cry, was determined to leave her past behind and let it leave no trace, to forget it without the slightest hint of suffering. As for Nuno, the impossible occurred, he cried and smiled in his father's direction, both happy and unhappy, feeling alone and at the same time crushed by the mass of people who knocked into his shoulders and pushed him against the rail. It was at that moment that he felt deeply aware of this, seeing himself so small and frightened and unprotected in the middle of so many strangers. He was setting out in search of his star, but no one had told him where to find it.

"What will Lisbon be like?" he wondered. "Who will be waiting for me in Lisbon and what future will they give me in that unknown and, now, unwanted city?"

Down below on the docks, watching the *Lima* pull away, Papa stood with his legs apart and his arms crossed on his chest. Rigid as a statue, Nuno said, and with his hat pushed down over his forehead because of the wind. His father's body would stay that way forever, a little bent and apparently indifferent to his son's fate. It's even hard to say whether Papa's eyes moved in search of Nuno as he lost sight of him in the crowd. Nuno kept watching the man's livid face from afar and experienced several contradictory sentiments: in freeing himself from that man, a discreet sensation of relief ran through him, but, inevitably, he began to feel quite the opposite as the distance grew between them. Today, on this side of Papa's death, the absence of that body lingers, that body with its excessively spread-eagled legs standing on a departure dock, the unremitting absolution forced upon us by our reciprocal guilt and the inevitable death of everything we know. Later, on the high seas, when nausea overtook him and he began to cry, he wanted only to hold out his arms and beg Papa to save him, to take him back to an eternal childhood.

While Nuno was to travel under the care of a very white lady with a sweet smile, but who had a very bad cold, and whose name was soon lost to his memory, Amélia knew at once that she was being abandoned. Nuno would be delivered to the first cassock who turned up in Lisbon, but she would have to resign herself to look out the guillotine windows of her first-class cabin, hoping that the nuns would deign to throw her a lifeline.

"Worse than injustice, it was immoral, sir. And coming from people supposedly so very concerned about acts of charity..."

The experience would prove to her that she was already being punished for her sins. She forced herself to believe that the nuns wouldn't abandon her to that sordid cabin, in which the air was unbreathable and full of the disembodied cries of other solitary women, their ceaseless, pathetic vomiting, and the braying of sick cattle. Could it be that there were, after all, legitimate explanations for all she saw — secret rules or reasons justifying the suffering of God's creations? She couldn't help but imagine, nevertheless, the nuns inaccessible in their cabins, safely installed in luxury and devouring their tea and cookies, embroidering linens for the altars of remote chapels and speaking always of the blessedness of the poor and how unfortunate it was to have traveled so far only to deliver God a single new acolyte, and possessed of a dubious vocation at best...

So it was by chance that we both left our home in search of our destinies: transported, though in different years and months, upon the same cargo ship, in its smelly, resinous, and dangerous interior. Each of us called, please note, by the distant and demanding voice of God — and each suffering so much from seasickness that to this day we lack the words to describe it. Each likewise enduring the most atrocious Atlantic solitude, unable to distinguish night from day or the light of the moon from the simple neon lights that turned our faces green there at the bottom of that galleon. In the middle of the journey, the sailors began to visit us. Seeing us so miserable, they tried to encourage us to take a little food, just the sight or smell of which gave our stomachs such cramps that it wrung their hearts to see us. The little water we were able to choke down we regurgitated into the basins and seasickness bags, and always with the terrible acid taste that our own saliva tore out from our insides.

Then we began to hear the voices of the creatures they call sea witches, hovering above the masts, so huge and malicious that they rocked the boat from one side to the other, as if it were nothing more than a dinghy, or an even lesser craft. Other voices, now those of the passengers, spat out the worst curses imaginable, finally assuring us that only Barbara, saint of storms, would have the ability to protect us in this time of mortal danger. Those who were happily immune to seasickness gave themselves freely to celebration, showing a continuous scornful glee at the violence and ferocity of the sea . . .

In what state they each arrived in Lisbon — I can't say with certainty. After five days at sea, without being able to keep anything down, and with the disgusting smell of the boat having invaded their stomachs, their lungs, perhaps even their blood, they both needed assistance climbing the stairs to disembark. And when the glass of a windowed door on deck served as a fleeting mirror, reflecting back their bodies in full, they saw the pallor, the hideousness of the shipwrecked; they saw the blue veins in their hands snaking thick as ropes through their scaly skin, and they wanted to cry.

"My eyes," said Nuno, "had dark circles around them; my bones protruded prominently. The terrible experience at sea stayed with me in the trembling of my fingers, in the hoarseness of my voice, in the first flowers of childhood that wilted in my eyes."

"Corpses were hunched over the rail, over the sea of Lisbon," said Amélia, returning again to the ostentatious rhetoric of her memories.

Her eyes were strained from lack of light. But she could, even so, distinguish in the distance a golden mass levitating on the horizon. It was a kind of yeast, like the one that Mama used to use in her great clay cooking bowls when she would prepare the Easter bread. And in much the same way, Amélia would see that mass rise, grow, gradually become filled with light, and turn white and luminous as it was revealed as nothing less than the magnificent Portuguese sun of that day.

Soon the towers of Lisbon also grew. These were the forms that had inspired the design of the great imperial houses on the shores of the River Tejo. The streets and roads came sharply into focus, became more numerous, irrigated by the movement of the morning. Both Nuno and Amélia could have sworn that at their sight of the first squares of the Baixa, they started to hear the sounds of another sea, albeit an urban sea, without water, and without nausea. Lisbon was now a great amphitheater of pink houses, with the Castle of Saint George at the crest of the Alfama district, with the little square houses of the rich who then lived in the Restelo neighborhood and with the enormous stone shadow that was the Monastery of the Jeronimos. On the far side of the estuary, lost in the fog, the starving Arab quarter of Almada peered out through the hills, all factory smokestacks and oil tanks. And yes, they also saw the innumerable, lofty, and silent towers of the churches of Lisbon.

"Just the towers," said Amélia. "Their only purpose was to support the weight of their bells as well as the weight of the memory of my passage through that bygone time. But, most of all, we were impressed by the silence of the city..."

Nuno had seen the sooty houses near the docks, and the sad clocks, stopped in their façades; maybe they weren't actually meant to show the hours of the day. The great red bridge between Alcântara and Almada didn't exist yet, thus there was nothing to unite those two Portuguese municipalities separated by a river. Thus too the Sunday suicides would have had to be drowning deaths alone, in those days, as one could as yet only jump into the river from one of the small boats that continually sailed between Cacilhas and the Colunas quays.

They traveled from the Azores to a Lisbon pier, intending to follow the road that people say leads to the testy grace of God. Downtrodden refugees just like the continental immigrants who arrived at the Gare de Austerlitz and flooded Paris with their wicker baskets, their cloth sacks containing the precious miseries of an entire country, and who cried and wiped their eyes on the black kerchiefs or on the hankies of that indefinable, terrible word *saudade*. They arrived in Lisbon and they were also immigrants: Amélia had a pathetic pallor; she was sixteen and dreamed of one day going to nursing school. Until she could enroll, she would live like the nuns; she would live a closed dream inside an egg, grow inside it, and then break the shell that separated her from the transparency of the world.

"It was without doubt the greatest happiness of my life, to come to Lisbon," she said, "in spite of the torrential rain. The sun lit up the rain and the rain swelled with an ethereal bluish tint. It delighted me to know that I was more Portuguese now than in that place on other side of that sea; that I was now far from its humidity, from the low sky of the Azores; from the days that had poisoned my life, now finally halted; far from the curse of my childhood on the Island. I immediately fell passionately in love with the European firmament, its high, vertical luminosity. I liked Lisbon so much, that blue octopus draped over the hills, its flat streets that go in a great circle from the end of the docks to the Bay of Cascais . . . And I started then to organize in myself all the reasons for me to want to live, to love being alive, to be a woman again, to start my days over again dating from this second birth into the world . . ."

"Besides this," Nuno pointed out, "Lisbon seemed to me right away to be a city of Sundays — even when, in time, later in life, they turned out to be those endless Sundays that I associated with the pain of poets. When I arrived here, there was a man in Alcântara wearing dark glasses and with hairy fingers who smiled at me in a civilized way and said he had come to meet me in the name of God . . ."

This was perfectly natural in a city with so many churches, with stone angels, eternal and immobile, in their aerial niches, on top of the buildings of the Ministries on the Praça do Comércio: one could see the arches, which needed a whitewashing, and the statue in the middle with the Prince's horse pointing one of its front legs in the direction of Morocco. I had already seen all of this in Rome, where in fact I'd never been, and in Madrid too, and in Paris, and in the little Greek cities on the edge of the Mediterranean — the world I had invented for my future life. It was only when the man with the dark glasses approached me invoking God that I awoke to reality, remembering that my destiny wasn't Lisbon, but the seminary. In fact, the man had come on Papa's orders, charged with turning me into a priest as quickly as possible, so that I could then return to the Azores and tell all the shipwrecked inhabitants there that I too had been baptized in the name of God . . .

As soon as we docked in Alcântara, I saw all the people dressed and shod just the way they were on Sundays in the Azores.

People wore shoes (in contrast to the barefoot men on the Island), wore ties, had the swaying gait of some other species of vertebrates that I had never had the chance to encounter in my homeland. My barefoot childhood, cold and frightened, neck bound by my first tie, was at last a distant memory, and I could see no reason to take note of the bucolic life that was dying inside me. I found everything to be exciting: the illuminated signs, the slender trains of the Estoril Line, the discreet smell of lavender in the taxi that the Man of God had stuck me in and then the aforementioned sound of that very solid sea, made of stone, populated by honking horns, by the roar of the electric trolleys in their troughlike tracks. And it wasn't even raining, though my sister wasn't so lucky when she arrived: no, I had a phosphorescent sun, a tepid November sky, bleached and cloudless. It was bliss to wake from the nightmare of seasickness, to be arriving at the immense mouth of the river of all the rivers of Portugal. Traveling up the Tejo, I experienced the pleasure of being present amid all the places and names from my schoolbooks — the sight of these now accompanying the ideas and beliefs I had memorized from our history books. The explanations and stories that lay behind the rivers, castles, and towers were now completed with the sight of their stones, in the same way that only roots explain trees and railway tracks explain trains. The world of theory, a world with no reality in the Azores, learned by rote from the maps and geography books, had finally drained away. I arrived with my ears full of dates, the names of strange kings, the river tributaries, railways, and mountain systems (mesas, plateaus, great ranges) of a country that wasn't real to me. I would check its teeth, as one does with a horse, see how it felt at a gallop, and come to know its body, its spirit, and its winds ...

In the taxi, I understood the familiarity with which the Lisbonites treated the man with the dark glasses. They believed priests controlled their destinies. After receiving orders to cross the Baixa, to drive by way of Avenida da Liberdade, Marquês, Fontes Pereira de Melo, República, and Campo Grande, and only then cut over on the diagonal toward the Casa-Mãe da Benfica, the driver smiled at me through the rearview mirror, caught in this vain complicity, and said:

"Right, little Father. Let's show you Lisbon."

We traveled along the Rua Augusta, passed the Praça da Figueira, and God Man asked the driver to stop at Rossio for a minute.

"Come and see," he said to me, "look how magnificent our pigeons are."

The women who sold flowers in the center of the park were faded, without beauty, with large misshapen breasts and legs covered with varicose veins, but they smiled at me in an impetuous way, perhaps because this pleased the God Man. One of them picked the best of her carnations and placed it on the lapel of the black jacket that identified me as a seminarian. Children, old men, and other women scattered corn and breadcrumbs and the pigeons dove down from the top of the statue to take what they could. They alit on the arms, shoulders, and head of the priest: he became a god crowned by these blue-gray, round, proud fruits.

"They're his angels," I thought then, when he flashed me a treacherous and annoyed smile. "He will wring their necks, pluck their feathers, suck their bones (like Mama did in the Azores), but he'll keep smiling and never stop saying that they are the angels of Lisbon."

I would myself become one of those docile and unhappy pigeons as soon as I entered the walls of the seminary. I would have to perch on his shoulders and on his head, every day and at all hours, kissing his hands, obeying him in everything, and, watching while those hands palpated my bones and squeezed my soul between their fingers, until my body was emptied of everything that had made me an Azorean boy. I would be a pigeon, belonging and not belonging to every flock, each time I traversed the mornings, the afternoons, and the nights, and later extinguished myself in the distance, taken by the wind. It would be impossible for me to escape God here, as I had in my childhood. I passed through silent, nameless neighborhoods, again in the taxi, sitting next to the man with the dark glasses. I didn't know what lay in wait for me in the distance, or where I was going, or what destiny I would be given by the king who was always waiting for the boats in Lisbon. God can certainly expel us from our childhoods, but not, however, from that great luminous wind every one of us carries within us after having lived on an island.

As for me, said Amélia, I stumbled through the crowd gathered at the docks, right behind the nuns, and I felt the old doors of our house in Rozário, the doors to all the islands close behind me, one after the other. Never again in my life would I be enclosed in that invisible dome, through which one could just see the sea, the motionless clouds, and the infinite distance. The horizon of each one of my actions was changed into a concrete line, and all I had to do was walk across. To seize time and to dominate it became the guiding purpose of my days. I was met at the boat with the convent smile of a freckled woman, Sister Teresa de Jesús, who wore tinted glasses with very thin frames. After I asked for her blessing and kissed her and the mother superior, Sister Teresa, opened her arms and drew me to her. She asked my name, found it funny, murmured it to herself until she got used to it, and then delivered a greeting that would be repeated for years, at rising, at meal times, at the beginning and end of our chores, and even at bedtime:

"Praise to Our Lord Jesus Christ, Sister Amélia!"

Astonished, I nodded, without knowing how to reply, till the little Mother decided to come to my aid: she did it playfully, but with a somber smile that revealed her first reprimand, prompting me to say:

"Forever praised, Sister Teresa de Jesús!"

The freckly Teresa de Jesús opened the trunk of the car, arranged the suitcases, climbed behind the wheel of a jalopy that seemed to cough and gag on the hills, and thus was I carried from street to street to the outskirts of the city. During the journey, the freckled one spoke incessantly, answered all questions, told me every detail of the daily life of the convent, fueled by an almost explosive energy. I was far from thinking that I would make her the only, the best of all of my friends, and that I would rely countless times on the kindness of that complicit smile.

Nuno experienced the trip out of the city in the dark. Amélia opened her eyes wide at the bleached morning and stepped into a circle of light. Sequestered in the convent cloister, she was stunned by the pulsing silence, the footsteps that fell in the corridors, and the glass clock with its peculiar function: experience would teach her that clocks, inside convents, are meant to stop time, not lead to the future . . .

Again, Nuno Miguel was taken in the opposite direction: his spirit left the daylight hours of Lisbon for the heavy night of the provinces. He crossed the country at a diagonal, in the company of two smiling men who over the three hours of the trip tried in vain to understand his Azorean accent. In the course of that infinite night, indeed in all that followed, they asked him dozens of useless questions, and he forced himself to answer clearly, hammering the syllables home and choosing, by intuition, the most suitable vocabulary. At the same time, he was careful to avoid the use of any unsophisticated sounds, deciding to imitate the rounded pronunciation and preferred phrases of his interlocutors.

When they arrived at the village and he sighted a large house in the distance, lit up in the starless night, a feeling of undefined terror ran through him. The house looked like nothing so much as an enormous tomb. The night that surrounded it felt like a silk funeral shroud. Nuno got out of the van and had to be guided by the shoulders to keep him from stumbling in the shadows. Exhaustion, fatigue, and discouragement added to his shyness and exposed him all the more to the ridicule and laughter of the others. Soon two priests with gray smiles and pearl-colored tunics would receive him. Their birdlike heads, shaved to the napes of their necks, were restless over the scapulars and the capes falling over their shoulders. The world was all upside down, because Nuno had only ever seen priests dressed in black. He'd thought that only black was up to the important task of being the worldly shroud of all priests, supporting their morose, crowlike aspect as well as the small holiness of their rituals.

They leaned toward him and cupped their ears, asking him to repeat himself and to speak up so they could hear him. He understood that they were accusing him of arriving two months late. They criticized his accent; they criticized the crude travel bag his father had made him out of strips of wood, with its broken aluminum clasp; and they chided him about being homesick. After his bags were stowed under his bed, which had been reserved for him in a corner of the dormitory, they told him to come downstairs. The rector waited for him there, at the foot of two flights of stairs. He was standing between the busts of saints lined up upon their pedestals, and Nuno felt as though he were being dragged into the presence of a stone colossus. They told him he had to kiss the rector's hand, kneel in deference, lower his head, and say good evening. Nuno was aware of the smoothness of the rector's skin, the bulges of flesh that cushioned the man, though he was mostly impressed by the excessive size of the fellow's hand. Looking up at him, standing far above, in hopes of seeing his face, Nuno could only make out the nostrils of a man who was still young but as tall as the ceiling. His arms ended in thick shoulders that were as prominent as angel's wings. Later, when he became a victim of that strength, Nuno would think that there was a perfect harmony between a man's stature and the almost divine power of his voice, between the heavy tread and the canonical justice meted out by the rector. The same arms that crushed him now to the man's bosom and lifted him effortlessly would in the end become those that educated him with countless beatings through the years. Administered without warning, in silence, the blows would open up clearings of fallen bodies scattered on the floor of the classrooms like beaten animals. Brute force, violence, and exhaustion, in addition to the punishment of being forced to recite prayers even during recess, taught Nuno to respect and to hate. Nevertheless every time it was his turn to be propelled off his chair by the power of those hands, he limited himself to invoking the holy name of God, knowing he would go on doing so repeatedly and in vain.

In the refectory a wave of enthusiasm greeted him as he went from table to table, introduced as "the Azorean." As soon as the director clapped his hands and the servile house master followed suit, demanding silence, His Reverence welcomed the candidate, deplored the two-month delay in his studies, and asked everyone to extend him the charity of their aid with mathematics and Latin. Nuno was finally among the many whom God had called and the few He'd actually chosen — with a plate of spaghetti and roasted meat in front of him, bone tired, and miserable. Without looking at the faces that surrounded him and started to lean toward him, he saw the faces. He took in the weight of all those eyes. To the first questions he answered that his name was Nuno Botelho, he was going to be eleven, and he had six siblings in the Azores. Politely they asked him to repeat what he had said. And since they kept exchanging glances and pursing their lips, always politely, he had the sad, lucid thought that perhaps they were actually foreigners. To be sure, they shared a country in name and religion. But as far as the pronunciation of that name, as far as their language and the origin of their saints, was a land without sea or boats, bearing no resemblance to the world of his childhood.

After the evening recess, he followed the crowd of seminarians to the chapel. Wrapped in the clatter of footsteps hammering the walkways and then the groaning of the chapel pews, he could hardly have been expected to know that, here, the hours of the day had all been drained away from their accustomed home in clocks. Time was only the brass bell, the interminable lines, the cult of silence, the religious prohibition of happiness. Nuno picked up a prayer book to follow the prayers that most had already committed to memory. He understood nothing, save that the Sleep of the Just, to which the psalm alluded, was already clamoring in the desert inside him. The fatigue of his body wracked his spirit, emptying it of all emotion. Later still, when the dormitory lights were out, he wished he could dissolve into the shadows and disappear into the future. The sound of the mattress springs, the whispering of his dorm mates, and the mousey squeak of the housemaster's shoes finally and definitively dispelled his inner silence and his desire to dissolve into sleep. He knew he would have to sleep many hours on end to overcome the sensation of still being in the boat, which lingered inside him like a sort of deafness that destroyed not one but all of his senses. He hadn't yet been told that on the next day and on all that would follow, a housemaster would always appear at six in the morning to wake him. He would walk along the row of beds, clapping his hands, and the seminarians would devoutly rise to their feet, crossing themselves shakily, while the housemaster's cold morning voice would call out:

"*Benedicamus domino!*"

We would reply in chorus:

"*Deo gratias!*"

When Nuno was almost about to melt into that sleep without beginning or end, from which his past would rise, the boat engines would start up again inside his head, along with the whining of delivery vans crossing the provincial night, and the voices of the boys who, on adjoining beds, kept calling him in low tones. They were tormented by the sort of curiosity that consumes lives led in secrecy and confinement; they wanted all the details of their newest companion's life, this latest fellow castaway . . . all the more so in that the mysterious companion they were now interrogating had really come from the sea, bringing — uniquely — tales of an Azorean childhood.

Nuno was terrified at the thought of having to stay there, abandoned in the presence of so many strangers. He was afraid to sleep among people who spoke the same language, who were supposedly from every corner of the country from which they all, in common, hailed, but who couldn't understand a word he said, and would never understand his way of thinking . . .

So that he wouldn't have to continue to answer their questions and not be understood, he decided to take his pillow and press it around his ears. His life could thus hide in the dark and silence, a place without depth or height. He'd never be able to go back to being what he had once been. Then he opened his eyes wide. He wanted to see and at the same time say good-bye to himself, to make out and understand the forms that were now taking shape in the dark of the dormitory. He wanted to love them with hate and hate them with love, perhaps. Shocking though they were, he wasn't surprised to see them, and soon he closed his eyes again tightly. A vision of his mother's illuminated face awaited him. She was surrounded by the halo of a saint, or perhaps it was just a star that was throbbing above her in the heart of the night. Swept up in this illusion, he tried to smile at her. But her smile was made of shadows. It was a smile that hurt him even more than the pain of being alive. It merited a sob or a convulsive laugh. Feeling his mouth twist into a howl, Nuno tried to contain his emotions. He promised that he would never again shed tears for the land of his childhood. And that he would be happy.

2

It had cost Maria Amélia a great deal to live through the sounds and sights of her last night in the Azores. The space and silence of the house shrank in the pit of her stomach into a knot of fear and guilt that didn't dissipate with the morning. She hadn't been able to sleep at all. Once in a while a sort of lassitude took away the weight and presence of her body, but it was just a state of apathy and absence that couldn't be confused with sleep. The pendulum of the clock in the living room became more than a sound in the monotony of the shadows; it was yet another supplication from Tantalus, because this oscillating noise ended up being confused with her own heartbeat.

When the clock struck five, she could no longer fend off the oppression of the day and started to cry silently. Today, living another life, no less confused, she swears that she had never had such a deep feeling of solitude as that night blackened by the thistles that were already budding in her soul. She tossed and turned on the mattress next to Domingas. Panting, she breathed in the insomniac rage of her vigil — and never as on that last Azorean night, she told me, had darkness and anxiety fused so completely into a single oppressive, interminable substance. In that complete and absolute darkness, the breathing of others rose to meet her, their slumbering peace, their ongoing, unbearable abandon, and the whistling of the wind grew louder as it swept through the cane fields, the leaves of the fig trees, and the holes in the wall in front of the house. Passing through the wind were the howls of the dogs that seemed to surround her in that nest of fear and fatality. The very roar of the sea that was always waiting for her stopped being the usual continuous rumble to which one learns to be indifferent; it had taken on the roar and menace of a lion.

In fact, all of this was typical for the Azorean night in those days: the wind in the fig trees; the pendulums of the clocks in the living rooms; the slime of the chicken coops in the yards; the nocturnal dogs, turned into sculpture by the cold; the cracking of the wooden boards in which, traversing and sustaining them, the future of the houses could be told; the heavy breathing of people falling asleep in various stages of exhaustion — and above all the sea within shouting distance. Every time her body gave in to the weariness of the hours and threatened to dissolve into sleep, a type of electric charge was loosed inside her that transmitted a nervous twitching to her leg muscles, forcing her to return again to her vigil. If it weren't for the cold, she said, I would have started to sweat blood, the way it happened to Christ on the great night of his passion. After a little while, since it was impossible to remain in that horizontal state any longer, she walked out into the night and began to cry by the beds of China asters and marigolds that surrounded the tank and found shelter by the garden wall. A sudden anticipatory nostalgia for those flowers, which she had planted herself, almost forced her to give up on the idea of departing for the Continent. Just before six, wet from her weeping and more exhausted than she could have ever imagined possible, she returned to the kitchen, rinsed her hands, face, and neck, and started to get dressed and ready for the voyage. Nausea overcame her stomach and forced her to vomit out saliva mixed with bile into the pig trough.

During the previous sixteen days in the city, where she had been initiated into the mysteries of the little nuns, she had pondered at length the paradox of her farewell. In part because she was so happy at the proximity of her liberation, she had been worried at the time that she might not be able to shed a tear at her departure. But if that happened, it would be shameful, even an act of ingratitude; she would be escaping not only the circumstances of her life on the Island but too the prescribed manner in which one was supposed to say good-bye to it forever. Whenever people left Rozário, this act of abandonment left in its wake a tide of cries and lamentations. The poor people were always noisiest, the exclamations of those happy people in tears being so dire that one might think they were bound for their deaths rather than a voyage to the unknown. However, when her hour arrived at last, the sobs flowed from her as well, in an irrepressible stream.

She was crying not for herself, exactly, but for all her brothers and sisters, knowing they were condemned to a future of hopeless waiting. Just imagining how their faces would look at her departure, she felt her heart contract until it was a small stone in her chest at this anticipated shock. She'd never really noticed the pumping of her heart save as a consciousness of its purely mechanical function, but now it felt like another body dying within her, softening her bones, commanding other unknown organs to wither. On the other hand, she could see before her the unfathomable land of her destiny: Lisbon would certainly be very big and crowded, but a desert nonetheless, made to the measure of her privation among strangers. Besides this, she would still have to sail the expanse of that infinite sea, perched not only on her metaphysical galleon but the other one as well, the one that had to weather storms and skirt both the oceanic abyss and the loneliness of the many people in her hold.

At the stroke of six, washed and dressed, she sat down again to cry on the kitchen bench and waited for Papa's arrival. She asked for his blessing as she always did. Papa answered her in sleepy voice that hinted of anger and disapproval. She rose to embrace him and to ask his forgiveness. But how should she do it? She'd never had any need to embrace him. At close range, the only parenting skill her father had ever displayed was the almost sagacious manner in which he whipped, scolded, and beat his children. She'd never known him to have any capacity for tenderness or for dispensing even a casual pardon. So she wasn't surprised to see him dip his hands quickly into the plastic basin, as if to make clear that he wasn't a man to give in to his feelings at the last minute. He lifted his dripping hands to his face and rubbed his eyes, his ears, and his neck. Apathetic, she thought; against the idea of making peace with me, with my disobedience, with the stubbornness of a daughter committing the cardinal crime of leaving home, like a refugee, to live at some suspect convent. Her father dried himself quickly with the towel, opened the kitchen door, and went coughing into the yard. Soon his carpenter's hands were rummaging through his tools, separating wooden beams that clanked like hollow tubes in the silence of the shed and the morning. His hands were working in a different way, without the determination of the days when, rising early, he would draw on a shaft of mahogany the outlines of oxen yokes, axle shafts, or break shoes. He was so engrossed in his carving tools, saws, bits, and planes that only Mama could manage to break his fast. In mid-morning she would take him a big pot of milk soup and waited standing until he designed to interrupt his work. That day Papa didn't seem lost in the construction of those wooden creations. Maria Amélia took it upon herself to try to retain, in the emptiness of the kitchen, the details of that offended and possibly ashamed face. For months she had engaged in a one-way conversation with him, always at the distance imposed by his stubbornness, cowering beneath his roars about the departure for the convent. Mama had to intercede on her behalf. Luís and Domingas tried, and then finally it was just Nuno who was able to extort a kind of family decree from him, while Papa made it clear that she could just as well go to the convent as to the depths of hell . . .

Well, now she was on the way to hell, on this dark morning of as-yet indeterminate weather, when Mama came down to the kitchen, gave Amélia a blessing, and started to cry as she embraced her. Nuno's memory of the event, which was formed as the two women wailed, still contains a luminous trace of that unexpected maternal tenderness. Her blessing took the form of her delivering Amélia's funeral eulogy in the same way that sailors like to list off, at the top of their lungs, the principle virtues of their beloved dead.

Thus, at this pivotal moment, Mama made herself an obstinate prisoner of the recitation of those adjectives that best described the character and behavior of her beloved daughter from her days of sewing and cooking. Mama alluded morbidly to Amélia's obedience and sense of responsibility, saying and saying again that the house would become dark as night in her absence. Mama would no longer hear that obedient and humble voice, the warmth of Amélia's uncertain and anxious breathing, and never again would that house show the results of her hard work.

In Luis's memory there just exists a mixture of perplexity and deafness on the subject, because from the shock of that pain, which did not properly belong to him, followed the emptiness of Amélia's departure, with moist kisses as she got into the truck, and then the return without her to the house where he would nonetheless on many occasions hear her reciting verses. I can say little about the others' memories. Domingas kept a distance from the many kisses and the endless, unbearable embraces. She was angry inside, though she didn't show it; the fact was, her sister was running away, she was separating herself from the bosom of the family, leaving Domingas to flounder in the hell of the pots and pans and corn sieves, condemned to the oven and wood stove. Linda and Flor, still so little then, stood stock-still in the middle of the house, looking perplexed, not understanding the unaccustomed display of tenderness and tears. Jorge, lying in his crib, had finally discovered that his body possessed two feet, and so he'd started the work of sucking on them, for which reason he protested noisily when Amélia lifted him to her lap and began soaking him with her tears. Then Grand Mama Olinda came, and started to tremble as if she had Parkinson's disease. She extended her hand to her granddaughter and, before she gave her a hug, passed her a folded piece of paper and said:

"This is for what you need most, my precious. There's no excuse for going without..."

She took off her glasses, which were wet from her own uncontrollable tears, cleaned them on her apron, and started to console the crying children. So wasn't it true that her granddaughter was going on to a better life? And suddenly remembering her absent son, she took on an air of disinterested widowhood, the resolute attitude that had enabled her to confront her manless house alone, the farming, the issuing of commands to workers and apprentices in service of the land. She put her hands on her hips, leaned over, and let her chin tremble again:

"So where is he? Where is that damn boy who doesn't even come to say good-bye to his daughter at a time like this?"

He was being crucified by the bitterness of his anger, rummaging in the bins to try out old tools covered with rust, without motivation or purpose. A strange trembling overtook his hands as well, and a terrible morning cough rattled around in his chest, spasms coming perhaps from his stomach or the depths of his soul, he didn't know which, as he continued to struggle, desperately, against the desire to allow himself the weakness of tears. When Nuno walked in and called him to the house to say good-bye to Amélia, he found his father exactly as he would a year later, when he went to him to ask his blessing and to bid him good-bye himself, when he left for the seminary. Papa had sat down in a corner of the workshop to stare into space and to listen to the darkness, and he had started to shred a plug of tobacco with his pocketknife in order to roll the cigarette that no one would see him smoke before eating. In Nuno's mind, his father was forever sitting there, through his entire lifetime, his eyes clouded by that same mute obstinate haze. Nuno went through the motions of their feeble embrace, his unconvincing request for pardon, and then he received his blessing bathed in the faint smell that he would always identify with his father, no matter where he encountered it, anyplace in the world, over the course of his years away — however many that would prove to be. And when he learned of Papa's death from a telegram sent from Vancouver and he tried in vain to reconstruct the thought, the image of his father inside himself, he could only remember that unmistakable odor ... but on the morning of Amélia's departure, Papa was still sitting there, and sitting there, just as he would on Nuno's own farewell morning, and it was impossible to imagine him ever dying. Time passed over Amélia's sharp cry, as she clung to him, embraced him without shame, and begged:

"Dear Papa, forgive me for the love of God and wish me a good trip ..."

Half of Nuno's life had passed since the moment he arrived there in the shed, asking for his own blessing, his face smeared with the saliva of his mother's and siblings' kisses as he opened his arms and was able to say nothing more, in a thin sliver of a voice, than:

"I have to go now so I don't miss the bus, father. I've come to say good-bye."

Time had also passed since it was Luís's turn, when he volunteered for the army and they sent him to the war in Portuguese Guinea at its worst, and also when, after he married, he fled from this Island again, going to another, chasing a dream. He opened his eyes wide and tried to see the difference between the sky of the Azores and this other sky, containing the same clouds, the same mystery as everything else, waiting to be deciphered. In spite of the fact that the same clocks separated times past from the future time of Toronto and Vancouver, he understood that he was not just on the other side of the world. He felt distant from himself and far from what he had hated: the dark earth, the damned howl of his memory of his father.

3

During the rest of the year, except for the rain and the earth tremors and the long nights when the hail and cyclones forced us to pray for our safety, nothing ever happened in Rozário. And then, with the exception of the rumors that formed in the air and that we later heard as they traveled from mouth to mouth in new and increasingly embellished versions, we had no other form of contact with the outside world. So we came to look forward, at beginning of summer, still well before the arrival of the seminarians, to the visits of the people who showed up, year after year, during the bustling feast days of Função, in the humid sun of our sea and the excitement of the first harvests of the year. They were always the same people, and they always came to us a little older, their bodies a little more emaciated by another year on the road. If there were no other way to measure time, it would have been enough to follow the cycle of those who came from far away to knock on our door and tell us about their way of life, forever on their travels on the road. Time followed the rhythm of pilgrimages, and then, during Lent, when the saints were in mourning, it followed the litany of our prayers to them, the arrival of happy students, notices inviting us to play the lottery, and little more.

First came the fishmongers hauling their catch — mackerel, blue jack, and sardines — to the salt tubs, in the season when the moons were round and propitious for the proliferation of the fish. Then came the men with the sieves and grills, those wanting to buy piglets, the women who bargained for embroidery, and the traveling salesmen who sold everything on installments or in exchange for bags of corn and sacks of beans. Very early in the morning the tradespeople started by gathering at the top of the Caminho Novo, and there they worked out the complex details of their positions in their procession through the streets. If it were wartime, nothing would distinguish them from an occupying army, with their staffs and cages, their wicker baskets and other implements hanging from poles. But when the cattle herders passed by them and everyone greeted each other, one could see right away that our coexistence with them was peaceful and as ancient as a religion without a god. The tinmen and fishmongers were always at the head of the cortege, and, descending the Rua Direita, they filled the streets and the houses with their metallic cries, as homes began to open to the morning. Merchants and toolmakers began the steep descent down Rua Mangana. Sometimes only the dogs and roosters answered, the music of their cries traversing the town. In spite of having traveled all night or slept akimbo in their carts covered by canvas tarps, our visitors neither wore the bleary look of insomniacs nor showed the least sign of fatigue.

As for the embroidery ladies, the northeast bus brought them in at six thirty in the morning. They came out of the buses, roughhewn women, somewhat obese, with monstrous elephant legs, always going from door to door chatting with the housewives from the sidewalk. Yes, these embroiderers with emaciated faces haggled over the pitiful price of needle and lacework. They were nearsighted and some were infected with tuberculosis. Everything set them apart from their prosperous customers.

Thus gathered this strange assembly in front of the church, disturbing the Mass, and that market noise hurried the tavern keepers of the place and called into the street gaggles of children still wobbly from sleep. The chorus of auctioneers, horns, and street organs mingled with voices until the time of the travelers' departure when they left behind not only the smell of gutted fish and a pile of decapitated tuna heads — for which our cats, crying shrilly, competed with our dogs — but also a sea of other offal covered with a cloud of flies. Above all, what remained was the sad silence of when the party is over ...

At the end of June, the few students from the high school arrived, fast as greyhounds, well dressed but generally pale and sometimes excessively quiet. Everyone always said they'd grown, that they'd matured, that their beloved faces were shining with intelligence, with evidence of their progress in their studies. Almost at the same time, a bevy of euphoric emigrants coming home for the holidays alighted from various taxis. Endless kisses flew back and forth and gift items that had never been seen before came out of their suitcases reinforced with steel bands that had to be pried open with pliers. Aside from their rude health, these "Americans" brought with them new or unfamiliar words; they called their spouses "sweetheart" and scolded their children in English: "Be quiet for a moment, Billy, I'm telling you! What a crazy boy, my God!"

Vigorous, flashy in their dress, and aggressive in their laughter, these copious consumers of black beer paid in dollars and scattered their money on the bars in a manner that was as ostentatious as it was philosophical. The Rozarians would approach these visitors little by little, in hopes of a glimpse of the presents they'd brought. In return, they would hear the repetitive, sad, vain tale of the world beyond and the unbelievable successes of these men, who, far from here, had conquered the ice of the North, a strange language, and the iniquitous injustices of the rich.

Even before the arrival of those monotonous and naïve student priests who would steal Nuno's sanity came the advent of that joyless circus of wanderers who, transported in trucks, set up wooden tents and booths and prepared the flat earth for the most fantastic machine yet invented by man: the wheat thresher. The stalks of the harvest awaited that thresher, which had traveled from municipality to municipality, pulled by a large tractor, and there it stayed for three weeks, plucking ears clean, vomiting the straw and the chaff to be baled. Its departure and the familiar, unbearable emptiness of its mechanical groan coincided with the beginning of the holidays for the seminarians.

On that distant July Sunday, when the eleven o'clock Mass was about to start, Nuno rose to his feet, like everyone else, and thereafter remained forever dazzled by the vision of those returning little boys that Rozário had dedicated to the future of the Church and the supreme grace of God. He knew, of course, of their existence, because Amélia had been insisting on recruiting him as well. But he didn't remember having admired them as much the year before. Me they left cold; they looked like a bunch of moles bleary from burrowing in the ground, with their downcast eyes and pale smiles, greeting everyone and blushing with shame if a woman spoke to them. Usually they walked in pairs, like inseparable twins, up and down, going and coming from Mass every day, and it seemed strange that they were so timid, unhappy, and silent. To this day I'm not sure if it's necessary to flaunt such austerity in order to become a saint — but from then on I formed an impression of saintliness as being related somehow to their whiteness, absent any facial hair, delicate in the extreme, and apparently asexual. I am, however, not a reliable witness in this matter, because, after all, it hadn't fallen to me to live out a life devoted to the minutiae resulting from the existence of God, but rather to my brother Nuno.

The Sunday I witnessed him falling under the spell when the two student priests left the sacristy right behind the emotional smile of Father Ângelo and followed by an enormous candelabra that the fragile little hands of the sacristan raised up to the niches where the saints rested. The priest's timid smile, his face discretely flushed by the lights and the noise of the multitude rising from the pews, abruptly confronted the eyes of the people. He was suddenly hot in his cassock and surplice; on his finger he wore that divine ring that was already beginning to hover over our destiny. The priests were very popular in Rozário, above all because they were different from the rest of us, and they were mingling with those who were anxious to receive their first priestly blessing, who were herding them from street to street, with laughter and jokes:

"There they go, the black coats! Give me your blessing, Father!" And they started to imitate the Lisbon pronunciation, its round sounds, sweet and sibilant and hard to master.

Nuno realized that a sense of gratitude took hold of his immortal soul at that moment. The appearance of those miniature priests struck him as being so supernatural that a kind of divine revelation overtook him until he was forced to return to the practical matters of life. Amélia had been unnerving him; she wanted to force him to study. And there was only one way to do this: enroll in the seminary. Now, happily, hope began to shine in him and fill him with a new and unfamiliar sense of clarity.

Contrary to what I'd always thought, those kids weren't simple apprentices of that dimly lit and shadowy office, parading in front of us during Mass with footsteps marked by angelic little bells. And they didn't just smell like the incense, nor did they limit themselves to following that mushroom dressed as a patriarch, as if they were his offspring. No, they also signified Nuno's entrance to Damascus. The boy, in a trance, followed their birdlike steps, listening to the voices of these Sirens of God, and he certainly didn't take long to be overcome by the sound of their melodious Lisbon-accented Latin as they sang Gregorian chants. The strangest thing is that, with the exception of the vestments and their almost effeminate mannerisms, the two little boys following behind the priest had little or nothing in common. One was thin and of humble carriage, and seemed almost submersed in the clouds of incense that belched from the thurible. The other was fat and proud, obviously nurturing ambitions to become a bishop; he embraced the missal almost carelessly, and he held the wings of Father Ângelo's chasuble. It even seemed that he was pushing that old sick man, who held the chalice of our Sunday Masses with trembling hands. The little bishop's gaze was cast high over the open-mouthed multitude and didn't seem at all intimidated by the shocked whispers that rose from the pews. In a certain way, it was as if he had just made his entrance onto the stage of glory itself. In part, he was right: we, who were of the same age, were sad, scruffy, and had little schooling, and thus we lacked his spiritual discipline, clearly visible in his eyes.

Just the approach of those two sad characters prompted everyone to study them from afar, fearing after all that not one or the other had the look of a priest. They would hardly have pardoned them for a hoot of laughter in public, or a gesture of impatience, but they also never put much stock in their piety. In the best opinion of everyone, these boys had entered the seminary just to flee the hoe and the plough, in the same way that others began to emigrate to happier countries only to escape the military. In fact, the profession of priest demanded the sharp eye of a partridge, capable of darting from God's direction back to the world's at a moment's notice, whereas these two were nothing more than pathetic sparrows, lacking the presence of mind necessary for nurturing ecclesiastical malice.

Nuno let himself be bewitched by those two angels dressed like priests, and he did his best to follow their every move, no matter how slight or casual, with the same sense of wonder. He marveled at their angelic posture, the luminosity of their faces and their almost phosphorescent cleanliness, marveled to such a degree, indeed, that he found them beautiful, important, elect. He thought the world revolved around them. If God had called them and chosen them to be His own, it was because He had preordained them to serve as an example to the human condition. The sacristan had hardly placed the candelabra on the main altar and rung the bells announcing the beginning of the Mass and demanded silence when Nuno rose to his feet trembling so much that he looked as if he were about to faint. The next moment, when the voices of the little priests responded in chorus, so wise and so sweet, to the Latin of the Introit, his eyes brimmed with tears. During the rest of the Mass, he remained as if in a levitation of his spirit, his face burning, his mouth giving out a series of sighs. During the sermon, high in the pulpit, Father Ângelo entered into a torturous justification of the vocation for the priesthood. He publicly praised those embarrassed and falsely humble little priests; he applauded their purity, the sacrifice of renouncing the pleasures of the world, and ended up singling them out as an example of the path that the other young men of Rozário should follow. At communion, Nuno was already lost to the earthly world and immersed in the other: distant and ineffable. In spite of not having made confession, he walked up to receive communion, and I saw that he did it in a state of innocence. I looked at him, saw his chin rest on the polished bronze of the paten: he was transformed into my blue brother, the fragile little brother, sensitive and perhaps inexplicable, forever suspended in the mysterious blue of his eyes. He started to live the impossible reality of God, and he continues to this day, I suppose, living not the days or the experience of the moments through which he moves, but just and only in a dream quite different from ours, and requiring different skills.

Now he claims he's agnostic, he is spiteful in his references to the ecclesiastical shoals, and even God, in his opinion, is nothing more than a palsied old man, emaciated and impotent. His life has become an obsessive reckoning of accounts that knows no end or motive.

As for the rest, father would never permit another son to escape the Island just to run around the world with priests. The way he fought Amélia's desertion discouraged any additional attempts at flight. But if Papa's obstinacy was enough to dissuade any one of us, with regard to Nuno, overcoming it that first time was nothing more than a game, a match between two equally stubborn players. Nuno's strategy consisted firstly of winning allies to his cause, and so leaving his final assault on the somber and unassailable fortress of his father's refusal for the very end of the contest. First he went to Luís, appealing to his sentiment, sensing that he had an ally there against the unceasing victimization of the children in our family. As for Luís, his personal philosophy rested on a fairly simple notion: if anyone in that house, anyone at all, deserved to stop suffering, and was able to achieve this end at any price, it justified everything, even the bizarre prospect of going into a seminary and walking around in a skirt. He needed no other reason to help; he wasn't the kind of man to begrudge other people their good fortune. Amélia, of course, embraced the news with open arms, seeing in it the result of the seed she had long since planted in the impractical spirit of her brother. She even tried to arm him with some additional arguments for the upcoming battle — irrefutable ones at that, to her mind. First, studying to be a priest doesn't always necessarily mean *becoming* a priest, but it does mean becoming educated, expanding his knowledge of the world and so opening the door to new opportunities. Secondly, what other prospects were there for Nuno's future, besides becoming a workhorse, being condemned to walk around barefoot with torn pockets for the rest of his life, and never being anything but an illiterate? Then, it was not certain that the family would receive the fortune or curse of a letter offering them passage to Canada. As for the little matter of priests being unable to marry, which was Luís's one notable objection, that was something one could safely ignore for the time being:

"The most important thing, Nuno, is that you pursue your studies. When you get the itch in your crotch, it's simple: take off your cassock, mount the girls the way God intends, and chalk it up to the salvation of your soul."

Luís tried to encourage Nuno with new guarantees. As soon Nuno arrived at the convent, Luís would spur a battalion of comrades into action, with the purpose of dissuading his father from disowning his brother. If needed, he would move mountains of stone, with faith in God and a palace coup. And since the country was so lacking in work, it would be easy to find comrades to work for the cause.

Sunday after Sunday, the image of the little priests continued to float inside Nuno. What fascinated him most about them? The Lisbon accent, the way the people of Rozário stared at them so adoringly during Mass, the tenacious bearing of Father Ângelo, who seemed to protect his flock the way he would the beached whales, so that his sermons gave life to the power of the sacred word. In August, when the procession of the patron saint went by, Nuno again was overcome with emotion. As always, the bands from Fenais da Ajuda and Algarvia had arrived, four priests from neighboring parishes as well as some singers of décimas, quatrains, and romances. The cumbersome cortege of offerings, led by the great silver cross and the blue banner encrusted with the gray dove of inspiration, marched at a languid pace, filling the streets with music and moving Rozarians to tears. There were litters, lines of haloed angels, payers of promises, men and boys wearing yellow, red, and purple capes. The metal of the band instruments sparkled in the brilliance of that August Sunday. High clouds, pushed by the wind toward the sea, hardly justified the pallia that sheltered the many priests Nuno saw passing by with the stiff demeanor of bishops. Trays were being passed around with rice pudding topped with cinnamon, plates of figs, plums, guavas, and meringues, in addition to chickens nestled in the laps of young boys and heifers being dragged along on ropes by those who were going to offer them to the priests. The mix of colors, the martial sound of the music, the miserable demeanor of the pilgrims and the people who kneeled in the ditches as the host paraded by, all of this infused further excitement and fascination in Nuno. Behind the priests, with their temperamental smiles and the majestically gilded vestments, followed the ecclesiastical pages; to the beat of the music, they seemed to glide in the midst of the sleeping multitude, one with the unassailable dignity of the enormous crucifix propped against his chest, the other girdling himself with the clouds of incense from the thurible. And so sure were their steps, the bodies marching in the sway of the wonder of the spirit, that there could be nothing in Nuno's eyes but the sweetness, the image, the mirage of the Great Dream of God. Years later, when he was a grown man, when he had run the complete course of his religious delusion, he would say to us with a mix of humor and bitterness:

"Some go to seminary carrying along their benefactors' money, the sick dreams of their grandparents, or the zeal of their old maiden aunts. I ended up there because of my older sister's vocation . . ."

He later said this into the microphones of Radio Azores, and he did it with conviction, thinking he might at last shake off the spell of an archipelago still mired in the religious mysticism of the sixteenth century.

When the cortege had passed and the procession reached the church and everyone surrendered to the luxury of the wine, Nuno hung around outside to watch the little priests and all the others seated at the Father Ângelo's table. He looked at them from the churchyard steps: the heat had prompted them to open the shutters of the priest's residence and to bring their chairs to the verandah. Some of us hung around there with him, gathered there to spy on the interminable courses of the banquet, the repeated toasts with crystal glasses, ogling the opulent desserts, the wine and other elixirs provided by their superior, ecclesiastical wealth. Nuno seemed stunned by the happiness of the diners' smiles, their faces puffy with alcohol, the cigars that always found their way into the guests' wide, grandiose gestures. They were the worst gluttons, hypocrites, and liars imaginable. They were, in fact, the very same corrupt priests as described by the great writer Eça de Queirós . . . lascivious smoke rings floated over their heads. Bursts of laughter erupted out of their fat bellies and came tumbling down over our heads. Young girls in headdresses, nieces of Father Ângelo's, with their little lace dresses and obsequious expressions, served trays bearing urns of coffee and glasses of brandy and liqueurs.

The next day, Monday, was a day when the markets held lotteries for bottles of sparkling wine, china dishes, and a special cake decorated like the Church of Rozário. It was a day of farewells and sadness, and as the bands left, accompanied by applause and laughter, and the last heifers were sold off, Nuno presented himself in the sacristy to talk with Father Ângelo. Taken into his presence, Nuno raised his eyes to the man in such a supplicating manner that Father Ângelo couldn't resist rumpling his hair and pinching his cheek. That very day, the priest sought out Nuno's teacher and asked him to intercede with Papa. Nuno was filled with courage by his teacher's gleeful enthusiasm at the prospect of this future priest giving confession to his first schoolmaster. Little by little, through these and other means that were no less tortuous, the whole neighborhood came to learn about Nuno's calling, came to offer their opinions and proclaim that, while God did of course hold all the wisdom of the universe, he had gone overboard with His choice to call to Him the son of the most dour, avaricious, and evil man in Rozário.

By the time this world of intrigue had reached his Papa's ears, Nuno had mobilized all the most influential opinions in his favor. Above all, he managed to present a serious dilemma to his father's conscience. If Papa forbade his son from going to the seminary, there would be those who would spread word far and wide about this crime against the Divine and so imply that Papa would be heading straight into the Pit after death. But he wasn't a man to give in to such blandishments — he began to take refuge in evasion, and, after a first wave of harassment, he was overcome with a blind rage at Nuno and began to treat him even worse than before . . . It was a short step from there to ranting about the idiocy afflicting his son and God both, as he assigned Nuno to the care of the cows and moved Luís over to the crops. Members of the family rotated, according to age, in that carousel of chores and responsibilities, between the sheep and pest control, between the care of the cows and cultivating the earth. Even Jorge, just in his first year of life, fruit of this exhausted, suffering family tree, was already promised to the land. Linda and Flor, still in their first years of school, had already forgotten what happiness was. Domingas and Luís, already long out of school, were still doing penance for having been born, a task aggravated now by Amélia's departure. The new threat posed by Nuno definitively ended the hope they all shared that they might someday jump the fence and away from that family prison...

I don't know how to explain in detail how so many hidden forces worked together to dislodge Papa from his obstinacy. Weeks after Amélia left, the news came that an American benefactress was offering to pay for Nuno's studies. The next week, our cousin the canon wrote offering to pay the price of the trip out of his own pocket. In the week following that, and coming from who knows where, a big bag of clothing arrived for Nuno to wear in the seminary. God could well have sent it, since the striped sheets, the nylon shirts, pillowcases, and excessively large briefs smelled of lavender and mothballs — which are, as we all know, the scents of which God's own breath is made up.

At this point Papa couldn't restrain himself any longer and slammed his fist down onto the table. He knocked over the oil lamp, swept plates, pots, and cutlery onto the floor, and began to curse the nameless strangers, en masse, who had already taken one of his daughters to a convent and now were preparing to pilfer Nuno's labor from him as well...

By now all of Rozário had taken the boy's side. The most daring of the island kids laughed at the "old man" at every opportunity, and the spinsters and grandmothers, coming by the house on mid-mornings during this last summer of Nuno's childhood, issued warnings to Mama that she shouldn't dare risk preventing the boy from following his destiny. And there was always another handkerchief, a black tie, or a pair of socks to add to the trousseau of the future seminarian. Mrs. Mariana Silva, godmother of half the children of the neighborhood, came out of her house, hid her hands behind her apron, and smiled, exaggerating her gold tooth. At the height of this malicious smile's glare, and under Mama's startled eyes, she held out a hundred escudo bill and said:

"This is for your little boy. On the condition that you invite me to his first Mass."

No matter where they came from, the self-proclaimed men of God on the Island pushed Papa into conversation at every opportunity, reasoning with him, saying they just couldn't understand why he continued to oppose the boy's calling. Who could say if God himself hadn't destined Nuno to be so weak, bony, and small as a pigeon, the better to suit him for study and, overall, for religious service?

A few days before they returned to their studies, the two seminarians who had so fascinated Nuno — invited by the boy himself — came to our house. I remember their bearing well: their cold eyes facing Papa's stony face; he looked as though he'd gone deaf, or perhaps been vacated by his spirit, which had traveled far away in the meantime. Not just because he was a little hard of hearing, was easily distracted, and would often lose the thread of a conversation, but mostly because the intense apostolic flow of their Lisbon pronunciation, full of unknown words and fashionable adverbs, escaped his understanding. Still, half his face frowned at the sweetness of their continental music, seduced by the soft, polite, and almost feminine manners of the seminarians. He stared at their dead smiles, their effortless gestures like sheets of paper fluttering in the breeze, the immense conviction they had in their own virtue, these angels who were speaking in Nuno's defense, speaking of the renunciation of worldly pleasures, of the worshipful, subtle, and sweet cause of God, the unspeakable sacrifice of eating the bread of the starving.

And more, the seminarians counseled him. The bed that Nuno would lie in would always be one of thorns, not of roses.

So be it then, my father growled in disdain, leaving them astonished and confused.

One thing was for certain, that God, at that time, wasn't dead — or, anyway, was somewhat less distracted than He is today. He had sent us the little priests at suppertime. He'd inspired them, made their eloquent words rattle in my father's ears, and empowered them to touch Papa's heart with a sword of fire. And if He hadn't sent them, then He must have come in person: he'd moved the mountain, lifted father's spirit to the height of the strong wind that in the old times brought nights of terror. The wind that had so often carried the desire for music, for relief, and for happiness, and so many other times had come to destroy our every illusion . . .

CHAPTER TWO

Nuno Miguel

The country taught us to be necrophiles by tradition: to venerate its dead heroes. It indoctrinated us into this elegant religion based on curving our blessed spines before people who've accomplished only one thing of merit: leaving this world. Though it's true that those who have passed on to the infinite darkness of death assume a supreme virtue: they've stopped disturbing the living.

It happens that death was actually introduced to us as being the dawn of a new, if obscure, existence. The declaration of a brilliant man — even if he is insulted on the eve of his death — serves more to honor those who are venerably mediocre. Thus, I was always fatigued by the lack of morals of the living. And this is also why the memory of my father can't draw from me anything more than a neutral, empty, blunted sort of testimony — certainly not reverent. Because if you're the son of a dog, the art of living is reduced to this: howling at the wind and learning to sniff it to discover what might be coming.

Of course, I forgave him everything, just as my siblings did! I forgave his absence in my life, the silence he cast over my future, the faraway voice with which he criticized each of my failures, and even the few things I did well and to him were meaningless, and everything else that served to keep my spirit fettered.

But there's something else, the invisible scars of his abuse: the cold distance I feel toward him, my renunciation of his indifference and the passivity with which, through the years, he came to accept my exclusion from the family. Perhaps the pardon I've given him is closer to a religious absolution than actual forgiveness. I'm still and always full of that sacred terror, the liturgies of that cult in which we were all educated to venerate the dead.

The fact is that I, unlike my siblings, let myself be carried away by an obsessive thought, the only one that occurs to me as appropriate to the world he put us in. I feel it working away, seeding my first white hairs and stretching out the tiny spaces that for the moment still separate the first wrinkles that will appear on my face, especially around my eyes. If I admitted to myself that I had a real father, then the unclean spirit hovering over my life would have to give in to the mechanisms of intelligence and reason. But to call him nothing more than a "dog of a father" is to acknowledge he will someday wind up, *ipsis verbis*, as a character in the book I'm writing here, and, as such, is perhaps something like committing a crime against nature. Or not a crime but justice: reflecting back onto his memory the same cruelty and lack of scruples that he exercised over us. And my personal feelings about him bother me just as much, today, as the medieval control he still manages to exert over my siblings, forever frozen in time: they grew up and left this place, but they still remain mystics, frightened of life, bereft of father and mother both.

I'm kind of the family eunuch, see? They castrated me, albeit without using their hands, and perhaps absentmindedly, never noticing how they were destroying me. They thought I was leading a charmed life in Lisbon. I was a stranger, engaged in an endless and incomprehensible exercise in style! It never occurred to them to think that I, being a dog, son of that dog, would have to bark, and that my barks would cross the night-sea, and I would never know the sleep of the just or the desire to be the son man...

"The great irony?" you ask. Do you really want to know what is the great, the greatest of all the ironies of my life?

The house. Everything conspired that it would be I, and not another, who would inherit it. Because the others haven't settled down. They live far away, will never return from the cold lands of their American dream. They will inherit the parcels of earth, the useless pastures, the brush, and the old orchards, and they'll go on to sell it to those other vultures who left here long ago and today buy up all the land. But they inherit the brief, tortured, and victorious possession of my father's things, and the names, and the miserable treasure of every mound of dirt — while I, owner of a roof that never belonged to me, will live out the dream of a house with trees facing the sea, any house at the end of a road that offers both repose and another future. I will return to Lisbon to put myself on the other side of myself, owner and master of the metaphysical house and a childhood locked away inside its darkness and unbearable emptiness. If I decide to sell it, or to exchange it for another, I will at least retrain the phantom ringing of the Azorean bells, the coughing of its old people, the sound of the horses that in the old days would shake the foundations of its houses. Wherever I might be, I'll hear the clanking of the irons and the thud of wood, the voices of passersby who would say Good Day, and the voice of the father who even now is calling me, making me hurry.

As a matter of fact, he was always so overbearing that we quickly lost the respectful restraint that marks other children's attitudes toward their parents. Our lives were being choked away in his presence, as if wiped clean by a sense of hopelessness. We were born, all of us, from the functions his loins, one after the other, two years apart. We were baptized by a robotic little priest, who was always full of good humor and would bless with a big smile the procreative function of fruitfulness and multiplication. It was Papa's job to give us nine unrelated names — not counting the children who died suddenly, or after a slow and torturous few days. And in the act of registering our births in those little booklets that gathered dust in the bottom of drawers, he always changed the order, purpose, and number of names we each received. For some of us he chose long, almost pompous names, choosing middle names from some bottomless stockpile inherited from who knows whom or why: Medeiros, Monizes, Tavares, Botelhos . . . For others he chose somber designations, the kind that gave its recipient a fair idea of how unlucky he'd been to be born into this world. For example, he wanted to call me Nuno Miguel Maria de Medeiros Moniz Tavares Botelho at first, with Carlos Miguel, my twin, getting the same role call for himself. This was finally too much for my mother, who spoke up in order to spare us those monarchical catalog appellations:

"I'm sorry, Emanoel! That's too many names for my head. Go on your way, find that teacher, Mr. Quental, and ask him to come over and cut out half of them . . ."

Furious, Papa muttered invectives against the stubbornness of women, too thickheaded to comprehend the ethical overtones of the names he'd chosen. Arriving at the house of his future compadre, who had showed him the world with his maps and set him against the Salazar government, he still couldn't leave well enough alone. Maria Amélia ended up with Botelho at the end of her name, Domingas got Botelho Moniz, Luís Miguel ended up as Moniz, I too got stuck with Botelho, a name I hate, while my twin was left with the problematical appellation of Carlos Miguel de Medeiros Maria. As for the others, Linda, Flor, Victor the First and Victor the Second (who went to heaven to join the angels, as did my double), not to mention Jorge Miguel, Mário, and Zélia — I myself couldn't keep all their dissonant denotations straight, during the years I was writing letters home from Lisbon. But it seems to me, even today, that our wildly differing names each contained a little prophecy regarding the different paths we had to follow.

Besides all of this, Papa abandoned us very early in life. Since we were all born two years apart from one another, that was the age at which the hugs and kisses ended for each of us. During those early days, when Papa returned from work, he was tired and depressed, of course, as he always was and would be, but not yet insufferable. As soon as a new baby arrived, however, those lean, muscular arms would never again open up to scoop us into his lap and give us the illusion we had been born from his love. When a new baby arrived, our eldest siblings became our father and mother, because at that point our real parents felt their work was done. Amélia, the firstborn, was transformed into a kind of aunt-goddess of the family, for better or for worse: forbidden from playing, robbed of her childhood, loved and hated by all of us. There was always a persistent, compassionate loneliness in her eyes, which the details of her life alone couldn't explain. The habit of being sad made the very idea of happiness impossible. Like us, Amélia didn't know how to be happy without tears, nor did she know how to laugh without feeling remorse for her joy. This was part of what we saw in her eyes.

We didn't have a mother. She was such a distant woman, with few opinions of her own. She scolded from a distance, where she was making the beds or carrying a bucket of bran and potato skins to the pig trough, but I don't think she did it on her own account. The love of this woman was guided by a strict obedience to her man. As for the rest, the family was just a chaotic nursery, growing to the rhythm of his lust. On winter nights, right after supper, he hurried everything and everybody — impatient, distracted, hands shaking, acting like a dog that the smell of a bitch has excited from kilometers away. He would rush my sickly sisters, who always dawdled over the salted fish or the fried pork rinds. For me, eating was death! I hated the hairs that stuck out of the fried pork, hated the baked beans, the cabbage soup, and the boiled stew. And I hated the fennel soup as much as, years later, I hated math and chemistry, hated the servile smiles of the little brothers in the convent, the Masses, the secret police, the ladies of the National Women's Movement, and our repressive country. Father soon lost patience with me. He would yank my plate away, hurl it to the back of the kitchen, and curse me:

"You don't want to eat? So let it go to waste! You'll never amount to anything. And if you're hungry in the middle of the night, go to the outhouse and eat shit, understand?"

Then he would send everyone to bed. A punishment. We washed our feet in a basin in the lukewarm water that came out of the kettle: barefoot, bruised by the stones in the paths that led to the land and the pastures. They were bleeding, were covered with scabs, had numerous ulcerated toenails, and were wrapped in rags to help stanch the flow of blood and to protect us from infection. Hardened feet, so damaged that I don't exaggerate in saying that they looked completely different from the rest of our bodies. They seemed like planks, because of their coarseness and flatness. All of us would have looked more or less fine if you didn't take our feet into the equation, but with soles like ours we were transformed into living refuse: forced to walk with the undulating gate of bulls, wearing hand-me-down shirts and pants that were too short, suspenders crossed over our shoulders to keep them up.

My feet were a mass of gnarled bones, stunted, wrinkled, and ridged like cement. Afterward they grew deformed. Stuck to my body, they were alien to what I considered the true nature of my being. I always refused to associate those lumps with the straw blond of my hair and the sky blue of my eyes, not just out of a sense of aesthetics, but because they connected me to the sordid earth of the corrals and the dampness of the pastures.

At that time, before they moved us to the loft, I slept with Luís in the so-called middle of the house, in front of my parents' bedroom. The girls occupied the space next to the kitchen, sleeping on a boat of forged iron, inherited from Grandfather Botelho. The littlest ones slept like ballast, on the floor, huddled as though they were a nest of puppies. Luís and I, and later Jorge too, coiled at our feet, would spy on that hardwood-floored space in front of us, which we were forbidden to enter. The altar of the house was where they made love, in the midst of niches and icons of saints, the image of Our Holy Lord Christ of the Miracles, a rosary, and a crucifix suspended on the wall over the bed. On the other side of the house my sisters squabbled, all of them huddled closely together, pinching each other, tucking the babies into whatever spaces were available in the bed. I recall perfectly when they began hurriedly covering their budding breasts, ashamed at these beginnings of puberty. Later, when I would come home on school vacations, in the second year of seminary, a space was opened for me, in the back of the house, in the loft. Then indeed my parents enjoyed the peaceful isolation of lovers. They made their last children there and the nightmare of hearing a bed that rattled ridiculously stopped. But before, as I said, we slept three paces away from that always open door that guarded us, and my father's hurry didn't give us time to fall asleep. First the husk mattress received my mother's body: a body that fell and then sank into the depths of a well of fatigue, without even the pleasure of the sigh that the exhausted release when they relax. We heard the murmuring of Mother's prayers while Papa was already getting undressed, and he would urinate in the blue enamel chamber pot and then place his boots in a corner of the room, near the window. He took off his jacket, pants, and shirt, and looking perfectly ridiculous in his flannel nightdress — dove into that nest of cornhusks that was refreshed year after year. Only much later, when he was older, did he, too, acquire the habit of praying before going to sleep. Mother's few religious convictions arrived via various mystic crises, during earthquakes or Lent. She made us pray the rosary around the table after dinner, but just as when she did this herself, alone, she was overcome with a consuming hatred, dead to the world, whispering invectives against the priests. Above all, Papa was impressed to learn that Christ was dead and waiting for someone to resurrect him once and for all. Papa never once, to my knowledge, followed in a procession, or even took part in all our pious novenas and kermises. The petitioners, the bazaars, and the rounds of the singers of improvised quatrains were exclusively for the benefit of the priests and the distant bishop. But I left early, as you know, and the family's behavior was no longer important to me. If our thoughts, despite the difference, ever happened to converge on any subject, I think it could only have been on the matter of the clergy ... the hypocritical Blessed Ones and our odious Dictator.

 The oil lamp would be snuffed out with one two three breaths. Outside in the Azorean night we would hear voices, singing, and whistling from those who were heading home late after card games in the stores. The rats started with their nervous squealing, pattering under the eves with rapid, blind, velvety steps. With the north winds came the rain. Everything was deafened by the sound of the water that dripped from the roof tiles and discouraged the house mice from mating, and in the midst of this almost perfect deafness, he approached her surreptitiously, initiating the always new and heady feast of her body.

 My brother and I pretended to be asleep, conscious nonetheless of the complicity and the secret of those two bodies touching, fusing and burning, consumed by the incomprehensible passion of adults. Papa would slap her on the buttocks, with increasing frequency and intensity as her white limbs were overtaken by the same excitement.

Once in a while my mother apparently had bouts of lucidity and distress, trying to bring Papa back to reality. She would ask him to leave her alone and let her sleep because we, the boys, were certainly still awake. Papa didn't believe her: he didn't want to recognize or believe in this possibility. If he sometimes got up to check on us, it was only to reassure Mother of the evidence: it was a well-known fact that children fell asleep as soon as they lay down, like angels. Above all, you see, Papa never suspected our rebellion, the mute complicity of his sons, the vigil of our panic, brought on by his possession of our mother...

My brother, so as to encourage me to pretend I didn't hear them, would turn to the wall and pretend to snore. I, small and terrified, would remain wide-eyed in the dark, just barely recognizing or guessing the nature of those sounds, those great couplings whose echoes traveled through the house. I tried to absent myself, focusing instead on the squeals of the rats and the continuous murmur of the rain, thinking however that even the house mice must have been affected by the same lust. Terrified, they ran around in the eves. They let out squeaks that echoed in the drum of the night, cries as mortal as those of pigs at the fairs during the terrible, frenzied January slaughtering season. The house began to shake in what remained of the silence. It raised wings, lifted into the night, flew over the sounds of the outside world with some effort. In the beginning, his thrusting was erratic, uncoordinated. Then his movements gained in rhythm, becoming almost frenetic, and Papa's sighs became labored. His tight embrace made her moan, asphyxiated by the weight of his body, and the mysterious words that we heard her speak sounded like the endless litany of repeated sins that so many, many times I was made to stammer in the confessional. Soon the bed simply went crazy. The house would again take flight, become lost in the space of night, hovering astonished like a great bird awakened from sleep over that very near, almost white sea, as you once described it. Father started to emit a perverse laugh. He mumbled absurd phrases. He couldn't contain his moans. He whispered: sweetheart, sweetheart, sweetheart! I don't know how it is that the bed never fell apart over the course of so many nights, so many years passing over the ancient varnish of its recycled wood, polished with tung oil. It never stopped being a perfect bed: low, with a very high mattress, filled with corn husks. Actually, I'm wrong: when progress came at last to the house, after my father's first return from Canada, spring mattresses replaced the husks, at the same time as he brought in a factory-made stove and a refrigerator, and sink and toilet replaced the primitive ones the family had been saddled with till then.

It happened then that my poor dog of a father barked with pleasure. Prisoner of that body, my mother was still suffocating, pinned down by the inconceivable and obstinate strength of his arms. Then he emptied himself into her completely with a lukewarm, viscous ejaculation. If they didn't repeat the act, and they rarely did, mother would at last manage to get up, would go to the basin and scrub herself energetically. By the time she returned to bed, my father was in a sound sleep. He slept the same sleep as the rats, without any memory or any remorse of having wounded us with those sounds, with the pain of our knowing that he was the only master and owner of that modest body he nightly profaned. Then the rain stopped coming down so hard — it was just plain rain again; and the animals that howled from afar, in the dark of their dwellings, and the chirping of the crickets in the oceanic night, and the hooves of the beasts scraping the stable floors, and the wind as well . . . all of this became as natural as sleep and death, in the unbearable succession of days and the eternity of that sea.

And I, filled with rage, could only cry. My brother, thinking that I was asleep, began to grope for the thing that was starting to come alive in him under his long nightshirt of rough linen, still facing the wall, and the groans, brief sighs, and grunts of masturbation began. My body bounced to the beat of his breath until the dizzying energy of his hand subsided into spasmodic jerks. His legs twitched, he sucked his saliva back in, and his body trembled in a feverish chill, a sickness that was still totally unknown to me. By this time I was as exhausted as he or my father. Tired of the excitement, the hatred and jealousy, and my own sobs, I fell into a restless sleep.

My whole life began to revolve around that primitive, atavistic passion. The axis of the world was my parents' bed, its secrets, their whispered conversations and orgasms. I started to see them in the dogs humping in the streets, in the sow who came down from the neighboring yard to receive her large, powerful male, in the eager chickens that squatted in the steaming dung heap. If one day I got married, my wife would have to be as white skinned as Mother was, with very black hair and intensely blue eyes. When Marta came along,

I learned to love her in his way, to enjoy giving her slaps on her buttocks, making her moan under the force of the same embrace. Years later, when I became shipwrecked in the stormy waters of my relationship with Marta and lost my footing in life, I presented myself to the craziest psychiatrist in Lisbon. His uncompromising finger pointed at my nose and left me petrified:

"You're inventing unhappiness and fictionalizing its triumph. You're like a nervous bride on her wedding night. We're going to do some scuba diving, my dear Pier Paolo Pasolini, and you are going to plunge into the mud of your little childhood. Understood? Good, then come along with me."

I refused with my entire being. I don't know if out of a type of stupid modesty or because of the horror of the evidence I'd have to present. Nobody really knows their own childhood: it wasn't time to open that chest and try and piece together the enigmas, the burned papers, and ashes of the past. I knew the secret and origin of my ailments better than anyone. I didn't want to believe in these newfangled, sophisticated, and probably sinister forms of confession. I just couldn't believe that psychiatrists would ever be able to transcend the blather and obsessional focus on obscure details indicative of the confession booth — winding up with just another version of the priests' censure without pardon in the seminary, their prescribed penitences, threats, and useless advice . . .

I was my own father, *you know?* And I became the father of children that were mine alone. I know that living and creating are the same thing. And I think, in the end, that nobody can resist the writers: they are the angels and the demons of our petty lives. That's why I'm here. To render accounts, as the poet O'Neill would say, of my blessed, tender little life . . . You get it?

Maria Amélia

I must have been around three or four — and I remember we lived in a small house, with a floor of beaten earth dark as pitch. The walls weren't limed, nor did they have any other adornment, and their stones showed through. The doors and windows too had never seen even a teardrop of paint. You could see the tiles over the beams mounted over a crooked double-T beam that crossed the house from one end to the other. During the day, the wind was marine blue. But on the nights when the moon was dark, it was a gray wind that moaned: it let out whistles of sorrow, a chorus of souls from the other world, seeming to weep for the old owners, the dead of the house. *Do you know what I mean?* Beyond the kitchen door to the backyard, on the other side of the dung heap, was the barn for the livestock, its roof so low that some animals had to live hunched over. Others, the larger ones, stayed in the open air, tied by the neck to the cane hedge around the yard. In the early morning, if you rubbed their backs, their hair felt crystallized by the night dew.

As you know, sir, animals are disgusted by their own excrement, not that of others. But it happens that those sad bony cows of my father's, unlike many that would come to the family during those years, devoured everything, wracked by a tubercular hunger and eternally sucked dry by battalions of flies. They not only ate the hedges that were covered with shit, but also the clothing hung there to dry by Mother, the hemp ropes, and even the pages of my first copybooks, To prevent such devastation, Papa would descend the nearby slopes, scythe in hand, bringing back a bundle of thistles with which he would crown the entire hedge around the yard. This had a second function too: it stopped the infiltration of mice that were attacking the corn bin.

To be able to get to the barn or to the street, the poor cows had to come through the house. But if their bellies were too full of the leaves from the hedges or from the pasture grasses, or if they were several months pregnant, they could barely get through the doors. They had to be pushed. The more temperamental ones balked at the sight of the spare furniture, suddenly drunk on the claustrophobia of that narrow hallway with the walls that, as I said before, were only bare stones joined by sand and cement. They were even afraid of the pictures hung there and the vases of daisies and hyacinths, afraid of the curtains and the mirrors and the doors, and so they hurried through like runaway trains without engineers, heading off a cliff. Taut, twisted, and with their snouts raised, they left the house riddled with flies. My mother would lead the troop and pull them with all her strength by the ropes that were tied to their horns. Papa, at the rear, whipped their hindquarters so much that it was painful to watch. The poor things, opening their hind legs wide and lifting their tails, shed brilliant tears that were as fat and shiny as pearls. Later, when they lost their fear of the things in the house, they started to try and eat everything, pictures, daisies, curtains, mats, and icons. Then Mama came from *inside, I mean,* from in there, swatting the flies with her dust rag her apron, or whatever was at hand, and she started to lament:

"Jesus, Lord of my soul! Who will get me a house free from all this traffic! The flies are a health hazard. Pests! They poison every place they go, demons."

There was a room upstairs that we called the loft because the floor was made of wood planks not beaten earth. Do you know those rooftop garrets in Lisbon where you can barely breathe, and the people who live there are like birds imprisoned in cages, forgotten by the world? Well, I would crawl into that dark and unprotected bunker, worse than those Lisbon attics, lie down on a little cot, and gaze at the leaden sky. A trapdoor served as my window, but it had long ago ceased to function, and it didn't protect me from those cold, damp nights. The rust had long ago fused the hinges, and I saw shoals of clouds brushing against that mud-colored opening with its crumbling, oxidized fixtures. I remember sometimes lying there counting the clouds and imagining that they had the shapes of familiar things. Some looked like cows lying in the pasture, because of their bent hooves and bent heads. Others, much bigger, were those frigates or ships run aground at the dock, perhaps even maps that would merge with other maps and form phantom countries — in a kind of dance, aerial ballet, or silent festival. If it were today, with my knowledge of the world, I would say that the clouds of that time were castles, or big mountains stretching from north to south. Now, *after all this time*, my hardscrabble life seems to continue much as before, burdened by the weight and darkness of those multitudes of clouds, eternally harried by the wind.

Without really noticing, I started to live alone. My siblings lived below, due to the fact that they were so young, Luís still a *baby*, and Domingas always upset because of nightmares. My parents too lived below. Poor me, I was sent to sleep far away from them, an outcast, close to the clouds, the attic rats, the rain, and the wind that formed the terrible cyclones of the island. Frightened, I would cover my head with the blankets and say to myself, as if I were still praying to an unknown God:

"Come on Amélia, fall asleep quickly. Close your eyes hard, pretend you've died: don't dream of nonsense that doesn't even exist in this world . . ."

I slept through the night, the truth be told. My head being covered had the advantage of my not hearing the squeals of the rats, the thunder, and the death cries of the seagulls. Besides, my breath was precious: it helped to warm the bed. Even today I can only get to sleep with my head under the blankets, full of fear, an inexplicable fear — not even the presence of my husband ever convinced me to uncover my head.

First Domingas was born, then Luís Miguel. I had just turned six when the twins arrived. I raised myself in the intervals between those interminable births, eating slices of corn bread swallowed down dry, many times without a piece of pork rind, bacon, or anything else to help get it down. If there were roasted sunflower seeds around, a little pork fat, or boiled corn, we all opened our mouths like famished finches, and Mama would get angry, insult us, tell us to settle down, tell us we were greedy, gluttons, the worst sort of scavengers. But usually there was just dry bread. Bread moistened with tears, sir, that even then were determining my future, as I will tell you.

I remember that around that time I started to visit the house of Grand Mama Botelho, mornings and afternoons. My Aunt América, the only unmarried woman left in the family, seeing me arrive with a piece of corn bread, would reach for the sugar bowl or tub of lard and spread the bread I'd brought either with sugar or with yellow fat, always the cheapest possible. When they started importing cow butter here and it arrived at Grand Mama's house, I craved it all the time. I swear I had never tasted anything more delicious. And if it was on a wheat-flour roll ... The honey I ate as a child was no more than this: first sugar and the complicit smile of Aunt América, then the roll with cow butter. *I repeat* never again would the taste of food seem so delicious. Even today it comforts me to have a cup of warm milk with a piece of bread slathered with butter. These childhood treats were sweetened with the infinitely kind smile with which my spinster aunt received me then. Not even the first wedding I attended, or my own wedding night, or the biscuits and *pancakes* of Canada, ever again gave me this mysterious and savory honey of childhood.

In our house, you know, everything we had to drink was acidic. The black coffee was bitter and full of grounds. The cows' milk, when they grazed on thistle or beans, had the taste of those strange green medicines ... the horrible tonics that Mama forced us to swallow on an empty stomach, for anemia and worms. My Grand Papa, always seeing me arrive very punctually, laughed with difficulty behind his habitual, asthmatic cough, through mucus like chicken fat. I saw him sitting in the doorway, with his head between his knees "to take a little of the air that comes from the land," as he liked to say; if Aunt América was inside or in the yard doing chores, he would give me a malicious wink and tell me to wait, while making an effort to suppress his smile.

"Listen here, girl," he would rasp with effort, as soon as he heard the kitchen door bang. "Bring the sugar bowl and butter Amélia's bread, poor little thing."

This last sentence caught in his throat and made him cough and spit through his knees. When the asthma attacks were most serious, his eyes glassed over, as if he was being strangled, and it terrified me to see it. My aunt would come over with her apron and wave it in front of her his face to give him air, which irritated him; she was always waved away by a dead hand with bones that shone blue under its translucent skin.

When I was four and a half I was ordered by my mother to take care of Domingas and Luís while she went to work on the land to help Papa or to wash clothes in the public tank. She always left me with the warning, repeated countless times, that I shouldn't open the door for anyone. One day, however, I opened it for my cousin Manuela; I wanted so much to play, tempted by the rag dolls, the aluminum pots and pans, the cradles made of baskets that belonged to my cousin. This miniature world had a charm far outweighing the meager world of our own little family, Mama's rags, pots, pans, and sewing basket! I seated Luís and Domingas on the mat in the middle of our house and we began to play pretend mothers, pretend wives. It was all done in complete innocence; we were pretending to be women with absent husbands, we were mothers with rag dolls. I forgot all my real worries. I'm not sure if I lost track of time or if Mama just decided to come home early — I don't know, and I can't say for sure. What I do know is that Mama, seeing the house a complete wreck; seeing Luís sitting in his unchanged diaper, with his mouth smudged from eating dirt; seeing Domingas with wet pants and a snotty nose; seeing everything in complete disarray, grabbed the bamboo cane she used to beat our mattresses and spent the rest of the afternoon whipping me. I remember her grinding her teeth, pinching me on the arms, her hands full of tufts of my hair. It changed everything: I had been a very tranquil child, even docile, but there she was coming at me again and again, beating me, blind with hate, as I wept and wept.

That day taught me about hate; I wanted to die, it was as simple as that. I couldn't really indulge in my self-loathing, though . . . The knowledge that Papa would be home soon kept me relatively calm. He came at nightfall, directly from working the land, along with the cows that had to pass through the house, and he quickly took stock of the situation and barked:

"You miserable child! You think that was a beating? If I get my hands on you, I'll leave you black with bruises . . ."

So even crying wasn't allowed. I kept my mouth shut. I was still in plenty of pain, mind you, from Mama's whipping, but that pain wasn't the worst of it, and there was no use making a fuss about the real problem: the fact that I was forbidden to be myself, the fact that I was forbidden to be a child, with all the rights and privileges due to every child: to rock a poor rag doll, to have the grace or the illusion of freedom, to be innocent and loved, to feel safe in the world, protected by the boundaries established by my family.

With the years, I acquired strange habits and never quite got accustomed to play. I lost my interest in dolls, lost the ability to behave naturally in a group and to laugh often or with spontaneity. People who knew me best said that my laughter was like a strange bark. My husband laughs at me when he hears me laugh. The Canadians stare at me and say, "She laughs for no reason, this one! *Come on*, Mary, please control yourself. What's the matter with you, anyway?"

I can't control my laughter, no more than I can keep from getting upset when I talk about my childhood. Even if, laughing at myself, I know instinctively that the worst thing in my life is that I've never had an experience that other people would actually find *funny*, or even worth a chuckle.

During the years I lived in Lisbon, in Nuno's company, he would get very sarcastic about my laugh — he'd say that he was beginning to worry about my intelligence, hearing me make that kind of noise. It really got on my nerves, at the time, much as I was irritated by his political convictions, about his always skipping Sunday Mass, about those ridiculous women who mooned over his blue eyes. Time taught me that those eyes of his were always fixed on a horizon directly opposite the one that the rest of our family was heading toward. But I needed many years to understand him. I really needed to replay, like a movie, that half of his life that I associated with mine, from the day the twins were born.

If there had ever been a Christmas crèche in that house, the sheep, the shepherds, and the very God-Child, they would not have had the innocence of my younger siblings. Nuno was tiny, weak as a newborn kitten, with straw-blond hair that was almost white. When his eyes turned a clear blue, he still had the face of a girl. Carlos, his double, seemed robust by contrast — hearty, blood surging through every limb, full of energy. There was nothing feminine about him; his hair was dark brown and his features better defined. Still, they were both premature, I think: they moaned more than cried, in a kind of feeble agony. Even the folds of a sheet weighed heavily on their little necks; even a light caress terrified them, giving their squeaks of protest an imploring tone;

even the air in their little lungs was almost too much for them to bear. They breathed with a thin wheeze that made them pant with fatigue. Of course, one of the most fascinating things about twins is how they mimic one another not only physically but in behavior, in action, machine-like, though each response is colored by the personality of the individual twin: whenever Carlos grunted, for example, Nuno would try to imitate him, though when Nuno let out one of his little soprano chicken peeps, Carlos's reply would blast back like a horn. It really did seem as though one must be a girl, the other a boy.

I doted on Nuno right away, because he seemed so small to me, lonely and incredibly fragile. He looked like one of the miniature figures in Mama's embroideries, with little fingers of filigree and a red mouth like a rosebud. Domingas resigned herself to keeping Carlos for herself, though her disappointment was mitigated by her fascination and pride in his masculine vigor.

I never understood why, since Carlos was the stronger one, but for whatever reason, thanks to whatever caprice of fate, he didn't make it past four weeks old. Carlos was predestined, we supposed, to be the guide, the worldly sun for Nuno. All reason said that if death spared them, sickness would devour them little by little, from inside to out, like worms eating an apple. For this reason, I don't know, still today, how to explain the reverse logic of the stronger twin's death.

I remember that Mama began to ask God to take one of the twins for Himself. There wasn't enough money to keep them both alive. In her opinion, their convulsive coughing was ruining them. The only doctor in Algarvia lived more than a kilometer away by road, and Dr. Arlindo Maia didn't much care to make the trip: during the rainy season, he wouldn't put himself out just to attend a deathbed. He sat in his office with its large shuttered windows opening over the immensity of his many acres of land and waited for death to attend *him*, rather than the other way around. They said he was the biggest farmer in the region and ran the strictest clinic on the Island. He only ever came to our house once, and that was the summer before, to diagnose Domingas with typhoid fever. It impressed me to no end to hear him whistle softly to himself as he palpated his patient's stomach, with a pronounced frown. He only interrupted his whistling to say:

"That'll be two hundred fifty escudos for the consultation and travel. Oh, and it's very possible that she will die."

It was February, pouring rain, and Dr. Arlindo wouldn't take his gleaming black car out on the roads. God wouldn't take long to claim the life of the least healthy and the most defenseless of the twins. And this was, quite clearly, my adored blue-eyed boy. I made my decision; if Nuno died, I wanted to go to heaven with him. I couldn't stand it when Domingas won our bet. Even though Mama hadn't taken sides, I sensed that her preference had always been for Carlos: he simply had a better chance of survival in the long term, working the land.

It was a terrible cough. It left them purple, stiff, on the edge of asphyxiation. Honey syrups, salves, and mint tea revealed themselves to be ineffective, while the specter of illness brought the inevitable death of the twins even closer. When the attacks became more frequent, they slept on and on, occasionally letting out a whimper that made our breath catch in our throat. Women wearing mourning clothes began visiting us, giving Mama endless advice. Barefoot men, the ones closest to the house, drew Papa aside and almost begged him to call the doctor since the boys were in such agony.

My sister and I limited ourselves to doubling our bets on who would die first. But soon we understood that there was nothing for us to do but get on our knees and pray around the cradle where the twins, minute to minute, were dying. Mama continued to ask God to decide quickly. Neither of the twins wanted to nurse. In desperation, I offered God my own life in exchange for Nuno's. Nuno was all I had in my life: there were no other reasons for me to keep on living.

On one late afternoon, as the rain thrummed down in a continuous torrent from the gutters, we found both twins burning with fever. They were in a kind of limbo, their eyes staring; sometimes they didn't even breathe. We decided, Domingas and I, to keep vigil through the night. Father was pacing like a crazy man, in his underwear, punching at the air, opening and closing windows so that the babies could breathe. Sitting on the bed, holding them in her lap, Mama blew into their faces and prayed to our Lady of Mercy. In a kind of trance, she said over and again that God didn't need to take both of them at the same time. She begged that divine mercy would permit at least one to be spared. Her eyes were bloodshot, desperate in the extreme. I drifted off, against my will, until I was jolted from sleep by Mama's voice saying: "Thanks to the Virgin, one of my little angels is now in heaven!"

Domingas stared to scream, kicking this way and that, even biting me. In tears, Mama tried to keep us from fighting, calling halfhearted threats to us from her seat. Papa separated us, stood us up without scolding us, and made us go to our beds. When morning arrived I saw that his face was greenish, pinched. In a little while we saw him leave for the yard, in silence, very pale, spent inside, without bothering to latch and bolt the kitchen door behind him.

Many times I found myself thinking that I loved Papa terribly, more than he deserved, and many more times I wanted to make him know that I hated him more than anything in the world. Yet later, following the death of each of my three brothers, whenever I saw Papa go into his workshop, every time I saw him choose the planks, the boards, the nails, and the rope handles for his sons' the little coffins, and then prepare the tools, shave the wood, take the shingle nails from his mouth one by one — I understood anew the incalculable pain of a father losing his sons and yet being the one responsible for building the small white vessels in which they would be buried. To build a coffin for the cold corpse of your son, to line it with a linen cloth and then lay the tiny lifeless body inside it, posed like an angel ... there was never a more terrible duty. But Papa wasn't a man to turn away from life; behind this lay his great honest courage, even coldness, which I never will cease to praise. But what torment, sir: to measure the body of your boy with your hand, to disappear into the back of the yard, to separate planks, beams, nails, and screws, and to plot out the shape, the interior space of their final abodes upon this earth... And then the gravedigger, and the earth falling onto the casket lid and producing that hollow sound, like a drum, and the cold roses and the rain and the priest's hurried Latin ...

Three times, as I said, I watched the construction of those coffins, after the deaths of Carlos, Victor the First, and Victor the Second. When Mama announced their deaths, Papa went right out in the direction of his workshop, worked all morning, and came back with a little box under his arm. He returned exhausted, subdued, and silent. The only visible sign of his grief was to refuse breakfast, lunch, and dinner on that day. I never once saw him shed a tear over the course of those years; he restrained himself to withdrawing into a corner during the wake, without a sob or a sigh. When the priest arrived for the burial, he would get up abruptly, pick up the smallest of us, and leave. I don't know how he didn't go crazy. Nor do I understand how Mama could stay lucid and even smile sadly, as the friends and neighbors came, filled the house, and admired the exceptional beauty of her dead babies. It always seemed scandalous to me that instead of giving their condolences, they would congratulate Mama and Papa for the death of those innocents — the boys had just gone ahead of their parents, they said. The boys were happy now, they said; they died purified, without sin, free from all the suffering they'd have had to endure on earth, and certainly they would watch over in Heaven those who had so loved them in this world. Papa and Mama almost smiled, thanking their guests for these congratulations on the death of their angels. Theirs was indeed a sweet death, blessed by a hypocritical God who made believers confuse misfortune with happiness.

Luís Miguel

All of us were born in secret. Our mother barely made a peep when she bore us, just little sounds like the murmurs of people buried underground. When Mama was about to give birth, we didn't notice her belly was swollen; the next morning we found her lying under a long sheet, looking empty and trapped. There had been no shouts or alarms, it all happened while we were asleep. It was as if we were forbidden to be born. Sometimes we heard my father hurry out into the night. But that didn't necessarily mean anything more than that Mama was sick and that he was going for help from Grand Mama Olinda. And since she always complained as loudly as possible as she limped along the road in the middle of the night, no matter what she might have been woken up for, we got into the habit of thinking that she was only coming to tend to yet another illness. She came when my father complained of a terrible pain in his stomach and then had to have emergency surgery for appendicitis. She came the night when he called us and wanted all of us around his bed: he was dying, he said in a tearful voice. He was yellow, covered with sweat, and his mouth was very dry — and then he had to be taken in a taxi to the hospital in Ribeira Grande, where they operated on him for a stomach ulcer.

She arrived wobbling like a short-legged stool, always making a fuss, pushing the night in front of her, and leaving the road deaf. The next day, the boys on the street made nasty comments and said horrible things about my mother's big hairy thing; it swelled, opened like a prune, and from deep inside her. It was inevitable for me to get into fights with them, defending our mother and those miniature people whose faces looked like ours; the same purple fingers, the same peach fuzz on their heads and backs, and the same strongly etched mouth. As for Mama, she must have been really sick, because sickness in our house was always treated with chicken soup and fried eggs with sausage . . .

We don't have a single picture left over from those days. Other families' children were normally photographed when they got baptized, or maybe when they managed to sit up without help for the first time, or maybe when they finally started crawling. Or else when they figured out how to stand up and took wing like little doves, tried a few steps, fell, and then got up again to walk. There are photos of their first and last days of school, the visit of the bishop who came to confirm them, the day of the military draft lottery, one or another pig slaughter, of parties and processions in which they were dressed as angels, or when they were crowned during the novenas of the Holy Spirit.

Yes, the big difference between our lives and the lives of others began with the simple fact that they were preserved in portraits while we were forgotten in the darkness of memory. With the simple fact that they could leaf through family albums and see how they had been happy, how they had grown and learned to enjoy life. As for us, there is only one dark past, with no differentiation between years, feast days, birthdays.

The few times the photographers came here, with their ancient cameras on a tripod, we gathered together to admire the way the man went about preparing his work. There was a sleeve of black flannel; the man stuck his head into it to look at people from afar. He came on the eve of feast days, installed himself in a van eaten by rust, and went from door to door asking for the children who were going to be dressed up as angels, for the men leading the processions and carrying the litters: didn't they didn't want to keep the best, prettiest, and holiest memories of their lives forever? Sometimes entire families planted themselves in the middle of the street, in front of their houses. They brought long benches and chairs, arranged themselves around the doorframe, and the photographer looked, looked, and looked. To a certain point, it was an art that demanded a great engineering of gestures, touches, and poses. He would emerge frequently from his flannel sleeve to adjust the angle of a head, move people together so they would fit in the frame, to better compose the position of arms, arch of a neck, lift of a head. During those moments of nervousness in front of the machine, the photographer became the master of ceremonies, the sole owner of those people. The grandfathers, born in another century, rested their shaky white hands on the boxwood cameras, in those days, came around to give us its blessing, from the height of my Uncle Martinho's six-foot frame (he was the tallest man I'd ever known).

He had come to Rozário to have a church wedding. His civil marriage, by proxy, to Aunt Etelvina could hardly weather eternity without first being sanctified by priestly blessing. Before returning to Canada to await the arrival of his wife, who would join him a little later, he began to anticipate his coming loneliness, to foresee the tears he would shed for her, for his nieces and nephews, and for everyone else he would miss once he'd left home again. So in the week remaining before his flight to Montreal, he assembled his seventeen nieces and nephews at the Canto da Fonte. He ordered them into two rows, putting them in size order, and urging them to lift their heads and look right into the sun. He took forever to double check that we all fit into his shot. After many adjustments of his lens's diaphragm, he squatted down and told us to look for the birdie to come out, and then he clicked the shutter. He signaled for us to wait, went into the house, brought out a big bag of candy, and began to distribute it to us. He left the next week, as scheduled, without saying good-bye to anyone, but leaving behind the promise that soon he would send us a copy of the picture. We waited for months, certain that the moment would serve as an eternal mirror of our childhoods — never changing or being effaced, like the images in real mirrors. It arrived the following Christmas, in a cloth envelope. It took Papa and Mama ages to find us in the midst of so many cousins. They turned up the lamp, and Papa asked for his glasses, and a long time went by before we heard him say:

"Look, there's Amélia! And that must be Luís, then!" Nuno, always the clown, stood there with his fingers in his mouth, like a perfect idiot, and Domingas was distracted, with her head turned away, staring off at the day before yesterday. Only after making many more comments and laughing at us did they permit the photo to reach our hands. Then we clustered together, shoulder to shoulder, to try to make out all the most important details of our existence.

As for me, I looked like a tower stretching up between my two fat cousins, and there was a visible difference as we posed for that picture squinting in the sun, between me and all the others. Nuno really did have his fingers in his mouth. Linda was frowning. And Flor was just a little speck trapped in Domingas's lap. Amélia was starting to take on the angular, sickly appearance that she still has today, and already her glasses gave her a long-suffering, serious canes, touched the tips of their moustaches, and lifted the brims of their felt hats, as was the custom in their time. The more distracted grandchildren were admonished to look straight ahead and to quiet down. The photographer emerged again in little jumps, walking on the tips of his toes; he spit into his hands, smoothed down hair blown by the wind, taming a cowlick or a twisted lock or badly combed wave, bribing the young with rag dolls or even with sweets offered by his dirty fingers.

"Look at the birdie, look at the birdie!" he repeated, again popping out from under his sleeve. "If you want to see the birdie come out, children, you have to be very still and look straight at my hand."

A good three quarters of an hour later, the man came back out of his van, shook the flasks of magnesium acid in the air, blew on the glass photographic plate, and then his frog's mouth ripped open in a wide smile. One could see a family with darkened faces, and astonished somewhat stunned expressions, like the coal miners of long ago. Then the portrait was ready to be mounted on a carpenter's board or a piece of framed glass that some, in time, would forget among other forgotten things. It was hung on the kitchen wall, over the dining table, or in one of their bedrooms, or even in the entryway, in full sight. It aged like a shadowy memory, lost gradually to reality, while some of those who were in the portrait became our ancestors.

Whereas my childhood and that of my brothers and sisters were erased from time, denied the luxury of such permanence. We were never angels in processions; my parents never bothered to acknowledge the supplicating voices of those photographers who came from far away and who guaranteed the preservation of human perfection as well as the art of lending daily life a little zest, a little romance.

We had, then, to wait for the years to pass, had to wait to drift apart from one another to earn the right to enter into photographs. Pretexts were needed, for instance the necessity that we be furnished with identity cards, that we meet the military specifications for being assigned our first passports. Aside from those exceptions, nothing, not a single image remains — as I've said — to remind us of whether we were handsome or ugly in those days, if we were thin or fat, if we all looked like each other or perhaps resembled some more distant blood relative. Mirrors don't give us this kind of information, you know; their images disappear with a breath.

Actually, no, I tell a lie: there *was* one time when the most modern of all countenance. Nuno and I stood out in the center of the picture thanks to the curly cowlicks sticking up from the middles of our heads, but also, in his case, because of his belly sticking out between his suspenders, and in mine because of my fine bones. That was when I saw myself as looking ridiculous. You see, we'd discovered some time before the picture had been taken that I could see better from one eye than the other. The doctor in Algarvia prescribed a pink patch to cover one of my eyes that adhered to the lens of my glasses with a suction cup. I didn't know how long I would have to use it. But even today, when I remember my childhood, I continue to present myself to life with a pirate's face, one eye looking at the future and the other covered; nobody had the presence of mind to take the thing so that I could appear in the picture with at least as much dignity and naturalness as my other siblings . . .

"Can you see my teeth?"

They're crooked and irregular. One day they started to crowd together, either coming out on top of or across each other. Papa would use a string, pliers, and his own nails, strong as pincers, while Mama held my head against her chest. He pulled, twisted, pulled, twisted. His fingers would get bloody, and I would scream in pain, as if they were pulling out my nails or tearing out my sideburns.

During all those years, during the my long life here and in Canada too, I was pursued by visions of those teeth, my crooked knees, excessive span of my shoulders, by the strength that made me different from but not superior to boys of my age. They called me *bow-legged weirdo*, *Dracula*, and *grasshopper*. Now I've got this big belly from Canadian beer, I've fleshed out all over, and I've had a limp since the day that mechanized saw tore into my knee. I fell, passed out, and an ambulance took me away to be subjected to anesthetic, the operating table, and the stitches of some quack doctor. Canadians stare, but my brothers and sisters take one look and then pretend they didn't see it, or else just change the subject. But I know what I was, what I always was and will always be — it's inevitable that it'll fall to me and no one else, the role of the fool. It happened in Rozário, and also in the army during the Guinean War, and above all in Canada — suffering everyone's jibes without understanding their language, without any tips as to how I could defend myself from their insults, hide away from the hell that was my life. I crisscrossed my little piece of the world in search of more money, *dollahs*. I was let go, *fiahed*, by more than a thousand bosses, mainly during the Toronto and Vancouver winters, when the harsh winter *snoeh* complicates construction work. I muddled through lots of "workers' compensation" and "insurance," and I was always an outcast, especially thanks to this butt-ugly face that God gave me. It all started the day that the Rozário girls looked up at me passing by at my six-foot height and averted their eyes, running on ahead of me or hiding their laughter in their aprons. Only one or two of the poor things, the ugliest ones, and one of them cross-eyed with a purple pimple wart on her chin ever condescended to be my girlfriend. The others, stuck-up princesses from Rua Direita, were happy to see me go: who cared that I was boarding a ship to who-knew-where, would be wandering through strange countries in pursuit of the perfume of *dollahs*.

"Suck my dick!" I said to one of them, taking my dick out of my pants and waving it at her. "Suck me and swallow it, or do it with your father!"

We all went through years when we worked like mules hauling cargo, the months passed by without Sundays, when on feast days there wasn't even enough money for a peanut cone or a cup of peanuts, and the times when my father was constantly in a rage, convinced we were useless and giving us the belt. Dressed in clothes that were too big for us, hand-me-downs from our uncles, we were children of parents who simply ignored us on the feast days of the Holy Spirit, turning away and pretending not to know us, just so they wouldn't have to give us a few coins for lupine beans and hard candies. In Papa's opinion, there were just too many of us, we were a liability to the household. I felt like screaming in his face, "Then you shouldn't have fucked so much when you were younger!"

I always heard him say that a child was an investment, a sort of vaginal business transaction negotiated on behalf of your family's future — but it ended up as a debit, if not an outright liability, when the goods arrived and proved useless as revenue or income generators. That's why Amélia and Nuno, deciding to flee to the Continent — so carried away by their callings, conveniently enough! — were such a big loss. For years they wrote from Lisbon asking for a little help, and their appeals fell on deaf ears, Papa's indifference clear for all to see in his slack expression, which only cleared up when he gave my mother those withering glances that contained his only replies to their letters:

"I'm hardly going to steal from the kids who stayed put just to help sort out the lives of the ones who jumped ship — who refused to work for the household or produce a damn thing!"

I don't know if he ever realized that things would change with time; I also don't think he ever took pride in any one of his nine children. The eldest, Amélia, *what a clever girl* she was in school, and she excelled in her profession as a nurse. I was strong as a horse, although I had my share of misfortune thanks to the two workplace *accidents* in my construction job. Domingas and Zélia, over there in America, are both doing very well. Nuno, no one should feel sorry for him; he got married to a peach of a girl, and he has a degree and is teaching in *high school* — though I don't understand why he didn't thrive and isn't rich and respected like *teachers* used to be. He has chronic headaches! Jorge, a master carpenter, is a big success. He's got men working for him in Toronto and he owns a proper Canadian company! And Mário, the most reserved of all of us, doesn't spend a *dollah* he doesn't have to, doesn't confide in anyone, and he screws all the sex-starved girls in Vancouver!

I'm the wild card, the ace in this deck of cards and the traitor of the family. I worked like an ox and suffered like a horse. When I married that girl who smiled at me one day from her house in Capelas, I went running to my father to ask him if he could chip in for the wedding and maybe throw in a little extra so I could start my life. He raised his eyes to a heaven that didn't exist and shook his head "no" twice.

"You should already know I don't pay for weddings. Wait till I die and you'll get your share."

Years later, when I was in Canada, I needed ten thousand *dollahs* and I went running back to Papa. I begged and pleaded: "It's just a loan, Papa!" He reluctantly agreed to give me the money for a year, with interest. Later, he regretted it, called me, and said he'd decided to invest the money in Portugal after all, where he'd get a better return, since the interest rate was higher. I was confused, panicked, revolted at the avarice of that old man. I reneged on my business deals, turned everything upside down, and took out a mortgage. That same day, at dusk, I went to his door.

"Here's your dirty little money back, Papa," I said, "and may you spend it in good health!"

He laid his very sad eyes on me, lowered his head to his chest, and, five years later, on his deathbed, he asked me how my children were doing, and then to forgive him for that unhappy episode.

Do you know what I did? I took advantage of the moment to forgive him for all the hell of my childhood, the many beatings he'd given me for no reason, the curses, the insults, the fact that he hadn't attended my wedding, had never liked me in the least, hadn't comforted me when I was sick or when I left for the goddamn Colonial War in Portuguese Guinea — as well as for all his deficiencies as a father and for all the reasons I could never be proud of being his son, the father of two of his grandsons and a serious man myself, dedicated to work and the harmony of my household. Our lives were the way they were, and not otherwise, because my father willed it to be that way. Even today, from the grave, he continues to impose his will on us, and we continue to obey him; his voice is everywhere. He calls all of us by name, giving us orders and warnings, advising and admonishing us. The only real difference is that he can't beat us anymore, because he's been transformed into a soul in torment, and nobody really believes anymore that souls can wield whips to flay and punish the living. Before he died, he asked us to let Nuno have the house. The land, the vegetable gardens, the hillsides, pastures, woods, and orchards were to be divided by lots among the rest of us, and that's what we did. During that last Christmas, when he had his grandchildren on his knees and there were more than thirty of us around his table, since nobody had died yet, we still had the illusion that maybe time could still run backward. We saw Papa acting nothing like his old self — laughing, playing with his grandchildren, telling them stories they'd never heard before, happy things that had never happened, or anyway not to us. He looked at my brothers and me, giving us a malicious wink. He knew what we were all thinking; that old age was the price of his change of heart. If he'd ever been this sweet, tender, and serene when we were kids, nobody would have been obliged to feel afraid of him. I wouldn't have married against his will. Amélia wouldn't have become a nun. Nuno wouldn't have had any reason to run away from home to study to be a bishop. And he also never would have had to dream up that ridiculous story he gave us to explain why he never became a priest. When he was around eighteen they expelled him from the seminary; he wrote us the longest of his letters and explained all the reasons he had lost his calling; how he couldn't stand the priests anymore and had decided, like us, to enjoy women. He was probably the only one of us who always had the luck of being able to disobey Papa, to refuse to come home and tell him in writing that he refused to be his mule, ox, or even his son. For this reason, Nuno could laugh at our story as if it were a good yarn. Told by him, sir, even we found it funny . . .

CHAPTER THREE

Nuno Miguel

The particular memory of this semi-fairy tale goes back to the days when I'd go back to the Island, year after year, every time the seminary closed for vacation. A woman who was as white as chalk, with deep blue eyes and the body of a clumsy gazelle, clasped me firmly against her large breasts when I got off the city bus — and that's when I always noticed some new and still unfamiliar wrinkle on her face, or another gray streak that was starting to appear in her hair. I thus witnessed her progressive transformation into a kind of bale of hay, becoming fatter and fatter, losing her teeth and assuming a resigned, melancholy air. Aside from that I remember her as a constant, flat, presence in my life. As abruptly as she would sing the few lyrics she knew by heart she would split the silence with an angry scream that would put our teeth on edge. When she laughed, it was a cackle, with shaking shoulders and a heaving belly. For her, life was a continual present that offered nothing to hope for.

On the day of my arrival, the family would assemble en masse at the bus station to wait for me. From up on the bus I would see this strange tribe looking for me with anxious eyes, waiting for me to stand up, smile, and wave to them, in terrible suspense at the mere possibility that I would be different, taller or fatter, after this latest year of absence. It was immediately obvious to me that they were the ones who had changed, not I. My older sisters were embarrassed by their sprouting little breasts; the faces of my father and Luís were even more chapped and sunburned. The younger ones, not recognizing me, hid their faces and refused to come to my arms. The babies born while I'd been away made faces, furrowed their brows, and let out cries of protest against this intruder who pinched their cheeks or tickled their noses. We disguised an undisguisable unease, reintroducing ourselves to each other like strangers, not like family. Aggravating the distance already put between us by my now-civilized demeanor, I spoke continental Portuguese, with its sweet, refined pronunciation, like a foreigner, and I was no longer burned by the island sun nor pickled by the salt that gave them all the look of burnished peasants. Papa was the one who broke the funereal silence of that uncouth tribe, submerged under his felt hat. He was so small a man that the wings of that hat seemed to dangle him in the air. A thick cigarette wrapped in corn leaves sometimes as thick as a boga fish drooped from his lips. He was always the last to come up to me at these reunions, and his limp embrace gave me not a father but a humid pall of sweat and tobacco breath accompanied by a trifling greeting that I got used to hearing from year to year:

"Bless you, son!"

My older brother, to disguise his discomfort, turned immediately to practical things. He picked up my suitcase full of clothes and useless books and asked me about soccer, since he was entranced by my description of the stadiums and the small Lusitanian triumphs. The girls, still shy, limited themselves to admiring my erudition, the rounded vowels of my Lisbonian pronunciation, and my happiness at being a man with hands as smooth as the pages of books.

In the middle of our home gathering, Papa emerged from the shadows of the kitchen bench. It was obviously difficult for him to overcome his reserve and to enter into conversation with me. What he really wanted to hear from my lips was how long we'd have to wait for the big bellied, ancient, and eternal dictator Salazar to die; could I perhaps share any new detail about his failing health, which I might have picked up from my place by his bishop's throne? Some new information as to how the man was managing to stay alive so improbably when no one ever caught so much as a glimpse of him from a single window of the closed airless house in which he resided, and which he identified with his country.

Suddenly Mama came on stage. She seemed to stand on tiptoe, to levitate from the floor, smiling with a barely-visible mischief at the corners of her mouth. She would open the doors of the pantry, my siblings would smile at the anticipated complicity, and there was always a clay pot there covered with a kitchen cloth.

"Look here, our dear Nuno, I made you sweet bread and rice pudding, just the way you like it. Fill up that belly for me, my darling son, and taste the pleasures of home."

Aside from such exceptional occasions, my soul is shut tight on the subject — it seems to refuse me even the simplest memory of that sweet mother, unflappable but hardly ever cheerful. It always impressed me that she didn't bother to remember our birthdays; we had no expectation of presents, of course, but we always thought we deserved a cookie or a smile from her. But there were never any celebrations of anything. Christmas presents were even less likely; sweetmeats and candies came randomly and from strangers. Wristwatches? They only came into the family when times changed and we were destined for Canada. Until then, we were stuck with the monotony of the wall clock pendulum whose swings sounded like sticks beating a box. It was impossible to guess at the correct time in its mechanical presence. Still, every time the great clock stopped, we had to wind it back up with a big key and readjust the hands according to whatever random occurrence: someone's guess, the supposition that it must be noon because the church bells were ringing, the appearance of the mailman, or the northeast bus. But this uncertainty about time never interfered with the rhythm of our life, or the way it progressed. At home we had hours to ourselves. On clear days, when we worked in the fields, far from people who had pocket watches, we stuck pieces of wood into the ground in a circle, in the middle of which a cane stalk projected a crooked shadow — and so our sense of time came from the sun and was never much more than guesswork...

But if there were no wristwatches, or birthday parties, or Christmas presents, the hope of getting toys soon disappeared as well. We made cars from melon rinds or potato peels, rag dolls hand sewn by the girls, tops and whirligigs of elder wood, oblong balls stuffed with floorcloths and strips of canvas. We invented substitutes for marbles, bicycle seats, and horse saddles. We mounted the branches of fig trees, plough shafts, and the cables of other farm equipment.

We wore shoes made of caked mud and cow pies. In the sea of the feeding troughs and the chicken and pigpens, we invented boats made of cane leaves wrapped in fiber. As far as airplanes or birds were concerned, we made use of the brown paper of the sacks of saltpeter and fertilizer and the strips of wood that curled out from the planing machines. Back then we fantasized that castles and mansions might grow out of the pebbles we scattered in the orchard, like in the fairy tales that we had heard about from Grand Mama Olinda. Imagining fish in an aquarium, we made nurseries of head lice, weevils, and fig tree bugs. Hair from the maize corn, wrapped in dried leaves, smooth and in aluminum containers, smooth and magically luminous, became cigarettes and cigars, and allowed us to play at being majestic, pensive smokers. We didn't know anything about pottery or sculpture, but we were resourceful enough to mold dogs and horses out of chewed breadcrumbs, we erected churches and birthed blind crèche figures from the mud. And since it was always forbidden to see the ocean up close, we used poplar boards to imagine ships on Atlantic crossings that got shipwrecked on the limestone cliffs, and we dug earthen tunnels traveled by foreign things, like invisible trains, or nonexistent exotic animals.

"So what was your life like?" you ask.

The best way to answer is to describe all the ways we were different from other families on the Island. At first, like the others, we went barefoot and we wore American style pants, overalls with breast pockets. But when rubber boots, Sunday shoes, or chamois leather jackets came along, we quickly saw that everyone else was leaving us behind. Other kids had the privilege of going to the barber, but not us: Papa had a rusty pair of scissors, a steel comb, and an electric razor that buzzed shrilly over our desiccated mops. On the occasional Sunday before Mass, that terrifying machine sheared off our hair and parts of our scalps as well, provoking a torrent of tears. We cried in silence, afraid of him, because Papa never believed that anything really hurt us. If we moved so much as an inch, a rain of blows would fall on our necks or throats, and Papa threatened to cut our ears off with his scissors and leave us lopsided for life.

We would go to the mirror afterward and see that we looked like badly-shorn sheep, shivering so violently that our faces were almost unrecognizable. The backs of our heads and necks looked as if we'd been bitten by swarms of insects or deloused like monkeys by the nails of our mother and older sisters. At the end of the summer, or any time that we became lethargic, which was a sign of parasites or worms, Mama would make us wear our clogs to bed. She kept us fasting until lunchtime and forced noxious syrup down our throats. According to her, the fast was as indispensable as wearing shoes on the day of the cure. If we were barefoot, the worms wouldn't die of the poison and they would remain in our bodies forever. Around mid-afternoon, with our stomachs roiling in a convulsive gallop and our intestines in turmoil, we would run to an open hole in the orchard, squat down, and from our insides came twisted coils of vermin that foamed in that deathly elixir. When they were doused with petrol and lit on fire, the pests burst like rats or garbage. They were, please understand, our odious offal as much as lice, their eggs, or ticks…

There was nothing sadder than to watch children playing with their worms. Poking their feces to find them, expecting to find the mythological tapeworm, the great green serpent or even fire-breathing dragon that might one day inhabit their innards . . .

The fashion for nylon shirts also passed us by. Polyester, chamois leather, and fake fur were fabrics we never encountered. Our lot was rough linen cloth, flowery linen prints, and fake taffeta; it was a time of thick gabardine jackets inherited from dead old people; canvas sacks folded into hoods flapping like fins or like the blinders guiding the bulbous eyes of our donkeys. But we didn't really think of ourselves, in our daily lives, as being miserable or impoverished. Mama taught us to take a very practical perspective:

"There are the rich, the saved, the poor, and the destitute. We, by the grace of God, are the saved. We have a house, land, and livestock. And there will always be money for our old age, or if we get sick . . ."

Misery was something quite different, it was spiritual. In my parents' hearts avarice grew like ivy on walls or clover in the fields. Dough would sit and go stale and moldy for up to fifteen days because to light the oven meant using some of our store of firewood. Milk that would give us calcium for our teeth and bones was only produced to sell at the factory; if we begged for a piece of home-baked bread with cow's butter, or even a slice of cheese with store-bought bread for our lunch, we got nothing. According to our mother, that sort of thing was food for the rich. We shouldn't let ourselves be tempted by it — the rich were cursed, you see. Do you know why? Whoever had pleasure on earth would suffer doubly in Heaven, and it was a proven fact that only the poor were entitled to dream of the Kingdom of God. Eggs? They were for those who bought them on Sundays in the church square, and only after they were emphatically offered to the priest and our teachers for Our Lord. Truffles, culled amid the terrible grunts of pigs, were ported about in the carts of traveling salesmen, while the gray peddlers with wine on their breath would measure flour and bag it to take it away in their ancient vans. The pregnant cows, coveted by cattle breeders, quickly increased other herds. Then came the money. It was folded, ironed, and secured with a clothespin. In the bottom of clothing drawers, it took on the smell of Mama's mothballs until someone advertised the sale of more pasture or half an acre of land.

In our household, Mr. Kafka, everything was always more or less absurd: we cultivated beets; Papa would travel once a year to the City in a truck carrying six tons of the stuff. When he returned, the coffee was still bitter and looked like it was made of mud. We owned innumerable animals of different species, but the meat always tasted like salted mackerel and we only ever ate lard in brine and bacon boiled in bone broth. The stew always tasted like sweet potatoes, and we ate it with corn bread and the awful roasted beans. As for me, I hated bacon, cassava, fennel, boiled corn, and stew; I was repulsed by their stash of money that grew or diminished according to the price of land and heifers. So many years later, when I think back, I see that herding sheep, cleaning shit, or digging up beets in the winter months was never any worse or better than harvesting corn, cutting down trees with a handsaw, or suffering my father's and my teacher's beatings. I was happy to be aging, traveling farther away from it all in time — I never once regretted that I was growing up.

I remember the first time I was taken to see the ocean up close: I was nine years old. We lived, as you know, two kilometers away from it; we could smell it; we heard its song, the cry of seabirds, the wind that pushed the frightening debris of shipwrecks up to the cliffs. Papa, however, always associated the ocean with leisure and laziness; he was forever opposed to our visiting it, as the other children did, to throw a little party, swim, catch limpets and crabs, or simply sit and watch it. When I finally got to see it for myself, I entered into a kind of ecstasy, as though what I was seeing came from some other, fantastical order of reality. Until then, I had only seen it from afar, from up here, from the heights of our land and walls, round and oblique and so formidably far away that it seemed to glue itself to the curved line of the firmament. The day I could admire it up close, it turned out to be surprisingly flat after all, so horizontal and level that it seemed to challenge the theories of the learned men, according to whom the earth, the seas, and the rivers were all part of an egg-shaped planet . . .

To give you an idea of how sedentary we were and how much we envied the few nomads we encountered for their good fortune in being able to travel, I only went to the Northeast Village on the day of final exam for fourth grade and when I left for Lisbon on a November day. When I boarded the boat, I entered the hold of a cargo ship that was full of cranes slurping up calves, goats, and timber. They accommodated me in a bunk surrounded by strangers; I was already suffering the first waves of nausea, dreading the continuous stench of salt and vomit. To this day I don't know if I have the words to describe the mercurial darkness of the high seas on that fearful voyage between Ponta

Delgada and the luminous City of Lisbon. Everything is confused with the turbid waters and the somber days of childhood. Happy are they who cross that space by plane. May they continue to be happy even though they don't know why. Fortunate are the children, young people, and adult citizens of this country of today; they meet the sea when they're born, they see it from airplanes and don't have to live under surveillance by the police. My generation ended the war in Africa, forgave the executioners, and returned the diaphanous sky of their dark country to the Portuguese people. You can die with an easy conscience; you did your last jump on the trapeze and landed on your feet; don't let anyone tell you that the circus performers are naked, or that the sun, the sea, and the days of today or of tomorrow are illusions.

Maria Amélia

The construction of the house is one of the brightest memories of my childhood. I don't remember the foundations being laid, or how the walls were raised, at what pace, or by whom. All I know is that it all started to happen on the day that some tired, very sweaty men hoisted the wooden slats from the lathes, and my father, up high, naked to the waist, nailed them to the beams. The house took shape on the day that the roof tiles arrived in a cart pulled by two men and were laid in an afternoon. My visions of the house were, in fact, both dreamlike and acutely lucid. For example, there were the walls: I remember them as being like the ones in the other house we lived in, without plaster and with the stones exposed. I don't know at what point the cement, limestone, and stucco appeared. *I mean, it's not easy at all.* It's not at all easy to reconstruct so many things in time and space, as you would like me to do. Papa and Mama died before their time, too young to go. It took them by surprise, just like you, and that's why we are still somewhat perplexed, and so rather passionate about mixing up facts with feelings. If only we'd had a few more years to prepare. But our feelings still betray us, our embarrassment at such sentiment. And until we free ourselves completely from that rain of tears that was our childhood, I doubt we can characterize ourselves as people who deserve to be happy. It's a gray happiness, between the black and white of our memories and our present lives, as if it had come to us poisoned and undeserved. But let's get back to the facts.

Moving day came. A cart drawn by oxen carried all of our few pieces of furniture, taking it along Rua Direita, and then unloaded everything in front of our new door. The dishes and clothing came in wicker baskets, and I remember that this happened at dusk, because several people came by after working in the fields to help and then to drink wine with cinnamon and eat a lot of pan bread.

"Carry Nuno," Mama said, bustling around euphorically; I'd never seen her like that before. "Take Luís and Domingas by the hand and start walking down. Your father and I will pick you up along the way."

She was happy, you see, because not only was it new, it was her dream house. It had a room for me and my sister, another for my parents, and a third for the boys. It also had the enormous advantage that the cows would no longer have to be herded through the living room. In the back, before the barn was built, a low gate with a latch was put up, which led to the livestock pen and the orchard. Yes, it was all ours: new, marvelous, and different from all the other houses on the Island. Even though it was modest, it was no longer that dark, squat hut stuck between big houses stuffed full of noisy villagers.

Mama was simply bursting with happiness. Sure, she was exhausted, with dark rings under her eyes, but the electricity was on, and she sang all day long, sweeping the corners of the house, filling up baskets with the dirt from the construction and throwing it in the corner of the orchard, where Papa had planted willow trees and a hedge. Dishes and clothing occupied temporary places because there were no armoires or shelves. The walls were bare, without any plaster. Our belongings lived with us between those stone walls crowned by a slat ceiling with the tiles showing, everything piled in the corners in complete disorder. Experience tells me, however, that women are always the soul of a house. They bring a special light to the poorest and darkest of them. Mama's gift for improvisation, during this period, when she was full of energy, imagination, and common sense, lent everything a place and a function that was immediately perfect. Papa was not as well adapted. Either because he rarely expressed emotion or was worried about the debts he'd incurred from the construction, he wandered about lost, with uncertain steps, like a caged bird, until he got used to things. Admittedly, there was a discreet pride in his eyes, and he wasn't always as angry and argumentative as before. We understood: this floor was "his," it was a boat upon the sea, a nest for his children and wife, the foundation of his future dreams. Soon he threw himself into a frenzy of work, possessed by an almost satanic energy that led him to craft armoires, tables, and benches and to finish projects only started the day before, whether they were window boxes, shelves, doors, or even pieces of flooring. At the end of the day, tired from the work in the hillsides he leased at Moio, he would arrive home with a bundle of wood or straw on his back, his forehead shiny, and his hair wet with sweat — a man bent under the weight of his obsessions. The next morning, very early, he left with a hoe over his shoulder and disappeared again into the depths of his leased land. He dug, cleared brambles, ferns, and ginger lilies, he planted cabbage and beets from the seedling beds. At quarter past noon, Mama sent me to take him his lunch in the same basket that once carried her newborns. By the time Papa came back with the cows, the moon was already out, and I saw him livid with exhaustion, his shoulders slumped, more impatient than sad, and I was filled with pity for him. The rest of us would go to bed. But he lost track of the time. We fell asleep to the sound of the lathe, the saw, and the hammer. When we woke up, there was always another chair, a new line of shelves, or a door on the china cabinet.

Early in the morning I walked to the school of my dreams. In the afternoons, I sat with Nuno in my lap taking care of the others. Mama would go out to do the laundry at a public cistern. Luís jumped around the house, crazy as a calf, or dragged himself along the floor, trying to discover the mysteries and secrets of a space that was unknown to him. Domingas, who had a mischievous nature and was a picky eater, would be reprimanded and start to scream and cry. She wanted to take Nuno from my lap by force; she hadn't forgotten God's injustice, which had taken the other twin and left her with empty arms. But then she'd turn her attention to Nuno. Won over by the tenderness of his very blue eyes and straw-colored hair, she begged me for a truce, whispering in my ear:

"Mélia, I know he's yours and yours alone. But I'd like to hold him a little and watch him smile just at me, for once . . ."

But he didn't smile at all! Nuno was what you would call a perfect mess. He drooled until he was four years old, only started walking when he was three, and until he was at least two his body was just a limp and boneless mass. He never gave us any signs of particular intelligence. He would stare at things, his gaze fixed in the distance, without following us or responding to stimuli. All we could be sure of was that he wasn't entirely brain damaged, since we could see that his eyes were expressive and amused. Still, though in a passive manner, he managed to get people to understand him. He would kick his feet with contentment when Mama chattered with him; he lifted his arms to be held. And he tried in vain to lift himself up, his spine arched, unable to lift his head. Mama was very worried about his weakness. She made him swallow cod-liver oil by pinching his nose; he would spit it back in her face, turn purple, and almost choke. Fearing he had worms, she made him take the parasite medicine, and Nuno would expel a yellowish slime, with gelatinous things in the mix. With time he started to get spankings because he continued to dirty his diapers and piss himself. Nuno peed a lot! As for talking, he only pronounced monosyllables, a nonsensical babble, and then clarified with gestures. When he wanted something, he'd pull my skirt, point his crooked finger and say: "uh, uh…" Later, he must have been four or five, something happened to him — I don't know what. He suddenly woke up, as if a flashbulb of intelligence had gone off in his head. From one day to the next, he gave signs not only of basic understanding but also of having discovered the nature of things. He became obsessed, spurred on by a desire to decipher the entire world. His monosyllables changed into clear, melodious words. Soon words gave way to perfectly articulated sentences. He progressed through the grammar of the world by grasshopper leaps, growing in spurts. It was a miracle. Mama couldn't believe it.

Uncle Martinho, from that time on, began to take him for outings. He'd give him piggyback rides up on top of his almost-six-foot-high shoulders. He could not, in fact, have offered Nuno a better vantage point on the world. Nuno was taken to the shops, the pig slaughters, and even to his uncle's trysts; Nuno tried wine with cinnamon, learned to wink at the girls, and soon he was gone for entire days. Sometimes, without telling anyone, he would sleep at Grand Mama Botelho's place, watching over that uncle who adored him so much and with whom he visited the cattle, the countryside, and the orchards. If anyone at our house remembered to ask where he was at that hour, since no one had seen him since the day before, a chorus immediately rose, with the complicity of Mama and the ire of Papa:

"With Uncle Martinho, at Grandma's house or in the stores!"

He hung around with our uncle so much that he started to imitate everything about the man: his almost rocking gait, he raspy laugh, and even his dirty words. We couldn't have suspected then that Nuno would learn about the world by sitting on those slightly hunched shoulders.

We would die laughing just listening to his discussions with Papa. At a certain point he decided on his own initiative to show up unannounced at all kinds of peoples' houses, regardless of whether they were enemies, neighbors with bad reputations, or people who were little more than strangers. When slaughtering time came around, in January, Nuno would knock on the doors of Papa's worst enemies and sit at their tables and fill his stomach, just to spite our father. One time Papa went after him, mad as hell, to give him a good beating.

"Listen here, boy!" he snarled, getting right into Nuno's face. "Didn't I tell you that I don't want you hanging out with those people? Wake up, look me in the eye: you know very well we don't get along with them! Listen here Nuno, get a move on!"

Nuno slowly lifted his head and stared at our father with a theatrical expression; he seemed very distant from the aggressiveness in Papa's voice.

"Oh Papa, it completely slipped my mind! Goodness me, what was I thinking?" he answered, opening his arms ingenuously. "But, look, it's hardly my fault that you can't get along with half the Island. This door I can go in, that I can't . . . you don't talk to anyone, do you? You just make enemies. Weren't you baptized, Papa? Aren't you a Christian?"

At that point Papa turned green, almost losing his nerve. Still, without taking another breath, he dragged Nuno back along the road and pushed him into the door of our house. That, however, was lost on Nuno. He listened, listened, and listened, but at the end of the sermon he didn't look a bit cowed and just started emptying his pockets. Out of them came pastries, almonds, and sweets, a piece of roasted meat, cookies, and even cigarettes. We all reached out for these treats, surrounding him in a circle of arms, and distributed the treats among us with equanimity. As for the cigarettes, he held them out to Papa and spoke, his voice taking on a certain scolding vehemence:

"Papa, stop your complaining! I know very well you like to smoke store-bought cigarettes instead of your usual lumps of tobacco rolled in corn leaves. So come on, enjoy, Papa!"

Papa looked nervous more than anything, inexpressive. Won over by the boy's wiles, he had no other choice but to flick his lighter and make a hasty exit, sucking as hard as possible on that enemy cigarette. A good part of Nuno's innocence was burned away by his investigating precisely those parts of the world he'd been forbidden to enter; and he showed the same sort of distance years later, when he would come home to the Island, never bothering to get mixed up in family intrigues.

"And what of his intellectual development," you ask me?

One day, when he was still a backward baby, Uncle Martinho gave him a good looking over and decided that all this drooling and babbling was clearly deceptive as far as his nephew's great intellectual powers. He decided to ignore the bottles and the bibs, trying to help Nuno understand that a man could never please women looking like that, dressed like a baby and with the disgusting habit of drooling every time you opened your mouth to speak.

"Jeez, Nuno! That's disgusting! I can't even stand looking at you. If you want to hang out with me, you have to blow the snot out of your nose and wipe the spit off your face. Got it?"

He taught Nuno how to unzip his fly and take off his pants when he had to do his business, to blow his nose sideways at the ground, and to swallow his spit. In a flash Nuno learned how to unfasten his suspenders and unbutton his fly, and he blew his nose continuously, and spat into the air in an arc or swallowed gulps of that same spit, which till then had drenched his chest in a permanent slobber. He took his uncle's warnings so seriously that he started courting Altina, a little freckly girl on our street, whose company he sought out with sick obsessive obstinacy. It didn't take long for this little dalliance to become a full-fledged passion. They sought each other out at every opportunity, went everywhere together, got themselves lost in strangers' orchards and backyards. Altina became Nuno's goddess. He invited her to the family table, kept little pieces of pan-bread cake for her, bites of sweet potato, roasted corn, or other delicacies. When he didn't show up at meals, nobody worried. Certainly he had decided to eat at her house. He became more refined in his tastes by eating over at her house. As soon as he got a taste of plum jam, honey, and cow's butter with wheat bread, he became fixated on sweets and dairy products, greedy as a bear, and preemptively declared to Mama that her cooking didn't have anything like the flavor or variety of the cuisine over at his girlfriend's house.

"So do something about it," she answered with feigned annoyance. "Why don't you just move in there? You're old enough to do what you like."

He became a pensive child, dreamy to excess, who cared more about supposition than reality. Surrounding himself with a wall of fiction, he absented himself from our way of life and started to live in a space that he had invented for himself alone. Everyone seemed to adore him and fear him, sure that a radical transformation was underway in his spirit and his body. From one week to the next his hair turned completely black. His eyes stopped being blue, or exclusively so, anyway, taking on some yellow streaks that gave them a greenish tone, between blue and honey. He gained some weight, but not enough to reach the bulk and size of boys of his age and height. Everyone teased him by predicting that he'd be a dwarf, comparing him with Uncle Sebastião. Yet for nothing in this world did he want to be associated with that tiny, feeble, and lazy uncle, who we all made fun of and who was quite the lost soul, walking around looking like a beggar. Barefoot and flat-footed and very patched up all over by Grand Mama, he looked at us with sad eyes and was certainly the loneliest person in the neighborhood.

Linda and Flor were born. Jorge was about to be weaned. In our house it had always been that way; the older ones were sooner or later deprived of their cradles, their parents' laps, and their right to innocence. When we were seven years old, we worked eight hours a day; at nine, no less than ten. After school, there was no difference between night and day, rain and sun: we were on the go fourteen hours a day, some of us cultivating the land, others taking care of the cattle, others doing housework, and so on . . . I was put in the kitchen to wash clothes and take the brunt of my mother's bad humor. When I didn't put in enough salt, or else sprinkled too much on the food, when I'd forgotten to sew a button on or hadn't swept the corners, the front path, or the middle of the house well enough, Mama, in those days, was so quick to hit me or to scold me that even today my memory of her voice is that of a permanent reproach. Never once did she let me off the hook about the salt. Besides this, the beds were always badly made, the floors poorly scrubbed, our clothes had never seen starch, and the pigs were squealing because they hadn't been tended to in hours. As I moved from one chore to another, I got nothing but scoldings, sermons, and spankings!

Without our realizing it, the chains that bound us and made us siblings began to weaken. With my departure and Nuno's, the first links of that bond were broken. We began to disperse, to dissolve into separate worlds. Our existence began to consist of letters full of spelling errors and paragraphs of badly phrased prose that we had to explain better in the next letter.

Because of his dreamy nature, Nuno never entirely freed himself from his reputation as a dunce. Papa decided to put him to the test, trying out some practical tasks. Papa explained and demonstrated what he wanted Nuno to do, and then made him repeat everything he'd been told. Since he always performed his repetitions perfectly, down to the smallest detail, repeating Papa's instructions using the same words and in the same tone of voice, the hardest thing to understand was why, when he stepped out of Papa's shadow, he did precisely the opposite. So in Papa's opinion, he was nothing more than a fool and wasn't good for anything. One day, he slapped him twice. On another he hit him behind the ear. When Nuno was finally assaulted with boards, canes, and cattle prods, he joined the ranks of outcast children. I couldn't do anything for him, except to watch and listen, without understanding that this abuse would define his future. Years later, in Lisbon, when we were living in part of a rented house, I tried in vain to bring back his sweet nature. Nuno had become filled with despair. He loved all women, except those in the family. He went to literary salons and political rallies. He was beaten by the riot police. He came and went from our house, but he never wanted to tell me where he had been. I never understood why, in the course of those three years we lived together, facing the river of the dangerous city, eating the same mud, and drinking the turbid waters of those times in Lisbon, we were leading parallel lives. We became silent and estranged. Without hate, without bearing any grudges. But always facing away from each other — do you understand that, sir?

Luís Miguel

The day that the purgatory of books and school ended for me, I returned immediately, head lowered, just like a donkey, to the hell of the lands and the tortured life ruled by my father. To work, in Mr. Quental's opinion, dignified man, brought the dead back to life and healed the sick; hard labor lay heavily in wait for me at the northeast bus station. I had hardly caught sight of my mother and my brothers and sisters, the neighbors uphill and downhill from our house, and a bunch of people who seemed to spend their time waiting for buses, when I started to feel miserable. It made me think:

"Saddle up the donkey of patience, Mr. Know-it-all! Now you'll suffer like a pig: you got nice and fat and you're ready to be slaughtered!"

My mother was then pregnant with the second Victor — who, like the first, would die of weakness, deaf-mute and unable to move — and she was carrying Flor around on her hip. She came out of that cluster of kids, a little agitated, already missing her two front teeth, her unruly hair turning gray, and she asked me:

"So my little man, did your exams go well?"

"Good enough, Ma'am!" I answered haughtily, trying to sound confident. The little ones looked disappointed, almost disoriented, straining to know the truth on the other side and hopeful that I'd soon produce a candy or a packet of cookies.

"I had no other choice except to excel," I said disdainfully, knowing that, to them, this would mean as much as my announcing that it was raining, windy, or that we were in for a bout of terrible, muggy weather. I wouldn't have the right to a congratulatory kiss, a distracted pat on the head, or a mischievous wink from her heron-blue eye.

"Very good, young man! You always were a sharp fellow, and I knew you wouldn't disappoint us. Isn't that true, our dear Luís?"

"Sure! Mother, you were the one you made me who I am. I had to take after somebody."

I picked up Linda and Flor, one on each arm, gave my book bag to Domingas, and we started down the road. My little sisters ran off to spread the news about my grades, and people started to come to their doors and windows to congratulate my mother and to say what a perfect, dear boy I was. The usual speeches were made, as had happened with Amélia and Domingas, and as would be repeated every two years, for the others.

"If there were a little justice in this world, Miss Luísa, this little one wouldn't have to leave school already. With a head like his it's a sin he doesn't continue his studies to become a doctor . . ."

"Ah, if only I could do better for these children! But this place is nothing but a mud hole. We break our bodies and shackle our souls . . . till we're dead."

Waiting inside, both the malevolent eye and the thin voice of my father reached out to stab at me — the first barb of many:

"Now Luís, you'd better learn how to dig in to your work here with your teeth and nails. Move on and don't look back!"

I sank onto the bench I found, eyes on the floor, ready to listen without comment to the orders, sermons, the venomous whistle of his imperious speeches, thinking — just to console myself a little — that in spite of everything it wouldn't be so bad to be back among the cattle, for them to shit on me, to be upset, consumed, trampled, and made bitter by them; the same way that training wayward oxen to pull their cart with discipline and devotion wasn't the worst punishment I might suffer. With a little luck, it might not be as dire an excommunication as all that, to be just eleven years old and forced to work fourteen hours a day; to cultivate the land, clear underbrush, bring in the harvest, carry beets and bundles of wood on my back while being so young; to be an ox like the other oxen, a drum player in a band, a dog like the other dogs while still being just, *you know*, eleven years old! Besides, I liked to observe the oxen, the dogs, the pigs, and the chickens to see how they were gifted with intelligence. Around this time I got a spotted puppy as a present. I had hopes of giving him a name and being his only master — as soon as my father was in the mood to let me think for myself. No, my fear came from something else; not only had my father been dealt to me by life's lottery, I could also bet that, in his opinion, the days didn't follow one after the other … no, there was never any tomorrow at all, just today and the work that had to be done. We weren't allowed our own sorrows, our own grievances, our own memories — only Papa's anxiety about everything that still had to be done.

If he'd heard that there were rock quarries at the bottom of the sea, if he'd heard that there was land there that could be cultivated, that there were submarine cattle or forests of useful wood awaiting our labor and his, nothing in the world could have stopped him from going right down to the ocean floor with his tools. He was more a convict sentenced to hard labor than a landowner: he was a slave to himself. He broke himself with work. And that's why he was never satisfied save when taunting us and making us squirm and suffer for not living up to his standard. At night we would come to the supper table dead tired, muscles aching, with neither an appetite nor any interest in much of anything. That was when he wanted to interrogate us as to where we'd left the day's work. If everything had been done, well, another, more difficult task had to begin. If not, we were just sloths, we weren't worth anything, a burden on his back. Of course we had to get up early the next morning, we wouldn't be allowed to laze around daydreaming about the day before yesterday. If more punishment was called for, above and beyond the beatings and verbal abuse, of course, it consisted of prolonging our work hours from Saturday afternoon late into the night. The other punishment — though not in Papa's arsenal, per se — was the rain. When it rained, we were forced to abandon the corn husking, but that didn't mean a vacation. Papa would put me in the stable to make bamboo-fiber ropes or to cut firewood. Nuno cleaned out the pigpens and would come back covered in dung. Amélia, tethered to the pots and the trivet, would get her braids pulled because she spilled salt. Domingas, who really was very spoiled, did embroidery for hire, under the supervision of a woman with the legs of an elephant who paid three hundred escudos for a linen towel that she would sell in the city for fifteen hundred. Other children our age, whenever it rained, would entertain themselves by howling at the rain, cheering the forced rest, and booing the work they'd been allowed to abandon for the day. We, however, were told: rain or shine, we have to eat and drink, and there are so many of us, so how could we expect to be supported if we were just a drain on the household and gave nothing back? Papa said this countless times, insisting that we had to ransom our lives, to the point that he actually convinced us: to be born in that house was a kind of debt that incurred interest and would have to be paid as quickly as possible. Years later, already in Vancouver, about to close his eyes forever, that man continued to conspire against tomorrow. In spite of his ravaged soul, and suffering terribly from his cancer, drunk and foggy from the morphine, he still had the breath to lift his head from his pillow, stare at us, and finish his will:

"I know very well that you're only thinking about your inheritance. Here I am dying in agony, maybe as a punishment for my sins. But my conscience is at rest. I've left two parcels of land to each child, a good house and a pile of *dollahs* in the Canadian bank. So you don't have any reason complain about me . . ."

The year I finished school we had two milk cows, three or four weaned calves, some sheep, and a pair of young oxen still not broken in to plowing. So that every year, at the end of winter, my father would buy bales of hay from anyone who was selling, sometimes as far away as Salga, Achada, or up at the foothills of the Outeiros. If there was no money for this, he told us to herd all the grazing animals to the roads so they could eat the grass around the hedges. Or they would eat moss, tender ginger lilies, and forest ferns in the mornings, or else, in the rainy season, all day long. There they hosed their feces on the cedars and the beeches, they filled and emptied their gullets and took forever to fill their stomachs. When they returned to the barn, they were filled to bursting, so round that it was a mystery why they didn't explode. But there was always my dear father in wait. He looked at them, furrowed his brow, and said we hadn't been diligent enough in making sure the animals were well fed, because he saw still saw concavities in their bodies, saw their bones sticking out. He wanted them fat, puffed up like yeast, and well groomed so they would sell for good money. When he sent us back again to the meadows with them, they once again became our world: some frisked about playfully, in the freshly harrowed ground; others jumped about, as if the devil were in them; and still others, frightened by blackbirds or a simple finch, broke herd in leaps down the hills, kicking or butting heads at invisible enemies. We must have been aided by the kindly ghosts of our ancestors, our dogs, or fate, because they usually returned on their own initiative. They responded to the cries of their young, were afraid of the pouring rain, and were stopped by our widespread arms blocking the stampedes and turning them back.

It happens that on the last day of school, everything that Mr. Quental had taught me in those years about arithmetic, history, and geography was swept out of my head. The fractioned numbers would turn into the rags that I had used to wrap my bruised feet and bloody toenails from tripping over the stones in the path. The surnames of the kings of Portugal would be the nicknames given me by those who liked me or didn't: to remember them longer, I wanted to give the names to the calves as they were born. But my father, not being a man who had much regard for kings, never approved any of those christenings. This business of naming dumb, meek calves the Conqueror, the Fat, the Wise, or the Brave could only be the work of idle hands, and that will turn everything topsy-turvy, with names hard to remember and without any history. He didn't even allow me to call my dog Just, in honor of the king who avenged the death of Dona Inés de Castro.

The tributaries of the rivers of the Continent, all born in Spain and for this reason, foreign rivers, would be the streams that I would cross in water up to my groin. And as for the railways, perhaps I would be reminded of them when I walked barefoot in the furrows behind the plow, without the strength to lift the dirt clogged handle. To turn it around I'd hitch it to my back, straining to prod the oxen on the flanks. When I fell to the ground more dead than alive, my chest was lacerated from top to bottom and my wrists were dislocated and my lungs were ready to explode.

I had never seen a train. But I imagined them going by to the sound of a thousand head of cattle of the richest farmers in Rozário. I imagined them later, when these people gave in and behaved like a line of ants, when they deforested the land and turned the hills into an enormous round pasture that no longer belonged to them. It was a train that disappeared into a tunnel and whose destiny became an exit to America. It was always easy for me to imagine trains everywhere — in the silent crowds, in the litanies of the pilgrims who made their way around the Island, in festival processions, in the people leaving mass, and in the voice of the Azorean wind — where in fact they did not exist, so that in seeing them go by into my future crossing the endless plains of Canadian lands, they did not surprise me, nor did I pay them the least attention.

I began to forget my letters and the curves and loops that I had learned to trace numbers on paper. Everything conspired to separate me from school and books. I began to be owned by the steamy breath of the flies and the animal shit, and that was my fate. It was true that to plow the land and sow new crops it was of little use to memorize the names of kings, trains, and the mountains of Portugal. And since we were cut off from the world by that dangerous and untraversable sea, book knowledge became a luxury. When women would come to beg me to write letters to Brazil or America, I would look at those sad faces, the mouths that were beginning to lose teeth in the absence of their men, and I felt lost. I was ashamed to be witness to their secrets, their requests for money, and their longing. One day I swore that I would never again write letters. But then Aunt Sonia, the silly woman, showed up, and begged me to draft a plea for help to the man who had shipped out years ago and had never again given a sign of life. I saw her squeezed inside herself, already aged and not old enough to be an old woman. I perhaps should have helped my distressed little aunt, but I asked her to be patient, to ask someone else. I, in any case, hardly remembered how to sign my own name . . .

She took offense, and started to make a big scene, and she carried on so much or so little that my mother rushed in angrily. In a huff, she pulled my sideburns and ears and slapped me twice in the face:

"That's to teach you not to talk back to family," she hissed into my ear.

She turned back to auntie smiling; she had fulfilled her duty as a mother, nobody could accuse her of not disciplining her children, especially when they were impolite.

"Give the letter here," she said. "I don't have more than a third grade education, but I wouldn't trade my mind for these dumb asses around us. Give it to me, sister-in-law Sonia, and dictate slowly."

In fact little or nothing set us apart from the illiterate; the only flame that we hoped to keep alive inside us was the precious art of signing our name. So we could receive an immigration sponsorship letter, do the paperwork to sail away; we have a name and know how to sign it. In the final crunch, any fool could learn how to do it on the spur of the moment. All it took was to line up the letters in a fairly straight line, with your head bent over and your tongue hanging out, your fingers clutching a fountain pen or a ball point pen and, done. The important thing was to impress the consuls, the lawyers, that entire band of people who tried to block our way and stand between us and America. Falsified documents, forged medical tests, or a bought x-ray to hide the sickness in our lungs, would open the way to the long-promised land.

I was one of those who counted down one by one, hour by hour, every day of my eternity in the Azores. When I began to believe in the miracle, I started to train myself to write, practicing on letters to uncles and an almost unknown godfather, in hopes that one of them would still remember what we suffered here from the first to the last day. Letters, letters, and more letters, understand? Most of the replies I received contained a folded, dirt-stained *dollah* and a hasty note containing the sermon of patience and acceptance; the Canadian government was making everything difficult, immigration laws had changed, and they were canceling visas and contracts. Besides, the relatives said, this was a very expensive country, a country of suffering, tears, homesickness, and regrets, with a piercing cold that made you lose sight of and chill your very soul. "What I'd give," they'd say "to turn back the clock, to return to my little hearth. I'd eat yellow corn bread with yams and bacon, without a doubt, and not have to cry these tears or be so far away from the sea and the land where everyone knows each other..." They had deep regrets for having crossed such a large ocean, from which they were still seasick and in agony — and we thought that they mocked us from afar, fat and shiny, laughing at us until they cried.

Worse was the fact that the letters dealt death sentences to our hopes and snuffed out the perfume of our freedom. Holding them up to our noses, we recognized the smell of farts and lies. They were people who were different from us, people who filled me with hate against selfishness, envy, and the petty intrigues that fed those who had once been poor. Unlike the rich, who banded together and liked each other, we learned quickly to hide our game; when we were well off, we laughed ourselves silly at those who were still slogging through the mud. My mother would speak ill of those deserters and rant: they could at least let our misery touch their hearts, those hypocrites, traitors, and bad-mouths! They've erased the memory of our sinful poverty on this crowded island, where it's even hard to breathe. Sea and sky, just sea and sky, she said. And they were full of excuses and ingratitude: they were consoling themselves in America, stuffing *dollahs* into their pockets. One of these days they would come back for vacation. They would have big bellies from drinking Canadian beer, and gold teeth showing through their smiles, and silver watch chains, golden skin, tanned by excesses of prosperity, and fat asses from sitting around in those luxurious Canadian and American homes that we saw in the pictures. She cursed her brothers, and the sisters-in-laws who had shamefully fled just barely pregnant to Brazil, and she would turn to my sisters and scream at them:

"God help you if you don't marry a fellow from a good family who can get you out of here! Until you do, I'll make you scrub floors and clean the barn until you learn to make a good match!"

My father would look at her askance, angered by such talk, struggling to contain himself from laying a hand on her. He would rise wheezing from his seat and go out into the black night muttering between his teeth:

"Shut your mouth woman. You're full of crap and you're talking nonsense."

CHAPTER FOUR

Nuno Miguel

I can't even say when my childhood sleep habits turned into chronic insomnia. I got used to five quick hours of sleep. If I try to stay in bed longer, my back starts to hurt. I get cramps in my legs. My mind becomes restless, troubled by the nagging suspicion that the world is lying in wait for me. Devoured by all forms of anxiety, I don't even know how to define "anguish" or to distinguish between words as flat as nervousness, or irritation. I distanced myself from others because of this cursed affliction. Discussing the obvious and gossip are perhaps the terrible pastimes of the bourgeoisie. What challenges me the most is the social convention of being polite to ignorant people and being tolerant of sects. I have always lacked the patience to listen to reactionaries. As for the rich who look down on the ugliness and filth of the poor, the intellectual assholes with square faces and thick glasses, and the pretentious and effeminate poets, I won't even go there! I escaped little by little into innocent drugs and the hypnotic of political activism. I would fall asleep too early and wake up fatigued, bleary eyed, and in a bad mood. I shaved sloppily at the mirror, cigarette dangling from my mouth, slicing the pimples and moles on my neck, and I appeared later looking like an obscene martyr before my children and students who snickered and passed notes in class. Looking at myself in the eye, I recognized that life had turned me into a blue-eyed dog, impatient with mediocrity and suffering from undefined ailments. I had begun to have psychosomatic symptoms of permanent dyspepsia and constipation that is typical for the sedentary and the mentally ill. I was unhappy with life, understand; out of step with the meticulously ordered and stupidly busy lives of others. I think I know a lot about what keeps some people who suffer from isolation from going insane. You had already written some minor books. They were mediocre and commonplace, the kind of third-rate literature that makes the writer feel a cynical jealousy of the success of other writers. You decided then to get back on your feet, turn into a vertebrate again and pick up what was original in you to create literature. You called Marta and revealed your plan:

"I have an open book inside me. If I can't write it now, I'll drown. Will you carry the house expenses or should we get divorced?"

You recall her great serenity. Only her enormous almond-shaped fish eyes seemed to flicker. She sat in front of you, took out one of her cigarettes, pulled in deeply, released it out of her nostrils, and pretended to smile at you. She remained like that for just a moment in a state between astonishment and amusement. Then she lifted her hand, as if she were going to slap you, then closed her fingers with the exception of her middle finger, raised her fist at you in a "fuck you" gesture.

"Climb up on this, sweetheart," she said with a trace of disdain in her smile. "Here the only open book is me. If you can't write about me, give it up. Or go cut the balls off fireflies in Eduardo VII Park!"

This book and all the others that you decided to write around your class schedule failed, and they took up time that should have belonged to the happiness and childhood of your children. You even continued to write them later, when Marta decided to give in and take over the management of the household, thinking she would save the marriage. From then on, your flight gained altitude, gave you a glimpse of the stratosphere, and made you dream of fame.

"You went up, up, up," the psychiatrist told me. "You succeeded in your studies, your profession, and your marriage. You can't now suppress your enjoyment of those achievements."

I never felt as if I lived inside the skin of a winner. That fat psychiatrist, perpetually drenched in sweat and covered with dandruff, had the small problem of never having traveled to the Azores. He assumed that walking barefoot and enduring beatings in the Azores was the same as walking barefoot and enduring beatings in any other part of the world. From my early childhood, my father's clogs clacked on the stone slabs of the shed, followed closely by my older brothers. We milked the cows, fed the calves and the oxen, and I went into the barn, freed the livestock tied up by the horns and led them to the path. They were dark and huge as trains. They went by me cautiously, pausing but not stepping on that tile floor. I believed they were floating over my head, levitating over my smallness. When it was my turn to tend them and milk them in the pastures, I saw the hoopoes and other blue birds pecking at the worms in the manure, and I saw them alight on the bony backs, or risk death under the tonnage of hooves. Only then did I understand that the cows saved me from death by instinct; because I too was a bird and lived from scavenging, removing and cleaning their shit.

Dawn had not broken yet; the cold was white and the cocks let out a nocturnal trumpet blast against the hedges. All the children, except for me and Luís, were asleep. He came along, organizing the herd on the deserted road, whistled for the dog, and headed off for Outeiros, to Mãe-de-Água, or Roca da Vila, faraway places where the pastures, the woods dark as graves, and the twisting rivers were found. It was my job to clean the stables. It was nothing supernatural and could have happened to thousands or millions of children. But since it happened to me and I was only seven, half asleep, barefoot, and upset that it was almost time to go to school, it's only obvious that I should talk about cow shit.

There were tons of that green sludge mixed with urine, flies, and the ammonia breath of the bovines. The solid feces looked like ropes, like coils of guts fuming in the straw. If it was solid, it wasn't so bad to pick it up with the pitchfork. But if it was diarrhea! The goddamn cows would squirt jets of fetid shit; it came out in spurts, running down their hind legs and dripping from the prominent vaginas that were as purple as tumors. Poor me, I would rake everything into a big pile, mixing awn, shredded straw, leaves or stalks, withered ferns, and lupine husks to enrich the manure. The lowliest profession in the world, I say, thinking now about the attendants in the public restrooms in Lisbon, about the Cape Verdeans with sequins on their breasts who traverse the nocturnal garbage piles of Lisbon. Damn that filth that I stepped on with the soles of my feet and where the pitchfork resisted in protest at my lack of strength to lift it. A brilliant boy, a conqueror, excessively well behaved — however smelling like cattle and shit during those four years of school. Much later during five years in Lisbon, I worked eight hours a day, and then took the bus to the University City for long night sessions in the classrooms of the Faculty of Letters. As a graduate student, I became well versed in the theory and semiotics of the texts praised by my clueless philology professors — yet I was still marked by the sensation that in spite of my academic success, I still stank of cow shit. And smelling of cow, scarred by the psychological calluses of the pitchfork I held as a child, how could I see myself as a winner? Throughout my life, whenever I thought of books, the smell of shit floated over the perfume of the flowers and everything else that supposedly enlarges a man's life.

It was a miracle, as you can certainly imagine, cleaning all the mud out of that barn and still getting to school on time at eight twenty in the morning. Because it wasn't just about cleaning the flood of cow dung and whatever the hell else; I had to make their beds all over again, spread the straw, awn, and stalks so that at night they could lie down on a clean floor. I filled the trough with sheaves of corn stalks that were stored in the loft, over the beams, where the rats were grey, miserable, and as numerous as crop pests. When I encountered them in their nests I would kill them with stabs of the pitchfork and raise them into the air, impaled creatures with their guts slipping out. The chickens down below received them with excitement and fought over the viscera and cartilage. When everything was done, I would close the latch of the cow sanctuary, leaving them in the shadows; I would run to the house, wash my feet quickly in the basin, swallow without chewing corn bread with milk still lukewarm from the milking, grab my canvas book bag and run, run. The absence of inner peace has stayed with me from that time, and I still live on the run, sleeping quickly, eating only the essential, and gulping it down. Sometimes I'd run into my teacher climbing up the Eira-Velha boat ramp. I saw his dark-rimmed glasses, the massive arms like a wood cutter's; I dashed around those huge haunches that contracted in the effort to climb the steep incline of the Rua do Ramal. Seen from the front, he had a very red, flushed forehead, framed by kinky hair like a mulatto's that stuck up in a tuft.

"Good morning, teacher," I proffered from the depths of my terror.

If he had come in with the tide, he permitted himself to return the greeting with a malicious grin. If not, he would just grunt a monosyllable and keep me at a distance with an annoyed look. Soon he would announce to the others which way the wind was blowing that day.

When he arrived, we greeted him in a chorus of chilled voices and wait for him to open the door and let us in behind him. Effortlessly he turned the key in the lock that none of us could open. First he set down the black briefcase with the thick plastic ruler poking out of it. His partridge eyes seemed to suck at our skin and cover our hands with blood blisters; then his entire massive body entered the room. Then, the man would stand up like a hulk next to the blackboard, bend over the portrait of General Craveiro Lopes, cross himself, and pray facing the grey nose of the dictator. He would sit down, play distractedly with the globe, and hurl out his first warning:

"I want you sitting down and quiet. Don't tap on your desks, don't scrape your chairs, and don't test my patience!"

Happiness was to see him ceremonially put on his lab coat, clean his cloudy glasses with a handkerchief, and blow his nose with a honk. He did this, understand, in front of me, if I wasn't late. Because on other days, when I got stuck in that mire of shit, I cried, seeing the desperation of my sweat mixing with the fuming torrent of those golden feces and saying to myself that life had nothing good or bad to offer. It was whatever God willed. I swallowed the milk soup with closed eyes without tasting it. I rinsed my feet quickly, without using the blue soap and hoping that the clocks were fast. Sometimes if my sisters heard me cry they would respond to my distress, full of pity. They came from inside, from making beds and singing, emptying chamber pots and basins of soapy water, from shaking out mattresses, towels, and sheets and singing — and they cried seeing me cry.

"Go on, sweet boy," they said, "so you're not late and the teacher won't beat you."

They took charge of the pitchfork and the golden feces, the sheaves of husks, and the extermination of the rats, the awn, or the ground straw — and sure enough, my time was up. Lost in time, I stopped washing my feet and hands and passed up the milk soups. The days were filled with the curse of marked time, by the relentless science of the wall clock and the inevitability of the bells that rang at the beginning, middle, and end of the mass. What awaited me was the violence of that religious man, on whose hands it had never been possible to detect the slightest trace of manure, not even a little dirt from that garden of roses and hyacinths that peeped out at the world behind the walls of an algae colored house. On those hands there wasn't a single torn nail, or a sign of any contact with stone, sand, or plant fertilizer. Their power rested on a scepter of India cane — and I never knew why exactly that instrument of torture came from India and not from any other country nearer to ours.

"Go on and eat a bit of corn bread along the way, dear heart," Mama would say in a velvety voice, while she twisted her apron in her hands and seemed ill at ease with showing me compassion. "Hear? Tell your teacher that you had to obey your father. Ask him to forgive you for today, for the love of God and your family. And listen: we'll give him an offering of plums and pears as soon as they ripen..."

I ran like a greyhound to the bottom of Boqueirão hill. Then from Boqueirão I climbed to the houses on the crest of Paloas. From the top of Paloas I finally could see Rama, and there I opened my eyes wide in hopes of seeing the Eira-Velha ramp.

"Excuse me ma'am! By any chance have you seen my teacher walk by?" I asked the first woman who appeared at a window.

"Glory me! He must have gone by a good fifteen or twenty minutes ago. Why are you crying, little angel?"

In a little while I was knocking on the back door of the school that led to a very flat recess yard, with rows of daisies and dahlias around the pumice walls and beds of carnations and sweetheart roses next to the gates that separated us from the world. Facing the firing squad of looks that greeted me and showed concern for my plight, I asked permission to enter, in a tight voice that seemed to come from an inhibited ventriloquist who had succumbed to my timidity. Annoyed, red with anger, teacher Samuel interrupted the grading of dictation and arithmetic problems. With a hooked finger he made a gesture of one summoning a lapsed debtor, and everything in his demeanor became strange; he seemed to smile, with an arched eyebrow. His eyes had a metallic and sensual glint and his lips were distorted with sarcasm:

"Here comes Master Nuno, always punctual, always on time for school! Would you care to tell us where you've been?"

I gave the excuses of the manure, my father's orders, the stomachache from the worms and other invented illnesses, and I mixed all of this up with an elaborate confession of guilt. My cries asked him, begged him for an impossible show of mercy:

"You really are hopeless! Am I not fed up with telling you that I want you here on time to start your school work?"

Nothing would change the reasons that were killing off my desire to grow up, to stand up to him and confront him with appeals for mercy.

"We'll have to settle our accounts, Master Nuno. You know what to do: put your book bag in your desk, just so, as I have taught you, then go to the middle of the room and wait. With your pants down, yes?"

As long as I live I will never be able to erase from my visual memory the sight of that cement hallway that had as its only function to separate the classes. In the front, at the bow of this ship without a deck, next to the desk, the world globe, and the maps of Portugal and the Azores, sat the older ones, who were already studying history, geography, decimal numbers, and fractions. In the back, the younger ones spelled out incomprehensible words, or they were memorizing their first multiplication tables. I'll never be able to delete from my memory the many times I saw of the older ones look around, laugh, and mock my terror. And I would see how my classmates opened their eyes wide and shrank from the same terror and moral pain that afflicted me. Most of all it burdened me that they laughed at my trembling buttocks, blue with cold.

I challenge you to imagine yourself in my place. The India cane starts to hum. The rough burls, intentionally badly aimed, imprint your backside with red lesions that in the early afternoon will turn blue and that at night seem to gnaw at the bones in your lower back. You are squatting and you don't know why. The machine of your body becomes those martyred buttocks. Towering over you, an immense man walks around you, biting his lips, furrowing his brow, and he whips you with all the hate of the world. You, however, are just a poor boy, and poor in the many unbearable forms of poverty — and he has the power to kill you. In other words, you are sentenced to capital punishment and will be hung. A rope, even if imaginary, is being tightened around your neck. What, in this case, would be your last wish?

You would have wished for, as I did then, the arrival of the white horseman, the wonderful, majestic white horseman who almost always shows up at the last minute and unfurls from on high, in front of the hangman, the divine pardon of the king. They did it, as far as I know, for Dostoevski, and I'm not sure if it was for Federico García Lorca as well. I wasn't there. If I had been, I could have only said to him:

Hijo mío, que te vas a enfermar de melancolía! Son, you are going to make yourself sick from sadness!

I also don't know if they did it to Franz Kafka or even Pier Paolo Pasolini, who as you know, played the dog and the tiger and wrote with his guts. Surely they did it to the very unfortunate poet J. H. Santos Barros, whose terrible verses and at least one highway casualty I know: *Os viajantes pensam: qualquer caminho / pode de súbito pertencer aos rumores das asas. / Será sempre o mesmo vento atravessando o rosto do mar? / O vento viaja para as nuvens e nem as palavras / dos mortos quando vivos o vento pode conservar.* "The travelers think: any road / can suddenly belong to wing beats. / Is it always the same wind that crosses the sea? / The wind travels to the clouds and not even the words / of the living dead can be saved by the wind."

I would wait for the arrival of the gunslinger dressed in black, like in the American movies, who would aim and shoot at my noose. That and nothing else, was my expectation. I jumped up and down and cried out—but my father did not come, my brother was not old enough to use a gun, and for this reason my buttocks began to get sliced up by the corrosive phalanges of the India cane. Nobody would bother to storm the walls of that cuckoo's nest.

"What about the people of Rozário?" you ask me.

As far as I know, the people were always on the verge of rebelling, blind, and thirsty for the blood of the tyrant. First, because word had gotten around about the beatings of their children. Second, because the children were young and ran the risk of being damaged for life. Third, since it was about a man from another Island, it was not given that a stranger would come there to mistreat the children of others without anyone being able to touch him. Finally, when they learned of his misogyny, they planned denunciations, humiliations, and other inoffensive moral platitudes suggested by their religion. Some threatened to denounce him to the school inspectors. Others would run him off of the Island, the way you do with cattle. But the supernatural thing was that the years passed, many of us got the cane, and nobody ever broke the teacher's teeth with a punch in the face.

A kind of glass case seemed to protect this man, shielding him from the slightest threat. It was the time when baskets of eggs and fruits appeared on the teacher's table. Then came the time of Christmas chickens and ducks, the salutations and places of honor in the church during Sunday mass. The teachers at that time were assured of the complicity of the candidates for catechism, the reverend priest, the Algarvia police, and the shop owners. When the teachers arrived at the doors of those very white women who had married rich men and presented themselves with smiles, they invited them in. In the Azores they had the good fortune of being public servants, godfathers of the future rich, their guardians and accomplices. The women, being in general smiling and malicious, irradiated a mocking beauty that made up part of their wealth . . .

I met teacher Samuel's wife up close and fell in love with her Cleopatra nose. I remember all the marks on her neck and her hair tied in a bun; I remember hearing men sigh as she walked by, made restless by the enervating scent of her apple perfume. These base passions were stirred by the vision of her impossible golden neck, her fleshy nose and beautiful legs. She was an excessively pale woman, with the suggestive transparency of glass, since the sun was rarely graced with her presence. And even so her skin, her phosphorescent, serpentine eyes, were made of that same crystalline sun and anyone who saw her smile received a haughty perfidious glance.

"Oh, sweet woman!" the boys would bray in lust as they masturbated hidden behind the hedges of the yard when she passed by.

Years later when I was far away, I could guess at the despair of that betrayed and shamed woman, when the cursed homosexuality of her man was discovered.

I will never forget that day with the copper sun and birds posed on window shutters and the intensely still sea, at the places where boats used to pass by en route to America. I had arrived early to school and went to sit in the front desk, assigned to the best students in class. At that moment my teacher began to sniff the air, right and left, and then turned to me to confirm his suspicion:

"And so you're the one who smells like cow shit!"

I shook from head to toe. The chestnut stains, already hardened, were clearly manure. The ammonia smell, since it was common to all of us, was the sign that we coexisted with the cows. But that burnished man, whose hygiene was scrupulously feminine, didn't forgive us our condition. When he discovered that I was the guilty one, he ordered me to stand and to walk to the last desk, at the back of the room next to the window, since he wasn't inclined to be around piglets. His laughter was thick, resonant, like turkey gobbles. Never again would any hallway be as long and humiliating, not even the ones in the cloisters or the naves of the chapels of the seminary and the convent. Sold out, betrayed, humiliated by the miserable stink of cow shit, the same way that many, I'm not sure how many, years later when I had applied for an assistant professorship at the university, a bay mare whinnied, gave me a disdainful kick in the back, and returned me to my philology professors.

It happened that by chance on that day of birdsong, copper sunlight, and calm seas in the distance, an ox cart came through Eira-Velha on its squeaking wooden axels. It also happened that by chance, José Silvana, who had been held back in third grade, was sent to the window with cardboard donkey ears. Moreover, and still by chance, the driver of the cart was Artur, and he was the boy's older brother. Chance made him look up and see, first horrified then furious, the little one bathed in tears of humiliation. Passersby were laughing. Some called others to see the show. Inside, we heard boys strike the donkey and call out about pack saddles, whips, and reins. After pounding on the door four times, a sweaty man with straw in his hair and an ox goad in his fist made his entrance. His pale eyes were streaming sweat, as were his enormous hands, thick as sledgehammers meant for pounding stakes and digging cisterns. We saw him make for the window, rescue his brother, push the boy struck dumb by shame and the laughter of the others, and we saw him tear off the cardboard with the nefarious ears and tell him to go home. In a tiger's spring, he raised his hand to the teacher's neck. Shaking him, he began to push him to the blackboard; he was a frozen statue, his white coat in sinister contrast against the black slate.

"I can go to jail for this, Mr. scumbag teacher. But first I'm going to rip your guts out of your ass. If I don't look after the people in my own house, I disgrace myself. Don't you dare laugh at our misery. If I have to beat anyone to death, it will be another man, not faggots and castrated dogs!"

The world fell apart right then. It crumbled like a house of cards, because this heresy whirled through the air and did not take long to become news on the entire island. How long it lasted, I'm not sure, nor do I know if it was then that the complete shaming of the woman with the golden neck began, the woman whose perfume marked the beginnings of our disquiet. I was far away; I was not given the opportunity to witness the commotion of his subsequent transfer to another island.

My definitive complaint against this teacher is however about the other side of his brutality, perversion, and the fact that he never forgave me for smelling like the cows. Listen to this. When I was sent over to Achada, to harvest figs, shoo away the birds, or move the sheep to a different pasture, I would climb up and down the churchyard walls. The widows and the old men would congregate there. I would see Calheta, the sacristan, whose light bony body was bent forward, as if he carried the weight of the morning on his shoulders. Then came his opposite, the heavy slow body of Father Ângelo stumbling along. A minute later my teacher appeared: tall, with his fat behind, the missal in his armpit, and the rosary looped through his fingers. I could never understand what kind of sins justified the fact of his leaving that beautiful woman so early in the morning, just to go to seven o'clock mass. I don't know if at that time it was an elegant and practical way of seeming different from other sinners. The damned limited themselves to visiting God on Sundays and holy days, and they did it crudely, without intelligence, with the look of captured crows in that cathedral of dull arcades that looked as if it were about to cave in and where the sermons were aimed at stopping the people from thinking. Not for the teacher: the daily mass was food for the soul.

However, the man who flogged behinds and legs and tapped his fingers on the ruler made of thick plastic, the same one who commanded me, his best student, to hit the bad students with all my strength and later was so proud to have been my first teacher — this man went daily and obsessively to mass! He took communion, he prayed the rosary, he left church and then opened and closed classes with a prayer to Our Lady of Rozário. He would leave mass, you see, to make us stand at the window so that we would look like fools. And he ground his teeth and exercised his sadistic cruelty on us without scruples. But on the day of my expulsion from the seminary, they told me from here, he spoke out about my betrayal of the Church, my family, and all who had supported my vocation for the priesthood. So that in Lisbon when I received the only one of his inquisitorial letters, to which I never replied, it was never possible for me to dissociate priests, masses, and papal bulls from the perversion of this hypocritical religious man. And when the idea of God paled inside me, it occurred to me that teacher Samuel contributed to my loss of faith. My father was a first, terrible, agent of God. The rector of the seminary was another emissary of God. The dictator Salazar was the symbol of this occult, unknown, and ignorant God. And our unmistakable American friends, infinitely more powerful than God, dispensed a passport, a luxury car, and a golden exile in a city that sheltered more than one deposed dictator: the ineffable teacher Samuel.

Maria Amélia

To the happiness of that new house was added another even greater one when I went to school. Papa made me a wicker book bag; it was very light; he varnished it and put a little spring clasp on it. I filled it with a pencil, two sheets of paper, a stick of white chalk, and a slate. School would take me from the house, the land, my chores, and the violent struggle with the animals. People could stop confusing me with the chickens, the pigs, and the dogs. I swore I would quickly learn the strange things that until then had separated me from adults: letters and numbers. I wanted to feel the pulse of the world, especially what was beyond the sea. The boats left the dock pointing to the rising sun. They disappeared from sight, tiny as egrets, and I would watch them disappear in the distance and think that one day I would also disappear on one of those boats. They were already my irresistible destiny. I had to go away in one of them.

The blackboard, on that first day of class, seemed possessed of a mysterious transparency. I don't know if I already projected the world of my dreams on it, as on a sea chart, or if the chalk marks were the meridians of my passage to another place on earth. My fascination with the globe of the earth, turning on an oblique axis on the desk and at the contact of the man who was there to teach me about the world, revealed great mysteries to me. I was in the presence of a wise man. Papa and Grand Mama Olinda referred to wise people as geniuses who were possessed of a particular madness. The hands of wise people were moved by magnetic forces. This is what I thought when I saw teacher Quental twirl the globe and point out the territories of Africa and Asia that belonged to Portugal. The map of the country, *my country* at that time, hanging in a corner of the room, our national flag, *I mean*, when I was still Portuguese, the portrait of the president of the Republic was to the right and Prime Minister Salazar to the left — all this harmonized with the scrubbed floors smelling of blue soap and with the rows of desks where other girls my age trembled and cried. I didn't understand why they were so frightened; while they begged to be allowed to go home, I was happy to be far from my house, out of sight and away from the demands of my parents.

It was obvious that the teachers had soft, superior voices; they did not shout to make themselves heard over the sound of hammers, cow bellows, pots and pans. They didn't have the hands of angry people who were always frustrated at life. The hands of the *teachers* were made of paper, endowed with nails that were not torn or stained with elderberry, but transparent as glass. Their eyeglasses were even intelligent, not at all sad, contrary to those spectacles that on other people always looked thick, uncomfortable, and ugly as the harnesses on the beasts.

I started to feel happy and to want to smile at life. I really wanted those years to pass quickly, to make me big in body and spirit and to help me discover the time and the way to take me far from the Island.

Have you ever had to wear glasses? Do you know how much they weigh, how much they irritate the bridge of your nose and make you look old? So then you can't imagine how they hurt me and how the first time I got glasses stayed in my memory...

The day that Mr. Quental discovered my weak vision, he found it strange that the numbers and letters that he wrote on the board became such imprecise, minuscule, and vague scribbles in my copybook. It was no problem to do my homework. All I had to do was to look for a light, put my copybook under it, and place my eyes as closely as possible to the paper. But the morning that he wrote a note to Papa, telling him I needed glasses, I suffered the first setback. Before even thinking about the situation, my father became furious at that new expense and started to scream at me. He screamed at me, please note, as if I had created myself and were guilty of being born defective. He cursed at his no-good children because they made him go to the bottom of the chest of drawers to touch his precious money: folded, ironed, and hidden like a relic. Glasses, he thought, were a luxury. I should open my eyes wider, sit in the front row, or simply deal with it, since God had decided to bring me into the world that way. He went on like that for weeks, postponing the decision and avoiding the issue. Until one day he concluded that the problem was easy to fix. He would pull me out of school, and he wouldn't have to think about it anymore. It wasn't even obligatory... and so my future would be to sweep floors, peel potatoes, dig up flax and beets, and for that nobody needed schooling. He did calculations in his head faster than a water cannon; the two incomplete years he had gone to school in the time of the kings was enough for him.

Well, I broke out into sobs, full of loathing, and I went to bring Grand Papa Botelho up to speed on my misfortune. He wasn't able to make up his mind. He turned very red, an asthma attack coming on, and could only say that he had nothing to do with the problems of our household. I quickly caught on that Grand Papa and Papa didn't speak anymore. They lived like deaf people, without an opinion, and they turned their heads when they passed each other.

"My father-in-law, give me your blessing!"

"My blessing," and that was it.

When Grand Mama Olinda, my father's mother, got involved, the conversation changed, and she sent me on my way. Mama had the idea of paying two escudos and fifty centavos to someone who would ask for donations after mass appealing to their charity to give us some secondhand glasses or some that they no longer used. Then my father's pride reacted and the idea was nipped in the bud. That's when Saint Joseph, the Carpenter, performed divine intervention, and Papa decided to take me to the City.. I was presented to an ophthalmologist who was in a hurry and very haughty, then to a man who was bending over a display case in a store, who showed Papa a sample of old frames and haggled over prices, styles, and conditions of payment. When I looked at myself in the mirror, it was terrible: I didn't expect that headgear to restore my vision. My eyes, frightened and very enlarged, looked like two crazy butterflies. The lenses were so thick they looked like discs etched into spirals. I understood that I had become incredibly ugly, different than other girls my age. I came to the realization that life separated me from them, because of the inescapable myopia and those lenses of various dioptrics. Countless times I changed the way I wore my hair, with the illusion that I would disguise the ugliness. I broke my glasses every two years so I could get new frames that would better suit my face. Every time I broke them, Papa would slap me. He tried every possible type of homemade glue to fasten them together, from gum Arabic to tabuga sap. The first time they came unglued I got another slap, and this went on until I convinced him of the inevitability of another eye doctor appointment. If I had to change prescriptions, I always had to wait for the festivities honoring the saints, the counting of the calves, or for September next year or Christmas. The result: between one consult and the next, my dioptrics increased, my face again became weighed down by those discs, and blindness lurked in the shadows.

When Domingas and Luís started school, a new round of notes were sent home announcing the same affliction. My father would go crazy, raising his voice and producing fearful tempests. We came to signify a triple need for trips, appointments, and changes of prescriptions. When he finally decided it was inevitable, he forced us to get up at dawn and set out with us on foot, down the road, ahead of the bus. The longer we walked, away from Rozário, it would pick us up on the road that led to the City and he would have to pay less. After three or four kilometers, our feet blistered in our Sunday shoes, we would signal the driver to stop and we climbed aboard. Papa instructed us to tell the ticket collector that we were two or three years younger than we were. The collector looked at him, looked at us, and thought it an impossibility that such a small man could be the father of children so big for their ages. It shamed me terribly to listen to him argue about the twelve escudos and fifty centavos, the price of a one-way ticket. But he was so tenacious that he was able to get what he wanted.

In the City, we stayed just for the indispensable amount of time, that is, for all of us to go to the ophthalmologist's office, to listen to Papa discuss and argue with him: it was not just, serious, or reasonable for the doctor to charge not one, as Papa would have it, but three consults. I again became ashamed to think that such avarice turned us into miserable beggars. He took advantage of the trip to the City to do some errands, to stock up on tools or other items that others had asked him to buy. He always left us in the middle of an unknown park, and we saw him disappear into that Babylon of paved streets, with stores on either side on very narrow streets, and a swarm of cars going up and down, along with carts loaded with beets, fish mongers' carts, motorcycles, bicycles, taxis, and streams of people. If it occurred to him to leave us in the Largo da Matriz, we would stare open mouthed at the traffic police ordering the cars, the bells, the pigeons perched on the stairs of the square, the street vendors, the persistent portrait artists who doggedly hustled everyone, and the taxi drivers who opened the car doors, sat with their legs stretched out of the car listening to the blast of Angra Radio Club or Wings of the Atlantic. That's when we took the pulse of the City: the smells were different and much closer. There were almost no barefoot people. And the world was much less sad on this side of the ocean. The shop windows beckoned to us from afar, with their illuminated mannequins in the grey day. There were forbidden dresses and shoes, sweaters in matching colors, flesh colored silk stockings, and an infinite variety of suits and skirts. Domingas lingered at the doll stores. Luís, who loved ice cream and sweets, followed the man with the hand cart in a trance, with the sad eyes of an exile, watching men holding children by the hand giving them cones of peanuts or cured lupine beans. That's how the hours passed until our father came back loaded with packages. There was a saw wrapped in brown paper and tied with string, boxes of nails and screws, and other little boxes of parts for the hoe and the ax. In chorus we begged for a six centavo ice cream, a roll from the bakery or a packet of peanuts; annoyed, he distributed the cargo between us and said angrily:

"Your mother sent food enough to shut your mouths. Make do with what you have and don't ask me for anything else."

If he wanted to look at the ocean, he'd take us to sit on the low walls of Avenida Marginal, and there we ate our snack: bread with roasted sausage, a boiled egg, and a wild apple that had been gathered from the ground. While we munched that dry, peppery food, Papa would wave away the shoe shiners, the city dogs, and vendors of contraband watches and bracelets. And we looked at the sea.

Lord, the sea! It was a consolation to see the boats docked on the other side of the bay. They were white, blue, yellow, and black, and the cranes grinded over them, above the empty decks, above the invisible holds, the beached dinghies, covered by canvas, and the gangways. Those about to depart carried cows, sheep, and timber. Others unloaded containers of merchandise, machinery, and boxes addressed to their recipients.

I knew then that my future belonged to the boats. Or I would die a prisoner on the Island, gone mad because of the boats. I did not have the faintest idea how that destiny would come to me, but my blood filled with a repressed shout and the salt of that sea that rocked under us, slapping against the concave sea wall on the Avenida Marginal. Little red fish came for the bread crumbs we threw at them, and we saw in all of this the wondrous, mysterious secret treasures of the sea. Papa then repeated the history of the City. Mixing legends with engineering works, he described the dimensions of the statues and arches, the symbolic doors raised where the sea had once been, then a pebble beach, covered with squid, eel, and crabs that was now the grand avenue in the shape of a half-moon. He remembered perfectly that time of the rocks, the fishing grounds, and the lighthouse. And he would again tell us the story of the construction of the docks, when again the blood of that sea would start to boil in me, and I would ask him full of hope:

"Papa would you please take us to see the boats up close?"

I tried to imagine the casks bound by thick ropes and chains, and the little cabins that floated in the fog, enchanted like maritime crèches, and the exhaust of those eternally bellowing funnels. I know today that the boats also exercised an irresistible attraction over him. But they were forbidden. He couldn't even dream about them.

"Take us, Papa, so we can see how they are up close," I insisted, losing courage, seeing the hours go by and that it was already time to go back. Father stopped the conversation, the same way he changed topics when we used to ask him to let us see the ocean in Rozário. When he finally condescended, we went down to the dock. The fascination of the boats made us important. We were never the same. On the streets of Rozário, old men, who had never left their land just a kilometer away from the water, wanted us to describe the boats. We were popular in school when we described the great dimensions of the merchant vessels that passed by in the distance, on the high seas. And for that reason, when it was my turn to experience it from within, I already knew everything about those floating gods that for a long time had been anchored in my blood.

On foot again, we walked along kilometers of road through overpopulated villages, with hordes of children loose on the streets that were darkening in the dusk and citizens sitting on their haunches in the humid air. Of special note were old people sitting on the walls, following us with their small oriental eyes, seeing us as strangers. We were from other lands, and each neighborhood signified a miniature country around a church, a square, and a public fountain. Women hanging out of their windows pushed us along with their stares and broke the silence only to call their children. And unemployed men, surplus humanity, stood at the storefronts, answering my father's greeting between clenched teeth:

"Hail, sir. Where are you and these little ones from?"

The same bus from the morning picked us up for the return; we were already halfway there, and Papa picked up his argument with the ticket collector. We arrived and our little brothers and sisters came to meet us at the station, waiting for the sweets and cookies; they were like puppies licking the hand of the man who was their father and owner, exceptionally happy with these treats. I ran to the mirror, saw myself as even more ugly, different from the others, and began to cry again.

In my lonely times in Lisbon, I was able to buy my first pair of contact lenses. I had finally earned my nursing degree. I was assigned night shifts and was paid double on Sundays. One day I went home richer than I had ever been. I laid out the innumerable bills on my bed, fragrant but sweat-stained with my hard labor. It was my afternoon of glory; I have an infinite liking for money. With pent-up hate I paid debts, bought a suit for Nuno and a piece of clothing for each of my other siblings — who had long been waiting for a package from me — and I tried to take care of my own appearance. The next month, I set out to buy contact lenses. It was all in vain. My eyes were protuberant: bulging, undisciplined, and chaotic as tumors. An irrepressible allergy overtook me, treated with blue collyrium and cortisone. But the lenses that were going to redeem me really did have to be thrown in the trash. I had to wait another few years, until I went to Canada. I treated the allergy, adapted to the gelatin lenses, and at least deluded myself into thinking I was less ugly.

My head swirls with the thoughts of lost time, and I continue to row against a visible and invisible current. Like the time I experienced the ships and then was taken to the convent by two nuns. Like when, against my better judgment, I left the convent and dragged with me lymphadenitis, vitamin D deficiency, and the despair of not owning even a skirt and blouse to change into from the uniform of a nun. I begged to be admitted to a home for troubled girls who studied for everything and became nothing. I studied with borrowed money. I ate bread with tears. I went through nursing school and paid all my debts from my time in Lisbon. I even bought a trousseau, having fallen in love for the first time to perhaps the only man in my life. I had received him like a prince, in Lisbon, and I lost sight of him late one afternoon at the Campo de Santana: he said "see you tomorrow," with a kiss on my lips, and he never showed up or called again. I got married later, became a mother twice, found an exit door to Luanda and another from Luanda to Lisbon, barefoot again, shipwrecked with two suitcases filled with clothes and the drama of having lost everything. The sons of the independence of Angola invaded my home, sent me away to fuck-all and called me a colonist. In the skies of Luanda rockets still shot overhead, bombs blasted, and fire spewed from the craziest machine guns in the world. All the damned whites were pushed to the airport and onto boats. The last dead lay in the filthy morgue. I had seen them by the thousands in ditches, piled on sidewalks, rotting in garbage covered by billions of flies — at the same time that over the skies of Luanda the tumult, the voices, and the booming of artillery persisted. Angola would become independent and all the whites became criminals and colonists. So I crossed that hell and tried to close my eyes. I had been too happy in that land for all of this to be the simple truth. When I finally felt happy to be alive, I was in a country that was about to become independent. I put my hands in front of my eyes and peeped through my fingers at the many dead, the terror of the whites who ran to shelter from the bullets: I kept that enormous pain that had filtered through my eyelashes. Before I boarded the plane, a son of the independence accompanied us. He pointed a weapon at us, demanded to inspect our luggage, our purses and wallets. He took away the little money I had. He tore up all my photos, my pictures on the bay, the memory of an Angola where I didn't even have time to protest my innocence, as did many others. I disembarked in Lisbon, violated once again, more ridiculous than ever, but already with another pang in my heart: Canada. The miraculous gates of a city called Toronto, on the way to another plane to Vancouver.

But before the easy things and my present happiness, sir, I scrubbed many steps of Canadian houses. I shoveled heaps of snow. I suffered with my husband and children the deathly cold and the white moons of Vancouver. And until I gained citizenship and the official equivalent of the nursing degree and could take shelter in the house of my dreams, everything happened to me. With tears, sighs, and rants I mixed up the pain, doubts, and closed doors of each dream. There was one time, and then another. In the sum of the disappointments and of the best days that happened to me, came the courage of being a woman born to be happy. I admire myself a lot, don't doubt it. And I like myself reasonably well. But I have come to believe that if one day someone wanted to put on paper, in every detail, the history of my life, it would certainly make a great novel . . .

Luís Miguel

We spent years watching people sell everything from one day to the next and then leave without looking back. People got out of taxis registered in other municipalities or from the buses and seemed to laugh at us, even though they were serious and already homesick. Others waited for their visa from week to week, deserters because they were going to escape this place. When a registered envelope arrived, they brayed like goats and immediately bought their tickets. And we were condemned to this: our feet stuck in the mud of this pigsty, knowing that these fugitives had never done a day's work and thought hard labor was beneath them. There were so, so many people waiting to leave that the land seemed like a beehive. The hoers could not get day work. They would go from door to door, like beggars, and come back with aching backs and injured pride. The answer was "no." But if the answer was "yes" it would depend on the weather the next day; then work for twenty coins, no food or drink, or for bags of corn and a quart of milk. The boys, hardly out of school, were sent to hang around on the streets, without work or master, until someone noticed them, verified that they were strong in body and mind, and then would contract them as cattle herders or minders of pests in the wheat fields. The winters were long and uneventful, with crowds of people filling the stores, looking at the rain, sipping from carafes of aromatic wine and shots of cane liquor. Wasted hours and days, because even the stonemasons and carpenters had no work, and for this reason they stretched out the work over the days when not even the clocks had any use. The church bells lied; it was never noon, or vespers, and Sundays were not the day before Monday, following days that were supposed to be Saturdays ...

In the midst of this time without time, there was the big bellied padre imagining he could undertake new, repeated, and lunatic fund drives for "his" church. He revived the idea of the repair of the roof, the pews, and the three altars. To convince the stingiest, he launched into an auction of sermons. It was always inevitable that God was angry with men because they had sinned. He prophesied cyclonic winds, torrential rains, floods, pests, earthquakes, the punishment of a cholera that would only be subdued if they were generous to the church. God's patience has limits. The mercy of the saints of health, concord, and agriculture don't just wander loosely about the world; it was essential to deserve it, and prayer and feigned repentance were not enough, like those who beat their chest, *mea culpa, mea culpa*, and are no more than pharisees.

Fire sermons, marked by shouts and long pauses, made the women sob and bathed them in tears. Others who were less impressed pretended to be disturbed, putting handkerchiefs to their mouths as they ran outside for air in the square. I saw them many times, trembling like sheep in the presence of dogs. Sitting with the men, the deacon turned around, putting his finger to his lips, and ordered the rabble to be silent. If a baby cried more than was permitted, he would lower his voice and, taking advantage of a pause in the sermon, shed formality:

"Get this child out of here. Go outside and show a little respect!"

From the pulpit descended a thunder roll that was directed at bad behavior, the luxury of calico dresses, the vanity of young girls of the age to marry, who, according to the priest, practiced shameless flirting from their windows, in plain sight of passersby who would turn a blind eye, and with the blessing of the mothers who didn't heed the voice of conscience ... When the fashion of women wearing pants arrived here, a lot more lightening flashed down from the pulpit! But at the end of the sermon, the sacristan came by with the offering plate extended from a trembling hand, his eyes fixed on whoever had the nerve to give small change: this wasn't a request for alms, such paltry offerings were an insult to the church! When earthquakes hit, nobody could restrain him, because misfortune always brought him a great opportunity. Then he would organize spiritual retreats and night processions, and visiting priests came to confess a multitude of sinners who formed a line that went into the square. There had never been so many sins; the women turned pale and fainted; the promise keepers, growing in number and affliction, wore rended garments, fasted, and bought candles the sizes of cart poles, to practice the via sacra, pray the rosary without end, and implore the mercy of their own death. Not satisfied with penance, they offered chickens, turkeys, and milk calves that were auctioned amid the cries of street vendors who called out sweets, bean grinders, cartons of eggs, and trays of guava paste, cassavas, and prunes. Hurrying back into the sacristy, the priest displayed a greedy smile and appeared dressed in the cotta, that white thing that priests put over their cassock. The sun shining in his face, he would shield his eyes, inciting one, stroking the pride of others.

"Come on, twenty more coins into the offering bowl," said someone from the crowd. "It's fer Our Lady!"

When the Portuguese money ran out, then the competition between the blessed Canadian *dollahs* against the American began — one after the other attacking each other like rabid dogs.

"It's for Our Lady of Rozário, Christians," the priest spat out, wiping his lips on his handkerchief. "It's for our patron saint!"

From the pocket of one of the "Americans" came a wallet full of pictures and credit cards. It was raised high in the air, above the heads of the crowd, so they would see the wad of folded *dollahs*, crisp new notes, whose owner was angered by the melee. Nervous, gesturing wildly, and foaming at the mouth, he took advantage of the astonishment and the silence:

"Take it easy! That's my money, understood? *My* money! The winner is the one who mans up and puts out lots of *money*."

In compensation, the losers in this fight over *dollahs* paid for rounds of beer, proclaiming into the ears of the skeptical that money — *money?* — was something they didn't lack. *Lots of money! Worked hard my whole life, that's for sure! But I've got no more money problems.* Because of this, on the very next Sunday, they had the right to special banns by his reverence, because, according to him, Dick or Harry had notwithstanding contributed, and generously, he stressed, with some large bills for the temple of God, or in honor of the dead or some foreign saint . . .

The result was no construction at the church, contrary to what had been promised. The poor and the sick were forgotten, and there wasn't even hope for the stonemasons and carpenters. Many times my father became offended, like a fool, without understanding why he was out of work and meanwhile carpenters were coming from outside, stonemasons too, even servants. The winter passed, the rainy days passed slowly until spring dried them out, and the outside workers left behind an unfinished church, cement showing and much still to be done. The incomplete project was providential; it offered new arguments for more fund-raising campaigns and new sermons. And meanwhile the padre bought a car or traded in an old one for a new one, wore silk cassocks in the heat, and cotton in the cold seasons, and his enormous white house, bought by the people, was discreetly renovated. No mention of big construction, so as not to draw attention. The verandahs were enhanced with forged iron, substituting split timbers; cartons of tile and bathroom fixtures were brought in; and baskets of dirt were carried out, as were the remnants of outmoded things, doors knocked down by hammers, and mismatched furniture. The people always said, although between clenched teeth, that he was the biggest thief in the municipality. Every time another nephew was placed in a school in Lisbon, it was evidence of his thievery. And the day that his ugly sisters, with their crossed eyes and deformed bodies and looking like defective pumpkins, were installed in the house, followed by their old parents and trunks of clothing, the people began to think without ever saying it that the representative of Christ was sent to them as a howling wolf in sheep's clothing. Meanwhile, the miserable sacristan, thin as a reed, covered up the game: starving, yellow, but self-important and haughty, he gave his wife and child fennel broth in portions that would kill a dead man — and he never let out a peep about the embezzled money and the desecration of the offering plate.

And it follows that despite all of this, the women did not stop giving birth. Rachitic children writhed and cried like skinned cats. They coughed and suffocated to death. Others came soon after, because the houses were filling up, the schools became nurseries of smocks that passed from child to child and the primers were held together with Arabic glue. The miracle of life came from the wild yams in the grottoes and stolen figs. We, the young boys, attacked vegetable gardens and orchards. The men acted at night, taken by a wind that muffled their footsteps. They poisoned dogs with grape vines. And when there was no dog in a household, they carried off chickens, sacks of wheat, bags of potatoes, *everything*. It was inevitable that half of the municipality robbed the other half. If the miracle of foreign countries had not come to us, we would have ended up eating each other alive, as my mother used to say. Even the air, according to her, would be difficult to breathe because of so many mouths suffering from the same illness, the poison of living without pleasure, the smell of the ocean and the white ships that never docked on the island. Others were saved by bird nests, rat holes, roasted in shameful secret, besides the yams and the blessed fennel. In spite of all of this we lived with some decency, through commands to the children: they went door to door offering the labor of their fathers for threshing days and breaking up stones with pickaxes, afternoons for clearing brambles, and rainy mornings to clean out the woods. Fortunately for all, there were always ferns and ginger lilies in the easements and coils of muskrats at the gates of the properties. During the time of the earthquake, when the broad beans and black beans were ready to pick, the flails came down from the attics and beat anything with a bean in it. Others, because they did not know how to or could not work, sold coal and firewood. And the last, after they had walked a long distance to call the doctor and to fetch remedies for the dying, dug graves and covered the coffins with dirt.

At the beginning of Spring there was no danger of the cows dying from the hail of the Mato do Povo mountains. The weather had changed color. The sun came in from the ocean, turning it a light color, without that blackness that had put it in mourning during the entire winter. It stopped looking like old rags, a sea of mops with flecks of soap foam, and it seemed peaceful, even if grey like a shaving blade. When Summer came, it became a blue and semi-transparent mirror. I would climb to the highest spot on the Island with my father, and from there one can see the ocean twice, on one side and the other of the land. If it was a clear day, we could see the little basket of plow furrows that formed the island of Santa Maria. I can't explain the feeling of our beating hearts and burning pulses just in seeing from afar another land lost in the middle of the sea. It was no more than a cock's comb illuminated by the sunset. But it was enough to understand that we weren't alone in the universe. That distant island represented a mute presence that watched us, always silent and luminous — a distracted God. In a certain sense it was a destination: from there the planes left that would cross the Atlantic, taking thousands of Azoreans to America.

We did as everyone else on Rozário: freeing the cattle, we herded them long distances, in the direction of the streams and forests. When we turned, they would grow restless, as if sensing they would be abandoned in those cold, lonely places. Raising their snouts, they sniffed the air searching for us and came to greet us at the bottom of the mountain.

"What was the idea?" you ask.

The idea was that they should graze loose, left to themselves during the summer. We wanted them to fatten up, to open themselves when in heat, to the bulls. We wanted the heifers to thrive, so they could be slaughtered for meat. There was no better pasture on all of the Island than Mato do Povo. The flies didn't go up there, or the illnesses, or the hot afternoons, and the cattle enjoyed the eternally humid grasses of the mountains. And for us it was a rest. There was never word of cattle thieves raiding the area. We were on an island; it would not be possible to hide a cow in another herd, since she would return to the house of her owner on her own.

When summer came to an end, we again climbed the mountain. It took several days to look for them sunrise to sunset, calling them by name, whistling ceaselessly, certain that from one moment to the next they would give a sign of life and answer our shouts. Kilometers and kilometers around, through the woods of Algarvia, Salga, Achada, even the Lomba da Maia, and many times we gave up, without finding their trail or smelling their scent. The next morning, or on the many that we had to return to the mountain to find them, God willed it that finally we would hear a lowing, then another and another, and finally a set of horns with tagged ears would appear in the fog. Little by little, a herd came to eat a tuft of grass from our hands. They were fat, shiny as worms, and seemed infinitely happy to have been reunited with us. My father almost always cried. For him, the Mato do Povo was a divine blessing. It signified the only abundance capable of taking the soul of the cattle farmer who faced the future on the Island with his herd.

CHAPTER FIVE

Nuno Miguel

"You're worthless, you'll never amount to anything," my brother Luís would say to me, I don't know if this was because he was angry or just being dismissive. He repeated it countless times, because he was very strong and I didn't even have the strength to hold a calf, a goat, or a sheep by its lead. He said it because I was afraid of the dark, the rain, and the large headlike shadows that the trees projected from the woods in the moonlight of the great white nights. He said it because I would run away, terrified, from the damned mare that Papa, years later, when I was already in the seminary, decided to buy from a stockman who was about to leave for America. He brought it as a surprise, when nobody believed in the miracle of this generosity, and introduced it into the life of the family as if he were dispensing a blessing. It whinnied, bit, and kicked so hard that sparks would fly. It was a reddish brown, and had two rows of tits that were dry and sterile as stones.

Papa started to rain blows on her because the cursed beast would straighten its ears and bare its teeth at whomever approached her. And since she was excessively thin, with knobby legs and a mean look, she devoured everything, famished even when it wasn't time to eat.

"Well if this is a devil from hell," my father would despair, scratching his sweaty head, as was his habit, "she's like a bottomless pit, this damn beast!"

And he'd deliver a kick to her stomach, while he tried to tighten her girth strap. Then he would beat her ostentatiously and with such cruelty with a pitchfork until she bled from the flanks so that even we, her principal enemies, considered the punishment excessive. The blows echoed in the distance, rained over the drum of that insatiable stomach that grass couldn't fill, and the swearing and repeated curses that Papa hurled at that animal were sad, noisy scenes that could be heard by the entire neighborhood. In our opinion, the spectacle of such disorder ended up giving the mare disproportionate importance. In order to mount her, I seduced her with treats, caresses on her neck, and words that were so tender that they would calm me too. Loading her up with pails of milk, sacks of squash, or bundles of firewood was almost impossible. Her diabolical intelligence enjoyed exploiting my fragility, but she submitted to the dominant will of my father and brother.

"You're not even worth the water you drink, you little eunuch priest," Luís Miguel insisted, beside himself with anger, at times when fury seemed to blind him and he would even start to cry. He would go over to the calves and lift them by their tails. If they didn't fall immediately, he would twirl them in the air, kick them in the neck, and throw them to the ground. He would grab the sheep by the wool on their backs, he would hold the goats by the tuft of hair on their backs, and with apparent ease, would fling them a long distance. This was his way of showing me how I should deal with those stubborn creatures. His blows, on those flying carcasses, sounded like random hammering, reducing the goats to brutalized lumps.

Since it was repeated to me so often, that sentence entered had my spirit and had the effect of making me withdraw. My nervous system weakened. I was always on the other side of violence, even the necessary kind, and it was difficult for me to separate the motives for my impulses. I never know if deep down inside me a little bit of moral courage exists, a nerve sensitive to modern aggression, or just a sliver of cowardice. Afterward, when even my sisters and the people in neighborhood lamented the small size of my body — and my mother fussed over my lack of appetite, weak bones, and absence of muscles — I was still unprotected. My father never tired of repeating, "What a pathetic creature! You'll never amount to anything."

Worse than any of those Island bells, that still today ring in my spirit from far away, there is always Luís Miguel's mocking voice, his scornful taunts, and laughter.

"You aren't worth the water you drink. You aren't worth the water you drink. You aren't worth the water you drink . . ."

So because I wasn't worth anything, not even the water I drank, I had to invent some kind of use for my body and find an outlet for my cunning and innocence. I didn't have the strength to milk a cow. I couldn't help the old man hoe rows of corn or weed the beets. In the woods, I suffered like the damned, until I'd fall by the wayside, full of crazy thoughts, my chest straining for breath, and then my father would start yelling and would exert more force on the saw to cut down the great trunks of the cedar trees.

You can't imagine, you can never imagine how hard it is; how it hurts until you think you are going to die, and how your chest splits open and your back breaks, and how much you despair. My father on top, me on the bottom, trying to balance myself so I wouldn't slip in the moist earth and on the steep slopes. Nevertheless I would trip on the bulbs of the ginger lilies, the resin of the logs, and on the yams, and father yelled constantly:

"Get some strength in those arms, you little shit! Wake up Nuno! Crying out loud, move it, don't make me do it alone!"

It wasn't just the sweat of the effort. I was drenched in the sordid affliction of weakness, the terror of those screams close to my ears, and the difficulty of keeping my balance on the swampy terrain that drained into unromantic streams. The narrow falls, on the edge of the cliffs, the ropelike torrents pouring into black pools, attracted me to the abyss. I was perfectly in reach of Papa's heavy hand, and I knew that death could begin there; if he reached out to strike me, I would fall screaming. I would try then to grab on to the small tufts of weeds, the exposed roots of the beeches to try to keep myself from falling to the bottom of that precipice. At the limits of my strength, exhausted and at the edge of death, I had to force my arms to pull me to my feet and not allow myself to cry. Sometimes I would fall over, breathing heavily. Cramps rippled through the muscles of my arms and chest and the weak cry of a puppy escaped from within me. My father would appear, out of his head with anger, his body twisted, bent over from back pain, cursing the hour I had come into the world to make trouble for him. Our Lord should have taken me, screamed, like the other one, or blessed him by paralyzing me and turning me into a vegetable. I had a hard time believing that he had not understood I was only eight, nine, or ten years old — and that my only fault was having been born from him, a twin, with my lungs damaged by the cough and the terrible fever that had consumed me as a newborn. Every time a tree fell, there was a crash in that shadowy cathedral of crumbling walls. I gushed sweat and tears, in the devastation of branches and foliage, and there my fiendish father cast dispersions on me, giving me angry slaps on the back of my head, hitting me with the handle of the ax that he used to clear the brush. The indifference of my silence irritated him, the accusation in my serious eyes that made him avert his gaze and stare at the horizon. Papa couldn't stand even the hint of the knot of hate in my distracted stare that was filling with memories and beginning to stumble into the future. In his opinion, I not only did not deserve the bread soup, bacon rinds, and salted fish that comprised my diet, but I was also not worthy of hating him as I did. When you have a god as an enemy, it's dangerous to look at him, or to even think of the profaning of his temples and altars ...

Following the noisy death of the trees, if the woods were accessible, the oxen would come to drag the logs to flat ground or to the road where they could be trucked out. If not, we sawed the logs into sections measuring twelve hand lengths, loaded them on our backs, my father in front and I following — and so, so many times I fell to my knees, crushed, run over by the inconceivable weight of those green bodies! Trampled not just by the trees, understand, but by the sap that was dying inside them, that silent blood, sweating and colorless.

"Well, so this is the day I die," I thought, noticing how my knees were shaking, as if my body was allowing itself to be crushed, vanquished by those logs.

I was sad to have to die this way, flattened, like a paste of bones with bits of flesh. I would have preferred to pass from this to any other world in a fit of coughing, or devoured by worms. Sometimes I appealed to a guardian angel named Luís Miguel. He always came from afar, after a long wait, seeing me moaning, trembling, under the logs, and he ran to lift them off my shoulders.

"Look here Papa," he would say fearfully, lowering his head, as if his conscience could speak directly for him. "This is too heavy a load for a small weak child like Nuno. Let him do what is sensible for his size, don't damage him for the rest of his life."

Papa would look at me with a final hateful expression, as he himself panted from the exertion, as if he had asthma, and exclaimed, "What he is, God forgive me, is a nuisance, a worthless piece of garbage!"

He decided then to try me out on lighter, conventionally feminine tasks. He put me to work taking care of orchards, giving me for company a spotted dog that barked excessively and that saw peach thieves in even the flies and birds. We would leave for the Chã da Cancela at dawn. We settled into the thatched hut that was reconstructed every year — and the hours turned into ghosts with an alcoholic stare and winged hands. The orchard was sufficiently scary to stunt the spirit of a child and to ruin the dog's sense of smell. It was in a ravine, surrounded by three hills of peach trees and apple trees, at the bottom of which a stream of the Achada River flowed from the mountains, from Mato do Povo and Outeiros, spewing its muddy waters. On the opposite bank cattle grazed to the sound of the bells. In the early afternoon the invisible whistle of the cowhands floated through the ancient trees. Everything was unreal and occult, like the very sun in its oblique, dun-colored sphere. Enveloping the peach and other fruit trees, the cedar groves were dark presences, tin-colored, put there on purpose by our ancestors if only to capture the stopped time of the dead. The strange nest in Grande Medo opened to receive my cold body. Then the family dead would parade by over the treetops, led by my paternal grandfather with his pale skin, the grating of his melancholy asthma, the whip of his weathered hands and in a permanent state of asphyxiation. Dead Aunt Flórida, mother's sister, traveled forever seated in the air. And her very blue eyes stood out from her face like the bulbous orbs of a frog. She had died of double pneumonia, strangled by her own lungs, after suffering the agony of a fish. For this reason, those eyes were always tumescent and glassy as marbles. My dead twin, poor thing, was a bird flying upside down, and he swam in the air on his back, over the pointed vaults of the great cedars. Sometimes he would pick apples, bite into a ripe peach pecked by birds, and he would tease me as I lay with my tongue hanging out.

Rendered helpless by the metallic blue cold, I wanted to drive them all far away from there. I lost the courage to hear my own voice. The dead harmed the fruit, filled the air with sulphur, and disappeared from my optical illusion. I still supposed that the family dead were amphibians, since I had heard them dive like frogs into the mud of the rushes. Afterward, their frenetic movements served not to distance them but to extinguish them in the bottom of the bog. Once the parade of the family dead stopped, then came all the others: old and young, ugly and beautiful, some with nests on their backs, others hanging from the anchors of shipwrecked boats, others still burning in slow, sulphurous combustions of sin, beside those who spurted blood, those who laughed at me and gave me the finger from afar, both amused and exhausted. I was reminded of the descriptions of hell, proffered in those Sunday afternoon catechism classes, and I saw the horrors of devil's forks, the crackling of flames, and the convulsion of those human pieces of bacon with their sweetish smell. My father had bought not an orchard, I thought, not even a stand of trees, not even that toilet of moist earth where seeds were always prolific and became infinitely numerous; he had bought the terrifying place of this transit that the dead watched over in continuous and long-suffering vigil. The spotted dog did not have the talent or the sense of smell to pursue the dead, because he didn't bark at them and his growls did not go beyond belches in his dreamless sleep.

One day it occurred to Papa that there was another use for me in that limbo. He ordered me to tether the ducks and chickens, and he threw the fowl into the bottom of the ox cart, releasing a cloud of feathers, in the middle of which bubbled weird cackling never before heard in the lands of shadow and light that sloped to the grottoes and the watering holes. The evening before I had tied up a cock whose spurs would certainly repel the kites, the hedgehogs, and the red rats of the swamp. Roosters with inflamed combs strutted among the horde of females with a martial air. My father's plan was that the rotten fruit, the grass, and the yam roots would make those stupid birds get fat and multiply. He called me aside and warned me of the danger of carnivorous animals, and he enumerated them: long-backed rats, bats, ferrets, red lizards that made nests in the ground, moles, and hedgehogs. He had less confidence in my ability to deal with this than in the rooster's spurs, the beaks of the adolescent chickens, and the proven efficacy of the watchdogs.

The next day, early in the afternoon, my sisters appeared without warning. They came bedecked with flowers, festive and rosy cheeked, sweeter than ever — they carried seeds in their aprons and caulis seedlings already starting to sprout and multiply their roots. When they started to sing, I saw them seeding the stone flowerbeds, and they were planting rows of dahlias, palms and amaryllis. Their hands were prodigiously busy; they planted cedar roots, lily of the valley, marigolds, and roses. It suddenly occurred to me that the box shrub and the laurels were already here, the fruits pecked by the birds and the dead, and they had come to bury me, alive and terrified, in that new cemetery of wilted scattered flowers. They gave the earth the sprouts from the gardens and the greenhouse. With basalt stones from the streams, they enclosed the beds where the chickens were forbidden to roam. They made cane fences, they populated the oblique border of the orchard with scarecrows, and they occupied themselves this way during an entire afternoon of roses, fences, songs of love and imaginary passions. Finally they came to meet me and covered me with kisses, always smiling; they asked me to watch not just the fruit and Papa's birds but also their dear flowers and seedlings. I should do this to ward off visible and invisible enemies, the same way that God and the angels listen to the breathing of the cedars, inhale their scent, and become the spirit, the honey, and the core of the cedar. In their opinion I must talk with the rose thorns, because they were also created by God, secret angels in the solitude of gardens and orchards.

When they said good-bye, they left me buried, waiting nightfall. The opening of the shed was my living mausoleum. The dog was like a porcelain figure, the kind always ready to take flight over the tombs in graveyards. The trees were once again sordid and lugubrious, just as the hens, ducks, and turkeys would always be stupid. Forgotten like other useless and discarded family things, I supposed that my soul had been separated from its physical form. For my body, I had cold food and rusty water of the Achada stream; for my spirit, the reverie of the luminous wandering dead, the far call of the concave stars, and my questions about the inexplicable forgetfulness of the world.

Contrary to everything I imagined, my little attempt at revenge didn't even bother the family. In fact, as everyone always said, I really was good for nothing. On the first day of my act of rebellion, I pretended to forget to call the dog and I decided not to take shelter in that mountain hut. I chose the rising sun, the absence of the dead, the silent clarity of the day, where the sounds of chickens and the whispers of a relentless inauspicious wind would not reach me. The next day I saw the kite swoop down on the capon and I heard from afar the croaking, the brief agony of the creature being quartered as it struggled against the power of those talons. In a short while, the rooster was just a shred of flesh hanging from the talons of a black eagle. I saw the evil, serpentine glow in its eyes, the strength of the mythical winged bull, the deaf clamor of horned demons in the stories told by Grand Mama Olinda. Afterward, as if the fruit thieves had recovered their nerve, I saw them crawling between the yams and the ginger lilies, hanging from the bent branches, carrying heavy loads of crab apple and sacks of firewood. The chickens, who before had been shooed away to the depths of the woods, invaded the orchard and scratched away at my sisters' seedbeds as they continued to be attacked by a new invasion of kites. To a point, they were sad battles, because the damned kites twisted their big black wings, swooped down on the round fowl, and flew away with the terrified beaked creatures. The mud rats jumped over the ditches and scampered over the cold mud bordering the forest. They came to devour the shreds of meat, the eggs in the nests, and the newborn chicks. They sometimes got a bonus of a few porous airborne bones.

When Papa arrived on a Sunday morning to relieve me of my post and to send me to noon mass, I finally realized the extent of the disorder around me. I observed it from a distance; I surveyed the torn up peach trees, which suddenly appeared yellowed and bent. I heard him calling the chickens, ducks, and turkeys. His finger pointed to the ground, he counted the golden backs of the chicks. He was a perfect Noah patriarch, as if in the time that, sensing the coming of the flood, he made the selection of the noble species and paired male with female on his Ark. Papa started to tremble, his rapid footsteps taking him to the profaned flower beds. Seen from above, from the place I was perched, his face took on the pallor of feces and began to swell, I wouldn't say with anger, understand? It swelled with sweat. In a rage, he pulled at his hair, swore without restraint, because he was offending God, he harangued the devil and seemed to shoot me, from down there, with the same frigid and unmerciful stare of the field mice. My head sank between my bony shoulders. He was going to kill me, right? He would kill me because his short legs were spread and his eyes were fixed on a bent branch.

Do you doubt he would have killed me? That was as obvious as the evidence of my guilt.

I watched how his body hung from the branch and swung one, two, three times, and then I heard the noise of the trunk splitting. Calmly, I thought about the thickness of those knots; I could not hold on to the slightest hope of my survival. I was going to die, and I could not think of motives, memories, even desires to escape. I was resigned to the logic of that promised death. Grand Mama Olinda had always said that death had a sweet side. When it happens to suffering souls and to the guiltless, in addition to being sweet, it is gloriously white and palpable. You fly to God's redemption and leave behind you a fiery trail of remorse, like speeding comets or lightening on rainy nights ... To die, at that point, was only to close your eyes tightly, stretch out your body on the ground and ask, under the darkness of your eyelids, how to get to God — a trip invented by martyrs, missionaries murdered in Africa, and above all by twin angels and chaste girls who fainted from anemia in the middle of Mass.

Do you know what I did? Do you really want to know how I prepared myself to die?

I called the forces of peace to myself. I lay on my back, breathing in the aroma of the green apples, like my brother bird did, and I prepared myself calmly to receive my father's punishment. I wanted the same blue posture of the angels, wings in repose, crossed over my body and impossible to be confused from the pink color of lips frozen in a half smile. I called softly for that purple death like the cold marble of altars, and I desired it to be as lucid and translucent as the days of winter. And that's how it happened.

I don't know, I don't remember the words I spoke to him. He was a father armed to the teeth, all-powerful, and I was not given the right to defend the slightest detail of my innocence. I, in fact, did not know what to tell him, since the habit of guilt and the habit of always bringing it on myself had suppressed the seventh sense of clarity. If it had been today, in this precise moment, I could have found a wise phrase, a verse of the poet Soares de Passos, for example, or a long paragraph read from one of the books that you published, in which death ceased to be temporal, to have weight, or to make sense.

Perhaps I would have said: "It's not worth killing me, Papa, because I am no longer here. And you can't kill a dead person, do you think, Papa?"

I only know that on that day began the few and all of the future miracles of my life. I suddenly moved from the kingdom of my father to not living in his sphere. My father's arms wilted in the air. He was snuffed out forever under my dark eyelids. Father accepted my surrender, and years later he embraced my body and cried bitterly over the past present and the present past of our reciprocal estrangement. Father swayed like a somnambulist. He bent over my body, lifted it on to his lap, and miraculously made it stand on foot in front of him. Then his father's bony hands ran with compassion through my unruly hair. Certainly magnanimous and a little proud of me, while he said,

"Go on to mass, little one, and pray for us to Our Lord."

Many times, during the years, I waited in vain for him to repeat those words. I waited for him in the distance, in the chaotic sum of my acts as a fatherless boy, in the difficult months when I was in Lisbon during the humiliations of a world that closed to me, on the very day of my expulsion from the seminary, for political subversion and lack of faith in God, according to what they told me — also on that early afternoon when I married Marta and became a taxpayer. I waited for him when I still had a bit of willpower in me, and at other times, when I was despondent, broke, and fallen out of love. I became an insecure man. And even when I lost my senses and beat my children and then abandoned my home and left the house full of remorse to drown myself in drink, I waited for him....

The hardest thing was to believe that I was a different kind of father, and a teacher different from all the old teachers, an attentive and courteous husband as my father did not know how to be, that my obsessions were not his and yet he was always present in how I became a man. And the difficult thing, believe me, was the day he arrived in Lisbon, on the way to his second and final return to Canada. He entered my house, sat at my table, and ate my bread. At dessert he looked me in the eye. I sustained the force of that gaze for a while, and tried to decipher it. But he averted his gaze and looked at the floor. He had never done this before, understand? Because I had always been the one to look away from him, avoid the sight of his mouth, the staring olive-colored eyes. We had never been this way, facing each other, but playing reversed roles, knowing we had a past that we could not speak about and that we had experienced separately. Everything was difficult, even to lose him in this last bet with death. This was when I understood he really was someone else, different from himself, but without the truth of having existed in my admiration. And when I heard him confess how happy he was with how my life had turned out, I saw in his big eyes the pride of being my father, father-in-law of Marta, and grandfather of my children. I examined his smile, listening to his absence, and answered him with the cold silent bells of disenchantment. He was, after all, as old and distant from me as a family daguerreotype, like one of my ancestors.

Maria Amélia

When she decided to go home to God and died of leukemia, Grand Mama Marta left a widower prone to allergic asthma, a distraught household heavy as the shadows, and six orphans. Mama was only sixteen and had not started seeing Papa. Once in a while she would talk to us about her. At those times, she would gaze into the distance, as if she were sensing her or seeing her sitting there in her hazy memory. Grand Mama was plump, white as milk, and according to her, had the same very sad eyes, the same jet black abundant hair, and that curse of the blood that ended up giving me anemia and lymphadenitis, and killed Mama with lymphatic cancer. As for Grand Papa Botelho, he died of asphyxiation and gasping with rage in his delirium, not knowing he was talking with his mute, illusory ghosts.

In his last days, every time we went to visit him as he lay dying, he presented that enormous fish body that later we saw covered with scales in his coffin. Perfectly still, they say, with wide-open eyes, glassy and hard as stone. In between his continuous wheezing, those crazy eyes kept looking for his wife, moaning for her and giving her confused orders. His affectionate name for her was Tita, the last two syllables of the diminutive Martita, and he said it with such discreet tenderness that none of us ever thought of using that name. Even Mama and my aunts and uncles had never called their mother Tita. And since it was an immemorial grandmother, of whom there was not one single photograph, that name was even lost to us. She was simply Mama's mother.

Already so close to death, Grand Papa decided to abolish all notions of time and place where his life would come to an end. After a long conversation with his dead wife, he started to call his children one by one, and distributed among them the innumerable chores of their once hectic household. Uncle Martinho, the youngest, had left secretly for Canada, but Grand Papa sent him to the store to buy a packet of tobacco, to get the thistle for the bunnies, or to grind corn and scatter it to the chickens. Uncle Antero, who had bad lungs and coughed like a fog horn, in spite of already being married more than twenty years, continued to be admonished about his courtship of the lovely but penniless and quiet Aunt Angélica. The other aunts gathered around him in tears and tried to calm those hallucinations and bring him back to his senses. This was, however, useless, and it threw him into fits of fury against poor Aunt América, who finally at thirty-five years of age had succeeded in marrying the inventor Herculano.

"Get out of here, girl, or go to bloody hell!" Grand Papa said, provoking the others to laugh at his outbursts and to cry in the corners, near and far from him, sad to see that time had stopped for him, like a broken clock inside his head. "You look like a barren cow, you damned girl! If a man ever looked twice at you he'd have to be blind in one eye or have his head up his ass!"

Two nights before he died, he confused the doctor from Algarvia with the vendor of water jugs and bowls, and so he started to haggle about prices and sizes of the goods. He ended up screeching that he didn't have the patience to haggle over prices of housewares with thieves and bums from the street. Dr. Arlindo, in spite of his well-known bad humor, applied the stethoscope to his chest and, unperturbed, whistled the latest tune from Lisbon. Tapping his chest and back with his fingers, palpating his belly, and peering at the whites of his eyes, kept whistling that spirited song from Lisbon. Then he scratched out an illegible prescription, arranged his instruments in the bag he took on house calls, extended his hand for the fee of his consultation, and pronounced:

"Prepare for the worst; he won't last long. Between today and tomorrow, say good night and turn off the light. Give him chicken broth and put a steaming kettle with balsam water near his nose. And don't bother me again: I have many people waiting for an appointment."

From the death certificate that arrived months later and during the hearing when the property was divided, we learned that Grand Papa had died of double emphysema. The day after the doctor's visit, when the priest came to administer last rites, he sank back into the chaos of those visions. Since he confused the cassock and the surplice with the coloring of the cows that used to go through the house on the way to the barn, he started to hit with his bony hand the animal that had come into his room and threatened to devour the bedspread, the sheets, and the mattress stuffing. Very flushed, Father Ângelo stopped the Latin and cupped his hand behind his ears:

"Well what is it? What is he saying ladies? Is he shooing cows? But what cows?"

So that on the day of his death, we all laughed as we stood around the bier, at the simple memory of his confusion, and we tried to think, like with all the others, that this was for us a happy death. Papa and Mama, always very serious and dressed in mourning, forced us to kiss him on the cheek before the arrival of the men who would place him into the coffin. My lips stiffened at the fleeting contact with the dead man's skin, and the funereal chill is my last memory of his face. The flickering candles in the glass votives, waving like firebrands in the wind, cast tongues of shadow over the scaly body and projected rose crowns and cedar branches over the eczema-covered skin. From that time on, death for me had a lot to do with the last joke, with the mental confusion of the dying, and the funeral elegy of their virtues, amidst the nervous giggles and sighs of people dozing near the body.

It was, however, the sound of the first clods of dirt that Papa forced me to throw on the coffin covered with flowers that I found most difficult about that death. Grand Papa's face must have frowned at the noise of the earth falling, and perhaps he was still fighting the living. Above all, I will never forget that we buried him on an unforgiving day of very cold rain. The earth muddied our Sunday shoes, the smell of the lilies faded, the scent of the asters and yellow calendula could no longer be detected, and the priest made mistakes and then corrected a Latin pelleted by the rain. Even though he was sheltered by the church umbrella, water streamed down his shoulders, splattered his square face, and soaked the transparent pages of the missal. The wind, which was continuously changing direction, mussed the strands of his grey hair habitually plastered to his head and shiny with gel; it flapped his cassock against his rheumatic shins. I'll never forget that we all left, tranquil and relieved that his long illness was over. We went into his big, honest, very poor house, with walls that had not yet known clay, plaster, and paint, just stones held together by veins of cements mixed with the black sand of Calhau. The house was still full of his presence and his life, do you understand, sir? Full of those bullish years sitting at the doorway and of his ancient widowerhood. The noise of the doors continued to be the same as when he started to cough and sat in the doorway to laboriously breathe the little air that could get through the sand of his lungs. Again we heard the scraping of chairs on beaten earth, the ticking of Uncle Herculano's fifty watches, the cock's crow in the evenings, the strong chewing of the sow in the wooden feeding trough — and all of this brought to my memory the times he'd receive me, listen to my troubles, and tell Aunt América to spread a piece of bread with cow's butter and sugar for me. Besides this, the wind and the rain of that afternoon, in the bamboo hedges, his large vegetable garden in the shape of a keel and squeezed between two walls, the public fountain at the back that carried the weight, design, and religious intention of the Padrão das Almas church — all of this was very much his. We had taken seats around his large cedar table, which ran the length of the kneading surrounded by the cabinets, and all of a sudden I had the vision of where he had spent twenty-four hours in the viewing chamber; flies the size of bats were continuously chased by a cane fan, the night was extinguished with the size of the candles, and the time of dying seemed unbearably empty in the very red eyes of my aunts . . .

We would then begin to eat him, this grandfather of the lands, the furniture, and the few decorative plates. Soup terrines and bowls, some broken and repaired with white cement and the pins of the repair men who came around in early summer, lay in the memory of the tableware. We would eat the grandfather of bell jars and mirrors, the music box with the dancing Spanish ballerina, the symphonic grandfather who revolved around this axis of poverty, the flint stone and the few saints in niches, whose sweet and suffering faces had always looked down on us through constellations of flies. He was buried and his bones were full of rainwater, but he remained alive amid the mute objects that grew in size and would be touched, examined, and discussed. They would have a price and would become the possessions of those who, even though they remained angry with him, would return to sit around his table. Subdued, still inhibited by the embarrassment of that house, the heirs looked like crows with shiny eyes. Covetousness made those eyes almost diabolical; they were familiar with all of it; they argued with the first prices fixed for the objects and began to distrust each other. With extreme slowness they rolled tobacco, returned to their crowlike demeanor with pensive, exhausted expressions, and had the useless idea to smoke the first cigarette of that Atlantic afternoon. The women had hung their shawls on the kitchen nails, taken the mourning bands off their sleeves, and decided it might be time to probe the promises that the house held. Mama got ready to grill some sausage, since no one had eaten for twenty-four hours. Even the older children had not eaten and hunger would not allow any more discussion. The caprice of mourning turned into the protest, the discreet tremor of the hungry hands, and the restlessness of the seventeen grandchildren of the deceased man.

Aunt Olímpia went to the cupboard and took out the dishes. Aunt Flórida, with dark circles under her eyes and unaware she would die within a year, went to the cutlery drawer and took out knives and forks. Aunt Angélica went to get the yellow corn bread and brought along with it two honeycombs. Aunt América, who was always with Grand Papa, told everyone where the wine and the mixing bows were, the platters and the jars, the water jug and the wine carafes. Then she asked everyone, without looking at anyone, if they would let her distribute to the little ones the last slices of bread with cow butter and cups of coffee with milk and sugar. There was a general nodding of heads, and then she told everyone where the coffee, milk, sugar, and bread were. And we were very happy; Grand Papa's death was a party, and for that reason a happy occasion, when suddenly her voice rose in a sustained pitch:

"That was the last of the bread of my saintly father!"

Sobbing convulsively with her thick shoulders shaking around her little bird head, in which even her eyes, in spite of being blue and calculating, seemed dead, she added:

"He was always so lonely, poor thing, and his chest hurt so badly . . . Oh my dear father, my poor dear father! . . ."

She quieted down in the face of the stony stares of the others, seeing all those eyes on her, disapproving of her mournful, unnecessary cry. After all, the time was now passed of crying for him and serving him, the hour of candles and flowers, and also the other hour, when they had returned him to the earth to the beginning of forgetfulness, among box shrub roots and the eternal shadow of the walls, of the cypress, and the big cedar with its evergreen leaves. He was already in the second phase of dying and the magnanimous hour of the distribution of property. It was not fitting or convenient to muddy the lucidity of this new moment of discernment with emotions . . .

After we finished our meal and the men had retired to smoke and spit on the floor of beaten earth, Aunt América, her face gaunt but lacking appetite, watched the flies hovering over the remains of bread and wine, saw that they were buzzing, ricocheting before landing on the table bloodied by wine stains. She saw the males mounting the females with abandon, in front of the children. She swatted them with a dishrag, called her sisters and sister-in-law, and embarked on a tour of the house. First they collected the gold hidden in the chests of drawers and then added it to the silver medallions that she herself had kept in a glazed clay pot. Then she showed everyone the chains with rusty crucifixes, Grand Papa's pocket watch, which passed from hand to hand so they could feel its weight. They examined the rings, the array of broaches, necklaces, and earrings of the unforgettable Grand Mama Marta. The greenish cast had taken over the clasps and had begun to disintegrate them; the gold was losing its weight and thickness, besides the shine that was supposed to belong to it; the silver had turned into a kind of tarnish over aluminum or tin; and in spite of this everyone was moved at the sight of old age, the hidden existence of this first death, and for this reason it drew a pearly smile at the corners of their mouths. When Papa, always the practical one, asked about Grand Papa's money, my aunt went straight to the china cabinet, moved around vats, terrines, cutting boards, and trays, tore the paper that lined the wood, and brought out a thick packet of paper, tied by a satin ribbon. Papa counted bank notes and Portuguese and foreign coins, six contos de réis, and an involuntary smile that on his habitually dour face looked like a nervous tic wrinkled his mouth and extended the wrinkle that traversed his brow. It was impossible to know what he was thinking at the moment that the paltry treasure of his father-in-law was spread on the table. Certainly a tiny feeling of revenge rose up triumphantly from his soul to his thin lips. It had been years since he and the dead man had stopped talking to each other, exchanging a reciprocal and never explained hatred. Nevertheless the supreme justice of time had decided to open to him and not his father-in-law, the forbidden door of that house. Never again would that stubborn, silent old man turn away his face to avoid him as he passed by, nor would he have to ask for his blessing. For years, when he walked by that door, seeing him sitting there and spitting on the floor between his knees, at the end of a hard day and in a state of exhaustion, his voice overcame the asthma, becoming even more breathless:

"Your blessing, my father-in-law!"

"My blessing!"

In the course of the rain that lengthened and darkened the day, alternating the great downpours with the dewy sun when witches enter into wedlock, we played with our cousins and listened to how the voices turned progressively more coarse and angry from afar. We played, and the voices came from the inventory of everything that had belonged to the dead man. They were inheriting his life, his soul, and his bones, all that remained was to divide the house, the lands, the forests, and the orchards. I sat in the midst of my elder cousins, who were silent witnesses to the zeal and measure and state of all the goods, when we heard Aunt América become moved again to acid tears and to implore the others, on the soul of her father, to let her keep the house. She had been a girl and a bride in that house, happy and unhappy, single and married, and she had always been surrounded by those poor cold walls . . .

Oh, sir, how miserable and miserly are the hands of the poor! When the objects were divided, in a raffle, Mama suggested that we, the children, pick out the little rolled up pieces of paper, on the pretext that only in our hands would perfect innocence reside. In this, all were in agreement, and so out of the jam jar came the numbers assigned to cast iron bed frames, chests of drawers, and keep chests, floor mats and clothing, china and other kitchen utensils. Silent, subdued, and unhappy, we witnessed the dismantling of the order and soul of that house. One of my cousins embraced the enamel chamber pot that belonged to Grand Papa and carried it down the street with a triumphant smile, as if it were a trophy. The dishes traveled to Burguete, in three clay vessels, while the trivets and iron cookware that Aunt América won in the lottery stayed with the pots and jars and the chickens. The sow was led on a hemp to the pigsty of Uncle Antero, who lived in the gloomiest of gloomy houses on the Rua da Canada. He himself came to get her, tied by the hind leg, and spit his dog phlegm along the length of that trajectory under the eyes of respectable people, who stood at their doorways to watch the second death of the dead man. Uncle Guilherme carried a scratched and chipped cabinet on his shoulders and then he came back for the drawers, the glass vials, and the water jug. The living room clock, the wardrobes, and the kitchen table were passed on to Uncle Martinho, absent in Canada, for which reason the attorney decided they could stay in the house under the care of Aunt América. As for us, we took apart the two iron beds and brought them, piece by piece, to be reassembled in the loft. They were much bigger than our former sleeping nests. Seeing them in their new places, Mama gave thanks to God that her children did not have to sleep on the floor anymore.

Sensing, as if she were just waking up, that the house was being pillaged by the family, Aunt América suddenly lost her memory of where things were, and she started to wander around the house like a big confused bird. They had contaminated her nest. Life was suspended and once again shipwrecked inside those empty walls. When everyone left carrying Grand Papa's precious belongings, she stood motionless and almost somnambulant, lost in those suddenly enlarged spaces between the walls, without noticing that the spiders were scurrying in the light and the absence of their hiding places. She didn't see them right away, only later, but the rat holes became visible with their nests in the cavities excavated inside the baseboards. Next to her, Uncle Herculano, the inventor, surveyed the emptiness, made a mental inventory of the wreckage, and once again returned to the feverish ideas of his inventions. Besides the things that were basic to life, the tools were left, and a measure of acacia wood had been forgotten in the stable trough. Since there were no cows, he could easily, with some imagination, modify the use of the objects and give them some other utility. He muttered this between his teeth and almost into his wife's ears, but she didn't hear him, even after he promised her that soon he would restore the house to its former dignity and function. For the lands, he had no vocation, as she well knew. Until then he had always been able to earn the indulgence of his father-in-law, and even his complicity, eating his soups, administering the income from the land and the pastures, without the need to resort to his inventions and patents. In recent years he had coexisted with the slow agony of the dead man, and had become accustomed to the whistling presence of the asthma and the visits of his clients. They brought him clocks and locks to fix, and they stayed to watch him take them apart and explain the machines, the incomprehensible mechanism of the gears, the steel cords, the notched levers that ordered and synchronized the hands. He had become so expert on the secrets of machines that, receiving them in an apparently irrecoverable state, he accepted the challenge of their reconstruction and sacrificed sleep to imagine new parts that would substitute those that had been broken.

Dozens of watches had been set to chime the hour in five-second intervals, measured by the chronometer. Aunt América, complaining of a headache, had escaped to the yard so she wouldn't go mad. The house trembled and vibrated under the terrible succession of the pendulums on the wooden gongs. Even Grand Mama Botelho, in spite of her admiration for her son-in-law's engineering skill, began to rail against that obsession of measuring time and reducing it with such rigor.

In time many machines arrived. Others were ordered on the basis of short descriptions. The system of milking with suction tubs soldered to rubber bags designed to be squeezed by hand; the cart to sow beets; the machine to hatch eggs inside an incubator with smoked glass hanging from the chimney... When there was time to spare, he entertained himself by making toys for the children, or he would draw their faces in real-life proportions, accentuating the cheeks and giving all of them such thick eyelashes that they looked like a new species of human. Since people were dying and others were going far away, people got very sentimental and asked him to reproduce a long-gone face from memory, of which there was no remaining photographic record. Besides this, the rich people had already started the fashion of hanging in the corridors of their houses frames etched with roses and the portraits of famous men, along with bucolic themes, landscapes with boats, and still lifes depicting the fruit arrangements that were starting to decorate dining rooms.

Unlike all the others, who considered him to be somewhat of a fool, I always believed in his superior intelligence, in the sensibility and inventiveness of Uncle Herculano. Even after he had come to our house to fight with Papa, I continued to admire him. Do you know why, sir? He was the only person in our family who appreciated my dreams and mad secrets. The others, who hated his capacity to dream, were always the first to forbid our friendship. Even Aunt América, in spite of laughing with some malice at her husband's daydreams, did not hesitate to have him draw her portrait with his coal stick. Seen in natural light, she looked like a kind of laughing cetacean, with languid blue eyes. But in the wood frame, the face settled in perpetuity over the torso, its half-smile was reminiscent of the uncertain serenity of Mona Lisa. That's why I'm saying that I never knew anyone who could better represent real and invented dreams. And since that was a time measured by madness, what people didn't want to admit wouldn't go beyond the obvious; Uncle Herculano was a little bit inside all of us. We all possessed a small part of his world, even though we didn't like it and were ashamed to admit it . . .

Luís Miguel

I remember it as if it were today. Sacristan Calheta climbed up the church tower and, with his hair standing on end and a runny nose, started to ring the bells so frantically that the people became so alarmed that even children women and dogs entered the fray. He was running around in a panic, gasping for breath, predicting new calamities, and proclaiming that the Pico da Vara had started to erupt, up there behind the round clouds that never moved.

The time that all of this excitement occurred I was very small, so that I don't even remember the event. It was my father who said that one night the Pico da Vara had started to spit flames and explosions, frightening everyone. He told us about the incident of a plane off course in the sky of the Azores, full of famous people from all over the world, and it got lost in the fog and crashed into that mountain with the twisted nose and ugly expression. It exploded and turned into a burning mass that even today recalls a huge iron slab encircled in smoke. That night Rozário arose en masse to flee the first tears and stones of the volcano, when the voice of someone who understands volcanoes reminded the people that neither was this the season for earthquakes nor did volcanoes erupt at random.

At first, people supposed that such a disturbance was a case of fire in the wheat fields, comparable to when fires surround houses, granaries, corn bins, and bales of hay, and the world sank into a burning, Lenten sadness. Later, when the people began to gain a clearer idea of what was happening, people came out to discuss it with the attitude of those who understand these phenomena, and to take sides, against and in favor, but all for different reasons.

As for me, I remember the stories of our talented Grand Mama Olinda, who liked us only when we were little and after we grew older never again offered us cookies or money for parties. A busybody like few others in this world, she grabbed life by the horns and spit out intrigues. I remember that she'd tell stories that would rob sleep from God's angels, and one day she announced that the world would end next Friday at dusk; it was sunny and raining, a deathlike heat that we hadn't experienced in many years, and suddenly there was a downpour, there were floods, and the streets were washed out. People seemed to walk around in a daze, without a thought in their heads, so full of anxiety it was as if an epidemic was starting. Nobody knew anything about the secret of Fátima, *anyway*. Sister Lúcia decided to join a convent, just like Maria Amélia, and she had decided not to reveal to anybody how the world was going to end. This being the case, one couldn't imagine what kinds of death would crucify races and *civilizations, I mean*, or when or how God would decide on the punishment of the beings He himself had created from clay, mud, or even *nothing*. Mr. Salazar, they said, was one of the few men on this earth who had been delivered a sealed letter containing the revelation of Fátima's secret. But since Salazar, God, and the Pope were one and the same person of our Holy Trinity, we continue to this day waiting to know our fate . . . The priest at the time shouted out his sermons from the height of the pulpit on Sundays and Saint days, a roster of mature penances, telling us to our faces that we were the world's biggest shits. We sinned by commission, thoughts, and omission of one thing and another; that is, we failed to act or think according to the Good. In the opinion of that stupid dog, Russia was assembling armies to destroy churches and to castrate priests, as if they hadn't been castrated at birth. In this regard, the opinion of Mr. Quental — the most respected person in the municipality — wasn't known. At that point it could have mattered less to the deaf people who turned their backs on the wisdom of books and only knew how to shuffle along behind the carts of religion.

As far as the catechism, I was more or less well informed. I had heard about the mysteries of the Holy Trinity and the Reincarnation. They told me, countless times, like a metronome, the story of the calf and the donkey, the Three Kings and the Star of the East, on the *Christmases* of old. But I never understood how the three things, Father, Son, and Holy Spirit, could join and become one person, or how the Virgin Mary, married to a carpenter with no balls, and impregnated by the Angel of adultery, could have given birth to a Son in a lowly manger and still be a virgin. Neither could I believe in the resurrection of Lazarus and Jesus and the ascension of Our Lady. These things were too confusing for my distracted head, like many other things associated with religion. The poor continued to believe in the Pope and the bishops. The rich have more than enough reasons to believe in the superior fantasies of God Our Savior!

It happened that the Bishop of Angra came here to administer the sacrament of confirmation to us on a day of a lot of rain and flowers and garlands, with ecclesiastical capes everywhere, banners and fabrics in the windows and on the verandahs, the streets strewn with calendula and wood chips, as on feast days. The people went to wait at the Canto da Fonte, where he emerged from a very long black car. As he set foot on the ground, people clapped and cheered. Afterward, as they had rehearsed with us the day before, we knelt in the ditches with our hands clasped, and that's when I saw a man with an even bigger belly emerge from the car, with a red cap shaped like a pipe on his head and an iron staff in his hand, curved at the tip like an umbrella. He smiled at us, the children, gestured a blessing as the men and women in the crowd curtseyed, and Sacristan Calheta, master of ceremonies, cried out:

"Viva to the Bishop of Angra, Viva!"

The people immediately repeated in unison, with great feeling,

"Viva Bishop! Viva the Bishop of Angra!"

Then we were all blessed by the smile and the bishop's red ring, from left to right, and automatically forgiven all of our sins. When he passed by, escorted by six men holding up a canopy who struggled to protect him from the wind, the women started to cry out in a burst of emotion. They came to the doors or appeared at the windows, old, sick, and written off by the doctors, and they too considered themselves automatically cured of their secret ills. Whoever owned a lame mare, a barren cow, or a dog riddled with parasites, took advantage of the occasion to put them in reach of the bishop's blessing, and soon the animals seemed to enter into a state of grace, improving from their illnesses.

"If this is what the priests' boss is good for," uttered my father inside the house, "then it's a shame that God only remembers us on the day of the bishop's visit."

We were confirmed standing in a line, with the hand of the little priest on our shoulder, in a sign of protection, and we received on our foreheads, by the fingers of the bishop, a dab of yellow ointment. Thus we became adult Christians. My alternate confirmation godfather was Uncle Guilherme, because my Uncle Martinho had left for Canada in a ship's hold. We learned from one of his letters that he had slipped away clandestinely and had arrived half dead in Quebec after three and a half weeks of seasickness. He sent two *dollahs* for *Christmas* and promised me the best confirmation present, a sponsorship letter. He never delivered on that promise; it's a long story and it's not worth bothering you about . . .

After attending but one catechism course, where the women catechists dressed in black and crumpled white handkerchiefs in their fingers, I was scared off from the church and the confessional by God's wrath and the sin of touching the consecrated host with our teeth — the Body of Christ! My father did not try to change my mind. He himself would turn away when a priest walked by. He went to confession each year, more or less on his Saints' days or when he had something on his mind, and it was always a private matter. It would have been, at most, two or three regrets, one or two lustful thoughts about women who belonged to other men, forgetting the Lenten fast or not paying the church tax on pork — and that's all, perhaps it was even too much. And the truth be told, either it was not a serious sin and the priest didn't require him to do much penitence, or he was not ready to fall on his knees in front of many of his enemies.

But the talent of Grand Mama Olinda, as I was saying before, was that she was always ready to predict disasters and fill us with the fear of God. In the last years of her life, they say, because I wasn't there any longer, she was always confused, forgetting her thoughts in the middle of sentences, mixing up the past and the future in a constant disorder in her head. She said then that the waters of the earth's beginnings and Noah's Ark would not delay in repeating the prophecy and returning everything to eternity.

And do you want to know how, sir?

Dust volcanoes would burn up the bottom of the sea. Rains as had never been seen before would traverse the continents, lash us with sheets of water with such brutal force that no living creature would survive the passage of the Second Flood.

"My word, ma'am," my father would cut in from his corner as soon as he heard her start these rants, thinking, as I do, that sickness in the head had started to fill the soul of the old woman. "My mother should allow herself to be silent. You're losing your mind, that's for sure!"

Her son's interruptions offended her. He made her mad. She would gather up her things in a pout and leave, dragging her clogs on the road and moaning about her rheumatism, so angry that she didn't even let one of my sisters accompany her to light the threshold lamp. And if this is at all relevant to our conversation, it is because on that afternoon of the bells and the agitation of the people, her stories were almost coming true. She said, cupping her ear and with her eyes lost in madness:

"Save us oh Holy Sacrament, because the punishment of the Lord is upon us!"

In order to see for myself, I asked for my father's permission to let me go watch what was happening. I wasn't even surprised to find him running ahead of me, burning up with the same curiosity. We arrived at the square where the crowd had gathered. The bull of a priest appeared, ordered the bells to stop, and bellowed an order for the people to be silent and to give the word to the local administrator.

"Fellow citizens," he yelled, cupping his hands with his mouth. And he repeated, "Fellow citizens! Salazar, who governs us from Lisbon, has announced to the people that the fallow lands of the Forest will no longer be a no-man's land and will be cleared to be converted into pasture land. This Forest of the People will be served by paved roads, public shelters, refreshment stands, rest stops, and milk collection stations. The machines will be brought in and there will be work for all, and God will grant long life to the one who governs us. Viva Mr. Salazar!

I saw perfectly how mouths dropped open, without expressing any opinion, just like spring traps, and this gave the administrator the time and the courage to continue his declamation. Besides the clearing machines, he mentioned the trucks, the sticks of dynamite, the forestry engineers, and the foremen, people from the outside. Because there was so much to do, they would need able-bodied men to hoe and make baskets, beasts of burden, oxen with their carts, and most of all faith in God and in the saintly intelligence of the president of the Council of Ministers. Job applications were open: men would be paid twenty-two-and-a-half patacas, weekly payment guaranteed, boys over sixteen would be paid seventeen patacas a day . . . From the heights of the churchyard, the priest walked up and down on the tips of his toes, composed a fat smile of great success, and nodded assent with his head every time the administrator linked God with Salazar in his speech.

People were starting to peel off into groups. Those in favor of the sacking of our Mato do Povo started to jump up and down, happy with the news, in a festival melee. They danced in circles, like schoolchildren, and they raised *vivas* and cheers — because Salazar had accomplished the miracle of saving them from miserable existences. They would no longer live from hand to mouth like beggars, always agonizing over whether it would rain and there would be day work. Those against began to get restless and to mass together. They gained in numbers and force. In a short while they linked arms. This was government robbery, the Mato do Povo had never had nor ever would have any owner other than the people of Rozário. How was it that Salazar had the right to expropriate it?

One voice encouraged another until all of them became discordant and confused. When women's voices joined in, chaos erupted in the square. The crowd became louder, arguments and insults flew. One pushed another, the other dragged the next one with him. Suddenly thugs entered the fray and more people fell to the ground. I realized that it'd become a riot. Clear spaces opened up, moans and the sound of blows and kicks, and my father pulled me out of a kind of whirlwind that threatened to swallow me up as well. I watched from a doorway as the violence dragged and swept the bodies; I saw spurts of blood and the cries of the women. Years later, in the Guinean war, I watched prisoners being tortured without averting my gaze; I felt no pity at the sight of them sweating blood and moaning of cold before dying. It wasn't necessary to feel pity: we were at war and everything was permitted. In fact, we had been prepared to laugh at those who died by our hands and to mourn the death of our own. And the way that the men of Rozário spit out their teeth and blood spurted from their noses, their heads hit the ground with the sound of bursting melons, all of this impressed me so much that it was not strange that I later practiced this in the war of Guinea. The only difference, as I said before, was that in the war, it was necessary to seed and to imagine the violence and the terror, to make us persistent and heroic. In Guinea, our crown of glory consisted in knowing that the enemy had put a price on our heads, so that I had to put a price on the enemy: so many times I was summoned to execute prisoners, to throw them off a cliff, to tie them to a tree trunk and set them on fire. My company commander would always come by and clap me on the shoulder, wink a red eye and say "it's just about killing, Moniz, it's just about killing!" In the meantime the memory of that late afternoon in Rozário, when a woman warrior started shouting from behind the crowd, where nobody could see the treason of her triumph: *Viva* our Governor! *Viva* Salazar! And this burst of courage de-escalated the crowd. Responses came from other hidden mouths in the crowd: *Viva the President of the Council, Viva, Viva!* between clapping, laughter, and running footsteps.

There is always the story of priests in politics, as you know, and it would have been best if that day had never happened when those assholes started to gnaw on the Salazar bone. In Africa, there were always newly ordained little priests to bless the dead, and they did it for ours as well as for the others, with so much religion that many times I thought, there goes the little priest to shout *vivas* for Mr. Salazar. People died and killed, then the priests came and prayed that the big cuckold Salazar would live long and eternally influence our decisions. Here they always called him the New Father, even when he already seemed to be rotting to pieces and dragged himself like a somnambulist in our midst. His name was Ângelo — my brother Nuno explained that the name means Angel and comes from the Latin. He had the angelic traits of a twisted laugh and crooked teeth, a big belly and prominent shoulder blades, like wings, a flat head like a pumpkin, and the always sweaty neck of yoke oxen. Besides this, nothing. All smiles, I saw him fling the blessing over that huddle of people, bless those who battled, the fallen bodies, the broken heads, and I saw him invite the faithful to enter the church on Sundays. One more time it was necessary to pray to God to prolong the life of the Wise, the Holy, the Good Professor Salazar, if possible by the grace of Our Lady of Rozário, patron saint of the municipality and protector of the poor.

Were you there, sir? Did you by any chance fall to your knees to pray and to give thanks for the pest and to beat your chest so that the wise, holy, and good Professor would continue to be a cuckold? I was there, and so were the others.

The same moribund religious women entered, dragging fussy children who preferred to continue to watch the fights and the arguments. The few old people who entered had been living by the difficult grace of God and nothing else. All the others lurched and squeezed through the doors inside the shops on the square, hiding their faces so that Father Ângelo would not recognize them, and there were rounds of beer, shots of cane liquor, and jars of Pico wine, because this was always, don't doubt it, the only Fools' mass in Portugal. As they dispersed, the men from the fighting rabble entered the stores, staggering, and then they left completely drunk, singing, and holding on to each other so they wouldn't fall down. In Portugal all dramas end in a big party and the pardon of mugs of wine. To a certain point, it's a happy country with wine: it likes what most embitters it, and it sings about what most hurts at the bottom of the soul.

My father swallowed the frustration of the revolt dry and signaled with his head to come along with him. He spent the whole way rallying those who were at their windows asking for details of the event. He told them that the Mato do Povo should be defended by pitchforks, for the good of the cattle and the dignity of the municipality. As for the rest, rumors were circulating about which lands were in a state of siege, and it was held as a certainty that the entire council of the Northeast had risen en masse against the tyrants of Lisbon. But this version could never be proven.

For this reason, I still don't know why my father switched so quickly to the other side and changed his mind. We had cattle, that's true. But they were a thin herd and they ate little. We could feed them well with the grass in the fields and forests. We also had land. At night, after dinner, he tried to seek the council of his compadre, Mr. Quental, who secretly organized the opposition to the Dictator. It wouldn't be difficult to imagine what he would have said: the deforestation of the Mato do Povo would be an improvement and would bring progress to Rozário.

When he returned, these and other arguments were buzzing in his head. Carpentry work was scarce. There were more than enough people at home to work the land: he, my mother, and the girls. For the cows, they were getting Nuno ready, quick as a rocket as soon as he got out of school. It was possible that even that idea, even coming from an ass named Salazar, was not so bad. Said and done. The next day, early in the morning, after a last exchange of ideas with Mama, he called me to his presence and said:

"You are going to give your name to the administrator, pick up your hoe, and pack a lunch to work in the Mato do Povo. You hear, Luís? You don't need to say that you are not yet sixteen. You are able-bodied and you already know how to work. They'll accept you on the spot, it won't be a problem..."

CHAPTER SIX

Nuno Miguel

What bothers me now is not knowing how many meters a plot of land measures, the worth of a good stand of trees or an orchard with ripe fruit, the value of the stream water running behind the old orchards, or how to assess precisely the quality of the clover, alfalfa, and rye pastures. It embarrasses me immensely to listen to my brothers discuss among themselves, in my silent presence, the precious trifles that were left from the death of our parents: the arguments about cash owed by those who got more land to the ones who got parcels of lesser value, the imaginary partition of the larger plots of land, longer or better located, all of the parchment of profane and other writings, the supernatural process of dividing the spoils, the memory and the spirit of our ancestors. I lost myself completely in these notions, of the useful love and the liturgy of the earth. I watch, in a panic, the dissolution of the family through the patrimony of its bones, knowing that the division of goods is the last act of this empty theater where my body grows cold. The actors move in front of me, in a square of light that is as white as the spotlights of the circus that always arrives on the eve of feast days and installs itself in the middle of the market place. In the shadows in which I find myself, I see each one of their gestures occupy this luminous and deserted space, where I really never had a place, even when as a child I saw musicians, fire eaters, men with sparkling tunics, and muscular boys juggling in the street. In Vancouver, before he died, Papa gathered his other children around his bed, propped himself with difficulty on an elbow, like a drowning man who surfaces for the last time and knows he is going to sink, and asked them to give me his beloved, honest, and healthy house in the Azores. I was not there; I was always an absent son who did not know the healthy house in the Azores. I was not there; I was always an absent son who did not see the decreasing countdown of his suffering, the man of little hurried letters who arrived in Lisbon without notice, a figure whose face accrued the pallor and neglect of casual portraits, in the month of Christmas in Lisbon. I really don't know if it was difficult to extract this promise from his children, or why Papa leaned on his elbow, lifted his green face a little, and justified such a wish as best he could. I suppose he had the illusion or the lucidity of thinking that I would be the only one to preserve the poetry, the culture, and the docility of the childhood lost in that house. Besides this, I was the only child still residing in the Portuguese territories. He knew of my passion for the simple, maternal, and primordial houses of the Island, and perhaps for this reason I am still perplexed and feeling unworthy.

"Inherit what, Papa, as if it wasn't this roof that covered my life or this house, or these secrets that gilded and then demolished the walls of my infancy?"

I inherit it because of the dead; so that one day I may hear the breathing, the shadow, and the nocturnal voice of its shadowy dead. Papa gave me his blessing and the penitence of his spirit because he will want me to be here one day, he will come down the creaky staircase near the kitchen, he will push open the door in the middle of the house and will sit down to see me sleep in the big bed that once rocked with the weight of his body. Sitting in the dark, he will again be the father of the night and of his children. It could be that then he will tell me the long story of his distant and unknown life, so that it might be the fable of an island named Ithaca, and on it I will live out my dreams. All this time, I experienced him through the false clanging of the Azorean bells, imprisoned by the fatigue of these misty places. Every time I returned to my childhood home, I saw it suspended in the imprecise design of the walls. There was a tree in the dreams of my days, and in this tree the god of the orioles and the doves had built a nest. But this nest had become a nursery for the dead.

Now the house grows over my life; it's large once again and I feel as if I never deserved it. One should only inherit what one helped to exist, what is a part of one's innocence. If you think of a primitive aesthetic, it occurs to me suddenly that I will inherit not a family house but a useless honeycomb that has no relevance to my destiny. I don't have the slightest intention of returning here. I fear the jealousy of the dead. To spend vacation time on the Island, with the mother of my children, would have been unbearably beautiful a long time ago, when the house was still the center of the world; perhaps if one had heard the small laughter of the old people, delighting in their grandchildren, the shouts of the children discovering the existence of doves in the granary, the chickens pecking for bugs in the manure, the pig grunting in the pigpen. Now, as I said before, the house lays the living and the dead in the same tomb, it's perhaps preposterous to think that time will return the physical reality of these suffering, lifeless walls.

Moreover, there is also the discomfort of having a finger pointed at you from the other side of the road, the tarnished sea like the lead of a shaving blade, the Sunday mass. One can't make sense of one's own feelings. In the eyes of this population that is almost unknown to me, full of old people dressed in mourning who call me by my family name, there is a silent accusation about the ownership of the house. They approach me on the street, like crows, and I feel the impetus of those who will peck my body and drink the color from my eyes. They ask me, full of greed, if I want to sell it, that it's for the asking, they will pay the price of the stone, the wood, and the shingles. They don't know and they'll never know that money can't buy or sell the myths of houses. They don't know what it means to return to the deep roots of the tree that gave its sap and body to the wood. If I told them I want it for myself, but for nothing at all, they would laugh in my face, thinking I'm being facetious, full of the stupid ideas of the newly rich . . .

Me, rich?

You know how sad it is to live in Lisbon and not to feel alive — without the landscape, or a single tree, so far from the sea and sky of the Azores? It's a mediocre existence, to spend your life between tall buildings that forbid us to love and look into the distance. In Lisbon, the horizon, contrary to here, is not flat or horizontal; the only possibility is to make it perpendicular, vertical in that luminous and almost always blue sky. Many times, I imagined that I should sell the Lisbon apartment, sell the house of my parents, and go somewhere else to play out my unbounded madness, a place where there would be fields, two trees, and any ocean in view. I would like to relearn the secrets of the earth, plant lilies around a wall, prop up small trunks with stakes, and see how the trees of my life grow. If possible, a fig tree. Do you know why? When I was small, there were always those trees with coarse leaves, to shelter me from the rain. The figs bled milk and split my lips, when the gluttony for the forbidden figs was bigger than the scabs on my scalp. This was what it meant to live the meaning of time. I also yearned for a cedar tree, a porous, tall tree that always graced feast days and the splendor of the music bands on the Island. There were processions of litters bearing the images of saints, with crowned angels, multitudes of red capes, the great golden pallium under which the translucent and solemn priests were sheltered. It was always Sunday when this happened, all were alive, and it wasn't necessary to suffer the solitude of my future Sundays in Lisbon . . .

The house contains the spaces and the lost footsteps of my life. The one in Lisbon, unlike this one, is a corridor with little landscapes hanging from the windows, soft footsteps on the carpets of the salons, the morose sanctuary of a master bedroom. My anxiety was populated little by little by the noise of doors slamming in the wind. The poet Ruy Belo, who died from writing verses, said: *in my country nothing happens; the land moves along the road* . . . For me, on the other hand, there was never even a road that led to the Island, because Lisbon cut off any possibility of such a retreat. I closed myself entirely inside that magnificent and moribund city, so that I never knew the names of those who were born after me. I did not know their faces or their time. And, since the worst for a man is the absence of these and all other memories of places, I don't know who I am here, and what I'm doing now in the Azores, or why I will inherit this ghost of a house. They say, those who live here, that I will perhaps be the first and last dead person in the family who still hasn't died . . .

Maria Amélia

Of all of us who were born and raised here, Luís is the one who has carried the longest memory of disappointment. We look at him and think that his eyes are very sad, burning with disbelief, and too innocent for a big bellied muscular body like his. You look at him and Luís is always motionless, as out of time and place as a Buddha in a foreign land. You try to hold him in your gaze, but he averts his eyes, incapable of sustaining your observation. Besides this, the serious aspect of his features seems to corrode him like acid; he has already shorn his thick hair, turned his mouth into an arc, and left a skein of wrinkles on his forehead. Even though he is still in the middle of life, he has aged more quickly than any of us, acquiring a translucent aspect, the demeanor of a castrated bull. His mood, when he wants to make us laugh and makes fun of everybody, is disproportionately violent. So much so that, if you watch him carefully, you will see that he has placed himself in the center of the family circus, turning himself into a caricature of himself, as if he wants to be more ridiculous than the rest.

As for Nuno, he assumes a different timidity, but one that is sensitive and much less spectacular. When he was little, he would express himself by crying a lot. Even at the age when he couldn't have had clear ideas about death, he had profound and unexpected desires to die. I vividly remember the day when he reached the limit of his ability to withstand these hidden emotions. Papa had given him a big blow with the handle of the scythe used to clear ginger lilies, because he was caught stealing green grapes in Grand Mama Olinda's yard. Mama started to yell at him, cursing the bad luck of having a fruit thief in their midst, and that's when Papa lost his head, hit him, and decided to lock him in the dark attic. We would take him his food, at Papa's command, in the clay bowl that we used for the dog. We climbed a stepladder with steps that were roughly hewn from cedar planks, between piles of sacks, plows suspended from the roof, and harrows stuck by their blades into the cracks in the walls. As we approached, the rats escaped through the crannies, crackling like fried eggs, and we had the sensation of crushing them with our feet. When we reached the attic, my little brother was sitting in the dark, his hands clasped, and his blue eyes glowed in the corner, alive like cat eyes. He received his food in silence, or limited himself to asking if it was day or night and how much time it would take for him to be pardoned for his sins. It was forbidden to talk with him. Papa even said that Nuno didn't even deserve from that time forward to use the family name. When we got the order to release him, I went running to free him, the oil lamp in my hand, lifted on the wings of a presentiment of disaster surrounding that docile, unhappy child. Nuno came after me, shielding his eyes from the light of the kitchen and asked for Papa and Mama's blessing. His hair was full of straw and his face was covered with rust, he smelled of wet hay, spiderwebs, and things rotting at the back of the attic. It was immensely moving to see how tears dripped from his red eyes, without his saying a word or releasing a single sob, to see my parents receive him with a tight smile, mocking, strangers, guaranteeing Nuno that the whole municipality would know the name of the new fruit thief. The people were authorized to set their dogs on him, to flog him with cart poles, and denounce him to the Algarvia police. He took all this seriously, shaking, his lips trembling, and he started to internalize the guilt and remorse of being alive without any dignity. In a fit of despair, he motioned me aside and, whispering in my ear, asked what was the easiest way to die; could he hang himself or throw himself into the sea or eat a mouthful of bread with rat poison? I started to scream, clamoring for Papa's mercy, to save our little brother from dying. He came running, but his response was to give him a mean and disdainful look, and without a smile, pointed to the sea.

"You really want to kill yourself? Then throw yourself off the rocks. You'll see how you explode down there on the rocks, like a squash. Try it, go on..."

Many years later, on the day they expelled him from the seminary, he still had that look of a whipped boy. He came running from afar in my direction, pulled me to his chest, and declared flamboyantly that he had been accused of being a "subversive" and of "having lost the vocation for the priesthood." He showed me the letter from the rector, addressed to Papa, then he tore it from my hands, shredded it to pieces and spread dozens of bits of paper over the limp plants of the gardens of Campo Grande. Then I observed his euphoria, I saw it deep in his doglike thinness, nervous and unhinged like his father, starved of the world and of women, and I thought immediately how difficult it would be for him to overcome his adolescence. It was the time when even street corners were suspect in Lisbon. It was the time of the war in Africa, of the cold and terrible days of the affliction of all boys his age. Nobody would give him a job, just because Nuno was eighteen years old and would soon be drafted for military service. With a little luck or some important influence of someone close to the regime, he might not be mobilized to the war zone. But since that was the destiny of that generation, not even he believed in such a possibility. Only a miracle would save him from having to climb the gangplank of a ship, saying "good-bye, until I return," as the others did, and then spending two years sending us letters with lies about the horrors of the African nights. Finally the miracle happened: Nuno went through everything like a perfect sleepwalker. The time in the barracks of Lisbon flew by, he watched all the companies leave, and said good-bye to all his friends. His turn went by, swept up in that heady time, and nothing happened to him. The moment that they ordered him to put on his uniform and leave, he took the tram to the center of Lisbon, got off at the Avenida da Liberdade, and walked on foot to the Praça do Comércio. He couldn't believe that the ships docked on the Tejo were real. He was not, he said to me then, either of his time or of his country...

But the day he arrived in Lisbon, from the seminary, there was a dying god in his eyes, in his tumultuous shyness, and in the will to kill it on the next Sunday at Mass. One could see that he looked around with alarm, like someone who discovers a flat and luminous world beyond the conventional walls and fences. If I hadn't grabbed his hand, he would have certainly fallen into depravity, into the disorder of the city. He would lose himself in the dangers that prey on birds escaping from their cages. He wanted to fly very high, without wings, to defy reason and finally be different from everything they had taught him to be. The first thing was to get him a job, so he would not have to go back to the Azores and submit himself to Papa's revenge. Like him, I was expelled from the convent, swept mercilessly from the tombs of those strange people who lived for God. I knew that the temptation to excess could destroy him. Above all I feared the influence of bad company, the prostitutes who pervert the best adolescents and the enemies of Mr. Salazar. These were the wolves lurking in wait for everything; they would not hesitate to take advantage of Nuno's rebellion and lead him to conspire against the government. Because my brother, you must realize this, sir, was still a very sweet boy; he still smelled of the deep waters of childhood and the streams of the Azores. He was a white sheep, but I started to hear him bleat for the wolf that would destroy him. I once again had the opportunity to become his mother, and I didn't hesitate to reach my arms out to him. I wanted to embrace him, to have him rest that starving head on my breast so he could sleep. I would take care of him, like no other woman, and I would wash his clothes, dry his hair, *and so on.* He arrived, however, thirsty for life, wanting to take his place in the world, and hungry for a woman. He even got to the point of declaring that I was hysterical and to tell me to my face that I was as crazy and cautious as a female in heat. Repeatedly I tried to manage the salary from the first job I got him and to introduce him to the serious girls who were in nursing school with me. Nuno, however, always thought they were ugly, saintly as nuns, and pious, too timid, and full of defects . . . One fine day, I came to the conclusion that I was wasting my time with him. The sweet boy stopped going to Mass, seduced freckly girls who were all too willing for my taste, and started to get involved with people in politics, some who had the reputation of being communists. Soon afterward, he was overtaken by the mania of literature. His incomprehensible philosophical poems came out on Thursdays in the publications of the Opposition. When he mingled with the writers and started to attend secret meetings, he was already on the other side of my life, launched to the destiny of books, electoral campaigns, and dangerous leaflets that protested against political prisons. I lost sight of him a little, because Nuno transformed himself into a clandestine night creature. I got used to the idea that one day, when I came home, someone would tell me he had been arrested and was being tortured. This happened to all his friends, and I think that Nuno almost wished for it. His stubbornness was becoming more desperate as time passed; it was very important for him to be arrested and to become a victim of his political penance. As for me, I'd lose my boy all over again. I feared for his safety, as much as I yearned to make him happy. I had to wait years and years for my own children, for the love I had to give them, for the marvelously beautiful way they look at me today, smile, and are magnificently happy and grateful to be in the world.

"Oh, mommy, it's *wonderful* having a mother like you!" my oldest daughter says every time I come home *dead tired* from work. I listen to their little *troubles*, I shelter them under my mother hen wings and make them smile again at the world and the life I have given them. I love my children so desperately, sir, that it's not hard for me to make up to them all the traumas and agonies of my childhood. I make sure that ours is a house of love, laughter, and understanding, never a place of fear, excessive respect, and sadness that hurts and opens wounds in the eyes and souls of children.

"Our house back then?" you ask me.

Well, it was very much like — *what can I tell you* — a cage of depressed birds, with a supplicating look and orphaned of their mother. Born only of their father, not from the ova or the heavy, plain body of his woman.

Eleven times pregnant, Mama lost two teeth with each pregnancy and ended up being transformed into a short, round, and very ruined women. Her hair was grey, her nails torn, and her muddy skin was fatigued. She was prematurely old, her features barely lit up beautiful blue eyes.

They were brutalized birds, the kind that look at the world through their wicker cages, are frightened by the wind, with the rain or even with the sun shining outside. Our house was what you could call a prison without bars; we all lived in it crouching on our haunches and afraid of everything. We were afraid of the humidity, of the day and night, the sound of the crickets, the howling of dogs at the cemetery gates, of the sea only two kilometers away from the kitchen window — everything gave us an undefined feeling of terror without motive or explanation. Little by little, without our noticing, fear became our most salient flaw, perhaps our only habit. It grew in our lungs and guts, it became a fear of being afraid and ended up giving us a special way of being sad. In Papa's opinion, we would never be better than ordinary, defective creatures, like the birds, because he always had to correct us and teach us everything over and over again. *So,* under the orders and angry voice of that bird tamer, we assumed the status of lesser animals, poised to serve him and obey his voice, without any other passion, and without any motive capable of explaining our life outside of him, except the fact of being alive. Like the orioles carried to the houses in the hunters' snares, they had stuck us in the family cage and also forbidden us to sing. Every time Mama clipped the chicken wings with her sewing shears so they couldn't fly outside of the yard, she was also disabling us. And when Papa went to the dovecotes that he himself had built and then hung from the corn bin, counted the females and the males and ripped out the feathers from their tails so they wouldn't fly away, he was also defeathering us of innocent illusions . . .

We were never noisy children, nor were we as boisterous as others on our street. At the end of the day, Papa and Mama had forbidden us to fly, to make noise, to run, to jump happily on the beds and chairs. To whistle, laugh out loud, wrestle each other, or express an opinion about anything or nothing, all of this was strictly forbidden. We couldn't even go to our neighbors' houses, or invite the children from the Rua Direita to our home. Even to get permission to accept an invitation to a pig slaughter, we had to ask and ask a lot. Apart from the cracked slate in wood frames, the old and outdated primers, cars made of melon rind and cornhusks, there were never other toys. Luís would get his ears pulled if he was found entertaining himself with the carpentry tools. Domingas and I would be swatted on the palms of our hands if we played with pots and pans or the colored threads of Mama's embroidery. Nuno wasn't allowed to dress like a scarecrow on Shrovetide because he might frighten the babies. We all became coarse, frightened, and timid as sheep in the vicinity of the guard dog . . .

What happened, or did not, in our childhood? On the one hand, it was the house in which they kept us closed in on rainy days when we couldn't go out to work the land. On the other hand, it was the street and the world that didn't belong to us but were, in spite of everything, the happy places of other children. Even on summer nights, when darkness had not yet fallen, Mama called to us from the door with loud shouts, because it was always time to wash our feet, eat supper, and go early to bed. The children of others still chattered in our ears until late at night, when the lamps were already out in our house. While they played hot iron, a type of bowling or horseshoes, and blind-man's bluff, we were lying in our beds, our eyes wide open in the dark, gauging with our hearing the happy childhood of the children on our street. Very early the next day, when Papa ordered us to "get up," it was the shock of this command that moved our bodies and made us spring out of our warm beds. We were not permitted a yawn, or the most fleeting moment to linger in the indescribable warmth of the cornhusk mattresses. So much, sir, that this memory has lingered in my blood, and even today my heart constricts, up north in Canada, the country of my perfect dreams, because now it is my voice that awakes my children who are going to *high school*, and I have to send them into that deathly *snow* of the city of Vancouver. I become upset just imagining that life could have dealt me the cruelty of interrupting the best sleep of my children ...

During winter, before Mama had made me the family cook and I had begun to suffer the solitude of pots and pans and the complexity of seasonings, Luís and I left with the cattle to Outeiros. We set out at dawn, barefoot and without breakfast, dressed in canvas sacks that we put on our heads like capes. The cold was fierce up there in the foothills of the mountain, and our feet would turn blue with the frost that tinges the grass with the color of steel. Later, when I graduated to the kitchen and Mama would beat me because of the salt or the tasteless food, Nuno took my place next to Luís. He was very afraid of the cows, just like I was, because they would pull at their leads and drag him along. The heifers and the young bulls, because they were more difficult to handle, would butt with their heads, tails raised, and only the dog dissuaded them from goring us. After milking the cows in tears, my older brother would become dizzy from the effort, and his wrists would be dislocated from the stress. Only then did the sun start to rise over the sea, first low on the horizon, close to the time we had to go to school. We tied the milk cans together with ropes. Hanging from our shoulders they were so heavy that they raised welts on our skin and bowed our spines. The cattle herders who passed us would be filled with pity and muttered that Papa was a murderous dog. We listened to them without comment, thinking however that they were gods in that rebellion glowing faintly in the darkness. When they took the cans off us and put them on their own shoulders, or accommodated them on the packsaddles of their beasts, God smiled from above and was again magnificent, as beneficent as the One who was promised to us in catechism class.

As a matter of fact, I don't know if Papa treated Luís any better than a dog. He won the sympathy of all the people in Rozário. Ours too, though in secret, because we were forbidden to be brothers and sisters to each other. When we returned with the milk on our backs, Luís always carried one or two cans more than I did. The weight bowed his legs. His bones even creaked. But never did this suffering take goodness from his heart, the caring and affection that he liked to give to young girls and little children. The times that his body rolled on the kitchen floor under Papa's beatings, the neighbors tried in vain to intervene. In despair, unable to do anything, Mama took refuge near the stove and sat with her hands clasped, looking up the chimney, seeking a spot of sky above that turbid bellow of smoke. Domingas and I hid, holding each other, in the sewing room. We saw a man with his teeth biting his lower lip, his legs spread wide, and a whip in his hands. While Luís writhed on the floor, like a beaten squid, we counted twenty, thirty blows and heard him scream,

"Oh Papa, dear Papa, oh dear Papa . . ."

The little ones came and went, frightened, crazed, between the front door and the kitchen, so they wouldn't see, even though they saw it all, what was happening. Papa was killing Luís, Mama prayed by the stove, until one of us, usually Domingas, couldn't stand it anymore. She would go straight to Papa, trying to restrain his arm, and implore,

"Dear Papa, please don't hit him anymore. You're killing our Luís."

He would torture him for insignificant reasons, as he often did with me, Domingas, Nuno, or Jorge. Once it was because he had stolen, with Nuno's complicity, wads of tobacco that he sold to someone to earn some money for the parish feast day. Another time it was because a man came to our house and complained about an inoffensive incident of rudeness and a heifer that had knocked down a wall, and another time because he had dumped a load of beets in front of the churchyard. Father Ângelo came, saw the pyramid of blows raining on the steps of our Lord, and started into a litany with Luís about respecting the divine. He wanted everything removed even if he had to drag him by the ear. And he talked so much that Luís sent him to an inappropriate place for priests and threatened to stick a beet up his nose. Papa didn't want any conversation or trouble with priests. That night he picked up the whip again, called him to the kitchen, and submitted him once again to the thrashing. He never needed a pretext to prove to the neighborhood that he disciplined his children and taught them to respect others. And, since all of us in fact always committed the same crimes and repeated them, there was Papa with his whip in his hand. We grew and multiplied. Papa, poor man, before he really died, was already dead, or at least moribund, in life and in our hearts...

I became sadder and lonelier, between the pots of boiling water and the firewood. I fanned the sparks that wouldn't light up the acacia wood or the green twigs, I saw the tears of sap boil on the flames, and my eyes would tear from the smoke. I was definitely condemned to be the oldest of six siblings born until that time, the most awkward and also the one with the least appetite. Can you die of disgust? My brothers and sisters quickly misunderstood the privilege of not having to work the land. Being given the role of family cook meant, in their opinion, an escape from the hell of farming and digging, sowing the corn, or carrying manure in a wicker basket. Domingas alluded to me with disdain and jealousy, referring to me as "the girl," and she didn't tire of pointing out the flaws in my domestic labors. Luís, half seriously and half playfully, wanted me to find a boyfriend, seduced or not by the idea of having a brother-in-law and becoming the godfather of the first baptism. And Nuno, bold as he was, took advantage of every opportunity to lift my skirts or pinch my breasts. If I had tried to explain to them how empty my life was, the reason for my tears and the sorrows that were starting to pierce my heart, I am certain they would not have understood my complaints. As for the pinches that Mama gave me and the way she pulled my hair and kept me in her sights all day long like a slave, all this seemed like a superior advantage over those who belonged to Papa's world and served him. I was, however, her "black girl," and I was subjected from morning to night to the censure of her hysterical shouts — the same way that a few years later, when I was a postulant in a convent, I would die of working in the kitchen to make the soup for the poor and to clean the cells, while the mothers and little sisters embroidered linens for the altar, snacked on cookies with tea and preserves, and expressed their doubts about my vocation for obedience and service to God...

From one minute to the next, seeing my pallor in a mirror, and feeling that my bones were weak and my stomach concave, I deduced that I was contracting a terrible sickness. My lack of strength and appetite became confused with bitterness, sadness, and the relentless solitude of my spirit. I wasn't in pain, because that would come later in the long nights of the convent. But I did start to sense that my body was fighting me. I don't know if it has ever occurred to you to feel your body, that is, to verify that the muscles and reflexes stopped obeying the orders of the nervous system. It happened to me, and that's why I'll tell you that death was sitting in wait for me. It opened its arms to me and I refused its sweet embrace and also its pardon, the day that a very religious doctor was authorized to examine me; he palpated me, did tests, and diagnosed lymphatic tuberculosis. Immediately thereafter came the decision of the Chapter; the little sisters of the tea and cookies pronounced in secret about my expulsion from the convent. I cried copiously! The mother superior entered, sat down next to my bed and took my feverish hand with which I closed my eyes and ears so I wouldn't see or hear what was going on around me. According to her, the Order had been deceived about my health history. Papa and Mama, seeing me condemned to lymphadenitis, had wanted to get rid of me. It was not fair or serious, or proper, or even civilized, that the Congregation would be forced to take care of me. It was decided I should return to my parents' house to recover, and thus it was.

"As soon as you recover your health, and if your religious vocation is still pure and intact," the mother superior condescended with a livid smile, "then of course we will open our doors again to you to our House, my sister."

It took a century for the water to boil in the iron pot on the stove. Far away from here, the day was slowly being born, coming from the ends of the sea. Already the voices of the roosters trumpeted it from yard to yard, while it progressed along its trajectory and unveiled the land crocodiles that came from the shore and floated in the waves with their snouts in the air. Then came the terraces on the hillsides, the deserted roads, the cane fields, and the walls. Everything was progressively visible as the days were born. But only when the sea left that muddy stain and presented itself in the tones of wintry mallow did the light of day present itself to me. Until then, I had remained in a state of torpor, wrapped in sleep and in the cold of the dark. Besides this, there was the awakening of the house itself. Nuno, still so small, came into the barn, carrying a load of twigs and shivering, and he started to scrape the cow shit into a big pile. Mama went out to the yard; she was going to spread the corn for the chickens, count them, collect the eggs they had laid overnight, put slop in the pig trough. Domingas, in a continuous yawn, full of distaste for work, needed an hour to shake a corn husk mattress and smooth two covers — always slow as molasses and with a smart mouth. Luís left sadly with the bony cows whose intestines had been emptied overnight on the straw Nuno had laid down with such effort. Papa, in the workshop, invented chores, poked around in the attic, said "good day" to whoever wished him "good day" and would greet anyone who passed for a little conversation when they saw him sharpening the spade or the saw. At that hour of the morning, when all of us were still dizzy with sleep, he already was philosophizing with strangers about the weather, giving them advice on the opportunities for the sowing or the harvest. In a certain way, he was a wise man to the others, while his prophetic judgments about us always seemed doubtful, fallible, or poisoned by his bad humor.

I set the table for the family breakfast, crumbled the bread into the bowls of milk, washed and dressed the youngest ones, dumped chamber pots full of pee into the compost heap in the yard — and I began, already then, to take on the color of muddy water, to lose strength, and to think I wasn't alive in the world outside. In practice, I had become the adoptive mother of those little birds; I cooked for them, fed them, sheltered them on my lap, and listened to their large and small complaints. When they sat at the table to eat my soups and salted cabbage and to chew the other tasteless food, I stopped to look at them and felt a ripple of tenderness inside me. If Papa demanded that they all eat in silence, it was inevitable that I think of meals in that house as a kind of profane mass. There were the cuckoos, who had already been dark orioles and descended directly from Papa, with his sad look and rigid silence. There were, on the other side of the table, the chicks with the little yellow cowlick in their hair that learned about life smiling in my direction. We had all been born different, predestined to radically different worlds.

The orioles were the ones that distanced themselves most quickly from beauty and happiness, condemned as they were to acquiring the features of cuckoos. Our manner of growing, in a continuous zigzag, some resembling Papa or then Mama, happened in spurts. At the beginning, all were very blond and pink-skinned, with round bones and flat noses. Then, they became dark-haired, streaked with moss, and finally their hair turned black and straight. Those who took after Mama — Nuno, Linda, Jorge, and later Mário and Zélia, born in my absence — quickly distinguished themselves from us, by their bright blue eyes of Nordic people and the diaphanous white-milk skin like Easter marzipan. They were born under the sign of an excessively clear sun, with transparent, metallic bodies where you could soon see the pigments and purple eczema that Mama treated with plasters of cream from cow's milk. They also had greenish veins, as deep as algae. The others — me, Domingas, Luís, and Flor — were born with darker skin, with Papa's big luminous eyes, and endowed with his slender, very cartilaginous nose. We were somewhat leguminous, vegetal beings. Besides this the mouths of some had fleshy lips, a little crooked and lascivious, turned down at the corners. In others they were thin as a wound, so that when they closed their lips, their faces took on a hermetic expression, like sad gypsies.

All these facts contributed to splitting in half our concept of beauty. I, for example, if I set myself to imagining our family perfection, regretted that God had not worked harder on the texture of our bodies, with elements of that paternal mix that favored us better. If I could have molded any of us in the image and semblance of our parents, I would have copied the lightly curled hair and the shape of my father's mouth — just that. Instead of his thickly lashed, excessively silky eyes, I would put in the angel blue and the shine of Mama's eyes. I would also take advantage of the intense blond of the first years, precarious in us as Autumn and certainly inherited from lost generations of Flemish. It had become clear, that is certain, that nobody wanted to inherit the dour face and brooding eyes that had made Papa a man so estranged from happiness.

I don't know if at that time our subconscious was at work in us. We all reacted to the slightest hypothesis of looking like Papa, that's a fact. Not only did we not like to be accused of this resemblance, we didn't even want to take a step in that direction, as if it depended on us. The passion for blue and the will to pass for the other side of the family dominated our childhood. At this point we all had our eyes trained on Uncle Martinho's free spirit and the malicious smile of all the children of Grand Papa Botelho and Grand Mama Marta. Nevertheless we knew that our blood had been contaminated by Grand Mama Olinda's bad humor, her rude antipathy, even her jerky walk.

Of all of us the one least conformed to this gypsy appearance was Flor, who always nurtured the hope that her eyes would change color. She wished that this miracle would occur on a Saturday morning, while she was looking in the mirror, like in the magic tricks of circus shows. She deeply envied Linda's eyes, who at that time reminded us of the American dolls that got off the boat here, coming in the trunks of clothing and toys. Her porcelain face, with her incandescent blue eyes and straw-blond hair, was a model of perfection, and could have come out of one of those enormous wooden boxes, tied up tightly with steel cords provided with clamps and spring locks. They came from Toronto and Vancouver, as well as from Boston and New Bedford, sent as gifts from emigrated relatives, and they constituted such a profusion of clothing and other wonderful items that it was enough to supply for another year a whole tree of families. Beautiful dresses that had never before been seen around here contrasted strongly with the extenuated shabbiness of our poplin. There were pants, thick vests that inflated when you blew air into them, shirts with many designs and some English phrases — all of them in perfect condition and hardly used. America and Canada arrived to us in these luxury items, smelling of lavender and mothballs; the frenzy of cutting the nylon cords that were tied around the bags with our teeth released an intense perfume of unknown flowers. Along with the clothing, accommodated in cardboard boxes with cellophane display panels, dolls with vivid blond hair and sparkling eyes imitated the beauty of my sister, Linda Maria. Flor envied them, as she did us, because they were the perfect artificial illusion of little princesses who in fairy tales always meet the slender princes, marry happily, and bear large children…

However, the world of these presents instigated a cacophony of horns, disorder, and wrangling in the municipality. There were noisy disputes over who could and couldn't use a particular piece of clothing or to whom the gifts had been intended. This mobilized the factions and opinions of entire streets. When these clothes were not identified with a note pinned on them with the name of the intended recipient, it was pandemonium. They fought over them like dogs in ditches, rummaging in the garbage of lives past and present and playing tug of war with those treasures that the sea had so randomly brought in, like bottles with anonymous messages or the wrecks that were pushed into shore by the mechanism of the tides. Fights broke out between the sisters-in-law and the daughters-in-law that made their nostrils flare and prompted them to hurl insults at wretched mothers-in-law, who were bone thin, dressed in black and with faces darned with wrinkles. Then the men would also enter into the fray, and cudgels appeared, stones and stakes were hurled, and bodies fell heavily to the ground, rolling under the blows. I saw, in that greediness, the miserable miserliness of the poor. Poverty had become odious and ugly, an ugliness that seemed to accompany the poor from birth until death and made them noisy and unbearable.

Nobody ever bothered to send us one of those *boxes* of clothes and toys — and for that reason we always hated the luck of those who had relatives overseas. Contrary to our uncles, the others kept, over there, the memory of the misery, desire, and the expressions of the Azorean children. Even Caritas always forgot us, even in the years of cyclones and locust plagues, as well as during epidemics of typhoid fever. In those times, men came from outside the island, all wearing dark glasses and with buffed nails. At Father Ângelo's suggestion, they divided the population of Rozário into very poor, poor, surviving, and rich. To the first group, they distributed a sticky, tasteless cheese that looked like soap; to the others they gave cans of flour and powdered milk, in addition to clothing, medicines, and plastic toys. To us, because we had cows and lands, and we were the owners of other pittances, Father Ângelo told them to give us rainwater and a mocking look that was very unreligious. At the same time, the lucky ones who were graced with the American treasures gave us their disdain and vilification, right in front of our door. Mama cursed heatedly, alleging that the recipients of these hand-outs were better off than we were, and they came to our house and stuck their tongues out at us, boasting of their presents. Instead of their cookies, cheese, and sweet milk, we ate crusts of dry corn bread, and we were out of the graces of Father Ângelo, the new priest. They would see, sir, that we were also barefoot, like all the others, and we, the girls, didn't have even two dresses of calico or poplin, one for each week. As for the only pair of shoes that were passed on from one to the others, Mama made us take them right off, as soon as we got back from Mass, and put on the cedar clogs that Papa had carved to fit the size of our feet. We wanted to jump and run, but those wooden shoes didn't permit a single joyous movement. Besides this, Mama would scold me, saying I was too old to be frivolous, and she ordered me into the kitchen to melt the pork fat for the evening soup, to fry the bacon and sausage, to mend the clothes, or to help her embroider a linen towel. Part of our lives, the lives of all Azorean women, went along those lines; fat ladies came to the door, discussed prices, haggled over the design and quality of the stitching, and took away from us days and years of labor to sell them to the stores.

There were, in that time, the great feast days: the Divine Holy Spirit and its devotions: that of the Patron Saint of every street, Easter Day, and the Feast of the Resurrection, the latter dedicated to Our Lady of the Rosary, patron saint of the parish. We adored these holidays because it was when our clothes were considered to be not good enough and our parents remembered to present us with a swath of fabric or some new shoes. But so that the old ones could be replaced, Mama had to see blood blisters on our toes. Then the new shoes would always be much too big. We had to fill the toes with newspaper or cardboard. As for the dresses, they were never to our liking and never in fashion. Sometimes Mama would buy them on layaway, without Papa's knowledge, from the peddlers with the vans who would come around the second fortnight of each month, and she would always pick the ugliest, cheapest, and most severe patterns. For this and other reasons, there was no possibility that the boys would approach me or Domingas to ask us to go out. Aside from being poorly dressed, we were all very sad, and we wore such thick glasses they looked like the bottoms of bottles. As for the rest, it was common knowledge that nobody wanted to call a man father-in-law who was so severe and who treated his children with cruelty. In his *mind*, courting was a question of the dowry that had to be negotiated between the parties interested in the business of marriage, the same way that, years later when I was in Luanda, I learned about the bride negotiations of the black women in the Luanda slums. The bridegroom came and bargained for the woman with goats, cows, fishmeal, and bottles of cachaça. He didn't realize, *I mean*, it didn't occur to him that love was after all the only serious matter of our lives. We were just part of his tribe, ruled by a whip; it was of no use to have the illusion of escaping, to be able to go far away from his control.

So that on the day that the little sisters arrived, and I asked them to allow me to go with them to the convent in Lisbon, he became very pale, almost offended. He wanted to beat me severely, threatening to cut my hair so I couldn't go out on the street, and declared that he was disinheriting me and would no longer consider me his daughter if I dared to bring up such outrageous ideas again. He wouldn't allow it; under no circumstances would I leave to become a nun and make him spend the rest of his life hearing about cloisters and convents!

Luís Miguel

From Outeiros upward, in the heart of the mountain, the world suddenly sank into mist and rain with a smoky blue haze rising from the whirlwinds. The sun disappeared for the rest of the day. We could barely bid it farewell, seeing it for the last time from the distance, in the place where the sea ended and the sky rose in those discs of clouds that were as still as eternity. There were, and always are in the Azorean sky, chestnut brown clouds and clouds the color of stone, and between one and the other roll rings of smoke and great masses of air full of rain. It was thus that I learned everything about fog, hail, and the shadows that come with the weather. I suffered the brutally cold winds, and their corrosive humidity like the acid of rust. To this day I will never know how to say it another way, because nobody explained the machinery of the world to me. But to me it always seemed that the winds crossed the island from north to south, taking the clouds and the sea itself from one side to the other of the coast. The wind tasted like salt, it burned our nostrils and tore our lips, and the cold was so cutting that it filled our bones with the humidity. This bygone suffering in the mountains was all very different than the hell of the snow and the very dry air that made me cry with pain in the early days in Toronto. My arrival to the Canadian winters, before I moved to Vancouver, where the temperature is mild and the city shelters itself from the eternal ice of the Rocky Mountains, happened in the worst moment of my life as an immigrant. In Toronto, I cried because my bones cracked from the cold, and I said that I was dying of frozen blood. I cried like a dog that had lost its owner, in a foreign country, moving from job to job, landing in work that was even more difficult. Just as I got used to the company and to the rhythm of those people who spoke English around me and drank bowlfuls of coffee to try to resuscitate themselves from the death of Toronto, there was always a man who came along whom we called "Boss," who very seriously and in a compassionate voice said the words that the immigrants learned most quickly and can never forget:

"I'm sorry, Lewis . . . You're getting laid off, laid off, Lewis!"

Everything would buzz in my ears: *I'm sorry, Lewis, I'm sorry Lewis, I'm sorry, Lewis . . .* and my tears would freeze at the contact with the cold or simply at the sound of that voice that told me I was *fired*. My eight-day-old beard would become matted with snow, frozen tears, and the sweat of my new affliction. I would go home, be greeted by the surprised look of my wife and oldest son, and I was a kind of out of season Father Christmas with a whipped look . . .

I'll tell you, sir, about the first serious cold that I ever felt. Sometimes I think my entire history is summed up in the curse of the cold that wounded me inside, in the depths of my lungs. It's locked in my heart, like a weight or a dead dog in my stomach, and I see it pass in front of my eyes again; it's a confused film, the infinite nightmare of my Azorean past.

At the top of the mountain, before walking into the fog and saying good-bye to the sea, I would sit down for a few moments to rest. The land descended in front of me, flowing down, from the summit of the Mato do Povo to the great falls on the coast, and far below you could see the landscape of those little fields of wheat, corn and lupine, all green and full of life — a consolation to anyone contemplating them. At the very bottom, two fingers from the sea, Rozário was no bigger than a stable, with its low little houses, the streets that looked like Canadian puzzles, the church with its round and heavy forms over the rows of houses, as if they were cut out of cardboard, the small trees along the road and other details of the landscape. I know I still see the island as I did at that time, because today it is so changed that I thought I didn't recognize it when I arrived. Even so, I always remembered, when I got homesick in Toronto and Vancouver, that aspect of a horse stretched over the water, as I saw it for the last time. When you are alone and suffering, you absolve cursed landscapes. My longing forgives one time period, but accuses the next, and there in all of those times a kind of pardon that extends to ourselves and also to others. Many times, from far away, I was tempted to forgive my father before his death. I wanted to forgive him for me and especially for him; after all it wasn't worth it to harbor that hate against an old man who worked so hard for our happiness and ended up being destroyed by the suffering of cancer and remorse. I was even tempted to give his funeral eulogy about his honesty and his example in acting like a man; he taught us courage, *you know?* He had a way of living with his head held high, and I think that, in spite of everything, the presence of his badness was preferable to this empty space, the unbearable punishment of his death. Every time that the "boss" came to fire me, and I was again back where I started, I would go home without the promise of a check the next week, and I felt like leaving it all and going home. To come back and embrace my old man, *you see?* I wanted to take care of the cows and the lands and even accept the winters of the mountain. Up there it would always be night, outside of me and within me, even at the time, though it contradicted reason. I thought that when we climbed so high, we would be closer to the sky and the sun, and the days there would be longer. All that darkness, however, wrapped me in rolls of fog, everyone disappeared in the balls of mist, whirlwinds, and constant bursts of rain. All around the air was difficult to breathe, watered by a drool of nitrate that in an instant soaked our clothes and chilled our bones. Sometimes at a distance of fifty meters you stopped seeing someone who had just walked in front of you, or you saw their shapes as ghosts, like in the mystery and suspense movies in the cinemas of Canada. You'd talk to them, shout at them, they'd reply, but their voices were invisible, lost in the clouds that lifted people outside of the landscape.

It was, as I said, in the time of the Mato do Povo. Convoys of people came through, and every week they got bigger and grew, like a line of ants, becoming so long that they connected the houses to those majestic cumulus clouds. They were trying to destroy the mountain, sweep it clean, and lop it off the top of the Island, as if it were possible to flatten the world. Salazar took away our mountains. He wanted people to tear the Island apart, stone by stone, root by root, as if this was to be their penance. I got to thinking — or I think it now, I don't know — that these crowds of dead people were walking every day into the inferno of the mountain, into the boiling pot of its steam funnels. With one particularity: these dead people were stealing the land from the living.

The very heavy machinery of the government had arrived, that little by little dug away at the mountain, filling up caves and valleys, razing dunes and small massifs. They did it with the same ease that God makes it rain or shine. Tractors and trucks dumped out the majority of those condemned to work in the mountain, taking them up and down. They didn't have room for the younger ones, who in an infernal scramble tried to climb on; the bigger ones trampled the younger ones, pushing off the old and the infirm. The lighter, more agile ones, as if they had wings, flew from the ground to the top of the vehicles, thus saving their strength for the hoes, breaking stones with sledgehammers, and the wheelbarrows full of dirt. Those who got rides jeered at the ones who they passed going on foot, bathed in the sweat of their ascent. Others hung on to the hooks behind the cars, running after them with clenched teeth, and withstood the jolts and changes of speed with clenched teeth, on the stretches of flat road. When they got to the biggest ruts in the road, the driver, who was a man from off the Island with a pockmarked face, turned back to look, always with few words and without any confidence in that band of workers; he told half of them to get off. If the tractor was still stuck, then all the rest had to get off and push, teeth clenched, almost lifting the vehicle up in a body out of the mud.

It was like remaking the world, I repeat: with pumps, dynamite, or antlike excavations. It was all too much for my strength and for my imagination. With the exception of the miller, who abandoned his mill in Achada and rode the wildest mule around, very few were the owners of the beasts. The horses came much later; sometimes carrying several riders at a time, kilometer after kilometer, they delivered and returned from the mountain entire families, five, six, sometimes seven young men waiting to be drafted or to be able to emigrate.

So it was impossible, and still is impossible, to say how many falls I took, how many miles I traveled, how many liters of sweat my body spilled on that damned mountain, from the time it belonged to us, to our people, until the days the government returned it to us, in exchange for an income and a new way of suffering on it. For six months, I was the poor slob who climbed up and down, in a back and forth that tore up my body and exposed our servitude. I carried my basket of food on my arm, my pants were rolled up to the middle of my calves, and the soles of my feet were cracked and had unhealed wounds. To shelter myself and to have somewhere to sit while I ate my lunch, I carried two canvas bags that I wore on my head, like a hood, and even when I was drenched by the rain, I didn't take them off and let them dry against my body. All of this adult suffering was in exchange for seventeen patacas, paid on Saturday afternoon, in damp bank notes and a few small coins that my father added up with a pencil on a board. He wanted to make sure that I had been paid the right amount and hadn't been careless with the change that was due to me! Poor me, trembling with fear with that big money in my pocket, knowing it didn't belong to me, would never belong to me, and that a simple pataca less wouldn't deserve his pardon or his generosity . . . It was good that the work didn't kill me; among the few who were always industrious and conscientious men, there were more of them who were shiftless and without any ambition, averse to dirtying their nails. Things moved slowly; it was under the supervision of the Salazar government, always so generous with hangmen and the university educated men. It was said that Salazar thought the poor had no ambition, all they needed was a little bacon with cabbage to be happy and healthy . . . On days when it rained a lot, we rested under the trees that were going to be destroyed, until the weather cleared. But since it never stopped raining, the foremen raised their noses to the sky, studying the clouds and the wind; they conferred among themselves and then came the decision to stop work. We ended up leaving with only a half day's pay. My father wouldn't forgive me for this; I had to go fetch firewood for the oven and the stove, put it on my back, and walk down the mountain quickly and without delay. To my great astonishment, as soon as we passed Outeiros and below, and arrived at Mãe-de-Água, the afternoons were always clear and bathed in sunlight. It was another world, completely different from the one we had left behind, up there on the top of the mountain where it rained, the wind blew, and electrical storms thundered with lightening. Many times, in the war in Guinea, I would remember those rotund thunder claps like rolling stones — either because I was under fire in the rice paddies and about to die, or because the sound of the mortars brought back the terror and the echo of the Mato do Povo, or because the African thunder increased in volume and exploded twice in my soul. I always had a great fear of war. I practiced the most terrible atrocities; I had, as I mentioned, a price on my head; my hide was torn by the electric discharges of the bombardments — but it was the fear of being afraid, even. I learned everything: to overcome my fear of dying, to pretend that everything was a lie, to suppose that we were just in the carnival of hell and that all were demons and angels at the same time. There were days that the death of others was a beautiful thing to see. On other days, it was an unbearable passion like the song of an assassin. I returned cured of all evils, or at least without their memory, but I brought greater ills with me: an open wound in my two eyes and a cold shiver down my spine.

I was fascinated at the time by the big yellow government machines that demolished everything in our path: mounds of earth and trees, rocks, and hedges, with those teeth of steel, the snout in gear, and a scoop that lifted into the air enormous cargos of crushed rock. In the rear, other big machines flattened the earth, pressed it down under their treads, leaving it flat, without elevation. Little by little the Island lost the spiked appearance it used to have, in the measure that it became rounded at its highest points, almost at the ceiling of the universe. Next to these animals of iron and steel, moved by gasoline engines, we were like fleas being commanded by the shouts of the foremen who came from off the Island. We carried stones, hacked at craters, and cut down trees with axes. The stone quarries, mined with sticks of dynamite, exploded with echoes that crossed the Island from one side to the other. Brigades chosen by the men of the forests planted cedars and beeches, cleared brush, opened trails in the direction of the future watering places of the cattle. We saw the Island change day by day, and this was extraordinary and unprecedented; we lost the notion of what had existed before in those dark mountains and we started to imagine the cattle poised in the landscape, their tails turned against the rain and their horns raised against the wind. Later, other changes happened on the Island. I saw this a few days ago when I arrived from Vancouver. I notice that now I don't see the rows of corn and beets. I don't see the lupine hedges or the expanse of wheat fields. There are almost no people here from my time, with the exception of those who were already old or about to die. The ones my age and younger were taken away by the wind, the planes, and the boats. I myself don't know what I'm doing here, or what has become of my youth or myself. I am Canadian, on paper, but I continue to think that I left my bones and my religion here. I will never understand what has happened to me, sir.

When, at the end of six months, my father ordered me to return to the coast, I missed that band of ragged men huddling from the cold on their canvas sacks, at midday chewing happily on the food stewed in pepper sauce. For the last time, I filled my eyes with that circus in which I was neither a clown nor a trapeze artist, but just a sad anonymous voice. I said good-bye to the mist, good-bye to the other side of the Island and to the sea at the south, good-bye to the villages that one could see there and had never gone beyond, a promise for my Azorean travels. I descended the mountain squeezed inside myself, alone among so many lonely men, and prepared to return to the destiny of the only man who, besides my father, was my owner and eternal master. I would begin to learn the new months, weeks, and days of the time of the land and the cows, I would learn about the manure, the seeds, the rows of the plow, the teeth of the harrow. I'd learn how the heifers were trained to pull carts or how dogs bit. Never had any man suffered more than I. Because, when you are a child and you cannot expect justice, a mortal poison seems to envelop the world from the present to the future. I say this because I lived it: I drank the poison and from then on I experienced its toxic effects. It served me that years later, when I went back up the mountain and tied up the cows, letting them graze in those new pastures, I could look into the distance and understand that I had long ago stopped being a man of this or any other place, or a simple creature of the earth. The time had finally come to find my other piece of the world.

CHAPTER SEVEN

Nuno Miguel

Believe me: it really was the work of the devil. It could only have been the work of that dark and wily animal. There was the bony ridge of the Feteiras road, with deep ditches, pools of mud, and basalt stones like eggs that the wheels skidded on, spraying mud in the September rain. But it happens that I was going ahead of the oxen, my goad on my shoulder, with the perfect calm of experienced cart drivers. This was my boat, and I was at the helm in that stony, muddy sea, when the collision occurred and the wooden axel stopped groaning. Looking at the oxen, I saw them sink in front of me, up to their snouts in mud, their eyes glassy, and their necks twisted. I wanted to call for help right away; the panic of the bovines, caused by such unexpected madness, was the fulfillment of demoniacal death, undoubtedly prophesied by the Hound. Besides, I still believed in God. I had given Him my innocence, the soul sickness of my age, the pathetic dreams I had then. When there were feast days, people sacrificed calves, chicken, and sheep to Him, and for this God didn't need to satiate on another's blood His temperamental thirst. I also knew of his immense mercy to animals.

My father, who was behind us smoking, lifted his hands to his head. He was dark, bone thin, and bent under his straw hat. He seemed to transform into a strangely distant being, amidst the collapse of the beet crop, the hedges of twisted willows, and the wheels spinning in the air, off their axels. The sudden image of a hanging man flashed by his eyes. One of the oxen had been garroted by the leather harness of the cart shaft, and he started to kick violently in agony at the unexpected choking. He seemed to be swallowing his own guts, because he was swimming in the air and was writhing in the agony of drowning. The desperation of the animal communicated with that of my father, and it penetrated my memory as deeply as the vision of all the family tragedies that had occurred to that point in time. For a moment,

Papa's eyes reflected the broken horns of the oxen, the grain fields destroyed by the mudslides, and the trees split by the action of cyclones or floods. The panting of the ox was the same as the otherworldly drone announcing the earthquakes. But when those nostrils filled up with air and the metal fittings of the harness broke, that was perhaps a magic trick replaying the black tides of a family shipwrecked in the memory of its misfortunes.

All of a sudden, I saw the animal free himself from under the yoke and clamber out kicking, in a great show of happiness. It was going through a second birth; it was once again a strong, whole male, energy running through his blood, primed for the sacrament of mating — the only passion of the bulls.

The habitually livid and sunken eyes of my father rested on me. He was hesitating between holding back his screams and ending my existence once and for all. I could see perfectly that he wanted to kill me because hate made him curl his tongue. At first, I thought that he would tear off a cart pole and beat me with it, the way he liked to do with the animals. Then, because he couldn't dislodge it from the willow hedge, he put his hand on the ox goad. He tried out its elasticity on the invisible body of the air and advanced toward me.

I remember it well; it was a chestnut ox prod, carved from a still green acacia trunk and straightened by fire and steam. When it was snapped over the long bony backs of the animals, it whistled and vibrated like a musical chord. I don't know how many times he hit me on the legs, back, and throat. When you get a lashing like that, without measure or reason, it just takes the first and second whistle of the cane or the whip. By the third blow, the body gets used to it and the spirit stops resisting the aggression. You howl and moan, but the body starts to receive commands from another source of energy. The pain itself is like a horse whinny, or the hollow groan of a conch horn. The worst, however, was that besides bending over and folding into my own body, the goad had the teeth of a snake. Its triangular snake head struck me with its bifurcated tongue. The nail at the tip of the goad, kept sharp by a file, forced the oxen to overcome the steepest slopes and strain under the overloaded carts. It even frightened the dogs and the horses. So when it was wielded with all my father's fury, I don't know how to describe it: the goad bites, burns, wounds with fire, stone, and salt, not just the flesh, but above all the impressionable soul of any child. I say this because father stuck the nail right through my buttocks, just above my anus, and it felt as if I was being cut to pieces by a mute instrument. Besides this, Papa clenched his teeth hard and skewered me with all the strength of his muscles and the clear intention of killing me. Then two lathelike blows rained on my head, and flattened me in the ditch. It's true I didn't die, but I lay there for some hours. So I wouldn't faint in the rain and the rising water, I howled like a dog in agony and rolled over sharp stones, brambles, and cow dung. Salt and rust flakes stirred within me the heroic cry of martyrs, a symphony of mourners at the hour of death. I lifted myself in the air, like an amputated reptile tail, and regained the consciousness of the moment of death. I was alive, you see? Without the fatality of posthumous funeral dirges, I watched the last moment of my human frailty from the sidelines. Spectator and spectacle of my own fantastic circus, with sequins in my eyes, the foot lamps, the phosphorescent sparklers, the firecrackers of this terrible fireworks that was the last celebration of being alive in the presence of my father . . .

However, and as you can certainly imagine, guardian angels do exist, and they are very opportune beings that are easy to invoke. All you have to do is call them, softly and to yourself, and they arrive flying in the depths of the silence to free us from greater evils. Many, many times I asked for help and pardon from these invisible birds, searching for a signal or any other news of my future. In the mirror of my madness there were already the mornings, the sky, and the water in this sea desert. Today, I have the past and the ignorance of all of these dream castles. I crossed through them with the memory of the swamps, and nevertheless the angels almost always took the right flight path. When they did land on me, they didn't do it out of joy. Other times, they were stubborn and absorbing as an obsession; in the seminary I got sick of them. I put little collars with bells around their necks and willed them to return to the infinite. They were so unnecessary that their protection almost took away our will to live. Outside of this time of being cloistered and asphyxiated, I can't complain about the desertion of those birds that are always on guard and at the service of God.

That was the case on that late afternoon.

I could never forget it. They came to rescue me from the mud, between the floodwaters and the September rains. A misfortune with rain always equals two misfortunes. And three would be the misfortune and the rain coming together close to nightfall, the delirium of the oxen, and a cart wheels up in the air. However, my compassionate angels of luminous apparitions became men in the persons of the ox drivers coming down the mountain. Barefoot, dismounted from their beasts, and leading the now calmed oxen, I heard them talking to them in such a soft way as only females can do. Seeing the upturned cart and the cargo scattered on the ground, their faces showed sudden and alarmed concern, thinking that the tragedy of carts is when they crush and bury the drivers. They came immediately to my aid. They were tall, with powerful shoulders, and by the determination of those divine eyes, I saw they censored the violence of my father and that they disarmed him of his acacia prod. To this day I recall their unmistakable voices, white with magic, and the way they lifted me up on to their laps and saved me from death at the hands of the man who at that time was my poor dog of a father.

The rain started to fill the night and it entered slowly, heavy as lead, into the hollow cylinders of my bones. I walked in the night, but without any consciousness of walking. I suffered from the rain, but I didn't know it was just raining inside me. I limped, twisted by the pain of that iron prod that had skewered me just above my anus, a puncture wound that to this day is stuck just above my anus, that iron prod that will always walk with me, stuck just above my anus, and it didn't occur to me that I could die from the simple bite of that ox goad. The arrival of night and the rain, the tetanus fever, and the anguish of being alive amounted to just the certainty of repeated beatings. In the body, iron is an abundant and supernatural presence; the veins suck it up, absorb it, and then blow it, with the violence of a gunshot, straight into the center of the heart. Mama had warned me of the danger of playing with the needles in her sewing box.

"Use your common sense, my little saint. The veins swallow them and suck them, and then you'll die with them stuck in your heart."

Passers-by, seeing me sway, didn't suspect I was dead. Everyone was used to seeing boys limping by in the dusk, walking in the rain, getting lost in the uncertain streets of those wet days, and crying for no reason. They had gotten used to seeing them go by like that, twisted and sad, because there had never been a time of justice, and nobody listened to them.

"Hey, boy! Hey, little boy," my Grand Mama Olinda called, in distress, from her window. "What did they do to you, boy? What happened to you, little grandson?"

When I knocked on the door to my house, and my older sister opened the door, the lame footsteps of Grand Mama dragged a clattering of bony spurs behind me. She had always been lame and had always walked too fast. She died in her sleep, at ninety-nine years of age, in the middle of an energetic breath, strong minded and light as a piece of paper. They found her smiling, with her eyes closed, and just a little more deaf than usual. Her mother, Great Grand Mama Aninhas, also entered death that way; a ball of wax seated in a rocking chair, little, cabbage-shaped, and intensely milk white. On the days of family visits to Great Grand Papa, I would see her invariably sitting down, with a shawl on her knees, even if it were summer, and her little ferret eyes, already without memory, were confused by my presence.

"Hey Olinda! Who does this boy belong to? It seems to me I don't recognize him."

"Gracious God!" Grand Mama Olinda would lovingly chastise her. "Can't you see that it's Emanoel's youngest? He was here just last week and I told you who he was, God be praised!"

Amélia took me to her lap and ran to the kitchen to sound the alarm to my mother. Grand Mama Olinda started giving orders and told them to take off my soaked clothes, give me a bath, and wrap me in flannel garments. Then, she herself lit the stove and put water in a kettle to prepare a milkwort tea. Mama called her to come help decipher the strange crater of blood where the soap water was bubbling. The usually silent eyes of my mother filled up immediately with tears and became bluer than usual, while Grand Mama's eyes opened wide like the maleficent flowers of a lethal smile and then became laser beams of hate against her son. As for my brothers, they were just silent marbles, overcome with crying and fear. In the waning lucidity of my feelings, I could still hear the cries mixing with voices and distant bells, and I understood I should resign myself. I had to prepare myself to die since this was the night of my final delirium. The candles came, with the flowers and the cold smile of my body lying prone with hands clasped. Soon there would be the black beads of a rosary between my fingers, a chambray handkerchief in the pocket of the blue jacket from my first communion, and a face tinged blue with the joy of dying.

In the first moment after I came to, the first things that came to my awareness were the anguished expressions of those witnessing my agony. In addition to having increased in volume, they were like eggs, and they floated around me with a gelatinous, supplicating expression. In the second, they lost again that affliction and reacquired an evil beauty, the mischief and grimace of laughter with which they had been born. I sank then, into a whirlwind of real dreams, separated from the world by the glass walls of delirium and agony.

I am not certain how many external lights were cast over the absence of sun in my spirit. I had not been able to hear the voices or make out those clouded faces. A mixture of darkness and disorder hampered the vital functions of my body. Vague monsters, similar to burning horses suspended in the air, entered me without the fire burning me. And wheels with teeth passed over my body but did not succeed in slaughtering me. Beaked clouds, in spite of impaling me like bulls' horns, continued just to float over me in flesh and in spirit. The rain was still dark, imponderable and acid like the great empty, timeless night. I could also tell you about the faraway choirs, the rattles, the obsessive sounds that alternated fragmentary music with dispersed sounds coming from nowhere. These were melodies impossible to reproduce and capture; if I could have retained them on a score sheet, I wouldn't know which instruments or voices would have to be invented. Surely you would see the genius and the sad beauty of the choruses and singers, the symphonies of hate and pardon, the murmur of water, stone, and metal. Long and magnificent preludes comprised the requiem of my demise, so that if I could reproduce that lake of music from memory, you would certainly be able to feel what it is like to die, and be able to write about it . . .

As for the rest, only later was I given the details of that time of limbo and forgetfulness. Mama would always remember the ten days I didn't eat, counted on her fingers, between vomiting of green saliva, explosive, fetid diarrhea, and great larvae of fever. I don't remember the chicken soup that women who had just given birth used to get; there were also Grand Mama's cookies, and the fancy treats that my brothers and sisters fought over later. Picky eater as I was, my pagan god rejected everything: the strained sweet rice, the cream pudding, the warm milk with honey, the cow's butter on pieces of sliced wheat bread. I also don't remember the honey fed to me by the teaspoonful, the eggs beaten with sugar, and the sweet, golden syrups that rested for a long time at my place at the table in the months following my resurrection. I think I recall the balsam, the unguents, and the rosemary. And I also remember the sounds of the harp, the clavichord, the old piano, the vibraphone, the speakers, and the turntable. I think I recall the cold apathy and Mama's hands when she put them on my forehead and said:

"God help me, this child is still burning up with fever and he's barely conscious . . ."

I remember the twisted sounds of the oblique world. I recall the hoarse prayers made of imperceptible words. But thinking that the family was kneeling around the bed, their hands clasped in prayer — no, that I don't remember. I have no recollection of the presence of Father Ângelo, or the Latin of the last rites. I remained suspended, lifeless, with the spider of death spinning its web of dreams around me. I don't believe I could have formed a single thought. I found myself flying on fiery horses; I felt loose and lost in the spittle of strange shadows. I was searching for forbidden birds, made of ether and alcohol, through the mist and high clouds. I crossed leaden skies, where memory is impossible, and I thought mine was a unique and happy death.

I was dying, and the idea of staying in space, stripped of weight and shape, became more enchanting. Little by little, however, the nightmares took on concrete forms. I started to become aware of when it was day and night. I knew where the voices were coming from but not what they were saying. Daybreak approached as slowly as the sand sliding in hourglasses or the liquid in water clocks. Even the monsters of my dreams changed color; they were blue, purple and magenta, and always melancholic. Kaleidoscopes turned, rainbow wheels coiled like harmless serpents. I recognized the smell of the ocean, and then the medicines, and finally my own sweat that was filling the closed house. They said one lady was called Mama, another was Amélia, and they said the names of those who were smiling at me and others, who just looked at me without smiling.

On the night I could open my eyes and make out objects in the dark, there was a cedar beam over my head that traversed the whole house. The world was suspended from it, like the pendulum of a stopped clock. I considered its ridges and the bulging form of its hexagonal body, and it occurred to me that, besides serving to hold up the house at the top of the world, it was also on that crossbeam that pigs hung during the January slaughters. The blood of the swine would drain for hours into a big clay jar and boil inside it like fermenting wine. I must have fallen asleep right afterward, because the images crossed each other and fused. My father's body little by little took the place of the hanging pig, and seemed to swing so softly as if in a soft breeze. Since it was tied at the wrists, it was logical I should confuse it with the Crucified one, since my father's head exhibited the same crown of thorns, the air of a martyr, and the weariness of the night of the Passion. The blood, though it was dark and clotting, ran along the fine wrinkles of his skin, since in his hands were the same nails that the Nazarene King of the Jews still today exhibits in that morose and tiresome crucifixion . . .

My whole body became fluid and joined in a single organ — my stomach — to produce the most anguished and cutting cry of fear and protest. Ejected by the spring of that cry, I sat up in bed, without depending on the action of my muscles, and my arms reached in the direction of the infinite, in hopes of still saving him from that torture.

I reached out for him and that was certainly the second repetition of my old miracles, from the time when he was alive and I was still a religious man. Papa was in fact standing there and had been for some time; he was holding a pot of flour broth in his fingers. His despair had become notorious, because of the way he repeated in vain the same request over the last ten days during my absence from this world:

"Papa wants you to eat something, son. If you don't eat you'll die of weakness, without any strength in your bones. Come on, Nuno. Come, my boy. Can a father let his son die of hunger, when there's so much to eat in this house?"

I didn't understand yet how I had saved him from being crucified. But when his muscular arms opened to my thin body, I felt that his chest was heaving, in finding mine. And, after being dead, I resuscitated. And, asking me again to eat, I took the pot in my trembling hands and began to sip, in quick, ravenous gulps, that delicious flour soup, the taste mingling forever with the sweet memory of my childhood. And his eyes, overflowing with tears, were finally happy eyes with tears. So you will forgive me the fact that my story also has happy episodes . . .

Maria Amélia

The nuns were very big women with apple-shaped faces and yellowish eyes. They came to us dressed in long blue capes over habits the color of pearl. Buried under the weight of so many fabrics, their bodies seemed to roll on invisible wheels, very straight and rigid, like statues when they are moved from place. They hovered, they did not step in the potholes or the stones in the road, since they moved in an almost levitating way that was without doubt graceful. Truthfully they looked a lot like frightened penguins, with their pendulum gate, and they projected such rigidity in their posture that people hushed and became frightened by the silence of their passage.

The youngest, when she smiled — and she did it often — revealed a badly disguised gold tooth. She had a voice the texture of flannel and a nose that was as curved as a hook. The other one gave us a little purple, cold hand to kiss, that was magnificent to behold because of its three rings from her engagements to Christ. They called her "mother" and said it with the devotion of paschal visits, when Father Ângelo went from house to house and became mellifluous with the sick and the elderly, carrying in his hands the bloody crucifix of the Passion.

They went from house to house asking for money for the Missions, distributing the prayer cards of the martyr who had the bad luck of being eaten by the infidels of Africa. They said "good day" to everyone, wishing peace on their homes. They were always very polite and spoke in a near wail, and afterward they asked if there wasn't anyone in the home, young boy or young girl, who might have a vocation for the Work of God . . .

I found myself at home alone, scrubbing the aluminum and metal implements in the kitchen and crying, when those statues knocked on the door and smiled at me in an automatic way, without doubt it was mechanical, yet sympathetic. When I encountered those healthy faces, blushing under the cap of their habits, my heart gave a leap. For the first time in my life, a strange white glow appeared out of the tunnel of my misfortune to illuminate my spirit with a holy light. In a certain way, I had long awaited that opportunity, full of faith, confident that one day someone would come into my life and talk to me without malice about a sea voyage and a boat that would take me from here to the Continent. I anticipated it from the bottom of my soul, by simple presumption, like in a fairy tale. I was waiting for God's coming, my enchanted prince, with the same convictions of the women who clamor in the desert for the arrival of the prophet.

I asked them right away to come inside, and I ran to the kitchen to find two chairs for them to sit in. When I returned I surprised the little sister with the gold tooth hovering over the flower stands that were surrounded by the family photos, touching them with velvet fingers and gestures of melting wax. The other one, standing rigidly, swept the house with an eye that dated from the Inquisition, searching for a crucifix that didn't exist, for any saint's niche, a music box of Our Holy Christ of Miracles, or simply to judge the details of our blessed poverty. I noticed her pink skin and her large almond-shaped eyes. She was not beautiful, no. But that porcelain face inspired me immediately with a supernatural sweetness. I was in the presence of a woman of luxury, *you know?* I had always been attuned to the genteel manners and glory of the rich. Then the mother started to ask me questions: what was my name, how old was I, and when had I begun to feel the Call, the Summons from the Lord. I answered all of this in a jumbled way, twisting my apron between my sweaty fingers, possessed, however, by a kind of religious gluttony and by an uproarious feeling of a state of grace. This was, in fact, my lucky day; God had finally come to the center of my life and was certainly disposed to putting me on His lap and taking me to His side. Until that day, I had been spinning a *fantasy* that dragged me little by little to the illusion of a single destiny that I intensely desired. I dreamed of becoming a nurse, and I harbored it with the persistence of someone obstinately embroidering her trousseau. I backstitched, in silence, the designs of this unrealizable dream, but I was always alert for the smallest sign of this miracle, made only of faith and secretiveness. If one day it would happen to me, it would be as if I had won the biggest prize that had to this day been raffled at the fairs.

After a half-hour conversation with the little sisters, I was already full of the vocation for the Cause of God and I started to reconfigure my plan. I had no doubt that I would go to the convent, to a prison of forced labor, indeed even to *hell*, if that path led me more quickly to study nursing. I had in fact heard that the nuns were given to learn the most varied professions, to better serve humanity. They offered themselves, for example, to the service of the poor, to whom they distributed the little charity of soup and clothing from Hell. Others devoted themselves to education and the care of orphans, or learned to cry with sincerity for the dead and to spiritualize the discouragement or rebellion of the unhappy. The rest converted repentant prostitutes, revived the spirits of the imprisoned and the bums, and they were very useful in diverse other pressing exigencies of Christian Charity. But for me, as I said, the temerity of the nuns only made sense in relation to those who became nurses. I imagined them always on the journey to the dying of others, running the risk of living among lepers, kissing the gangrene of men mutilated in war, or cleaning up the bloody sputum of those sick with tuberculosis with a frustrated smile. There was, in fact, a double advantage in the risk of living with the contagion and disgrace of others; I could either one day transform myself into a martyr, and thus merit canonization, or surely prepare myself for a dignified world-recognized profession in case I should opt to abandon the convent. Nobody can read the future, *you see*, but one must keep an ear tuned to its great distant night . . .

I wasn't seduced by the opportunity to go on faraway Missions, because in Africa, they used to say, the climate devoured the living and the dead. And besides this, at this point the cannibals didn't merit my slightest sympathy . . . I would choose nursing, not the cloister or the mystical marriage with the Crucified one. The few times that the public health nurses had come to Rozário, I envied their luminous bodies, the painted smile, the elegance of their fairy hands that injected us with vaccines. I immediately liked the smells of alcohol and tincture of iodine, the cold of ether, and the competence of the tweezers. My destiny began to link itself, even from a distance, to the syringes and the gauze in the little yellow dispensers; I was seduced by the liturgy of those magical instruments.

The little sister with the golden smile noticed meanwhile that a shadow had fallen over my face. Seeing me so vulnerable, with my awkward, useless hands resting on my lap, my teary enormous eyes behind hugely thick lenses, she wanted to know if I had talked about this with my parents and if they were willing to consent to my leaving. I was then an anemic seventeen-year- old, with an excessively unhappy face, a lonely mouth, and I began to lament the emptiness, the absence of religion in our house. I told them that Papa and Mama lived in mortal sin, with dark consciences and without the grace of pardon of the sword of the Angel. They nodded in agreement with their heads, very politely and with furrowed brows, thinking exactly as I did. To them it was becoming clear this was the signal of a divine calling, since God had the habit or caprice of choosing His in the bosom of his enemies and those indifferent to Him. His diaphanous hand always picked the best lilies precisely when they were blooming in abandoned gardens, the same way that He had known how to choose among the thistles and the adverse spirits of the evangelist Apostles. As an example, they told me the story of Peter, the one about the cornerstone, and they narrated the episode of Paul on the way to Damascus. Then, and without even changing their tone of voice, they delighted me with the parable of the Sower; some of his wheat seeds fell among the brambles and were immediately eaten by the birds. Other seeds were taken by the wind to the rocks and the sterile lands, and immediately the force of nature that gives life withered away. But the one who could find the good rich land, that one quickly sprouted and grew in the direction of the sun and multiplied into millions of new fruits. And I was the good land. Papa and Mama would have to come around, for better or worse, to the will of the Sower. The only problem still was, according to them, that I had to be put to the test and pass the test of the principal and rigorous virtues: obedience, humility, and meekness. They also needed to test me in the spiritual secrets of poverty and in other less subtle skills of human behavior . . .

"It's indispensable," the mother interjected, with her little hand in the air, her fingers pointing upward, the way preachers do, "that you stay with us for some time so we can put you to the test. You need to be observed for your temperament, you understand. You will provide service and submit to some of our sacrifices. Only then will we judge your vocation . . ."

So they proposed that I talk with Papa and ask his permission to spend two weeks in Ponta Delgada. Once I was there, far from the disturbances of the world, I would enter into spiritual retreat. As for the cost of the voyage and my upkeep, I shouldn't worry; everything would be taken care of by the Congregation from the funds for recruiting new postulants.

When they left and resumed their rounds from door to door, with their uncertain penguin gate, their polite knocks, and saying "good day" to all the people, I remained buried in a great square drum, happy and unhappy, moribund and reborn — just like the bird reborn from the ashes. That crucial step in my life would force me to face Papa's terrible eyes. I immediately burst out crying to myself, tears of fear and affliction, knowing I would be caught in the family web — and never again, since then, have I stopped crying. The journal of my past life, sir, became filled with pages and pages of abandonment, written out of anxiety and revised by my many mistakes. I leaf through it with great disappointment, and those useless memories are no more than footnotes at the end of my family's story.

Papa started right in with his huffing and puffing, pacing, and never again stopped being a caged man. He nervously traversed the open space in the kitchen, back and forth. His chin and his eyes trembled; he said I must really be completely crazy. If I thought he'd let me run away, with his blessing, I was thoroughly delusional. When had anyone seen such impertinence? Then I had decided for myself, without rhyme or reason, to leave home and go off with a nun, worse yet to a cloister, a dull place with no profit? Mama didn't restrain herself from joining that funeral mass. She said and repeated, on that night and for the rest of her life, that she needed me for kitchen service. Now that I was raised and ready for work, what a stupid idea, she couldn't even believe what she was hearing. My brothers and sisters laughed, amused by the idea of me dressed as a nun. Later when Papa got angry and alluded to my sixteen years and then went off in another direction to find reasons to be angry, they suddenly became very serious. Everything to this point had happened to him in this miserable life of a dog: years of cyclones, lost harvests, dead or lost cattle, and now comes this foolish girl, with a stupid idea in her head, to tell me stories of nuns and convents? When he stopped enumerating all the disadvantages of my departure, the whole house was shaking, like a boat on a stormy sea; I was crying, seated at the table, asking forgiveness for existing and for being that way, and I was torn about whether to wish for life or death. This was because Papa, always instigated by Mama's asides, ended up forbidding me to bring up the subject. If I did, he'd whip me with his belt or a good stick, and it would take me a lifetime to recover. The matter closed, he'd gone out for the night in a huff; then he stopped talking to me. I became "Mother Amélia" to my mouthy, laughing siblings, the same way that Nuno, a few months later, got the nickname "little castrated priest." Those mocking, gilded monikers stuck with us through the years. The family became habituated to always speaking, thinking, and distinguishing between "us" and "them"; even when we became professionals with diplomas, they never completely forgave us our ecclesiastical past. Luís Miguel even got to the point of declaring the injustice that we would all inherit equal shares while ignoring the fact that we hadn't worked as much as he and the others for the house. *My mother used to say* that Nuno and I should be more conscientious in this respect; after all, our education was a good inheritance, we didn't need those patches of land. They simply forgot about a useless and small detail: I ate bread with tears, I spent a sleepless life, I treated my lymphatic tuberculosis with the kindness of strangers. I begged the doctors to give me, out of charity, the free antibiotic samples; I spent hours and hours of my life waiting in lines, standing powerless at the doors of the Social Assistance agency. They would listen to me distractedly, always in a hurry, telling me to come back next week. I appealed to the priests, who heard me in confession and then would give me a letter of recommendation to some public charitable institution. One fine day, Papa decided to offer Luís a weaned calf, because he was becoming a man, he could start to provide for his own future. If he married, he had something to start with. I was at home after the expulsion from the convent, and Mama would wring her hands because the doctor in Algarvia prescribed very expensive medicines. She took it upon herself to make the selection in the pharmacy, always deciding on the cheapest and most innocuous ones, and forbidding me to verify that they were specific to combating my disease. What's more, I didn't let go of my obsession to return to Lisbon. Even when I was sick and looked like death, I persisted in my determination to get better and return to my nursing program. Then I thought of proposing to Luís an honest transaction; he would sell the calf and lend me the money. After I got my nursing diploma, I'd pay him back double . . .

"Don't fall for that stupid idea," Mama interjected with such spite I still can't explain it. "Amélia, who is an invalid, can die from one day to the next in Lisbon, and you'll be stuck with no calf and no money. Keep your eyes wide open, son."

Luís was astonished. He looked at me, seeing my eyes filled with tears, looked at Mama, and stood up. I never saw him so indignant.

"My mother is soft in the head. That damned calf can fall into a gully and I'll lose her anyway. But at least my sister won't die because she lacks medicine. Keep your money, Mother, because I don't give a shit about that fucking calf!"

He stormed out of the house and didn't come home that night. Later, when I was almost dying in Lisbon, he faced my father's obstinacy with identical fury, snarling at him and looking straight in his eyes, so that he'd see he was dealing with a man, and he said:

"Why do you want to keep your money in a drawer while your eldest daughter is dying without any help, as if she were a beggar? If I were closer to her, Father, I'd give her the best I had — a good dose of my blood in her veins — and I'd not let her beg for money anymore!"

As for Nuno, what happened mostly was silence. The letters became more infrequent, just like the visits, because Nuno was working and studying; he taught Latin and wrote poetry. He ran from night school to clandestine political meetings, became slowly angry with the world and with life, and began to think that his father, his mother, and God no longer existed . . . All the evils of the country were summed up in the existence of Mr. Salazar, his secret police, and the Censorship of blue pencils that forbade the publication of his poems. There was the overseas war, and Nuno thought about fleeing to France. But while he was deciding whether to leave or not to leave, he faced the riot police and turned yellow himself, with dark rings under those terrified blue eyes, hunted and still full of cunning . . .

Between Papa and me, from the day he stopped speaking to me, a kind of grave in fact opened between us. For twenty-five years we limited ourselves to exchange phrases of greeting and farewell, not more than that, and sometimes with intervals lasting decades. The last time we were face to face was in Vancouver, on the eve of his death. Finally I had become a nurse, without his consent and in spite of his blind opposition. I had conquered English and won the recognition of my degree by Canadian schools. I had in my favor a secure income in a very large country. When Papa, on his death bed, saw me approach, he tried to smile and felt in my arrival the presence of his angel. I brought him morphine, and I represented sleep, the rest from delirium and pain. He smiled at me with an expression of gratitude on his ashen face, but it was a smile where the wind, the wolf, and the dog of remorse howled. He couldn't talk any more, and couldn't see more than three meters ahead. He recognized me by the smell and efficacy of my drugs, but he continuously searched for me with the emptiness of those translucent eyes, attentive to the slightest sound or a simple signal of my presence.

On the twentieth of August, after the morphine injection, I sat next to his deathbed and felt a bony, greenish hand hold my fingers. I recognized his death by the fetid breath of the dying, by the cloud over the defeated eyes, and by his remorse. Not that he could give me a single word of gratitude but because he felt himself dying from the power of my fairy hands. The greatest irony of our lives transpired through this axis of vanquished and victor. I suppose that he just wanted to smile at me and tell me that I done well to persist until I had defeated his will. I swear that it didn't occur to me to harbor any fantasy of pardon, either me to him or him to me. It was perhaps our longest conversation in my forty-two years of life. It happened wordlessly and without any other form of expression, but it was just as deep as my love for him could have been, if everything had been different between us. It's a conversation that still goes on inside me and that will certainly last for many more years. It could be that this has to do with the fact that you and I, sir, are here now, sitting in front of each other: incredulous, perturbed, and looking uselessly into the void . . .

Luís Miguel

Whoever has had the good fortune to live their childhood and not be able to remember it with gratitude will have a hard time accepting that the body and the soul have a well-defined age. I think that about myself, every time I look in the mirror at the yellowish white of my hair, the habit of arching my eyebrows and wrinkling my forehead, and the way I talk to myself; my voice is that of a man angry with life. My wife doesn't know, and will never understand, why I don't look at her when I talk to her. Our children, every time I scold them, shrink away, tremble with fear, thinking that my voice is the size of my body. I've never hit any of my little ones. I promised always to look at my past and think twice before punishing a child of mine. I planned to educate them with respect and not with fear, completely the opposite of my father, who was always in the first line of my intentions. Nevertheless, the oldest continues to compare my strength, the thickness of my arms and the volume of my muscles, with the *strong men* of Canadian television. I also never got used to saying, even in jest, the phrases that Canadians dish out to their wives when they happen to call them when they're out drinking and I hear them greet each other on this side of the bars where they continuously suck at their beer mugs.

"Hi, sweetheart! Are you OK, sweetheart?"

Two years in a row, and in the same month of November, I herded the cows off the Caminho Novo road and put them in a line in front of the few houses that were there, and I watched the passage of the blue buses that took Nuno and Amélia to the City and to the boats. Not once did I look inside them, afraid to see my brother and sister and to see them crying, with swollen, red faces. I preferred to lower my head and look at the ground, so that they wouldn't take with them the memory of this new emptiness that spread through my life.

Without knowing why, I got mad at the dumb beasts and let loose a dozen lashes of the switch that sent them running down the road. My revolt was against myself, because I'd stay here like a dumbass while they had figured out how to be much more calculating and smart than I was. I stayed here, incapable of any vocation, without incurable illnesses or physical defects that would relegate me to sitting in a corner catching flies and spiders and looking at the day before yesterday. According to my calculations back then, it would be another good six years until my life changed. The army was as certain as death. But while it hovered out there, the months continued without Sundays, the years of rain revolved inside me, and I stuck around with my eyes wide-open, like an idiot, without music and without hope. I was fated to be the biggest fool in the world at the beck and call of my father . . .

Every time he yelled at me and beat me, punishing me by making me work on Sunday afternoons, and every time he threatened to hit me on the head with the hammer, I imagined, one by one, all the possibilities of getting out of there. Even when I volunteered and they sent me as punishment to the worst of the Guinean war, I always had the illusion of not being very far away from him. The very day that I presented myself with my orders at the barracks in Arrifes and everyone started yelling at me and giving me orders and telling me to do everything at a run — his voice was still present over me and in my core. I had left him completely dumbfounded, scratching his head, for having done everything in secret just to get away from him. He wanted to beat me one last time, to mess up my life, disinherit me and throw the worst curses on me — but he was afraid of how I raised my head and stared at his left eye. Everything had been said between us. Did Papa want to bet that he'd never lay eyes on me again? He was suspicious, with angry eyes and shaking hands. If he lifted a finger at me, in the state of mind I was in, I don't know if I wouldn't have flattened him against a wall. I was seeing everything red, understand? I was blinder than a pig's balls, and I was just praying to God our Father that he would turn his back and go to mass at another church.

And it happens that those despicable sergeants, as well as the officers of the day, were all from Lisbon. They ordered me around in their strange accents to do cleaning duty, sweep the barracks and clean their latrines. They used the same words, insults, sneers, and tone of voice that I had taken from my father for the last six years. The electric razor that shaved my head and the punishment to spend the weekends on guard duty or standing at the security gate were exactly like the drudgery, the shouts, and the forced labor at my father's house. The dog of the second lieutenant, who I had the misfortune to punch in the eye, had a face that was almost like his. The idiot battalion commander, who was more or less his age, with that body like a cart pole, the same thin nose and narrow shoulders. He ordered them to write up charges and almost sent me to Lisbon to the military tribunal.

"Oh sir, please sir! Sprinkle a little holy water on this, Commander, and don't ruin my life!"

He got mad as hell, and even pulled me by an ear and got into my face hurling gobs of spit at my mouth. The thing was I had some issues that had been badly handled with a neighbor of mine, a guy named Chora. I beat the shit out of him because of him going after the boobs of my sister Linda, and I would have killed him if they hadn't pulled me off him. So there goes Chora, he gets advice, talks to people, goes and files a complaint. The commander launches into a long-winded harangue, all stiff like, talking to me about aggravating precedents; I had already spent ten days in jail because of that attack on the second lieutenant, and because of this and that I was on the way to the Beja Military Prison. Yes, sir, Commander! It helped that my brother Nuno put a bunch of priests on my trial. And the thing would have died there, I thought, if the Commander hadn't been a dumb beast. He withdrew his charges, said yes sir to the priests, and I wouldn't be sent as a prisoner to Lisbon. But so that he could appease superiors and civilians, it would be best if I were sent to scalp blacks in Africa . . .

Before this, however, listen to what was behind that time of war; it was a stagnant, rotten time, dirty with blood. At first people came from outside to help. They'd knock on the door, call my father, and try to keep him from killing me. When I was working the fields, men would stop their work on their land and stare in shock at how that man punished his poor oldest son. The ox goad left my neck black and blue, as if I had been bitten by unknown insects of Guinea, and I rolled around on the plowed ground, under the heels of his boots. What most disgusted the men wasn't even the brutality or the reasons, but the endless duration of those blows. Normally when someone hit their kid in my presence, it was a matter of brief anger, arising from mischief or bad pranks. The hands of those fathers were shaky, even hesitant, to strike a blow. Perhaps for this reason, the children were almost never forced to cry. They limited themselves to lowering their heads, as a sign of respect, and they weren't yelled at or pummeled with the sermons and earthquakes that my father carried on for entire afternoons. His nerves took a long time to settle, between curses, insults, and slaps, and one could hear our cries from far away. Besides this, while other fathers reconciled quickly with their children, with us it was never possible to receive pardon, a kiss, or peace, or to recover our innocence . . .

Many of those poor men ran to my rescue, while my father tugged at the steel chain that held the cows and stood wide-legged over me trying to kill me. You can't imagine how much it hurts to feel the coils of the steel snake on the middle of your lower back? You don't know, you can't know, how it cuts your clothes, bites deep into your skin, and sucks the best of your blood. I know from direct experience, from the first to the last of those six years when he ordered me to shut up with the crying and swallow my tears, what it is to feel disgraced and revolted. At my side, the oxen tied to the hedge panted like bellows, their tongues hanging out, a trail of saliva running from their mouths to the ground. Irritated by the flies, crazy with hunger and exhaustion, everything startled them. The plow dragged along, and I, hanging from the reins, was pulled along after them. My father carried the hoe and I could immediately see his green face change color, turn grey and blue, distorted by nerves. First he hit the oxen with the goad that he took from my hands. Sticking it in their flanks, the iron prod scraped their hides, and the great coils of their guts seemed to empty themselves into the air, turning them into hollow drums, when Papa kicked them repeatedly with his muddy boots. Then, because I was always the only one to blame, and I never did things the way he had ordered me, and I wasn't even capable of holding the plow handle, and I was a worthless shit, and I ploughed uneven furrows, and I didn't have the strength or the knack to guide the oxen or talk to them in their ears, and because I had never learned to turn the plow at the end of the row — he'd turn to me dripping in sweat, grinding his teeth, his jaw bones cracking, and land two slaps on my mouth. I immediately fell down flat, knowing I'd have to protect myself: curl up into a ball, put my arms around my neck and head, and defend myself as I could from the blows of the ox goad or the chains. Dead tired, my muscles all sore and beaten, but always, in his opinion, doing things backward, and never right. In spite of this I began to assume the responsibilities for the tilling little by little. I'd come home later and later every night, wet, barefoot, and cold from the winter chill. I'd wash my feet in the hot water of the basin, quickly change clothing, and sit by the fire. I was as sad as the big night during those six years, feverish and treated like a dog.

Of course I started to eat like a starving person. A hunger tormented me that even the roasted beans with milk bread couldn't sate. The others laughed at the huge portions I took: I had three servings of the soup; I would crumble half a loaf of bread into it and Mama would start laughing, amused and frightened:

"My word, it's a comfort to see you eat, Luís!"

Before sleep overtook me, I had to give accounts for everything I did that day; what was done and what still had to be done. I saw that my brothers and sisters turned pale with pity for me, fearing he'd start to beat me again. My ears burned like a candle because my father was and would always be right. The more I did, it was infinitely too little. I had to listen with my head lowered and my mouth shut. He swore he'd cure me of my laziness and make me a man. A man, see here, sir! When he seemed to be possessed by the devil, hysterical as a woman, nervous and mean as I'd never seen him before, I wanted ardently to be a man, yes sir, to look down on him and have the ability to frighten him. I swore I'd grow a lot and quickly, I'd become a very strong man and force him to swallow his words and never think of raising a hand to me again.

Six years passed, without Sundays or holidays, and I wasn't aware if it was sunny or raining, or if it was night or day. Around five in the morning I'd climb to the highest places on the Island, walking barefoot for kilometers and kilometers, up and then down again, with three large cans of milk on my back. Then I'd put the hoe on my back and go to the fields, from the early morning to the middle of the afternoon, to hurriedly hoe the corn growing on mounds of dirt, to hoe beets, beans, and the world that was growing and waking up to the summer sun. At a quarter past noon, they brought me food, potatoes mixed with the damned salted fish, and bitter coffee. At four in the afternoon, I left again for the pastures: to herd the cattle, milk the cows, and to carry the same three cans down the mountain. Now the sun was already setting in the distance and the sea turned from grey into a rusty red river of blood spreading over the water. The water of my blood.

I didn't measure my time as a crippled, sleepy donkey on clocks or on calendars. Like all young boys my age, I counted the new hairs that sprouted over my lips and the beginnings of a beard, first a ginger red and then blue back. I also discovered the females that I desired in the rapture of three daily masturbations. At that time my old schoolmates excited me, as I saw them growing up, and they provoked me with their way of walking, the waves of their iron-curled hair and the false shyness of their lemon-sized breasts. I possessed them in my very sweaty dreams and pursued them with a great, unrequited passion. On Sundays and late afternoons and especially on holidays, I tried to talk to them at their windows. I must have declared myself to at least half of those rosy, distant young girls, guided by blind passion, always hopeful for a courtship that would lead to marriage and escape from my father's house. Then I realized they were all laughing at me. If I followed them down the street, they'd quicken their steps and duck into the nearest neighbor's house. If I approached them at their sewing windows, with their flowerpots, they'd slam the shutters in my face, calling me repulsive and ugly and sticking their tongues out at me. They'd scornfully talk about my bowed legs, and they didn't pardon me from being the son of that man that half of the municipality talked about. When we walked by we were always the sons of the Hound, the sons of the executioner, the sons of Emanoel Demon, and everyone associated us with his legal issues regarding inheritances and parcels of land, the innumerable visits to the court house for offenses and disorder, complaints against filchers of fruit, firewood, and fines rescinded against the will of the administrator — even when this was no more than his imagination, his anger, or his scheming. We were his sons, *you know?* But we were also held guilty of his crimes and accused of his defects. No one thought of the possibility that we were, after all, his first victims.

When the partition of my Grand Papa's estate was being done, Papa angrily confronted the lawyers and his in-laws, and forced bitter disputes over the value of the lands and the house that dragged on for months and years. This chronic distrust offended the other heirs, making them pale with anger. But Papa always insisted that others were not behaving responsibly and were trying to deceive him. Miserly and accusatory, he reversed decisions, turned over things that were already settled, and walked out on meetings. One night, Uncle Herculano, the inventor, came to our house; they started to insult each other, exchanging threats, and ended up challenging each other to step outside to reckon with each other. Mama started screaming to the neighbors for help, very afraid for him and the children. But people around us had long ago tuned out the noise of the shouts and wails coming from our house. So my father stood up, fuming, his back up like a dog's, facing that wolf of Alsácia who was the inventor Herculano. They tackled each other, butting each other like bulls, banging their backs against the doors in the middle of the house, rolling around in the hall, and that's when I noticed that Uncle Herculano was almost lifting him bodily into the air and had him by the neck. My father struggled against the steely grip of those fingers. He tried to knee him in the groin and couldn't do it; then he raised his hands to Uncle's throat and dug his nails into his gullet. The inventor let out a fearful bellow and tried to shake my father who was stuck to him like a wasp. He was so big, but he couldn't find a way to free himself. Both of them, stuck to each other, barreled into the bedroom like dogs and fell on the bed, then rolled over the wooden floor. Pictures fell down, night tables were toppled, the flower pots on stands were knocked, and even the chamber pots came rattling down with the sound of cans falling. Then Mama pulled us all into the street and made us yell:

"Help, they're fighting! Help, they're fighting! Help, they're fighting!"

The neighbors from up the street and down the street came. The men returning from their stores who were about to go home to bed, came. They filled the house with their opinions, some siding with my father because he was in his own home, under his own roof. Others argued over who had won or lost the fight and examined the destruction. The inventor's face was all scratched up, his nose was bleeding, and his shirt was torn to ribbons. A well-aimed punch had given him a purple runny eye. Sitting on the bed and restrained by two men, my father sucked in air, very pale, drooling over himself and saying in a panting voice that he was going to kill that dog. The first chance he got he'd clobber him over the head and finish off those damned crazy inventions. The other gave a twisted little victory smile until he was dragged out to the street by those who advised him to go home. The next day everyone came up to us on the street and in the fields, wanting to hear the story again to then pass it along from mouth to mouth, each time more distorted by the new versions embellished by fantasy and imagination. They laughed behind our backs, feeling vindicated by the hands of the inventor; after all, they said, that was what my father needed, someone to confront him, bust his face and shake him around in the air like a rattle . . .

I began to feel divided. One part of me said yes, disagreement between heirs really did quiet down, and it well could have been that the punches of the inventor had tamed his bad temper. The other side of me was in turmoil, and I found myself taking his side. Everyone was laughing at us and at me in particular, because I was the oldest son. But I swore then, the day would come when I'd be the strong man in the house, or even on this earth, and I wouldn't allow anyone else to make fun of the old man. I swore to wage war and settle accounts with the thieves who stole our fruit, the filchers who stole into our yard at night, fed the dog a piece of hard bread, and stole corn from the bin. My father, who was a light sleeper, heard the rustling, grabbed the scythe, and ran after a burlap shadow that flew down the hills, but he always came back empty-handed. In a certain way on those nights of chicken thieves, I was full of pity for the old man, even though I didn't want to say so.

The first time I confronted him man-to-man, he had lost the courage to beat me. Respect continued to forbid me from touching him, and I suppose that I would not have done it under any circumstances. My wrists had suddenly become thick and I had grown to a height of a meter eighty-eight, and I was sorely tempted. I had won all the bets playing strong-arm and the contests to lift weights and loads. I had wrestled the heifers in the pasture, holding them by the horns and forcing them to lie down on the ground. Even so, I wasn't certain that I had the will to challenge him.

It was around that time that I announced my first girlfriend. The girl was what you could call a poor soul; she wasn't ugly and she wasn't pretty, the daughter of a respectable family that had the small defect of being poor. The family had a gaggle of kids, and they lived in a dark house, with a beaten earth floor and a thatched roof.

"So that's how it's going to be, my dear man!" my father immediately harangued me. "You'll marry a poor girl, who will come and chew on everything I have built with so much sweat to leave to my children? Either get rid of her or I'll disinherit you in a flash so you'll learn not to fall for the first woman you see . . ."

He started to make me work until all hours of the night so I wouldn't have the slightest chance of meeting her. He gave me so much work and doled out so much shit that I became furious, and I tried to prove to him that he'd either have to leave me alone or I'd go for the girl and we'd go as far away as we could. To prove to him that I was in control of my life I stopped listening to him give me work orders. I said goodnight after dinner regardless of what he said I had to do or should do the next day. I took the responsibility for certain tasks on myself: the selling of the heifers, the purchase of hay *and so on* . . . Then, he opened his sad old eyes, lowered his head without a word, and went to bed. Moral of the story: I stopped living under his command, but my girlfriend broke up our engagement. She had heard of my parents' opposition and decided herself to break up. I was left worse off than bereft. I was orphaned. A widower, an orphan, and out of luck. From then on, every time the poor little girls turned away their faces and told me to ask my father first, I became blind with fury, as if there were ants in my blood and holes in my heart...

I can't count the times when I found myself miserable because of these disappointments in love. Deep down, I wasn't better than a lonely stray dog, because my father poisoned everything in my path. On cloudy days, I got up with a bad taste in my mouth and the desire to argue with everyone and everything. I began to leave for work the way you go to war. The day we harvested beets in the Moio district, there were two other day laborers with us. It was heavy work, without doubt, but nothing that could frighten anyone with two arms and a good back. My father and I went ahead pulling up the plants and trimming the beets. Behind us, Mama and my sisters collected the harvest into the baskets. The men carried the yield to the road, so the factory truck would take them the next day to the City. Those two rascals were getting on my nerves. They were very slow and talkative, eager for the time to go by. They were good for nothing; bent over from the weight of half a basket of beets, they called out for someone to help them lift the cargo up on to their backs. Suddenly I saw red; I brandished the pruning hook in their faces and said I'd teach them to get serious and to be more conscientious with the people who were paying their wages. I filled the basket to the brim, and stuffed in a few more, packing them tightly. That's how I wanted to see them, fast on their feet, because it was going to rain soon and nightfall wasn't far off! They shrank away like sewer rats, saying that no man in that municipality would have the strength to lift that horse's load. I must have been half blind with rage; I put one hand on top and the other on the bottom of the basket, and with one heave, set it on my shoulders. One hundred and some kilos on my back, and they stood there with their hands on their hips as if witnessing a miracle. My father started to harass me from a distance; he was screaming at me that I was going to break my back and be worthless for the rest of my life. No, I wouldn't! Everyone should be aware by now that I was already the strongest man in Rozário. I could lift tree trunks that not even four men could load on the ox carts, and that was an everyday thing. And in the first fight that I found myself involved in because of him, I proved forever that I was not and would never again be afraid of anybody: here in Toronto, and even later in Vancouver, where we moved in our third year in Canada.

It happened that one day my father came full of complaints, dishing out some of the humiliation he had been subjected to on that morning. He had gone to Moio very early to drive the sheep to a new pasture and pick white figs. When he got there, one of the Dimas brothers, those idiots, was up in the fig tree, happy as a lark. When he was reprimanded and chased away, he started to laugh and to make fun of the old man. He stuffed figs in his pockets, broke branches on purpose, and farted; he was about to make target practice of throwing green figs — still full of milk — at my father's head; they say that they give you ring worm in your scalp if you scratch it. The old man returned with wounded eyes, deadly angry and with hurt pride. This heated up my blood, more so because those damned people, who belonged to the Dimas clan, were terrorizing the municipality with fights, robbery, and evil pranks. Joined at the hip, they were always in collusion with each other. If one was in trouble, the others would come to the rescue, armed to the teeth. And they laughed diabolically when they took revenge on us and everyone else, without taking into account the situation or the weakness of their victims.

That night, after taking care of the cows and eating dinner, saying nothing to my father, I went to Furtado's store. By some miracle, the Dimas boys were there. They spent their afternoons there drinking cachaça and messing with anyone who was minding their own business. If you didn't want to be annoyed and get into trouble and make a ruckus, the best idea was really to go another way and not look up. So I went in, had my glass of wine, and started to feel my blood boil. There was going to be a procession and a high mass. The Dimas boys had split up into the two rooms of the store. The youngest and the oldest were playing a game of whisk with two other men. The other three were talking endlessly about cows, lands, and sponsorship letters to go to Canada, because around here we didn't talk about anything else. I asked for another glass of wine and sat down at the table where they were playing cards. Then I asked the youngest of the Dimas if he hadn't by any chance brought along a few ripe figs so I could eat them with my wine; it had come to my ears that lately the boy entertained himself by robbing figs, breaking branches, and doing target practice on poor old men who didn't have the strength or the stamina for a good fight. Then the two of them looked at each other, very maliciously, realizing right away where I wanted to go. The first who made a motion to get up to call the others got a punch in the forehead and almost flew backward to the wall. The second picked up a bench, lifted it a meter from the ground, but he left his stomach unguarded and went rolling, with a punch, on the floor full of spit and cigarette butts, turning very yellow and retching. That was enough for an inferno of voices to rise around me, everyone getting out and running to the street. Others, spoiling for a show, took sides or started to hiss at us, the way you do with dogs: "Psst! Psst!" Poor Furtado asked me calmly not to destroy his business and finish off the store. When the three Dimases approached from the other side, one of them had a crossbar in his hand and tried to pin me to the wall.

"Watch out, little guy, because I'll tame you too," I said.

Instead of shrinking back, as he perhaps expected, I jumped forward and disoriented him. That was enough for the bar to miss my head and fall from the counter. Never in my life had it felt so good to plant my fist on his little porcine nose and then to grab him by the collar of his jacket, stand him up, drag him to the road, and flatten him with a knee jab to the stomach. As for the other two, I grabbed them both by the hair and knocked their heads together like two pumpkins. And I landed so many punches on those noses, sir, that I felt that I'd settled the score for good. It took six men to pull me off that gang, I swear. The shitty mess my life was in at that time was full of violence and taking justice in my own hands; I didn't even know against whom or what I was avenging myself, whether it was my childhood, or my father's hands, his yelling, and his bad nature. Because of my own stupidity, my chest was bursting with hate against the world. I had turned myself into a mass of muscles through hard labor, eating like an ox, and running like a horse. I needed to give this strength a direction and purpose. Rejected by the girls my own age, without a single friend, I was forced to take a big jump to the edge of the abyss. I landed feet-first into a bottomless pit. No sponsorship letter ever came from Canada, contrary to what I had always thought would happen. If I wanted to get off the Island, I'd have to swim, who knows where and in which direction. Some had the luck to join the military in Lisbon and they would come back singing about the marvels of the lands they had visited. Nuno and Amélia had found another future, and they came less and less frequently. Jorge, because I was of draft age, was being groomed to begin my cavalry all over again: the same tears, the terrible meanness of my father, and the martyrdom of being young and so hopeless. What's more, he was small and full of aversions, like Nuno had been, and too weak to squeeze a cow teat. In a flash everything passed before my eyes again. Jorge had had the bad luck of being born long after me, in a time that wasn't mine, and on top of this he was so weak and so white that he seemed to be made of glass. These were things my father didn't forgive his children. As he got older, everything turned sour on him: his stomach, his guts, and his tongue. Everything and nothing turned into an altercation. He avoided arguing with me for reasons I've already told you, but then he took it out on the younger ones. My poor sisters didn't know where to hide when he approached, as frightened as sheep at the sight of a dog. He made them do heavier and heavier work; he shamed them with his shouts and insults and made them cry with repugnance. Some of them were at the age to have their first boyfriend, an age when women stopped working on the land and went home to embroider their trousseau and sing. They dreamed of that day with the happiness of the other girls their age; in the morning, just like the others did, they would open the blinds of their bedrooms, water the flowers, and dust or make the beds; they would sing morning songs. That day kept receding farther away from their reach; I was going to the army, Nuno and Amélia were still absent in Lisbon and there was no news from them, Jorge wouldn't grow up and become a man to take care of the farming and milking the cows . . .

I felt a cramp in the pit of my stomach, just thinking that the poor boy would soon inherit the hell and the sea of excommunication that I was leaving behind. My father had begun to train him in everything. He took him along to the cows, taught him to pull by his wrists to take the milk from the cows, to put the cinch, the packsaddle, and the cans on the beast. When he didn't pay attention, lacked the strength, or started to cry, my father would become irate and shove him, or pull his sideburns. "You sack of shit, God forgive me," he muttered between his teeth, with his eyes wide open and shining like beacons. I could barely restrain myself from putting myself between the two of them and telling my father to cut it out, feeling like giving him two or three hard punches in the ear. From a distance, Jorge's eyes called to me for help. They looked at me through tears and begged me to save him from this affliction, but I walked away so I wouldn't see or hear anything. It was still early, time was continuing to mature inside me.

One day, high up on the mountain, in the Salazar pastures, I ran into Jorge and my father going after a frightened heifer who had seemed to evaporate in the middle of the fog. The little boy circled him on one side, my father on the other, and the dog was following it too. Papa was shouting, Jorge was crying with terror at the crazy cow that was pointing its horns and going off trail.

I was still far behind them, but I saw everything was repeating itself again, like it had happened a long time ago, when I was Jorge's size and age and was suffering as he was now. My father became blind with rage again and started to blame him for all the evils in the world. When I saw him grab the steel chain and move toward him, I started to run and told myself I was going to commit a sacrilege. Papa would have to deal with me. The first lash on the legs toppled him on the ground, and I heard his mortal cries from where I was in the distance. I ran through the pastures, jumping walls and hedges, until they were finally just two hundred meters away from me. I don't know what strange madness had taken over that man, because I suddenly had the sensation of confronting an assassin. He had aged a lot, he had certainly lost much of his manly strength, but he had become a hysterical, unbearable human being. Mama already was saying the same thing, alluding to his irrational, uncontrolled temper. This time, he had crossed the line. He was about to pick up Jorge, throw him in the air, and let him drop. The body, when it landed on the ground of wet foliage, produced the sound of things falling into a bog. It was easy for me to conclude that he was taking out his revenge on the boy for his lack of authority over me, Nuno's escape, his sexual impotency, and the demands of the young girls to be allowed to marry.

I pulled Jorge away from him, held his arms and again had the clear sensation of being in front of a mad man. And I swear: it was the only time in my life I was about to hit him. If he hadn't been prudent, I would certainly have landed my fist on him. If I had, I would have put all my strength into that arm, resurrecting all those years, from the time when even before I was of school age, I began to walk behind him, under his orders, his blows on the middle of my back. With the desire behind that energy, I really don't know if I wouldn't break his back. Now, sir, it makes me want to cry, just thinking about how my shitty life got me into that extreme situation. I don't even know if I could ever be forgiven after this. I picked up Jorge, wiped his tears, and pointed him to the far end of the Island.

"Go home, little brother. If our father lays another finger on you he'll have to deal with me!"

There was no longer room for the two of us on this Island. The day would come — and this is the worst curse — that I wouldn't be capable of containing the strength and rebellion in my blood. For this reason, when the draft lottery came up, I volunteered. Portugal was at war with Africa. The Americans were at war with Vietnam. I was at war with myself and with him. When I informed him of my decision, he opened his eyes wide, shrank into himself, and said nothing. Finally he shrugged his shoulders with resignation, started coughing nervously, and went out into the night. One of the times that I was on leave, I came back to another disgrace. A delinquent from our neighborhood had tried to molest my sister Linda, as I've already told you. Finding her alone at home, he pretended to come to borrow an ax and tried to fondle her breasts. I ran to knock on his door, I pushed him out to the road, and I left him lying in the ditch with three broken teeth.

When I returned to the barracks, I found a complaint waiting for me. According to the papers they served me, I soon realized the commander couldn't give a shit about Linda's honor or shame. He wrote an order in a doctor's crabbed handwriting to send me to the war in Guinea as punishment. Then a boat came along full of troops from Lisbon, and along with many other Azoreans, I boarded, got seasick, and walked off into the worst of the war, the crater of the volcano. I was there to replace a soldier who had died in combat, but I didn't have the slightest intention of dying. I always said I'd return alive, and I'd split open with my own nails the man who had insulted my sister and sent me to this hellhole.

Hunted like an animal and incorporated into a band of ex-convicts, I learned to be a wolf among wolves and to howl as much or more than they did. In war I didn't do any more than what they had taught me: I practiced hate. Authorized to exercise it, I clamped the bit in my teeth and took another leap forward. With a machine gun, a knife, or a grenade it was, "It's about killing, Moniz! Just about killing!" the captain would say, clapping me on the shoulder. I just continued to follow the call of that old and new hatred, the arms, the prisoners in the bush, the suspect houses in the middle of the jungle, and the illusion of assassins or heroes who don't have scruples or reason to kill.

Look at my hands now, sir. The whole war went through them. You can't possibly imagine the nausea, the terror, the danger, and the anxiety, a time without end and the frozen hours of those days of blood. I will never be able to reconstruct the terrible glee of our crimes, or the taste of that other wine, or the drunken sprees, the fires in the huts, or the delirium of the bombs, or the risk of the machine guns — much less the strange and unbearable silence of the dead. They were big black men lying on the ground with their heads blown open. And old people who would run burning like torches from their straw houses. Children would be trampled under boots, women slit open with knives in cold blood — all because we were on the side of the "good guys" against the "bad guys" and we were beautiful, powerful, and invincible...

I don't have one white memory of this time. If I had imagined you, sir, would come here to listen to me, I might have made an effort, and it wouldn't be so hard to relive this again. But since my life really should be forgotten, I limit myself to opening my hands in front of you and asking if you can see if the curse of the war passed or didn't pass through them. And what can I do with them, in this part of the world and in the time left for to me to live?

To this not I, not you, or anybody, I'm sure, can give the answer. As for the rest, I have no illusions. I ask just to ask — do you believe me?

BOOK TWO

Third Person Singular

I

When he looked closely at the portraits, Nuno thought the face of the provincial looked like a death mask; his ugliness was to a certain extent caused by his stern expression. It was much more severe, in any case, than the pictures that had been placed everywhere since the provincial had been appointed to his post. His little pigeon head was prominently displayed in places of silence and vigil, as well as on the walls next to the image of the Crucified One or the morose visage of the founder of the seminary. The pictures were in the study halls, the cafeteria, and in the two long attic lofts, which were used as a dormitory; there were rows of beds under small windows, night tables, and chests secured with padlocks. The provincial's picture was placed under two martyrs, and his expression was opaque, almost sweet. His mother-of-pearl complexion, very much of this world, was neither sad nor saintly, but he didn't look like a real person either. We only knew that God had chosen him and that his life had already been chronicled by the masters of philosophy.

Summoned to his presence, Nuno Miguel noticed that his features, in spite of being glorified in the portraits, were lacking almost everything: youthfulness, a spark in the eyes, wonder, warm-bloodedness, and presence. The teeth were small and sharp. The gums were thick and prominent. The mechanical way his smile buckled his face and divided it into a livid grimace, like that of a corpse, didn't distract the eye from the honeycomb of pockmarks on his face. In the craters of that wrinkled, flaking parchment was frozen, like a clot, a purple boil. But even that sign of stagnation was habitually erased from the daguerreotypes.

A small and very light boneless arm tried in vain to embrace him by the shoulders. Nuno recoiled at the contact of the little clammy hand. He felt it touch his neck and understood that his time had come. But what did that mean? Normally, when a senior priest pressed against the body of a seminarian, and if he did it with such unexpected intimacy, it could only mean expulsion, or worse: he had come to preach insulting sermons to him, the kind that mortify the body and leave the soul fouled in the limbo of death.

His time had come smoothly, confusingly, and completely unexpectedly. It would no longer be important to think that there was a difference between the real face and the very light, false, and useless coloring of his portraits. From this time on, this man who had until then been supernatural, whose existence was confused with the saints' prayer cards, the figure of the diocesan bishop, and the roseate marble bust of the Pope, would always be just a spirit who had come from far away, from unknown altars, to change his future.

It was forbidden to go to his presence. The rector of the seminary took it upon himself to lead him to the other side of the fence that separated the big seminary house from the three low, long wings, in the shape of a fork that comprised the convent. Only the novices and philosophers, and also the few who were already studying theology, were privy to the rare appearances of the provincial. The head priest even dissuaded the younger friars to go to him directly to confess their sins. This was because the monks were bent, impetuous creatures, and they took time to invest in their misery and pain, the great torment of sinners. Nuno Miguel had let himself be impressed, once, at hearing from the mouth of Brother Pio the most heartfelt confession of faith in God. One late afternoon he saw him arrive with a hoe on his shoulder, exhausted from work in the fields and covered with dirt. Brother Pio stopped to listen to the sarcastic exchanges of the older seminarians, put the hoe on the ground, tried to straighten his back and opened his tearful eyes wide. He raised a hand in the direction of those astonished heretics, held it shaking over their heads, baring himself to their ridicule — and that was when Nuno retained forever in his memory the most terrible statement he had ever heard:

"Brothers, look at me in the eye and listen to what I have to say. If any one of you proves that God doesn't exist I will certainly be the most unfortunate man in the world!"

The provincial had been forewarned of his visit on that early afternoon, a "pureblood" from the islands — and not a model of pliable virtue that his potter's hands could mold quickly, and so on that very day they had decided to expel him. The very wise rector had reported to him in detail the history of the boy's behavior. He was notorious for taking long detours before getting to the point. Experience had taught him that expulsions of the older seminarians require an almost consular wisdom. The secret was in modulating the voice to a suitably soft but persuasive tone, capable of defusing these dark moments. He behaved like a dancing bird, circling his fish in a game of hypnosis and seduction. When it was sleeping, he'd pick it up in his beak and fly off with his stunned prey.

He started by talking about the Azores and his last pastoral visit there. There he had cast his apostolic net to fish in the shoals of religious vocation. And no, he wasn't very successful, no sir. He said it with pain wrapped in the velvet of his voice, lost in the memories of the patient courage of that pilgrimage, as if he were imparting an intimate secret. Nuno was so close to his mouth that he smelled his intense breath, caught the treacherous gaze, and once again was threatened with the return to the desolation of his muddy home. It was precisely the mention of that trip to the Azores that put Nuno on the alert.

II

The moment that the arm reached around his neck, and the voice became even softer, and His Reverence changed tone "to talk about serious things," the boneless arm around his shoulders felt like a snake. Almost immediately the pressure of the arm pulled him a little closer, forcing him to lean against the priest. He couldn't escape the contact, the heat of those soft flanks. He felt his bones adjusting to the pressure of the fat body of the priest. With a shiver, he suddenly remembered the other one, that pink little priest who lured startled young boys with red faces from their first pimples to his room; he offered them cigarettes, smiled as he unzipped their flies and, still smiling, led them to the delirium of masturbation. He never noticed the strange complicity of the cigarettes with the tremulous light of the oil lamps, nor had he ever guessed there was a relationship between the mysteries of the mass and the profane god of that pink, smiling priest.

Then it all happened very fast. The voice of the provincial gained strength, still magnanimous, softly chastising him. At first he spoke at length about hypothetical behaviors, where it wasn't possible to discern either wrongdoing or missteps that could be corrected. A kind of verbal fascination calmed him, under the protection of the arm and the contact of that man's body. He had never been so close to him, and had always imagined him as a hidden, beautiful, and indescribable god in the shadows and on the throne of the

Mother House in Lisbon. He was aware nevertheless that the provincial was powerful, elect, and distant, but not as decadently ugly, or as dark as the disgrace that he had come to denounce. Every time Nuno had the occasion to see him at close range, the provincial had always been transformed into a liturgical figure; he wore the sacred vestments, performed the Easter rites, or came to perform the closing ceremonies of the annual retreat of the two communities. On those occasions it had just occurred to him that perhaps everything was wrong: the bird body disappeared inside the excessively large vestments; his purple face became shinier and his crow's voice was strident. He emerged from the sacristy as if he had arrived from the other side of the earth. Lacking the haughty dignity of the patriarchs, he swayed inside the costumes of the Mass. In Nuno's opinion, he didn't deserve to be called "Father" by the common priests, just as he didn't deserve the bows and prostrations of the two wings of habits when he walked to the altar and became the ship, the rudder, the water, and the angel who announced the resurrection of Christ. Nuno Miguel saw him from a distance, his hands raised and with his sliding gait, with his air of a false bishop — and that was when the Gregorian chants of the friars once again lent him the supernatural air of the portraits. It smelled of the incense in the thuribles, the mute flames of the Paschal candles. And his hands, holding the ciborium, seemed majestic. Then the voice little given to oratory started to resound in the arches of that small convent church. The sermons were hardly divine, one could say, and in general terrible, a harangue that frightened, offended, and brought to tears the youngest seminarians. The only positive thing about those visits was the improvement in the lunch menu and the reward of an extra hour of recess after the spiritual retreat.

Because he rarely appeared, he took advantage of the entire time of these pilgrimages to demand more discipline and to alter all the rules and schedules. On his surprise visits at the seminaries and convents of the province, he carefully examined the accounts, taught theology classes, and stayed long enough to give confession to the senior priests. They said that his pastoral journeys, enduring the cold and running the risks of discomfort in the provinces, were not only marginal to his mission but they didn't appeal to him at all. What he really liked to do was to go to Rome to talk with the Pope, to cross the peninsular sky in the planes that took him to Madrid and Salamanca, or to earn the long monthly audiences of His Eminence, the Cardinal Patriarch of Lisbon. Aside from this, he came only as an exception, called by the rector or the head priest; he personally reprimanded errant priests, defrocked some, excommunicated or pointed the pathways of the "world" to a few, who in his absence had interpreted for their own profit not the teachings, but the error and excesses of their philosophy . . .

Nuno Miguel didn't know right away what was more shocking — whether the sudden revelation of his disgrace and the conviction behind the words of the provincial, or the fact that those accusations left him speechless and irremediably lost. The voice had changed again, erasing the moderate tone of the beginning of the conversation. From one instant to the next, the space was filled with a silence that darkened Nuno's senses. Then he allowed the last of his hopes to resurface. It could be that His Reverence had not even come there to expel him. It happened that the provincial not only took care of those extreme cases but also of those of conscience; he enlightened confused spirits, admonished the sheep that had strayed, and prescribed penitence to the finalists and the novices. Those who wanted to accelerate their vows of chastity and poverty also came into his presence. The deacons experiencing a crisis of faith asked for transfers to other communities. The new priests, wanting to have other experiences, petitioned to let them discover how the miners and workers lived. Some even left for the African wars as chaplains; others went on to specialize in canonical law. Perhaps what awaited him was a simple change of direction — because Nuno Miguel was not prepared to be expelled. He had not definitively decided if he wanted to follow the path of the "world" or to accept that his life would be carried out inside the walls of the monastery. At a minimum, he thought he would enter the monastery, change his name, and be invested with the habit of the Order. He was also seduced by the mystery of the thick books, written in Latin and containing great treatises of philosophy. To be thrown out into the "world" was as frightening as sinking in a ship on the high seas: aside from being as immense and turbulent as the ocean, the "world" was a kind of foreign country where any seminary student would be singled out. Once there, he would always be an outcast and a weakling. He would never be a man who had the worldly experience and knowledge of others.

"Such a state of spirit," he thought, "hurts deeply. It hurts more than a crisis of faith and mindless despair. This is called anguish, these bas-reliefs of time, the terrestrial curves in which the great mountain range of my future is beginning to take shape."

His life was sentenced to change direction. For this reason Nuno Miguel looked beyond the heights of the pine forest and tried to listen, for the first time in his life, to the distant roar of the "world" that must exist somewhere, on the other side of the forests, the valleys, and the walls. For years he had taken refuge in the seminary and was protected by the natural wall of the strange landscapes, forbidden to dream about them or to know them. Even when he was taken to the sea, he had always made the crossing at night, so that everything would continue to frighten his religious spirit; the great trees silhouetted in the darkness, the bustle of the cities at dawn, the departure of the boats, always very early, in the direction of the Azores. The Order was always as scrupulous to hide this "world" as they were in revealing the knowledge of the life of God. No seminarian knew what the features, the expression in the eyes, or the energy of the fingers of the God of contemplation and grace were to be able to move the "world" of others.

"Was I denounced," he thought "caught in flagrante for thinking?" as soon as he heard the news of his expulsion.

His moments of weakness, he recalled, were on his knees, at the confessional, and into the ears of the rector. He had never revealed any deep secrets to anyone, fearing being denounced by the seminarians that spied on the behavior of suspect individuals. He had said to his spiritual mentor that the worst thing about God is when he possesses a man who is in agony. In a state of agony, God is a corrosive larva; it churns the stomach of his hosts, it sucks one by one, all of his bones, it's a rodent. But this was said in a moment of despair, when he was asking for advice about the senselessness of an existence imprisoned inside the walls of a seminary.

"Doubts, my son, crises of faith, hours of anguish," answered the little voice of his confessor through the grate, "who doesn't have them? The priests, the bishop, even the Pope have them. Only weak spirits don't ever admit to the lucidity of doubt. Go in peace."

So, he'd been caught in flagrante delicto for thinking. Seventeen and a half years saying the Creed in the secrets of the confessional dissolved suddenly in the certainty of that moment when he would be taken to the presence of the seminarians by the hand of the rector. This habitually occurred in an almost theatrical form. The bell ringer convened everyone to the assembly hall, and the seminarians ran to sit on the benches, on the windowsills with their vaulted shapes; they even occupied the stairways to the classrooms or leaned on the railings. That was their preferred theater. Normally the rector fiercely gripped the arm of the condemned one. The other hand concealed in the sleeve of his habit a cedar paddle with little holes in it. He assumed in full the function of the hangman that accompanies the last steps of the condemned; fear made the eyes and shoulders of the lonely boy tremble — the one who had the little luck of writing indecorous words on the walls or on the bottom of plates. It was a merely physical fear, dissolved in the time and memory of an inquisitorial church. The courage and glee of having sinned was pooling behind his eyes, in the deep axis of a new passion that would change into hate against the harshness of the new inquisitors. A dog howled with pain from the mouth of the expelled — a twisted dog was excommunicated from the presence of the mute seminarians.

None of this happened to Nuno. The provincial asked him to remain calm; he would personally inform the other students of his expulsion. When Nuno mentioned that he would like to say good-bye to his friends, the priest nodded his sad pigeon head and responded that it was never allowed, in a religious community, to choose "friends" because this meant discriminating between brothers. Besides this the presence of the expelled suggested the parable of the tumor that can invade and create disease in the collective body. If he wanted to maintain one or two of these relations, he should do it discreetly by letter. Nuno Miguel knew that the letters came and went after being opened and censored by the seminary prefects. He had lived in these six and a half years of seminary with crossed out sentences, without the right to privacy, and with words underlined in red. Thought was stripped naked in the inverse order of the other forbidden nudity in those walls; the condemned body, the damned desire of the flesh, the crime and punishment of that sinful instinct. Whoever wanted to become a priest should, first of all, forget his own body. The body was a vice; the spirit, a virtue — so that sainthood was acquired in this strenuous physical fight, often obscure, but always in awareness of the infinite . . .

For a moment the fierce smile of the provincial seemed to savor the effect of the surprise that had overcome the boy in the middle of recess, where both had been taking the air. Nuno's perplexity now confronted the contrite expression of his accuser. One would like to think that this face was filled with sorrow and desolation. The hated and odious clairvoyance of those hawk eyes were trained on the last phase of Nuno's religious adventure. He had alluded already to the systematic avoidance of confession and daily mass, the poor performance in his studies, and his bad relationship with superiors.

"Above all," he added, "we have been of the opinion that your habit of isolating yourself from others is destructive. You have formed suspect little groups around yourself. The fact that you write poetry is an obvious affront to the priesthood. If only you had some talent, and had thought to exalt the Faith in your poems . . ."

III

He couldn't imagine how that man, an absent stranger, could possess the vision and knowledge of what was going on inside these walled, silent kingdoms. But the sensation of being the object of this scrutiny, spied on even to the most insignificant degree, became suddenly uncomfortable because it resembled an act of public nudity. He was at the sensitive age when the spirit moves between accusation and the feeling of injustice; never again, for the rest of his life, would he possess such an ability to so profoundly distinguish the equivocal notions of Good and Evil. For that reason, he wanted to summon the only jury available to him. He believed only in the impartiality and dignity of his peers. He wanted to be taken to the presence of all those who prayed the rosary inside those walls, so they would witness the good-bye and the humiliation of one more expelled seminarian. Half of the faces might become livid with anger. The others would blush and lower their eyes. He himself, in the course of those years, would experience many times that mute alternative, blushing or paling while the rector, the spiritual leader of the month, or the student-prefect of theology opened the door of the student lounge, rolled up the sleeves of their habits and clapped their hands to ask for a silence that had been in force for a long time, a silence that would always exist and had to exist. There were those who would leave "on good terms" and those who would leave "in dishonor." In the midst of these, some had decided to "change vocation" and to return to the "world" for good. Then one could hear the buzzing of the flies in the silence of the enormous room, hear it in the empty eyes of those newly condemned to the "world." You could hear the rain dripping from the gutters, coming from the tiles high on the roof of the big building, the night of the pine forest being whipped by the wind and the distant howl of a lost dog in that windy night.

The only sign of the real world that reached there came occasionally from the trucks carrying wood or pine needles and the echo of the power saw destroying the eyes, the heart, and the hands of King Dom Dinis (*oh, flowers, oh flowers of green pines* . . .). Everything else was the simple and forbidden landscape that the seminarians thought they recognized in the trains they took at night to go on vacation or on the hygienic excursions during exam week. For most of them, abandoning the seminary meant happy train rides, forgetting the obligation of the weekly confessional and the obligatory invention of sins, and to know that never more would the daily mass at six thirty in the morning mean violating their sleep. These were heroic journeys across rosy provincial landscapes and the undoing of the fascination for the cities that had always been promised to them. They had been trained to live in the silence of the cloisters and the shelter of future monastery cells, not to take part in those rebel heroics that were taken as symbols or examples of Evil. So much so that he gave up on insisting with the provincial to take him to be judged by his peers.

Nuno Miguel had always suspected that the euphemistic phrase "change of vocation" hardly alluded to a last cockfight. It was the laconic and evasive language of religious protocol, not appropriate to the embarrassment or ferocity of new expulsions. Many times, sitting in the lounge, the cafeteria, even in Latin class (*qui, quae, quod!* — old Father Vincent repeated irately), or even in the middle of daily mass, the gauzy voice announced to all a new equinox of God with the "world." Made of gauze, cotton, or felt, the voice took advantage of the opportunity to ask everybody to pray for the brother not to lose the Faith or the practice of Good. All wore guilty expressions. But for the major infractions there was corporal punishment, before the culprits were sent to pack their bags. Homosexuality, stealing, or profanity were never spared the rector's rod. Nuno watched from the sidelines as those terrified colts were castrated. The shoulder blades of the rector started to quiver. His hair stuck to his forehead. His upper teeth clamped down on a curled tongue. He counted thirty, forty, fifty blows in each hand, he panted with exhaustion and raised his voice to say:

"Let this, young man, give you a lesson for life. And God have mercy on you, wretch!"

Precisely, God was all inside him, but in the position of a statue. It was a bull-god, voluminous and judgmental, muscular but with little or no mercy. So as not to watch the spectacle of that madness, he hid his head in his hands, plugged his ears; a repulsive, shameful sweat poured from his bones and dripped out through his fingers. Then he ran from the room, tripped in the potholes, fell in the dark, and inevitably threw up in the nearest bathroom.

Happily, he thought, my time came discreetly, diplomatically, and without fireworks. They had prepared for him another kind of violence, another river of sweat in the dark twisting paths of his childhood. A train merged into the tunnel that led from day to night, leaving behind familiar landscapes, the solid colors of the wind, a past that would live eternally inside him. Provincial Luís had told him this a little while ago, very softly and just to him, and always with that confidential arm over his shoulder. If he had found any dignity in this, he would have dropped to his knees to beg for pardon for his innocence. Of course he was guilty of being innocent, like all the other seminarians. They were guilty of having grown up, of having felt the wings of anguish spread inside them, that stupid bird of clarity. They were guilty of allowing the bird to traverse the time of their growing up and ascension. However he was not yet prepared to cry. Revulsion suppressed the initial impulse to cry. If he cried, he would condemn himself to intensifying his stress. He would not bear the shouts and insults or they would destroy him.

At this point, he still nourished the hope of bypassing adversity. With a little prudence perhaps he would obtain a commutation of his sentence. He knew that the priests were open to supplication. He wanted to confess to Provincial Luís all the sins of that innocence, and he'd do it with his hands clasped, with the imploring eye of the penitent. Moreover, it was holy week; Christ would be resurrected the next day, and that was always decisive for the good humor and spirits of the priests.

Had it not been for the third day of the annual retreat of the two communities, the playground would have been noisy and full of boys at that hour. There was a silence outside and another inside him. Flocks of old pigeons traverse the afternoon sky, that ball of sky that he knows will become part of his distant past, the bell tower, the two wings of the smaller seminary, the fork of the cloister. His memory marks the trajectory of the pigeons because his gaze follows them on their path across that space of sky that had been and in a brief time will cease to be his. He looked and said good-bye to everything because he was about to leave for the eternity of other places. The places he had known would become distant forever and forever eternal inside him. If he returned to them, it would not be a reunion, but a change that would be produced by him and inside him. Destiny would always be another thing and in other places. In spite of everything it had been good to live here all these years. His dreams had been born in these walls. He couldn't and shouldn't betray them.

A vertical good-bye, he thought, to the tall, long buildings that followed the curve in the road, behind which the world of travel and time were hidden. He bade another farewell to the convent and the yellow turrets, oxidized by the wind of the pines. The only time he had gone inside there to watch the novices don their habits, the heavy corridors of the monastery were already dead. The creaking of the doors was as austere as the Gregorian chants of the friars, like the philosophy of Socrates and the *Summa Theologica* of St. Thomas of Aquinas. The peacefulness frightened and seduced him. Like a continuous sigh, the light of the stained-glass windows colored the silence and the cloistered atmosphere. He wanted to see where the dead and the living of that monastery were hidden. He saw them from a distance, passing through the outer doors of the church on their way to captivity. They were so light and so subtle that he had the illusion of seeing them pass through the salmon-colored walls. He was duped, however, by these shadow beings that changed their names, put on a white shroud, and professed vows of poverty, chastity, and obedience. Since they usually adopted names of saints, they came to be called Brother Tiago, Brother João Baptista or Brother Paulo — and Nuno Miguel didn't ever come to understand the strange, secret, and tortuous Road of Damascus, or how it locked them in the depths of the monastery and forbade them definitively from coming out to look at the weather in their little piece of the world. The most supernatural thing, he recalled, wasn't the silence, but the voices, the chants, the mystery of very thick books full of wisdom that they passed around shyly, tucked tightly under their armpits. On the other side of the wire netting, God wore sandals, coarse mantles over his robes, with a scapular and a cowl. He was certainly a barbarous, strange God, to whom one prayed only in Latin . . .

IV

"Because worst of all," said the provincial, still trying to be delicate but preparing to get to the point after all of his circumlocutions, "was that you never knew how, or didn't want to train and overcome your distress. On the contrary;

you gave it wings, you let it fly. And it flew so high and so far away from you, my son, that it turned you into a doubter of the faith. You have even become a political subversive. I don't have the least doubt: your vocation for the priesthood is definitely lost."

"He went from the plural to the singular," Nuno noted to himself, with the same concentration as he applied to the memory of that day. A cold, dry March whitened the rose marble of the mornings with its frosts and then turned the afternoons a deep blue. The nights still fell suddenly, and they continued to be long and to sink the dormitories into a wintry, even tomblike darkness. The oil lamps, with their mortuary flames quivering in the air drafts, suspended time in this disciplined and endless season. Inside it was always winter; the months of sun were rapidly extinguished by the window shutters. Mold and mildew were a part of that permanent penumbra, where it was forbidden to ask to borrow a comb, to answer a question, or even to yawn noisily. Worse than these prohibitions were the sins of insomnia or laziness; the crimes of masturbation or nudity could only be redeemed at the confessional, if not also with physical punishment. The prefect of the week used to punish the ones who walked around naked by refusing them lunch, or putting them on bread and water for a day, or forcing on them the little whip for self-flagellation . . .

In the course of the three days of annual retreat, themes and times for meditation had been proposed to the two communities. An enclosed garden of silence and prohibition submerged that entire religious complex in the fear of God and the contemplation of the signs that had been affixed there the year before. Even the sound of the chimes and the bell had been substituted by soft handclaps and the creaking of an old water wheel. They ate in silence, walked with rosary beads in their hands and a great silent tension dragged behind it the sobbing of Gregorian chants. It would have been sweet to die in one of those days of retreat, because death had been converted into a symphonic movement. As for the rest, our own sins, in spite of being innumerable and even more monstrous than the week before, dragged us willingly to the confessional. Doing penance was moving and put us into a new state of grace. It settled our blood.

The provincial made him stop again and turn toward him. It's true he had nothing more to say. But he wanted to peer into Nuno's eyes, and dissuade him from challenging the order of expulsion. It was as if he was luring him to his preferred battleground, either to fight him or disarm him. He still had an arsenal of arguments, in case the boy dared to contradict the superior logic of that decision. The fiercest reasons he kept for the emergency of that possible misguided opposition. He often used the tactic of taming beasts whose pride had been wounded. The boy knew it and that's why he turned his eyes away from the pustules on that face and fixed them on the receding horizon. From the place he was standing he could see the signs that were peeling from the humidity of that definitive March. The sentences written on them seemed perforated by the ridges on the wall just under the bell that rang the times for meals, classes, recess, or prayers. Nuno didn't need to strain to read them from that distance. He admitted to himself that perhaps he knew by heart everything that had happened and everything that went on inside that space, where the years and the hours always had been the same. Now, however, he interpreted the deep meaning of each thing. For example the phrases: HERE YOU WILL EAT THE LORD'S BREAD. REMEMBER THOSE WHO ARE WITHOUT. Next to it, on the study hall wall, another legend recommended: SILENCE IS GODLY. STUDY, MEDITATE IN SILENCE, AND YOU WILL BE WISE AND HOLY IN THE SIGHT OF THE LORD. Inside, at that hour, during the afternoon Bible study, the world was continuously being threatened with floods and destruction by the waters. Along the breezeways they walked through during the rainy season to reach the chapel and the dormitories, and, on the very pillars that held up the night and day of that house without foundations, nailed on boards or stuck to the walls, the signs from the previous year multiplied: NO TALKING, NO TALKING, NO TALKING ... On the second day of the retreat, at the hour of morning mass, when the seminarians formed a procession of two lines to take their places, they were surprised by an implacable sign, written in blue chalk on the chapel wall: FUCK IT, EVERYTHING IS FORBIDDEN HERE!

That had cost everyone two extra hours of prayer, with the advance promise that those who had profaned the temple would be found out.

And now, startled, Nuno wants to be accused only of this minor sacrilege. If that were the case, he could still kick his way free of the noose, and believe in the pardon of the king. But it wasn't worth clinging to that illusion; he had been sentenced and soon he would feel the final blow. If he had not written it, he had at least been a moral accomplice of that nocturnal phrase, as he had been on other useless and anonymous pranks. And the heavy thought struck him, for now and forever, that everything in his whole life had already been forbidden, from the act of being born to the moment when he was becoming an outcast from that little stagnant world between the walls. The other world entered there in a filtered and distorted manner, without the news of censored letters or the echo of its tiniest daily detail. There were also the behavior police, and the final grade at the end of each quarter. Everything was forbidden: filthy money and care packages from home — and happiness, and the visits of the nuns who might present a glimpse of generous breasts. And books not catalogued by the librarian, and radios, and cigarettes, and sports magazines, and cries that were not always possible to suffocate, and saying there was just one month to go until Easter holidays, and writing poetry, and taking pictures to send to your parents, and saying My homeland, My house, and also not liking the stew of bread with boiled fish served at Monday lunch, and saying I'm hungry, and saying Fuck, and other and other of any one of a list of small crimes: masturbation, possession of magazines with very sweet, half open women's mouths, stealing fruit from the orchard, forgetting the black tie to go to Mass, and not knowing the declensions of *rosa-rosae, templum-templi, corpus-corporis,* and having a mustache and beard before others of the same age, and above all thinking out loud and saying what you were just thinking out loud.

In the most intimate recesses of his being, he can't, he shouldn't reject the evidence. God is dead. He is just a fetus decomposing in the nest of his guts. Realizing this, even though it doesn't surprise him, leaves him in a new state of excitement. It was precisely with this obvious yet invisible death that the new inquisition was already punishing in his body. But said in this way, by the less than enlightened voice of the provincial, it is like a physical aggression. A punch by that little purple hand would certainly not leave as devastating an effect on the walls of his stomach. He wanted to shout just about anything, raising his voice and becoming physical in his rebellion. Just as in his dreams, it was like being in a nightmare; he wanted to run away from there and not feel the ground under his feet; he tried to speak and found that his tongue was stuck to the roof of his mouth, just like butterflies when they are impaled by a wire and submersed in jars of formaldehyde. Or it was like fish fighting uncertainly with the terrible harpoon tip of the hooks. It was, however, the time of rhetoric, the time of the iron arm of the obstinate, powerful rule of the old priests, and he knew that the little hand of Provincial Luís had the power to expel him not just from the real world, but from the invisible reality of the seminary. At a minimum, now that everything was definitive, he would try to have his expulsion announced to the others with a smile and not in between clenched teeth. Worse than the twilight, he knew, was the curse of the Order. With a little luck and a dose of humility, perhaps he could come to benefit from the second protection of his metallic arm, out there in the world where he would be exiled. There was no difference between dealing with a priest of the Order and calming a frightened horse. It was all a question of softness of touch — or the whip.

"It surprises me, it hurts me, Father Luís, sir," I said when I could compose myself after the shock, the sweat that was starting to run down my back, my neck, even the corners of my mouth — "that you have come to such a sudden decision, without warning. I thought your reverence would agree to hear me, to understand my reasons. I suppose that it's even my right . . ."

He could see perfectly well that his little hawk eyes opened in astonishment, showing something between surprise and indignation. Upset again, he felt his knees begin to tremble, as did his voice, his brow, and his fingers. It would cost him a great deal to remain submissive and humble, once again reverent and small, in front of a man who was as tiny and bent as only grandparents are. This man had suddenly started to grow to an almost unprecedented height. Then, from on high, a disdainful smile flowered from that body. The face became again somber and deathlike, and Nuno understood he had gone too far. He wouldn't be able to hold out another minute before letting out his hate. For years he had limited himself to domesticating the dog of hate. He knew that if he let it out of the kennel, that dog would gain inside him the force and fury of a wolf.

"I don't have to know why," the provincial retorted standing on tiptoe. His heels rocked back and forth, lifting and lowering his body as if moved by an imaginary pulley. At that point Nuno couldn't avoid a malicious thought: he would see the priest take flight, turn into a dove and fly to heaven. God would receive him distractedly. He would put him in one of the innumerous pockets or let him slip into the folds of His magnificent blue robes. He would do it with disdain, because God's biggest problem was that the world had too many priests like this: tiny, blind, and temperamental. "It shouldn't be news to you that we've had you under observation for a long time. It's been a matter of days, months, or even years . . . And don't forget: where men can't see, God always has his two immense, supernatural eyes looking down on them!"

"I won't deny, Father Luís, sir, that I'm a little distressed and in need of spiritual help. I may be in disarray with my share of moments of crisis . . . but about losing my calling? The Order is usually tolerant; it has allowed others to always say the last word in these cases of conscious. So what about me, Father Luís?"

I could have sworn that his eyes lost the brilliance of the hawk and started to pale. I couldn't have offended him, in spite of everything. He was just flailing at the beginning of his first shipwreck on land. It was as if he was becoming tangled in the net of a new and still unknown nakedness. His reverence stopped hopping about, the steps of a mole, the instinct of a bird that had alighted on the authority of the minuscule body.

"So you'd like another chance, is that it?" he brayed, in a shout that didn't disguise a fit of anger. "One more little chance, and there you'd be doing it again. You'd make fools of us, who after all these years of study gave you a good bed and the best food, and perhaps some manners! Tell me this boy, how many times have we pardoned your lack of humility, the heretic poetry, and crises of faith? Go on, tell me!"

His face swelled with blood. Humiliation spiraled upward into the center of his face, suffocated by a rush of tears. He waited for the impulse to cry to pass. He was at the mercy of that man; destiny was nothing more than an intense moment, the panicked agony of the dying. If he jabbed him again with a simple expression of censure, he'd be summarily executed. He knew the finger was on the trigger; Father Luís would not hesitate to call the kitchen servants or the monks. If he whistled, those dogs would come running to the master, who would order them to throw Nuno's body, spirit, and his miserable clothing to the other side of the walls. For this reason, even today, with the distance of so many years, he can't explain anything of what happened back then. A type of nervous breakdown, perhaps, and an evil wind made him start to scream. The hate of that day took him hastily to a dark train station. The train made all of his bones rattle in the expectation of misty landscapes at the end of which would start to emerge the shapes of tunnels, churches, and bell towers of the city of Lisbon. Lisbon happened at a quarter to midnight that night. The electric trams clanked on their iron rails. The hum of the traffic flowed in a continuous stream. The crowds at Santa Apolónia station roared under the great arches that held up the building. On the other side of the street, the boats swayed to the steady wind crossing the river. It was a translucent night, sparkling with the fatuous colors of neon signs that gave this maritime, fluvial city an unreal aspect. Like the first time he had come there, transported by the fog-shrouded boats from the Azores, he would get lost again in this city where nobody was waiting for him. The fathers had forgotten about him, and Nuno didn't know where to go or whom to seek out. He let himself fall asleep in the atrium of the station, curled up on the first empty bench, and he continued to hear the shouts and confusion that had made him lose it.

"What opportunities, Father Provincial, sir? Every time they took me to the presence of the rector it was to slap my face or humiliate me because I didn't even pay tuition for my studies and I was a poor ungrateful slob! And now your reverence comes and throws everything in my face again! I'd like to return everything to the Order: the Latin classes, the religion and morals, the hosts, the missals and the Sundays, and the grace of God for my present disgrace . . . To my rector, I'd return the slaps, the denouncements, the scolding, and intelligent insults. Believe me, your Reverence; I'd only want to have my former innocence back. I want my life back. I died from the work and the secrets, the years spent here and in the machinery, the discipline and penitence of this Order . . ."

Hands, knees, and chin all trembling before and after: in front of him and later in the atrium of the Santa Apolónia station. He had never before been so at the edge of saying everything he was thinking; the blackmail they practiced on him on the pretext of his terror at being returned to his father, year after year; the discrimination, the difference between his continuous and extenuated poverty, the son of poor people, and the baskets of fruit, the wineskins, and the turkeys offered to the reverend fathers by the parents of the rich students. Everything still has to be said, he thinks even today: the days of scorn for his strange Azorean accent, the furious disdain for the poetry of the Literary Contests, the nothing and emptiness of a daily routine that was slowly replacing innocent peace with Doubt, sleep with the insomnia of Anguish, the act of praying to real saints with the voice that got lost and became metaphysical . . .

The sons of Apostolic Action and of the Conference of Laypeople were returned to a certainly inevitable world, however they were wrapped and hidden in the cellophane of smiles and the discreet fraud of their diplomas. Golden boys, happily expelled from the seminary, carried letters of recommendation to men who then fired grey slaves and long-suffering women who had lost their beauty just to guarantee work for these privileged graduates. They were always scrupulously Catholic, their quota of devotions up to date, but eternal debtors of mysteries, miracles, and blessings to their reverences... In a moment of confidence with the older ones, the rector lifted the edge of the veil about resistance to the Dictator. He said it with vanity, swearing that he would never abandon an ex-seminarian to his fate. Did they need a home or a job? In the morning he would run to Lisbon, enter the translucent city, and God would always be where he was needed. Was the Dictator screaming orders to send people who didn't have the age or vocation to die in Africa, to fight his silent battles that were obstinately and forever inglorious? The little cart went back to the road, in the direction of the border and carried the theologians of military age; the night before, the rector had obtained the complicity or benevolence of Catholic officials and border police — the same who afterward hunted for crouching shadows and sent dogs after the simple sound of footsteps. A passport, a tranquil journey on one of the many peninsular trains — the only commitment of the ex-theologians with the Order after the journey across those supernatural frontiers was to return the habit and the breviary to a convent in Salamanca, Rome, or Paris. They unfrocked themselves quickly, stopped being shy little boys supposedly going on to continue their studies, and then they were picked up by organizations that protected political exiles. Very far away, guarded by the impenetrable shadow of the Pyrenees Mountains, the future theologians seemed like exiles at the entrance of the secret escape tunnels. They were the future. They saw it, waved at it, but the future dissolved in the grey fog that fused with the fleeting shadows, as they became forever invisible.

In the Lisbon night, Nuno's destiny became as round as a paper moon. He was in the center of it and everything had become equidistant. If he were returned to his father's house, the black nights of the Azores would again become filled with the dogs, the eternal rains, and the cries of the Atlantic shearwaters. If he stayed to inhabit the hardships of Lisbon, it wouldn't be long before he was mobilized to the African war. With that paper moon at his back, in the country of fear, in the time of the very old Dictator... Life was a twilight overtaken by belligerent dogs. He thought of all of this, while in a state of agony. The priests had again refused to come for him. Not only did they not hurry to find him a job, but also they would never risk sending him across the border. This curse would always be with him. He had come from the malignant and enigmatic shadows of the Island. His birthplace had lost him the protection of his confessors. He had also lost the forgiveness of the women who had paid for his studies — his benefactresses — gone was the voluptuous smile of the cousin the Canon, the protection of the rector who opened up borders to sentential exiles. The Lisbon night would become transformed into the countdown to being drafted to the colonial war. It would also be the time of his return to his nameless Azorean poverty, of the present and the past that was permanently etched in his memory.

Twice, in the summers that his father had refused to pay his way back to the seminary, his cousin the Canon had saved him from being retained in the Azores. In offering him the money that Nuno had gone to beg for in the company of his mother, he had warned him, smiling, that he should settle the debt not with him but through a direct commitment to the Church of God. Thus he couldn't have the slightest illusion: his cousin the Canon would never forgive his ecclesiastical treason. In the first and last letter he would ever receive from him, he read the curses, the veiled insults, and the twisted handwriting of an exasperated hand. He also read all of this in the correspondence exchanged later with the rector, who continued to excommunicate him and chastise him from afar for a long time. He read it in the last letter from the benefactresses, who said they felt betrayed and ashamed. And he read it especially in the silence of his old friends and schoolmates, who avoided writing to him, fearing to be found guilty by association with him. Consequently, the only luck left to him now and in his future in Lisbon, was the simple fact of staying alive. It's true, he was far from his family, without a diploma or a single friend; but he was committed to the oldest and most lucid of all disciplines of the living — the beginning of a great passion for life.

V

For the last time, the little purple hand tries and succeeds in drawing him close. It now has an almost bony weight, like a phantom serpent. Nuno falls under its spell without suspecting that the triangular head of this reptile won't hesitate to inject him with poison. The snake would nest and lay eggs in his guts, on the walls of his stomach, and certainly in his bones, liver, and lungs. The unique and multiplying venom of the snake immediately started to invade his blood. It was a symphonic snake, whose music seemed to hypnotize him and slow his movements. The voice of the provincial went on near his ears, in a mellifluous and calming oratory. He seemed to have turned into a supplicant, without any arrogance, forcing him to propose a second marriage with the Order and the truce of reciprocal understanding. He also proposed a new courage now that he was going to know and live in the "world." Nuno's attention started to wander from that speech. He was holding back convulsive tears. To contain them, he looked out at the yard. Down there, at the back of the playground, where endless times he had kicked the ball of the rebellious ones and had tripped the priests and some of his enemies, there were groves of orange trees, furrows of earth that had become prickly with weeds, the apple trees, the garden with cabbage and lettuce, and the box-edged beds with roses that supplied the chapel and refectory of the senior priests. Even the elderly little monks, with their bent spines and bony frames, continued to give the garden a silent and passionate order. They took care of it and loved it as if it were part of God's work. When he spotted them, still pressing their hands to their backs but with faces glowing in the devotion of that penance, he felt the first tinge of remorse. He remembered again the tragedy of Father Pio and his declaration:

"If you ever prove that God doesn't exist, I will be the unhappiest man in the world!"

In the course of all those years, above all in the years when he was still growing, he had stolen from the monks, and not from the Order, the oranges and apples that sated his night hunger and the clandestine appetites for that fruit that the rector had reserved for the oblong seminary table but never for the seminarians. Many had been discovered and then expelled because of those night raids on the orchards. Nuno had watched them through the holes in the fence, camouflaged by the dark of those nights of fruit raids. He saw them fill the folds of their shirts, the pockets of their pants; he saw them dip their heads into those dunes of apples, wrapping themselves in the furious joy of the great forbidden pearls. He heard the sound of their teeth, their laughter, and the squeaking of the mice. It had been easy for him to quiet his conscience. After all, it was in the time of hunger and jealousy; only the oldest ones could have seconds of spaghetti, rice, or stew. The others were served with ladles, their plates held out with shaking hands. Their imploring eyes were always met with the heretical energy of the prefect of the week, who ordered that the last servings, scraped from the bottom of the pots, be divided among the finalists at the back table. So that in the week of the expulsion of those fruit thieves, he had given a convincing plea of his innocence before the interrogators in the wake of the inquiries initiated by Father Francisco. He had even refrained from confessing this sin to the man whose ear was glued to the confessional grate. In his opinion, only the monks deserved his secrets and guilt; those were the fruits of their labors, sweat, and suffering — he didn't have to expose them to the pardon or the censure of the confessors. He had watched the expulsion of those mystics of the night, closeted in the conviction of a second innocence. In panic, he watched them pack their bags; he saw them stand before the entire community with downcast eyes and very red ears, crying again. The rector prescribed thirty-five blows with the ruler on each hand, and Nuno watched how their bodies writhed and their faces became contorted. With relief he saw them disappear around the first bend in the road, shamed, straight as poles inside the seminary van. He sensed that he heard, or dreamed that he heard, the whistle of the trains taking them back to their homelands ... He was alone in the dormitory night, wracked not by the remorse of the priests, or the passion of those who had been expelled, but by the gaze of the younger friars.

And now that the provincial thinks he has tamed the horse and the spirit of the boy, Nuno limits himself to acknowledging the effect of this subtle change. The competence of the beginning of old age that had led to his being elected by ecclesiastical scrutiny, he used astutely to quell the revolt. He had no difficulty in making him take an excursion back in time. He talked to him about an examination of his conscience regarding those years in the seminary. He wanted, he said, to arrive with him to the evidence and the bright light of the motives that justified the decision to expel him. He knew, obviously, about crises of faith, of the scientific times of torment and the apparent death of dogma in his spirit.

"The big detail of the existence of God," philosophized the provincial, "is the whole story of His death inside us. See if you can reconstruct it. Maybe you yourself will come to the conclusion that it's much better to close that door, and to open another and fulfill on the other side all of your capabilities."

For Nuno, however, the existential vicissitudes of God had become associated with the convulsions of the big parasite that had started to wriggle in the throes of death. God had been born far away from there. Not in his parents' bed, but in him and inside him: in the egg of the first intestinal worm. He had felt It grow, become a tapeworm, then a serpent or scorpion, then a dragon or dinosaur. It was in the final stage of metamorphosis that He had thrown him into the supreme fire. Before this he had heard the fathers baptize Him with different names. The ancient Latin professor had nicknamed Him, a little morbidly, as *Creator Divinus*. And to better characterize Him, he had added: *quia omnes res a Se fiunt et magnae sunt*. The professor of religion and morals decked Him with complex designations: Doubt, Affirmation of Personality, Crisis of Faith and Values, Aptitude for Inner Growth. But the priest who taught philosophy, in addition to being an alcoholic, decided to accept the challenge of this problematic existence. He called him Anguish, a word that mixed with his wine breath and seemed to boil in the complicity of a plural voice. He said it with the same forthrightness as before, to the astonished ears of his superiors, that the "annexation of Goa by India" was not at all the annexation of Goa; the Angolan warriors of February 4, 1961, were not the "bandits," the "terrorists," or the "pirates" of the chronicles of Mr. Ferreira da Costa. He pronounced other truths. In the weeks when he was designated prefect, at the lunch hour he allowed the students to listen to the radio broadcasts of the apoplectic tales of the servants of Salazar about the attack on the ship Santa Maria, and also the protests, the voices, and the supplicating choruses of the Living Forces of the Nation about the dismantling of the nest of vipers that was the Portuguese Society of Writers. The father of philosophy pushed Anguish to the front of the line, knowing that it was necessary and organic to feed his parasite, feel it alive in the guts and the stomach and not to disturb its growth. One day, he was defrocked. News from afar said he was alive in strange lands and cities, following the call of passions of a European moment that had not yet arrived in his country.

"What do you think the priesthood is, boy?" the provincial asked suddenly. "It demands much sacrifice, total obedience and complete humility. Or do you think that our brothers," and he pointed below in the direction of the tiled roof of the cloister, "have your freedom, and your lack of concern? They pray, they study, and they learn what you can't even imagine about the mysteries of Life. And what freedom do they have? Only one: to choose between silence and perdition. They turn their backs to the world, not just because the world is full of temptations and deceits. Not you, you chose the world, so you should abandon your service to God. Do you pretend to have a vocation so you have access to an education, so that later you'll shut the door in our faces? You have to understand that tolerance has its limits . . ."

"Have mercy, Father Provincial, sir! Is your reverence insinuating that I came here just to get an education?"

"I'm not insinuating anything! You made a mistake, we all made a mistake about your future in the Church, and that's it. There is no room for insinuation."

"Then listen to me, reverend Father," and I felt my voice start to tremble as I was being abandoned. I was on the threshold of definitive defeat. I knew I had started to surrender. That soon I would become a beggar. "I ask you, please, to look at me and listen. Listen to me just for an instant."

Provincial Luís seemed surprised. His eyes became suspicious, shifty.

"Your reverence came here. You called for me. You said I should pack my bags and leave on the first train for Lisbon. Is that practicing charity, dialogue, and tolerance? In my opinion, it's not. It's making a top-down decision. Why didn't you ask me if I was ready to abandon the seminary?"

"Because by the looks of it, you never wanted to make the decision yourself. That's why we decided that we should make the decision for you."

"Which is far from the truth. Especially because of something I'd like to tell your reverence if you are disposed to listen . . ."

"Go ahead, I'm all ears."

Then Nuno felt his throat dry up. They were standing still again, and the provincial put his little golden eyes on him. The boy's body shivered and this was discernable only in his tremulous guttural voice. It was a sad, rebellious voice. His body leaned slightly forward, in the beginning of a bow. His face swelled again, about to return to his previous state of bloody congestion when he was about to cry.

"It's that I," he said, as humbly as possible "still want to ask your reverence's pardon . . ."

"I don't understand. Ask for pardon? What does asking for pardon mean?"

"Pardon for myself. I am the only one guilty of having led my superiors to think that I had lost my vocation. I had a moment of weakness. But that's over. I have found myself and I'm at peace again."

"So does that mean, if I understand correctly, that you lost your vocation and now you've found it again?"

"Yes, precisely. And I ask you humbly to believe me."

"When did you decide to recover this miraculous lucidity, may I ask?"

"Last February."

"You're joking! We have nothing more to say to each other. Go pack your bags!"

"I decided, Father Luís, to follow the way of the Lord and never to stray from it again. I just want you to believe me. There are moments when everything is decided inside of us. Your reverence can't deny me this last chance. Give me, for charity's sake, six months of probation. You'll see that I'll prove myself."

When he looked up at him, the provincial's mouth was hanging open with stupefaction, and he was forcing himself to breathe through closed nostrils. A lengthy shadow passed across his confused face. A few other shadows followed. His face wrinkled up again showing his little sharp teeth again. Perplexed, his eyes rolled on the livid surface of a face suddenly touched by discouragement. Nuno's, because he was about to explode, turned bright red, and held himself stiffly.

"Either you are very clever, and trying to have fun at my expense, or I really don't know myself."

"What's happening is that your reverence also has doubts. And you are starting to admit you may have been mistaken about me. If you kick me out into the world you know I'll lose my way and enter into disgrace. But your reverence will not be able to sleep well . . ."

"I won't accept blackmail!" yelled the priest, standing tall and wagging his index finger. "Anything but blackmail. Right? Deep down you've never done anything except shuffle and deal out the cards again. Now tell me, be honest: why are you so afraid of the world, boy? What are you so afraid of?"

In the simplicity of the question, Nuno again recognized the subtlety, the experience of the hawk that opens its wings, flying out of that body, and then hovers over its frightened victim, flapping its wings. In fact, he thought, what could be scaring me so much on this first afternoon of the world? When God is dead, there is still the big sea between Lisbon and the Azores; there is still the metaphysical sea that I will sit in front of with the same sensation of being on my haunches with my tail showing in the middle of the desert. I would look around and be a beaten man before the people of Rozário who always had said I didn't have the "look of a priest." For them, that would be the supreme triumph. For the family, it would mean shame. In the mouths of those people, studying for the priesthood was to go to a school run by those eunuch tyrants. But to be expelled by them was much worse, knowing that lust, silent laughter, and revenge had to be a part of the excommunication.

The provincial continued to wait for him to say what was scaring him most about the world, but Nuno felt lost, drowning in his own questions. If he could he would just say that he was about to turn eighteen and he knew nothing about the world. Life was a tunnel between the big holidays on the boats and the successive years of reclusion inside the very high walls of the seminary. He couldn't remember any other landscape or people. He had seen the sea from above, from the decks of the ships. He had known the trains that come and go between the provinces and Lisbon, but not the other sea on land: the sea made of time, pine trees, pilgrimages to Fátima, corridors, railings, bells striking the hour, music and the words of psalms, the bell at the start and end of classes — and always, always those eternal voices who murmur on awaking every morning:

Bendicamus domino!

Deo gratias!

"What do I know, or what can I know about the world?" he thought, knowing this was useless. "I don't even know what part of the earth is destined for me!" He still had a brief, perhaps fleeting illusion of being able to express himself better to that man. He wanted to move him, dominate that hawk's eye, stop those eyes from spearing him. He had finally become an inoffensive prey whose strength was ebbing. He was a bird, the provincial was the serpent of enchantment, melodious and perfidious. The more he ran, his body would always go to the encounter of the dusk of that seductive, hypnotic god. "I think," he thought, "that I've never been so alone in my life as now."

"What frightens you, I know all too much. It will take you some effort to become a man with a purpose and personality. Just that."

"Forgive me again, your reverence. But while I say that my destiny is in the priesthood, it's true at least for me. I just wanted you to acknowledge that hypothesis. That your reverence may be wrong about me . . ."

"You continue to insist on making things difficult. Your pride has been injured. You've never listened to our warnings. You didn't want to mend your ways. Well now the door's in front of you and you can follow the path you chose."

Then the provincial hesitated for a moment and seemed to become pensive. Sadly, his arm went to his pocket and it took out the piece of paper signaling his victory. Opening it in front of Nuno's eyes he said in a pious voice:

"We've even bought you a train ticket. Pack your bags, take your things to the gate house and Brother Gregory will take you to the station. When you get to Lisbon, our priests will be waiting for you. You will go to the Mother House where you will wait for the first boat to the Azores. Go on, son. You don't have much time."

Nuno let his arms fall and lowered his head. The provincial interpreted this as the obedience that was owed him by his position that he was elected to and he threw him a blessing over his head. He saw him walk away with hesitating steps, as if he were swaying. Nuno guessed that at this precise moment, dozens of heads and eyes must have been spying on him from afar, inside the study rooms. He supposed that mouths had begun to whisper among themselves, spreading the word about the new expulsion. His eyes filled with tears. His mouth was twitching in a grimace of crying that was impossible to control much longer. Suddenly the provincial saw him turn back and walk toward him. Then he stopped and tried to contain his tears. When he was able to, the boy lifted his arms to his chest, interlaced his fingers and crossed himself in supplication:

"Provincial father! Have pity on me. For the love of God don't send me away. I swear, I promise never again . . ."

At a gesture from the priest, however, the voice receded. It extinguished itself in the same proportion that many tears started two flow from his eyes, becoming thicker and thicker. The priest then needed to summon an indefinite and remote courage to nod his head in a sign of negation. He did it in silence and waited for Nuno to turn away. He saw him cross the entire space of the recess yard and enter the door that gave access to the dormitory of the older seminarians. He thought he heard the sound of his feet on the creaking stairs that at the same time pounded like a drum in a deserted house. Then he took his breviary from his pocket and started to read as he walked: *unus ex discipulis meis tradet me hodie: vae illi per quem tradar ego. Melius illi erat si natus non fuisset.*

VI

It always comes from where the inhospitable winds blow, from where the skies are high, curved, and certainly as immortal as the vaults of temples. One enters through the door of an enigma named Santa Apolónia. There is that approximation of a rigorous and exact form like a forgotten science. That's when iron scrapes against iron. Then the landscape starts to change from low houses with grass on their roofs and whose doors look like old women in mourning weeds. By day men appear in caps or with their caps askew over their ears. Children in pinafores sometimes forget the routine of watching the trains pass by and raise a little hand purple from cold to wave to the faces coming from the provinces. For these little ones they are exhausted, apprehensive dead people. They don't know how they will live in the city of Lisbon. The boys will resuscitate after they pass the last houses on the line, at the place where the noise of the railroad cars ceases and the buildings facing the Tejo are now that dull ochre color. At night, the windows of the houses are shaken by a long blast. A whistle passes in the direction of Lisbon and that is the destination. Then you can hear the very silence. Because the silence is before the trains pass, never after. When they stop in the station, way ahead, the night vibrates under the light. For the ones coming from the provinces, the solitude is sudden: it's in the strange faces, in the unknown arms and the thunder of many footsteps heading out of the station.

For Nuno, solitude means sitting on one of his suitcases, looking in every direction and concluding quickly that no one had ever been there waiting for him. It's past midnight. The noisy stream of people drains out quickly. One doesn't know if the crowds are eager to get into Lisbon or if it's the city that opens itself to each one of these guests who in the taxis, vans, and private vehicles talk about where they have come from, what happened to them in the provinces, and then they ask everything to those driving them wherever they happen to be going. What's life like in Lisbon, what things go on through the years in a city that they say has a river, square parks with yellow lights on poles, clocks stopped on purpose on the façades of the churches, and always bands of pigeons sheltering themselves in the niches of temples and statues?

When the last electric trolleys squeal by, there are only sleeping faces inside. The bodies of those faces travel slumped over, they are cold and tired, or they are heads that barely move and stare straight ahead. Then, at the Santa Apolónia station the last doors bang shut. The windows are locked. Railroad workers in dark brown uniforms approach the exits suspending lunch pails from the hooks of their fingers. They stare at him with suspicion. For an instant, Nuno stares back with a distrustful expression, without any hope that one of them can save him from this enigma called Lisbon. The little doors of the kiosks are also shuttered down. The lights go out. And suddenly, there in the depths of the shadows, the trains are just shapes that are cooling overnight. Someone comes to tell him he can't stay there. He has to pick up his bags, go to the end of the platform and sit in the waiting room at the street level. They don't ask him any questions. If they did, they would hear from Nuno's mouth that anything can happen to a boy expelled from the seminary. Besides having no money, he knows of Lisbon only what is in front of his eyes. He feels the closeness of the river because he recognizes it by the salty wind and the boats, whose keels are sharply profiled by the shadows over the anchor chains. He's not afraid, just cold and tired. He knows that he's in a moment of his life that will be precious to him. He doesn't want more than to feel himself on the threshold of happy years in Lisbon. He desires the city with an identical conviction to the newly released from any of its prisons.

It's a safe country: nothing ever happens. For this reason the night watchmen and the police on shift walk by rattling their keys and whistling to themselves. They won't bother him because they are used to seeing boys from the provinces in the waiting rooms of all the stations in anticipation of the days, seduced by the distant siren voice of the city. For them the boys are no more than recruits joining the Army by deluding themselves that they won't be drafted to Africa.

He can't even call Amélia because of the early hour. If the phone rang in that enormous sleeping house, a drowsy voice would answer that he should have the decency to respect the rest of others; it was no time to be calling for any student and no emergency would justify such action.

He is able to call her at eight in the morning. Amélia was leaving for mass and for a shift at the Hospital dos Ossos, but she hastily canceled all her commitments. She tells him to take a taxi and to meet her at Campo Grande. Nuno hurries to the meeting place. Warily the taxi driver tells him he doesn't have all morning to wait there with him and threatens to impound his luggage. Seeing her finally approach, Nuno sighs with relief and lets out a sarcastic comment that the man pretends not to hear. Before hugging her he is surprised by her pallor, the wan smile, and the sickly obesity of his sister. It's not a happy or a sad smile, just stupefied. Just like him, she was expelled from the convent. Accused of not having the constitution for the work of the Divine, they had banned her like a leper. But that was three years ago. Half that time she had lived in fear in the house of the Azores, without medicine, forbidden to dream of a return and barely tolerated for her ambition to cling to books and take the high school exams in Ponta Delgada. Now she was in nursing school and she made her living doing shifts at the Hospital dos Ossos and giving home care to a lady who was convalescing from a femur bone fracture.

It doesn't take much to notice her starving sadness, the angry energy of poverty. Suffering but not rebellious, she had accepted the persecution of the Order, the miserliness of her parents, and the charity of public assistance in a solitary fight against lymphatic tuberculosis. As for the rest, it's immediately manifest in her tenacity. She brought perfectly designed plans for Nuno. They would live together. She had a few contacts, and she believed that it wouldn't be difficult to find him a job in Lisbon.

"Don't even think about going back to the Azores," she insisted. "Anything but going from being a horse to a mule. And Papa has to calm down, he has no choice."

He knows that he will quickly love her and hate her for this. Maybe he will surrender to this maternal instinct, the way she had always protected her younger siblings. But he will hate the imperative tone of that voice that continues to be resigned to her unhappiness. He will not be able to tolerate listening to her give so much suffering to the Divine, or to believe as she does that only God will cure her. In the train he had more than enough time to plan his escape from God's sphere. He had decided to disobey Him in everything and to give himself the excess of living the life on this side of the walls. He would start by forgetting Sundays.

How do you win with God? By indulging in the diabolical forbidden fruit of women, by beating off during mass, by smoking cigarettes freely, far from the snitching of spies or the eyes of the prefects. The God of the expelled and the outcast is also defeated by the company of his first friends, above all those who were immersed in the secrets of the city. You win when you don't need to depend on His grace but on a job and a monthly salary. He needed to give the finger to the Azores, where his father demanded he return to work the land. There are many ways to reduce God to an equivocal figure. Nuno swore he'd do it fast, without suffering and without remorse.

VII

In the course of the following months, still Nuno goes along with the entreaties and threats of his sister, by whose insistence he puts up with the horror of going to Sunday Mass. A whirlwind of opposing forces buffets him: revolt and obedience, hate and indifference collide inside him. The insecurity comes precisely from this contradictory coexistence. Sometimes he would circle the church of the Largo da Anunciada. Strolling around the neighboring avenues, he avoided the Mass and tried to take the pulse of a city that offered only the alleys and not the exit door that he longed for. Those excursions could only be measured by the strength of the doubts that assailed him. Something unspoken always made him return to the square and forced him to stand in front of the temple. He saw the eternal beggars sitting at the door, the real ones and the fake ones, and he saw the old ladies in mourning who came in and out and crossed themselves with holy water. He asked himself what that meant, what the crippled were doing there, and which ones made a living out of Sunday charity. Other times, he entered the church with slouched shoulders, immediately recognizing the rites, the crowlike faces of the faithful, the whiny, imperative voice of a very tall priest, with the shoulders of an ox and a disgusting pink sheen to his skin. Something inadequate and repetitive imbued everything. The body of the priest was too big for his effeminate voice. The old women continued to stink of something rotten, wrapped in their sweat-soaked Sunday veils, and all this was the same as what he had gone through for so many years in that chapel in the provinces. The same young women wore glasses, they were ugly, all of them excessively virginal and with very white hands that shook under the weight of the missals. Even the men seemed different from men there, with their sebaceous and equivocal mannerisms. He imagined them making love to the very religious women, fornicating with them as if they were practicing the Eucharistic sacrament, and there would be something mystical in this sexuality, a kind of sacrifice in which both offered to the Lord the betrayal of the pleasures of the flesh. During the years of all of his future social experience in Lisbon, Nuno would many times have the sensation of moving among sects, participating in their cultish practices. At dance shows he would always be surrounded by the same virgins in glasses, the same well-behaved couples, fat old ladies who fanned themselves with Chinese fans of mourning black. The culture always seemed ugly, myopic, and sectarian to him. In the theater, the male actors oozed with affected mannerisms and gestures. In newspaper circles, there were viperous tongues and mouths thirsty for whiskey. And among the ineffable writers, it was even worse: they compensated for their unequivocal, perpetual physical ugliness with intellectual boredom.

In addition to being ugly, the culture of his country wallowed in an attitude of systematic malice, and the sentiment that dominated it was always motivated by jealousy. It was a petty, competitive culture, pretending to be humble to better hide the little vanities of their circus.

He began to hate that his sister liked to walk to mass arm in arm with him. It was how she gave him a love that was reserved for Sundays. On the other days, she criticized him for the mounds of laundry he gave her to wash, never being at home after work, the suspect men who asked to borrow money from him and then avoided him in the cafes, and who was the questionable young lady she had seen him have tea and toast with, and where had he been until all hours of the morning on Friday when he came home euphoric and almost drunk, and what was this about writing poems and stories and publishing them in newspapers that were against the regime, and what happened to his old plans to take up his studies again, be a man, and prepare himself not to be drafted into the army — and she threatened again to return him to the Azores and to their father if he didn't get some sense and kept up with this madness of keeping company with Salazar's enemies. Amélia hated politics, not for herself, but for the fact that it was taking her brother to the frightening world of political subversion. She feared he would lose his way to the Lord and to completing his studies, and had the premonition of these threats turning real. Her feeling of impotence made her angrier every day and forced her to shout that he couldn't count on her for anything if he ran into trouble with the police. Nuno threatened to hit her, alluding to the hysteria of the terror that was abominable because it refused to be enlightened or intelligent. In his opinion, Amélia, who would go off to a corner to cry, personified the concept of the golden sheep of the Portuguese flock. She thought that you shouldn't meddle in politics just and only because it was forbidden and because in Portugal the prohibitions were not to be discussed; what was outlawed meant a duty as sacred as a divine commandment.

He wanted to explain to her where his revolt had started and how it was growing. He made her sit down in front of him and he began to talk: in the seminary, he had studied with the same obligatory books, and had even been an above-average student. He had gone through all the subjects in high school: mathematics, physics, foreign languages, a dead language called Latin, solfeggio, religion and morals, and civics. And suddenly, as if by a cruel joke, all of this was swept out of his life. The cardinal patriarch of Lisbon didn't recognize those studies for any of its expelled students. If they wanted to continue high school and get into university, they had to start all over again, wrapped like garbage in the useless paper of the seminary diploma. And nevertheless, these metaphysical studies of the expelled ones made them eligible to serve their country and make war in Africa; a superior beneficent state received them in the offices where they could be clerks, designers, cashiers, tax collectors, all of this at one thousand seven hundred and fifty escudos per month; charitable bosses, all very aligned with the politics of the Dictator, agreed to employ the ex-little priests because, in addition to being very religious, they believed in their virtues of discipline, in the timidity of subservience, and in the inferiority complexes of these workers.

Amélia wouldn't give up. The logic of decisions that couldn't be discussed soon gave her the illusion of being able to solve all of her brother's problems. What couldn't be helped, couldn't. But what could be done? Nuno was perfectly able to walk away from those affronts and decide to go back to school and sit for the exams. He could make up his high school equivalency in two semesters and then go ahead and finish his seventh year. He refused. With that sister he was always going to be speaking in Latin, they lived on different wavelengths; they'd never be in synch. He had been liberated from the trenches of the ecclesiastical censors, of the weekly sins he had to invent to justify confession and the vigilant eyes of the prefects; but he was delivered to the prejudices of that little nun without a habit, whose mentality was forged in the cloister and domesticated in the convent! From then on, all the women who smiled at him could only be prostitutes or simple opportunists who would not hesitate to take advantage of Nuno to get pregnant, forcing him into an apocalyptic marriage. She tried to introduce him to what she considered were "serious girls," who always went to mass and wore modest little dresses and translucent veils. When they removed their veils, they revealed defects of being big-nosed, freckly as carrots, pimply in adolescence that they hid with rice powder — but, countered Amélia, they offered the guarantee of virginal purity, good moral principles, observance of the Faith, and promises of matrimonial fidelity. For Nuno, whatever she tried to force on him with these nubile novices didn't go beyond church weddings and the virtuous tunnel that collided with the availability of his passions.

One Sunday he put up with the mass until the beginning of the sermon. After the reading of the Gospel, the priest clasped his hands, closed his eyes, and assumed the seraphic posture of preachers. He started to discourse about the ways of Faith, Hope, and Charity. He had the effect of opening in Nuno's heart all the wounds that had started to heal during his time in Lisbon. He decided, meanwhile, on an unorthodox and combative faith, made of parables that allowed libertarian interpretations. He couldn't stand the supplicant fanaticism of the preacher who asked the faithful to pray for the salvation of God's enemies and our governors. God's enemies and our governors were excluded from the number of the elect of the Lord. They had immense defects: the materialism of carnal pleasures, the instigation of hate among the Portuguese, the betrayal of patriotic designs, the venom of heresy. In Nuno's mind, he was witnessing the hope of hearing the Church of his country denounce the crimes of the Dictator, the violation of human rights in the person of political prisoners, the genocide of the colonial war, and the exploitation of workers. In the seminary, the defense of this attitude had long ago been assumed by the "new priests" who started to pressure the hierarchy. The "old priests" held all the priories of the Order: they were rectors, provincials, masters, and clock keepers of the time and the temples. This deaf war had begun between two generations of priests, but the country went no further than a boat off course on the sea of the arterial sclerosis of the eternal bishops and the few who benefited from their excesses. The crew of the boat was constituted by the offspring of accomplices who venerated an invisible Dictator from afar. There were sanguine generals, a cardinal patriarch with a maternal smile and colorless eyes, docile politicians like widows surprised in sexual misconduct and a civil contractor with a toothpick stuck in his teeth. Other accomplices descended the nautical pyramid, populating the promenade decks, the lower decks, and the deafening party of the bingo salons. Others still tried the wine and drank it on the infinite birthdays of the father of the country. But there would always be the bottom of the hold, asphyxiated and silent, where you could hear the continuous clamor of the shipwrecked of this unreal or apparent country. Nuno learned to hear their moans and rages, the sobs and cries from behind the muzzle, and he learned also that silence can lie behind silence. The church of hope and justice had betrayed in him this apprenticeship of the country. The bishops continued to bless the ships, the cardinal patriarch would come to die just of this, the fatigue of blessing so many pilgrims in Fátima — and that father of the church of the Largo da Anunciada would never know that he was just touching the nerve and subversion of Nuno.

It became unbearable to remain there any longer. He left convinced he was making a definitive break from the church. He said this to his sister's astonished ear, who rolled her eyes and tried to stop such a disaster. The morning was magnificently lit by the early summer sun. Walking down the Avenida da Liberdade, Nuno discovered the inestimable importance of being alive in this white city, under its diaphanous blue sky. As he advanced in the direction of Rossio, he found the country that only exists far from the temples and their murmurings. He saw it in the shoe shine boys who crouched at the doors of the cafes, their eyes on the shoes of the crowd. He saw it in the florists, the paper boys, and in the proud passage of the legions of foreigners who carried cameras over their shoulders, and he saw it above all in the young people his age strolling with hands clasped who certainly shared some of his anxieties.

The vision of these young people in love raised his spirits. He knew from them that he was already a participant in this passion. He would live in defiance of the dark little world of Sunday masses and against the shadows that had come to him still from a past that had been imposed on him and not chosen. He wandered downtown for the whole morning, forgetting Amélia, lost in a reality that was even illusory and suddenly projected over another time in Lisbon. For the first time in his life he felt lucid. He had stopped missing God. The family had transformed itself long ago into a lost and unnecessary tribe. The country was there to be invented, since it couldn't be called country if it persisted in the fable of explaining the existence of dead heroes and maimed martyrs. He had the upper hand of being a new arrival to these notions and also to the new fatality of those days. He saw it with his body, felt it in his bones. There wasn't a single organ of his body that wasn't ready to react against the achievement of those innocent, distracted, and poisoned years. At the same time, a kind of double play entered his spirit. One part was born for hate and was filled with rejection of the God of the seminary and the Sunday masses of Lisbon — and against a country that wasn't at war, didn't obstruct the thought of thinking or the feeling of feeling. The other part learned to distinguish between love for one's neighbor and the love of a woman.

It had never been as clear as it was now that he was undergoing a change of life. In his childhood he had suffered a similar but less-pronounced impulse. When he was going on nine years old he had felt a strange clairvoyance that made him understand from one instant to the next the arithmetic of the world. Now this light rekindled with new intensity and told him it was time take the leap to a better place.

VIII

He knew her smile, the color of her hair, the sound of her firm footsteps, and each detail of her body and her existence — but perhaps all that was missing was to see her come around the first corner, follow her, and offer himself to her. When such a thing happened, he would certainly tell her that he knew her and that none of her mysteries were unknown to him. He knew the story of her childhood, and thus passion is nothing else but a long, mundane childhood. She had been born from deep inside the earth. He watched over her sleep, heard her first sobs, and soothed her night terrors. Always and everywhere he would distinguish her from other women by her crown of stars and by her silent presence. That's why he was faithful to her.

It wasn't even necessary to idealize her. The Woman was inside him, sublimated and possessed by his imagination, so that it was enough to consummate an image of her. With the exception of this presentiment about the woman who would come to fulfill his passion, nothing important happened to him in those Lisbon years. He needed the grandeur and courage of this unreal, unfathomable woman, and he tried to find her. One part of her coexisted in the illusion of Barbara's happy eyes. Another part seemed to fulfill itself in the other illusion of Áurea, the priestess of that time who refused Nuno and rejected his love. He wasn't into Inês, the tiny hairdresser's apprentice who had rough fingers and a big solitary green in her too sad eyes. When he was able to make a date with her, he found himself in front of a mute, frightened little girl. She didn't say a word, but her eyes cried, a type of panic made her small breasts tremble, and Nuno deduced that no passion could thrive in this cowering presence. Another part of this Woman hovered over the luminous head of the young store clerks, in the supernatural breasts of a maid who had come from the provinces and said "I can't, I've got the curse." Surely the presence of Woman was fooled in the bed of a sacred prostitute called Anjos. She was very thin, called him "son," and then forced him to take five doses of penicillin. As in an apparition, he found her in the proud students whom he courted in vain until he felt ridiculous. He met them in homes of young boys with beach towels around their necks and well-dressed men who rode in luxury convertibles and whom they called "godfather."

Amélia had given up understanding her brother's life. She resigned herself to his coming in very late, drinking milk from the fridge, and going to bed with a lit cigarette. Through the partition that separated the bedrooms, she could surely guess that he was brooding in the dark. She heard sighs, the squeak of the mattress springs, and finally the heavy breathing of restless sleep. She never suspected he could be in love. As for the rest, she couldn't explain to herself how he could believe in a passion that he suffered for an invisible and nonexistent woman. Nuno, on the contrary, didn't doubt this for a minute. His conviction resided in the fact that he knew he wasn't going crazy. It could be a strange clairvoyance; but what hurt him about this still unknown woman was the very idea that she had made him up. The time was nearing when she would come into his life because new details were revealed to him about the goddess and how he would meet her.

Amélia rejected the simple hypothesis of being introduced to those vapid, shallow, and money-grabbing females. Her daily life was almost completely separate from her brother's, with whom she came to an agreement about the rent, food, and other monthly bills. Nuno didn't concern himself with these things. His dizzy fixation on women was now the only way he had to learn about the world. If he dissociated himself completely from Amélia's life, this meant he would be more available for the Woman with whom he allowed himself to fall in love. He wouldn't be beholden to his sister, but to Her, the one who had come to save him. He decided to look for her in books, because it could happen that she was still fictitious and would grow until she became real. What he could not doubt is that the Woman would arrive, out of a page or around the corner of any street in Lisbon, born to be loved by a man like him and by no other. When she arrived, she would be, perhaps, young, and would need to mature. Then, he would have the happiness of teaching her everything, the names of things and of streets, the political situation and the Stone Age, his perhaps useless knowledge of Lisbon. The Woman was all he needed in the future.

He stopped suffering in the measure that his passion grew closer to this truth. In truth, everything was strengthening in his spirit. Small but systematic triumphs were coming his way. After he was promoted at work, he felt the comfort of a bigger room, in the home of an eternal widow who continued to mourn her dead husband. He started to take on Latin students who always tripped on the plural genitive of the declinations and who would never get the conjugation of irregular verbs. He discovered literature. With time and once he had never let go of his commitment to the Woman, he deduced that he had invented her. She was written in the pages of his poems, just as she could be on the canvas of a painter or on a music score. He saw in her a definite transparency. She could be a dove and fly out of him, in case she weren't forever announced in his writings. He was absolutely sure that all she had to do was wake up and walk out of those pages. Then he would bask in her luminous smile. The Woman would walk on the paper, with her firm steps, and the wind would lift her hazel hair. Nuno would close the door and open the window, to see if her eyes were deep, dark, and determined. And holding out his hand, he would just be a happy man in front of his goddess. She came wearing a crown and she had a name. Nuno practiced saying it, he liked hearing it, and he limited himself to repeating the name: Marta!

IX

Twenty-one years later, there were the same sagging beds, with mattresses that sunk in the middle, and Nuno remembered everything again. There were the same chipped iron studs on the walls, and the shutters still hung from the roof and blocked the view of the street; there were the same square houses with little porches where the women, who were now old and widowed, would sit in the afternoons, and the same parochial church. It had been decrepit and in ruins back then, and he found it as it was before. The only difference resides perhaps in the clarity and wonder of things, in the naked forms of peace or in the extension of the new ruins. In the extreme north of the bedroom, the mirror over the washstand is still streaked by rusty spots, on the glass as well as the thick frame, which is starting to shed flakes of rust. The attic loft extends just as it did in his time, the whole length of that room. Two dozen gutters, dripping randomly in the ruined silence of the building, bring back memories of the rainy nights, when he woke up and found his bed soaked by the leaks.

The empty loft was still gloomy, and still held the terror, passion, and fever of when he had peered in the dark and listened for the slightest noise. The others had always left for vacation and Nuno had stayed there delivered to the night. There were trains to Minho and Trás-os-Montes, trains for Algarve and for Beiras, but not to the Azores. Not even boats or planes at Christmas or Easter. He felt alive in the grave of the big seminary house, listening to the laughter of the priests in the distance and in the evenings, the cracks of the wood columns supporting the roof, and the quick steps of the rats in the eves. Terrified by everything, he waited for the prefect to come to the room at a corner of the dormitory; then the fear passed and he could sleep.

Because of a lack of candidates for the priesthood, the smaller seminary was closed a few years ago. As for the cloister, those who crossed its threshold rarely stayed long and it was emptied of those who had studied about God inside its walls and had lost Him in the same fashion. From this remote community, once concave with the hum of Gregorian chants, there are still two foreign priests in residence there who speak in French, five little brothers with frosty eyes and bony fingers, a hive of nuns in the kitchen, and a few sandaled friars who now prefer grey robes to the heavy tunics of the cloister. So that facing the sudden emptiness of his present time and his memory, the hallways are deserted tunnels where footsteps vibrate and shadows project themselves on the wall. Even the voices seem to rise up from the bottom of abandoned mines, museum catacombs, or profaned bone yards. The interior patio, where the box tree had been, and the roses and holy fountain of knowledge, had yellowed irremediably with the new fake plastic and dried weeds. People wander around there lost and perplexed, crossing hallways in which doors groan and the wind whistles as it comes through the shutters or the broken glass panes. Nuno had seen these people from a distance, shuffling in the depths of the building, and they seemed like scuttling snakes in these absurd labyrinths.

To survive, the community had decided to convert the smaller seminary into a boys' home. Nuno had seen them, not long ago, at recess and in the cafeteria. They were orphans, sad little bastards, drug addicts trying to climb up from the bottom of the well to regain their will and connect to the world around them. He was surprised by the fact that all of these faces frightened him; suddenly he thought he recognized himself in the somnambulant bodies, the sharp profile of their bones. If he could have seen them face-on, he would have been transported in time and would now be in their place: seeing the procession of visitors and listening to their applause at how well the boys were being domesticated there.

What remained to him from that dark past was one single friend, and through him he had been invited to participate in a reunion of ex-seminarians. They had left Lisbon early, and his friend Fausto showed him long forgotten valleys, the unmistakable aroma of eucalyptus and cedar that mixed again with the acid air of the paper factories and with the noise of the saws, the names of the minuscule villages filled with old people and children, then so close and today gone from his memory. Year after year he had resisted the insistent invitations, fearing an encounter with the embrace of those nostalgic pilgrims. In the faces that approached his, he dreaded above all their sickly color and cloister-like voices. As he observed them from a distance, he guessed at their lazy marriages and their conjugal frustration that was fed only on the Sunday Mass. He also got a sense of their bitter view of the world and their anxieties about the threat of the demon Democracy. At the same time he allowed himself to test his reinvention of himself there. He wasn't sure he had killed the God dragon inside himself. Perhaps he had just been able to avoid its fiery breath . . .

He was not surprised by the faces that he recognized without difficulty. In truth, he had kept them inside himself, sublimated by the memory of childhood and adolescence. It didn't even seem strange that the priests had not aged in proportion to all those years. They looked just a little more bald, a little deaf and cranky, but still maternal in the way they embraced and welcomed each one of these prodigal sons. It also didn't surprise him that many of the ex-seminarians knew almost everything about his life. Written in the wind, it was certainly transcribed in all its versions and commented on in the reunions of previous years. Every time he ran into one of these people in the streets of Lisbon, he had forced himself to listen to the account of the vicissitudes of the others. He would then be in contact with the triumph and glory of a dispersed sect, albeit a wandering one, but that above all could pride itself on few martyrs and many winners. The "world" continued to be that old circus ring, with its deceits and pitfalls, the place where all of them had been threatened with extinction.

Alone in the dormitory, twenty one years after that cold March when he had been expelled without mercy, nothing had changed. The sinks were still like the watering troughs for the cattle of his childhood. There were the same faded, dirty, and poor colors. The columns that held up the attic loft had the same cracks, dents, and gaps. But in the places where there were no longer any beds or chests locked with padlocks, there was now the garden produce: sacks of potatoes that were starting to sprout, bags of onions and garlic, and baskets of fruit. He allowed the smells to penetrate his senses, along with the disorder of clothes hung on nails, the crime of badly made beds, and the specific and unforgettable nocturnal odor of this place of sleep. Everything had stopped being real and unbearably flat, incriminated like a nightmare that had never been resolved. He himself might not have been there. His existence was confused with that of fictitious people, with the actors standing in the shadows, the forgotten voices, the hand of the one who throws the net and harvests dead souls from the waters of time.

And he was submersed in the tumult of those years, when the orphans and bastards arrived there. There were many of them, dirty, cowering and shallow-eyed. Their heads had been shorn by an unskilled pair of scissors — certainly the same one that then was exhibited by a truculent seminarian whom all designated as "the barber." When he faced the solitude of those dull eyes, he didn't have any doubt. He was looking at himself in an old mirror. He saw himself in the body, the patched clothes, the mundane poverty of each one of those orphans. Just as in his time, the achievement of the bastards consisted of being in a world organized by others, not in their own reality. Just like when the wolf confuses dogs with her young and decides to nurse them. Perhaps for this reason the priests wore tunics, not pants — to give the seminarians the maternal illusion of the wolf or of the ladies with goat's hooves. They certainly imitated the smiles of nonexistent mothers. But the sweetness was always caustic.

He tried to talk with them, to capture the anguish of their faces. The orphans were sly, however, with invisible smiles, and it wasn't possible to penetrate their sadness. He was filled, this is true, with an old and a new affliction. The little ones were just waiting for the first opportunity to escape his presence. They hadn't left out of politeness. He decided for that reason to let them go. Sticking his hands in his pockets, he pretended to turn his back on them and he felt them slip away to their hiding places. In a little while they picked up bucket, brooms, sponges, and cans of sawdust, and they started to clean the dormitory floor. Others threw water on the cement of the lavatories, picked up scrub brushes, and flushed toilets. He observed the obvious: they did it with the same lack of joy as in his time. During almost seven years he had been there as a form of punishment. Not to study and to become a priest, but to be punished with latrine duty, just like prisoners in penitentiaries or the recruits in the barracks when they are given cleaning duty. They were assigned to clean, he thinks now, what could never be clean and to take care of hygiene that would never hide the filth, the moral pus, the sinful solitude of the inmates of reformatories and seminaries.

There in the bowels of the building he could hear the clattering of pans in the kitchen. At the same time the cars that continued to arrive let out euphoric horn blasts and from them emerged ex-seminarians with sunglasses and emotional smiles. Many brought wives and children. The beautiful cars, the rings, and the blue suits spoke of a new prosperity and self-sufficiency. Nuno was made uncomfortable by the long embraces, the unexpected familiarity of the priests who continued to address them as "son" and the festive air of these reunions. Before each embrace they stood for a moment studying each other, trying to recognize in those bodies the prankish childhood and lost complicity. Then they burst out into raucous laughter. That was when time definitely stopped, caught up in these emotions. Then they immediately started to recount everything that had happened to them in the "world." The studies picked up or abandoned, the professions, the conquests of prosperity and intelligence. All had been excellent students and were considered to be persons of talent. Nuno noticed that the teachers tried to maintain their joviality, in spite of their skepticism, their tired eyes, and bald moons. Men of luxury, in rigorously knotted ties, practiced law in Lisbon, Porto, and Coimbra with elegance and distinctiveness. The psychoanalysts took off their jackets and tried to seem uninhibited and superior. He heard them talk about their patients, in an obscure and voluminous jargon, and he learned that life was a theater where everyone knew the role of others by heart. Muscular businessmen forced themselves to suck in their big oval stomachs, as if they were trying to match the elegance and fluidity of the speeches. And the doctors in social sciences arranged their faces into philosophical frowns before carrying forth on the evils of life. As for the rest, they stayed behind the group and hid their dirty nails. Nuno saw that they had bad teeth and for this reason they didn't smile. Embarrassed, they smoothed their thin hair toward their necks or adjusted their wool caps on their foreheads.

"Those are the ones I like," he thought. "I like their almost rural loyalty, that shyness that burns for a drink to feel dignified and secure."

He liked them and not the self-assuredness and talent of the others, because the seminary was doubly unjust with those men.

At twelve thirty, according to the program that had been distributed, there would be a welcome reception in the old gymnasium, after which a luncheon would be served. The afternoon was reserved for what the priests continued to designate as time for "spiritual reflection." Each one would speak of his "experience in the world," which was intended as "an exchange, always enriching, of points of view." Since he still had a half hour, Nuno opened the windows of the dormitory and looked out at the landscape. All of it was the same, vivid and as if no time had passed. To the left were the same pine groves spread over the small hills, with eucalyptus on the slopes and ancient groves of olive trees on the rocky ground. To the right, the same gardens of cabbage and lettuce, where women bent over who certainly were already old during his time as a student. The same bicycles continued to go by on the dusty road.

At this point the orphans started to communicate with each other. They did it with monosyllables or gestures. Since he had been watching them, he had not heard a single complete sentence. Nuno's presence intimidated them to the point where they didn't want to raise their eyes from the ground.

"Perhaps I'm in the position of the old benefactresses of the seminary," he thought.

It was the visiting day for the VIPS; the rector took them on tours through the study rooms, the dormitory, the kitchens, and the refectory, offering them food tastings, and a place of honor at the reception and the recital of the students. These prodigious spiritual godmothers thanked him with an emotional smile. They praised the cleanliness, the sweetness, and the educated manners of so many angels. This was when the magnificent rector blushed with pride:

all of this was his work. Now he's in the place of these haughty, vain, and in part also magnificent benefactresses, because the orphans suffer the same shame or revolt that he experienced there. Never had he been as close to them as now. It's in the age, the shabbiness of the clothes, in the discipline of the small hands that grasp the broom handles angrily and push the water around the floor. He had started by working in the latrines to learn humility and humiliation. He had understood the goodness of Christ in scrubbing the floors of the chapel. And all of this had happened especially on feast days when the benefactresses came from far away, from places where it wasn't necessary to suffer, to approve the expenditures and new orders and to receive in return the prayer cards and blessings of their saints. Nobody even told them how life hurt here, inside these walls, facing the pines, listening to the bells striking the hours, and sighing for the unknown. Life hurt, not because of those daily chores, but because of the happiness that was forbidden there, the solitude of the saints and everything else that was absent.

He would not know it any longer. If he had really lived that last day of the orphans or had at least persevered the rounded hours, the gyration of the carousels, the roulettes, and the wrist watches . . . he had wanted perhaps to flee from this and all the days passed without ever looking back. If he did, it could happen that one of the orphans would continue to look at him from the bottom of a well and beg him for an impossible rescue. And if it were not for the look of an orphan, it would certainly be that of the shipwrecked sailor that had always been inside him. Only that it wasn't always on the sea or the rivers, but in that cursed wind that followed him. He dragged his whole life behind him, submerged in the numerous, unbearable tumult of voices and footsteps. His happiness moved from the bottom up, from the past to the present, from childhood to adolescence, and from there to the center of a city that could be called Lisbon or Marta.

He had also understood that the Woman had arrived to become the exact center of his life. She existed in a space where there had never been such loveliness. In spite of having come from the impossible, she had transformed herself into a presence that perhaps preceded reality. But to believe, it's necessary to touch, to press. Those cannot be her hands, and there is not in this Woman a unique voice that only belongs to her. She was born in the future. But hail, the time of his grandmothers also arrives, and hail, she breaks into the mischievous virginal smile and wisdom of all mothers.

Marta had crossed the shadows of cold landscapes to arrive in his life. She had overcome the resistance of these veils of darkness and had burst into flame like the lantern that heats the house and lights the profile of a man's face.

And he knows that love is exactly this, the impulse of drowning men clinging to driftwood, the instinct of newborn creatures that stand and wobble, a certain art of being born and another of entering the world.

X

When she left for Luanda, Amélia said good-bye to him in tears, in a crying fit that was offended and at the same time driven by the idea that her happiness had to be found in Africa. He saw her board the Vera Cruz, in the midst of the few civilians who were emigrating, and only then did he dare suspect the reasons that had led her to such a decision. In the midst of the troops she followed men of all ages in khaki uniforms, boys that had been mobilized and promised a small plot of land in the woods or a job in the cities of the South, and women who looked like officer's wives joining their men at their posts. Amélia took her place near those women. Her long straight hair, tangled by the afternoon wind, hid a face convulsed in tears and also the rest: the enigma and despair of that sudden departure, a decision taken in just a few weeks.

It occurred then to Nuno to ask why his sister was leaving Lisbon, particularly why she had lied to him about a supervisory position in a clinic that included an apartment facing Luanda Bay and two trips a year to Portugal. Then Marta took his arm, leaned closely against him, and returned the smile of mysteries previously unveiled and felt safe confiding in him.

In a short while the atmosphere of the docks became dark, an unbearable cacophonous confusion. The boat was backing away from the dock and the crowd advanced, pushed by a shout that started as a howl and then became multiplied in shouts, cries of seagulls, and wails and laments rising from a pain that echoed the suffering of that time. Here was the replay of the anguish of a country that didn't understand why so many boats were leaving for war. Nuno's immediate thought was that he could not bear to hear the shrieks of those women: mothers, lovers, and sisters reaching up, hidden behind their handkerchiefs as in a painting by Malhoa. Later, the men dried their eyes on their handkerchiefs and bit their nails and the police shouted at the crowds to stay away from the edge of the pier . . .

He had seen it innumerable times, every time he had witnessed a farewell of friends mobilized to those obstinate wars; in Portugal everyone had a friend, a neighbor, or a son on those boats. And they would have them still for many years. The radio and television broadcast the daily news of one more contingent of troops leaving for overseas on a mission of conquest. Now, everything was doubly awful; his sister waved a limp handkerchief ever less visible in the distance, and she herself was extinguished in this crepuscular vision, in the middle of uniformed men who gave up saying goodbye and limited themselves to see, to feel in their bodies, the strange undulation of the sea.

Seeing him so disturbed, Marta suggested that they find a place to sit down. She ordered a hot tea for both of them, saw in her husband's face the same expression of perplexity, and judged that there was the weight of some remorse in his sadness. She opened up to him in confidence; she said that Amélia had simply decided to leave behind the loneliness of Lisbon. Because a woman like her, she said, wasn't made for such a treacherous, obscure time, with boats leaving and arriving full of troops, a country where nothing happened but this. She wasn't made to lose the love of men she fell in love with. The last of them had proposed; she had assembled her trousseau, picked the date of the marriage, and put a deposit on a house — the fiancé, an affected guy, went on strolls with her hand in hand, approved everything, said "until tomorrow, at the place we agreed, my love," and never appeared again or even called. So she conflated the displeasure at living in a small country where you couldn't save any money, walk with your head up high, or be happy, with the fact that she had no friends and couldn't count on the presence or affection of her brother, and she decided to go to Africa. She would try to recover the illusion of promised love, impetuous fortune, and the need to see the other side of the sun. And that's what was going on with his sister.

Nuno began to understand everything. The marriage with Marta was just a way of her taking over his life, little by little, along the invisible pathways of his family. He had transformed her into a confidante; it had not just been Amélia. Because of her, he had stopped writing to his parents and siblings who were still in the Azores. It was a family slowly dissolving, as much in the letters of farewell as those that came from Canada and America. They forgot to send wedding presents, Christmas cards, pictures and other signs of their existence.

Luís had gone and returned from the Guinean war and didn't remember ever having received a miserable airmail letter from his brother. Domingas and Linda had sent pictures of their babies — but Nuno wasn't moved by the image of those rosy offspring and the eyes that still only looked within. His mother had stopped complaining, used to the questions about "What ever happened to our Nuno in Lisbon?" and never receiving a reply from anyone.

He had gone with her once to the Azores. Many of his siblings had left, led on by their foreign marriage; perhaps they were happy. Even so, he had made the trip to the Island to prove to his parents that he also had triumphed with Marta's beauty and her eternal, still nuptial love and by the happiness that she had given him through those long years of absence. On the return, there was again the uninterrupted time of Lisbon. Nuno set about living it through this essential ageless woman, who spurred him to practice life not because of necessity but out of a tribute to passion.

With the years he was struck with the strange notion of this flat marriage, without surprises, between happy and lonely, which was managed and celebrated by her and whose vicissitudes he participated in with concentration, only and just to deserve it. He had studied because she had insisted on loving a successful man. She believed in his talent because this goddess demanded enlightenment in the body and spirit of her man. And in permitting herself the risk of seeing him conspire with marked men, conspirators in the subversion of the dictatorship, she decided that these dangers made him more mysterious and infinitely seductive . . .

Instead of a woman, he had perhaps married a caster of spells who had seduced him into make two children for her. But the supreme contradiction of life was that he never had to act because of any suggestion or demand that she made. Everything was turning out all right. He didn't tire of her intimacy. He loved her without obeying her, for the pleasure that her pleasure gave him, for the happiness that made her happy too. In a certain way, marriage with Marta was a calculated achievement — in part desired by him and also in part by her consent. It would be inevitable to admit one day that the grammar of that marriage gradually lost the amplitude of the tense and mode of verbs, and that this conjugation didn't go beyond an almost absence of personhood — that could, in fact, be confused with the third person singular. When that day came, Marta's voice would perhaps be different, or perhaps Marta would be another version of him . . .

BOOK THREE

Mama's Last Breath

1

The access to the living room of that big Canadian house is up some stairs that have a somewhat unusual Z configuration and that below lead to the basement, behind the front door. Flor, the hostess, extends her arm in greeting over the railing, inviting him in. Nuno accepts her invitation with a shudder, knowing that what separates him from the cold eyes of the Dead One is just the brief ascent up the stairs to the family enigma. He doesn't know if he ever anticipated this moment. He will never know. His idea of family had for a long time been associated with dormant, empty houses. They are scattered people, shaped by shadows that suspend them between the light of the living and the unreal night of the dead, which is still difficult to understand.

The stairs stretch upwards, almost in a spiral, following the caprices of a highly polished mahogany railing that glimmers under the lights. At each landing the railings look like heavy sculptures, where the molds of the lathe give way to bulging stone vessels, rustic amphora, or just nautical forms that are completely unfamiliar to him. It's as if he had been taken on board a ship. The living room is suspended, like a quarterdeck, and is disproportionate in size to the rest of the house. A discreet smell of ammonia comes from the sinks, the mirrors are warped, and the kitchen smells mix with the heated air that is suddenly unbreathable for someone who is not from there. That's why the roses look greasy and the windows are very fogged up. Flor must have taken great pains with the arrangement of the vases. The lavender air freshener, mixing with the kitchen smells, give an aggressive tone to the innocence of the colors. But the naphthalene and the incense give away the illness, the medicine, and the approaching death of our mother. It's an egg-shaped house, at the same time maternal and tomblike, but with an interior that's like a ship. Its round, hermetic portholes look out at an invisible sea, certainly a fictitious one, but which possibly is the source of the unmistakable, persistent odor of algae. Nuno has the sensation that he is hearing the drone of engines. People are inside the heat of the house like fish asphyxiating in a dirty aquarium. He thinks about the boats, and he does so obsessively, because his senses have always been assaulted as he entered the thresholds of strange houses with those same disturbing, wafting smells — along with the hidden vibration and the enclosed quarters of the ship to Lisbon, when he was about to die of seasickness. Only much later, when he will wake up from his first night's sleep here and become reconciled with this new reality, will it occur to him that the distant whine of those turbines come not from inside him, or from the obsessive and embittered contemplation of all boats, but just from the central heating of that big Canadian house. He looks up, just for an instant. He doesn't know if he's looking for his Dead One, if he can see her peeking through the banister, or even if he wants or can stand the idea of sensing her presence and first fit of weeping. With a nervous glance he also notices over the skylight the shadow of a cloud in the illegible skies of Vancouver. He doesn't know if the tree rises from the back of the house and extends a branch over the locked glass hatch. But he isn't surprised that a bird is distractedly perched at its top. That's how he learned to define death. A crow poised on the crest of a cypress tree, exactly as in the verse of the poet Soares de Passos.

As soon as Flor pauses with the embraces and kisses and starts to weep, someone turns on all the lights. The varnish of the banister sparkles under the lights and the sea-green walls fade. Grave faces emerge from the shadows of the pictures and start to watch him. They see that Flor is showing him the living room. They see him turn red and listless as he starts to climb the stairs. The people don't have bones and their footsteps are silent on the marine moss of the carpets. Nuno still hesitates for a second. It occurs to him that the flowers in the vases can't be real. He slides a trembling finger along the varnish of the banister. If he could, he'd go mad right now. Sitting on the next stair, he would put his head in his knees and just say that he doesn't want to ask forgiveness from the Dead One, because he will not be able to take the shock of seeing Mama transformed into a china figurine. He stops the thought, he doesn't even have to go to her presence. He feels it in the silence and the lamentations of the living, and he feels it in the air that he breathes and in Flor's voice that suddenly addresses one of the children:

"Son, please lower the volume on the TV, would you? We don't want to disturb old Grand Mama, ok?"

He feels it especially in the limits of his body: his cold fingers and shaking knees and the acceleration of his heartbeat. He wants to think that this is due to a small excess of adrenaline, not that he isn't frightened or anxious. He is no longer even tired. He just needs to stop drowning, to rise to the surface and fill his lungs. He also knows how to turn on the social smile that Lisbon life taught him to display every time he was in an unhappy situation.

The next moment, at the top of the stairs, he is faced with her blue knees. He just has to lift his eyes to confront the definitive evidence of his Dead One. When this happens, Mama is just the sitting corpse who suddenly smiles at him from up close, but just with one half of her mouth. From the other half slips an ashamed pursing of the lips, which is perhaps the beginning of an almost happy cry. He doesn't know if this cry smiles at him or if it's the smile that cries from the right side of the mouth — because her eyes express the indecision of her mixed feelings. It will be a fleeting vision, one that shrinks away from the acknowledgment and clarity of his senses. He can't remember ever being able to associate the memory of that body to the smell of peaches that comes from her breath, the medicines, the incredible blue of her lusterless eyes, and the fuzz that now substitutes her gray hair. Nor does he recognize the volume, the heat, and the mystery of those sixty-eight-year-old bones. Besides this, Mama's voice comes from a distance beyond time. When she lifts herself up with effort, with that half-smile, to greet him, she only shows how weary of life she is. If he pauses for a moment to listen to her voice, it will become plaintive. She will start to mourn him as if he were the dead one. Or her grief will be as subterranean as the bells that toll for the dead as they visit each other's graves. He prefers to prolong the voice of his memory of her in a dream, returning her to the years when she called him by name, asking him to wake up from his deep sleep in the Azorean night. Every time he imagined being taken to her presence, Mama's unreal mouth limited itself to mimicking those inaudible words. In the dreams, the movements of those lips were lost in an almost supernatural fluidity: the absent voice, but at the same time one illuminated by the auditory memory of words. In spite of having appeared to him repeatedly through the years, always unique and ubiquitous, he had just fallen into an optical illusion: this woman had existed, without doubt, she had lived her time, gotten old, and now was about to die, but she had not belonged to him for a long time. So that now, finally face to face, in the middle of the stairs that lead to a living room of a Canadian house, he can do nothing more than accept the inevitable return of this stranger: to see her dead eyes, smile at her with the same frightened smile, and become bitter from her bitterness. Then he feels himself pause. That he does it out of instinct, afraid to open his arms and to press to his chest the weight of that cold, rigid body.

"If I do it," he thinks, "I'll have to embrace my premature death. I will start to die from her second death."

He has a presentiment of the rigidity of her facial bones. The smile that in vain slips through or is traced on her lips is also cold. Her forehead becomes lined with the steel that gives color and shade to sharp metals. Mama grasps the beads of her rosary. She lets it slip between her swollen, purple fingers, their grape color between the deep green and blue of new wine. She has a great cloud in her vision, thinks Nuno. She had stopped praying but she is still an obstinately religious woman. She definitely looks like the grandmothers who, in addition to being religious, are always excessively cold; she has worms in her cloudy eyes. Mama will say later that they are not worms, nor are they in the eyes. She will say that death bites from inside; it's a scorpion that squirts poison into the mushroom of her intestines.

So he doesn't hesitate, he reaches for the bannister and holds it tight with both hands. Now he is indeed frightened and shaking again, taken by this vision of devastation. He can't, he will never be able again to lie about that illusion. Now he is faced with his real mother, he won't confuse her with saccharine dreams of Mama. He refuses to see her again like this, a clay figure looking at itself in a pool of water blackened by clouds. He looks for the once blue eyes, the vivid black hair, the satin whiteness of her throat, heavily speckled by moles. But in the place where there should have been the body of a heron poised in its nest, it's only possible to discern death sitting on a velvet throne. Bolstered by pillows, the body resembles a boulder: oblique and twisted by immobility. There are two sleepless eyes, and a deep suffering, and extreme misery — and there is this mask that has the hue of lilies, and a trembling of the lips twisting slowly into the half-sob of the mouth. One side of her face is frozen in a vertical smile, unlike any other form of smiling. It thus becomes clear that Mama is a woman divided between a sob and a smile. Her right side comes out of the cold and desires, forces itself to express joy. The other remains frozen. And then a sweat of tears, perhaps tender and anxious, bubbles over and finally runs from the immense, vanquished sweetness of her eyelashes.

He hears her murmur his name, as if she had started to pray again. He hears her and obeys, approaching now to the call from the depths of the earth of the dead, and not from her mouth. Two paces from that body, and he doesn't know if he should embrace her, or how he will do it, because the thick legs, bound by the snakes of old varicose veins, are two tree trunks that can't be budged. Resting on the thick folds of the synthetic down of the heavy, Canadian blankets, are two feet with no shoes on next to the unplugged electric heater. They are, however, heavily bandaged, excessive in their thickness, inside short socks.

There is another source of anguish, perhaps even a wounded rebelliousness. This is the kind of feeling that the blood segregates and gushes out, which doesn't yet belong to the real dead but is already in the unbearable torpor of those church tapers that justify Mama's existence and go out little by little in the countdown of the minutes. Nuno doesn't know if she has submerged, if she has accepted the fact of abdicating, or if she still hopes that this son has come from very far away, from where it's not possible to return, with the mission of seeing her and resuscitating her. Mama had called him by telegram; because only this way would he believe she was dying. She had asked for help from one continent to another, from the Pacific to the Atlantic, and he had obeyed promptly. He had traveled from Lisbon to Toronto, and from Toronto to Vancouver, as if he were flying to meet everything that had been pitted against time, in the inverse direction of clocks and time zones. Now the violet eyelids and the pockets and protuberances of her face mix with the age of the dead. Her hands, preparing to receive him, are wooden and sad. They follow the arc of the breasts, the weight of those shoulders of a bird felled by a bad shot.

Nothing is sure, Mama. Never was anything more certain than the moment when your eyes fell into a slow, lucid death, and your arms tried in vain to freeze the same terrible, sweet, odious mortal embrace. He sinks into her body, hears the sigh of the great night of that mother without a name, the mother of the lost years and his eternal and absurd absence of mother. He recognizes not her real smell, but that of his dreams. And he inhales the gray breath of the still woman and her suppressed aura, and the physical nature of her life. He realizes that he knows nothing about her as he separated himself from that breath and body that still breathes him in twenty-seven years after the time he left home. But the best in this woman is simply the fact that he had once been her son. He has no memory of any other honey milk, this is certain. Nor does he recognize the crunching of teeth chewing on the sugar of her cookies — nonetheless he embraces her and breathes her in, and an unfamiliar groan rises from the sobs that embrace her tears.

It's possible that Mama would much prefer suffering the pains of a second labor. She rests her blind hands on the mass of that son who came from far away to resuscitate her. Mama thinks he won't refuse to save her. She thinks that her time has come again, because she feels it in the contact with her ravaged groin. She palpates him. By the way she touches him, Mama sees him through the dark. She believes that he is again emerging from inside her, so that she desires him because of the pain and passion of that second birth. She thinks: he came from Lisbon, he came very quickly, only he can save me. If she doesn't know it for sure, she at least has the final illusion: maybe Jesus had taken on the destiny of that son. He was crucified in his name, in his distances, in the mysteries of his Portuguese existence.

Still, he is just a son without tears. Fragile, bereft of confidence, he is now murmuring into her ear:

"I can't, Mama. No one can do anything for anybody!"

Then Mama, who is fed up with her inglorious, sedentary death, who is forever in a wheelchair and without the hope of deserving a little of his happiness, tries to lift her face. She sees that Nuno is just a boy, that Nuno has refused to grow up during his absence, and that in Nuno's hesitation is the smallness, the suffering, and the need to learn of a newborn. Because Nuno is as wrinkled and purple as a fetus, exactly as on the day he was born. Mama has an absolute, undeniable need to think that she can still protect him. If she could, or if she were not already dead inside, she would put him on her lap again, and certainly life would return her to the time when she wanted to teach him the only two syllables that she doesn't remember him ever saying: *Ma*-ma! However, Nuno will always confuse, in the gray wilderness of life, the word *Mama* with the lack of stress on the syllables of the word *Mama*. Precisely for this reason, due to a lapse of orthography, he is missing concepts, experiences, sounds, and rules. It's not possible to take the measure, to know the music, to taste the many other words: lap, nipple, nectar, milk, pardon, guilt. Perhaps because of this, he can't and doesn't know how to link that past present and the present past of the body and eyes of his mother, and even less to the life of his Dead One.

2

It is perhaps this second and incomprehensible dimension that forces him to relive everything so he can write about it. He knows that it will repeat itself, at least from memory.

Living is definitely a very different act than writing, even when this coincides in the same person.

He has said it countless times: *writing is the moral food of life*.

Now he feels this without emotion, just with a part of him that is thinking. Oh, the great, beatific, and mummified poet Fernando Pessoa!

And there is an expression that fuses, crystallizes, and confuses, a superposition of his writing on his life — write to survive.

It's almost certain that Toronto has no resemblance to Leningrad, cities of metallurgical countries, with iron landscapes over which the very air is metallic, inhospitable, and the color of cold. First, Leningrad is unique, sitting on the islands of the delta facing the Baltic and crossed by the green waters of the Neva River. Secondly, Toronto is much closer to Mama's death. Every time there's a mother about to die, all cities announce it sadly. What is it like to die in Vancouver, a distant city that is three hours away by plane from Toronto? In Canada, God has a mechanical, trimestral ear. He allows the trees to resuscitate along those imaginary rivers of Ontario. He can't hear who might be praying for Mama's soul. Nuno had never experienced the passage of one time to another. Much less to have to explain it to her, the mother who doesn't want to die, offended by the distance and without his forgiveness. Rui Zinho, Nuno's double, uses this pseudonym because the modesty of books demands it of him. Only the books will force him, years later, to transpose this hollow reality and to open on it the doors that exist in the threshold and preludes of his doomed music. In every one of the small books he published, the writer Rui Zinho always limited himself to freeing the doves and letting them die far away, in the space that crosses and goes beyond the white oceans of Nuno's childhood. When he thinks they are lost from sight, the doves are still a point on the horizon. Nuno's days and years are composed of the distance that the eye can follow them. From now on, the time, the writing, and the madness of Rui Zinho will surface.

Is it inevitable that he live Nuno's autobiography? A perplexed writer, he gives himself the task of reconstructing the logic, the murmurs, and existence of his double. He suddenly takes his place at the table. Nuno's youngest son was celebrating his sixth birthday that day. In the afternoon, his little friends from school had come over: the party was made of ribbons, balloons, streamers, big slices of cake, tubs of ice cream, camera flashes. Marta commanded the chaos, in the middle of the shouting and crying (the writer Rui Zinho, unlike Nuno, doesn't give this any accent of tenderness). At night, when the children were in bed, their friends came over for a drink. At eleven thirty at night, when it's only three thirty in the city of Vancouver, Nuno's mother opens her eyes wide and has the premonition that she's doing it for the last time. With a shock of recognition, she sees death seated by her side. She wants to shout out, to call Flor. She tries to move in bed to escape the nightmare — and ends up finally exhaling her last breath. Flor recounted this in tears, hours later, on a phone call to Lisbon, with a desperation that Marta tried in vain to console.

It must have been a mere coincidence. If it wasn't, the writer Rui Zinho has free license to give Nuno's life the shock of this additional fantastic episode. The moment that Mama died, Nuno's arm accidentally knocked a glass to the floor, breaking it. He didn't find it strange that his friends clapped, because breaking glasses at parties had long since stopped being an act of superstition. Nuno's strange presentiment flew, however, in the direction of Vancouver. Years later, Rui Zinho, who is his double, feels the same chill run down his spine. He tries in vain to channel this feeling into the impulse and thread that he must follow in his writing. He can't. In fact, between them is a third individual. This one changed all the names, invented faces, and joined Nuno and Rui Zinho in the lie of his pseudonym; it is he who will put his name on the cover of this book . . .

He resumes everything again. He needs to repeat it and write about it so that he can't go back or relive the time and pain of his mother's last days. He absolutely needs for the readers to be accomplices with the play between his mother's death and the love of Marta for her husband.

You don't know Marta?

There are more than enough reasons why she enters the story again. Marta was always Nuno's second childhood. But it is by Zinho's hand that she now enters when Nuno's mother dies.

Shall we begin again? On the trip between Montreal and Toronto, he meets

Jorge, who will accompany him to Vancouver and point out to him: "These are the Rocky Mountains, that is the Pacific Ocean. You can see Seattle in the distance, to the south. This is America, brother."

3

The Rockies appear to us this way — sculpted over the bluish background of the planet — those translucent landscapes, somewhat desert-like and very still. They don't have the characteristic smell of the earth, or its memory of dreams, and there is no concrete way to define them. The landscapes are carefully composed, like canvases, symphonies, or books. They fulfill the dreams of their creator.

For someone who travels at thirty-four thousand feet, on the way to Toronto, life is nothing more than that infinite Canadian landscape that we cross on the metallic morning, the dream of a bird suspended from jet engines. Everything is confused in the cross-country trip; not even the aspens and the birches resist the clouded iris of the end of winter. The forests are fish skeletons that lift up bony spurs to point at the absence of God in those wastelands populated only by pine groves. Occasionally mysterious little cities emerge from the plains, blackened by the cold — but there is always a kind of mist that envelops, tarnishes, and almost crushes everything. It isn't the desert for the simple reason that this very white sand, plowed over the black soil, isn't swept by continental winds. The dunes and rocky surfaces are arid. There are areas where ice floats in the midst of the waters, profiles are blunted, houses without owners have a low profile, and the kilns of big factories rise on the side of the roads. Afterward come the interior seas, the water deserts of the eternal lakes of Ontario. The sun lies low. Clouds of gauze roll in and then hover over cylindrical forms, suspended like hanged bodies in the emptiness of this eternity. Every time the sun crosses them and lights up the snow, a phosphorescent grey tinges the polar tongues and stretches to the mirror of the lakes.

Judging by the way the trees revive from the depths of their violet death, there are frozen riverbanks leading to Toronto. It is almost depressing to look for too long at this last breath of the grasslands, the blue destiny of those primitive waters, the still uncertain end of the long hibernation of the flat forests.

In half an hour, Toronto will appear: a city he is not eager to visit. The voyage had been made in the opposite direction of the rotation of the earth, in the inverse direction of the movement of the hands on clocks, as if it were about going against the order and convention of time zones. It is common knowledge however, that traveling to Toronto, and going on to Vancouver, is as absurd as linking the future to the past of a family, with the only present being Mama's last days. He had never experienced this landscape from one time zone to another, much less having to explain it by the fact that Mama had called him, not wanting to die without the guarantee of his forgiveness. The truth is that the family had begun to occupy an almost fictitious place in his life. Some of his siblings had even stopped leading a concrete existence, lost as they were in eighteen years of absence. For this reason, the perplexity of his gaze seemed to fix on imagining their features. The great strangeness of life was in this feeling: he had had parents and siblings, he had known their names, but they belonged now to a previous existence. Perhaps even to another genealogy.

He had hoped to recognize them by the ambiguities of physical resemblances and by the exercise of memory, with intervals of sporadic pictures, letters, and all the signs that he had filed away in Lisbon during a time of scrapbooks and memories. After eighteen years, the disorder of these pictures didn't go beyond a daguerreotype of his closest ancestors, organized into an imaginary tribe...

It occurs to him that he needs to reconstruct the family. He does it face by face and imagines it in a frame, with his parents at the center, sitting with the uncomfortable smile of old age — and the hardest is to recompose their mournful posture, the look of precocious grandparents, the neutral way that their faces would express the passage of time. His brothers would possibly be big-chested men, with large wrists under sleeves rolled up to their elbows, their thick, muscle-bound necks like those of the tame oxen of the Azores. Nevertheless, the eyes would remain a temporal, bewildered in the middle of a childhood that had never been graced by innocence. His sisters, if he could see them standing in front of him, would certainly be women in dubiously fashionable clothes that contrasted sharply with their provincial hairdos, their bellies worn by childbirth and disappointment. Next to them, he forced himself to place nephews and nieces with the look of properly baptized children, whose presence was simply a trophy of the marriage bed. As for brothers- and sisters-in-law, he knew of their existence more from their names than their faces, but everything indicated that they would speak the Azorean dialect of the old ox drivers, the unforgettable clamor of the harvest, a speech now corrupted by an untranslatable English. Sometimes he had been able to join one or another of his brothers in the Azores, on the occasion of his infrequent visits to the time and house of his childhood on the Island. Other times he had received the visits of the younger ones in Lisbon, the same way that his parents had decided to say a final good-bye to him, Marta, and the boys. Father had already been condemned to prostate cancer, Mama complained timidly of lumps in her breast and groin.

Strangers, lost in the past, and suddenly reunited by a telegram announcing Mama's approaching demise, more than four years after Papa's painful, distant death. He didn't believe in anything anymore. A few minutes from Toronto, where he would rest before continuing the trip to Vancouver, flying in the metallic eagle that crosses the morning and starts to descend the steps of clouds, landings of wind and structures of ether in the freezing air, and the glaze of the Canadian cold, he is aware of the inevitability of being introduced to a family of strangers. Certainly he will ask Mama to do it, so she will confide to him in her dying voice:

"Here they are, your brothers and sisters. You may kiss them: Amélia, Luís, Domingas, Linda, Flor..."

It was ridiculous to have to embrace them without having met them before. Luís would certainly still have the strength that he had used to pick up calves and horses and to carry the great baskets of beets, and for this reason he would lift him into the air, so light and thin, and always good for nothing, without being worth even the water he drank... Amélia wanted to open her arms to him, as in the old times, to gather him in to her displeasure. The others were frozen in the time of the orchards: they would shrink into a corner, full of the same shame that children show in the presence of strangers.

"Tell me who they are, Mama. Is it they, or are they are someone else? If they were once, or if it has to be that these and not others are my brothers and sisters from the Azores. I don't remember having seen them be born, or how they cried or smiled. I don't remember their voices calling me, or how they laughed at me because I was studying to be a priest. I remember nothing at all, Mama."

For that matter, who was Mama, this dying woman whom he had come to honor? How would he express his disgust at seeing her so old and ruined, if there had never been time and it had never been possible to understand her vocation for motherhood from each and all of these children?

His concept of family hardly went beyond a sacred puzzle that had to be put together from primordial pieces. If he could fill in so many empty spaces, and could decipher the nostalgia of so many enigmas, he'd be just a solitary player, sitting as he was in the window seat of his future airplane and watching the lakes, the woods, the bifid highways, the desert of the few houses lost in the infinite Canadian landscape.

He suddenly felt longing for Marta, the children, and his house in Lisbon.

The inevitability of the encounter with Mama's death enlarged the great delta of his anguish to the point where the pain of being alive became a bearable feeling. He had never known anything concrete about the death of mothers. Women had always signified life, the sun, the pleasure of giving to the limits of energy. Their opposite is refusal, because all of them invest in this firmness much more than simple rejection of a man. He had learned from women what they themselves, and only they, had decided to teach him. Like forgiveness, for example. When he began to know his wife's body intimately, he tried to inhabit it in all its natural amplitude. He loved her always not just because of desire but above all because of fascination.

His relationship with Marta was the long story of intimate contemplation, because what he most liked was to spend a long time taking in the vital complicity of her dark eyes. Most of the time, they didn't even have to talk. Every time a message was transmitted by a glance, there was in the silence the almost mystical clamor of passion. He knew it was inevitable to brush his hands over her face, along the satin surface of her thighs, and the almost swaying fragility of her buttocks. Then his hands became even more sensitive. They burned, fascinated and eager, in a kind of amazement, as if they didn't believe in the existence or mortality of that naked body that had never been shared with another man.

Sunday mornings it wasn't even necessary to think about the injustices of the world. No friend had ever committed suicide in a hotel room, and Marta sang in the kitchen while she made pancakes for breakfast. There was, in her morning song, the happiness of a woman who had been well loved on Saturday night, loved without the hurry or tension of a pressured ritual repeated on workdays. They practiced a perfect and primitive love, as slowly as possible, without time, and sublimated until the definitive corporal possession, when the spirit inhabited the body in its plenitude.

Marta loved to be taken from behind, and for this she would kneel with her knees on the mattress, hugging the pillow. Nuno's hands traveled up her body in circles from her buttocks to her shoulders. Then they closed around her neck and from there slid down to take possession of her small breasts that were firm and unequal. He thrust himself on top of her, forcing her down on the mattress and molding her under the prison of his inconceivable manly weight.

Seen from behind, Marta was like the stray dogs in heat on the back alleys of the Azores, with her gray anus, the pubic conch cleft in the middle with its very acid smell, the magnificent petals of that same corolla that the oxen of his childhood licked and smelled before losing themselves inside it. Then the temptation was irresistible to become the dog and the bull of that sweetly prone female, who in spite of everything waited and remained submissive, listening to her husband's secrets. His scepter slowly explored her anus, with discreet and sensitive friction, and Marta closed her eyes, sighed, and signaled she was ready and open to be penetrated by her man. She had the superior advantage of having a mouth of honey, every time he offered her his tongue or bit her at the corner of her lips. Her tiny head twisted to receive this soft bite, and also to beg him to penetrate her deeply with his staff. Nuno asked her for a little more time. He loved to feel his hands wet from her intimate juices, and he filled them with the mucosa, the coarse nest of her pubic hair. The moment of penetration was intensely desired by both. His phallus rubbed against the lightest resistance of the walls of her vagina, elastic and muscular, until it disappeared completely into its conical form. It was the perfect, absolute junction of their bodies, and almost their fusion. Then, holding her groin, he made Marta his little cart. The movements started slowly, somewhat lazily, in the long tip of his penis exploring her clitoral hood. Then they started to move into a rhythmic cadence, and Nuno's testicles slapped against Marta's anxious fingers, and her anus was like a wrinkled prune. As pleasure spread through her body, Marta opened up like a flower, offering herself to the contact and tenderness of her man. They stopped to kiss. They spoke words, absurd phrases. He rested his body at the edge of the bed, without being able to hold off any longer the irresistible and deep knowledge of his wife. He turned over to be able to repeat the pleasure of penetrating her again. He plunged into her until forgetfulness and darkness, because Marta had transformed her body into an enveloping ring. Her legs wrapped around his back. His arms encircled her neck and taking her with his full weight he flooded her with three powerful spurts, and also with a deep, grateful cry, his very life entering the flesh and blood of his wife.

4

The customs official only has to look at Nuno's pink hands and almost haughty face to know that he doesn't have to lump him in the category of those who are behind him in the customs line, with their impoverished appearance, their noise and disorder. Nuno notices the difference in the sudden tranquility and sweetness of the very blue eyes, but also in the way that the customs official's hand rests, distractedly, over the stamp of the entry visas. He is a small, blond man, with cropped hair and freckled skin. He is almost a redhead. Nuno supposes, however, that the zeal of the immigration officers hides their apparent indifference. Behind him, coils of nervous people continue to drag their suitcases behind them. Nuno hears them scold the children, the dazed children who still don't understand the gravity of the moment. While he waits his turn, he looks askance at the thick fingers and dirty nails of the Azorean immigrants. They hold their open passports, with shaking hands and anxious eyes. Others wave at family members waiting outside the customs areas. They shout out their first messages; they say and repeat "thank God!" and the others agree, nodding their heads.

For Nuno, it's a repeat of experiences in London, New York, and Moscow. Especially London and Moscow. As he disembarked from the ferry that links Calais to England, he wore a three-day-old beard from the three-day crossing from the Peninsula and France. The same guards with blue eyes and uniforms had confused him with illegal immigrants, not believing that a Portuguese teacher would be mixed up with people carrying big bottles of wine, sacks of salted cod, and Tupperware with dried sausage. He had been surprised how the immigration officials renounced the English port, transforming themselves into Latin men — stupid, violent, and radically nationalist. At this moment he understood everything: Europe had discovered the third racism. Xenophobic Europe rejected, scorned the Portuguese immigrants, with the same ease that a son of the Supreme Soviet Republic had stared at him disdainfully for five uninterrupted minutes at the Moscow airport. Rui Zinho, his double, had been invited by the Writers' Union to represent Portuguese writers, and he was faced with a glass box, where a human crocodile stared at him in a cold, immense airport, echoing with the sound of boots and uniforms in transit. It was racial profiling, because the immigration guard must have been studying his bones, the color of his spirit, and his past and present. The interpreter struggled to explain to the crocodile that the writer Rui Zinho was part of an invited delegation — but he did it with a strained voice punctuated by invisible sobs. So that after five minutes of that contemplative silence, when the stamp pounded, it was done with the boom of X-ray machines, and Zinho concluded that all of his organs had just been put on film.

Racism was universal: he had seen it in his own country, exported from Africa, arriving at the New York airport on a freezing morning, on the streets of Paris, in the London wax museum, written on the political billboards of Lisbon, on all the television images, and he knew its face, its skin, and the smell of its breath. The Azorean immigrants of New York, London, and Toronto faced the third dimension of this Biblical sickness, and Nuno's spirit vacillated between panic and hate. His nerves are suddenly assaulted by a vague feeling of guilt that seems to swell his heart. Years and years had passed since the absolute control of the Portuguese police. His country had turned away from this obsolete tension, turning to other problems. But Nuno had never known how to explain why he continued to feel distressed and confused, his voice faltering in front of a simple immigration agent.

He decides to open all of his suitcases, as he sees the others do, and he knows that he does it from sheer nervousness. When he extends his passport to the official and tries to smile, his face is that of an ambiguous man, full of shadows. In London, he had been confused with terrorists and had been subjected to an interminable interrogation. In New York, an FBI agent had wanted to see his wallet and had counted the dollars in it. Afterward he apologized, he had confused him with some Latin American . . .

The Canadian police, however, gave him a conciliatory look. Along with the blue shirt and the royal blue epaulets, the gaze says, You're welcome sir, and reassures him about the luggage. He only wants to know what brings him to that faraway country of strangers and perpetual immigrants and asks:

"Why are you here, sir?"

Nuno resorts to a tortuous English, which he thinks is scrupulously grammatical, and responds:

"I've come to see my family. My mother is very sick, and I must see her before she dies."

Instinctively, the official shrinks back and retreats behind his glass cage. Before stamping Nuno's passport, which he does with an identical thud as the crocodile in Moscow, he still wants Nuno to declare his profession. Nuno hesitates for a moment, he doesn't know if he'll say I'm a Portuguese writer, but he ends up settling for the mediocre option of high school teacher. Then the official opens up a millimeter of a smile over his magnificent teeth and asks if he has anything to declare to the Canadian customs. Nuno alludes to the Portuguese tobacco, the sports jerseys for his nephews, and the ties for his brothers and brothers-in-law, and the small gold trinkets for his sisters, mother, and sisters-in-law.

"That's okay," the official interrupts. "Souvenirs, right?"

"Of course, just souvenirs."

"Any liquor, sir?"

Since he doesn't understand the pronunciation of the word *liquor*, the officer tries to be more explicit: "Oporto wine? Madeira wine?"

He answers, "Nothing at all, sir."

Then his passport is stamped and he hears the man wish him a good visit to Canada. With a wave of his hand he indicates that he should clear away his open baggage from the inspection counter. Nuno drags the bags to the wall that separates the customs area. He sees the anxious crowds pressing against the exit barriers. He senses immediately that Jorge, Teresa, and the girls have already identified him. He doesn't want to see them yet. He feels their eyes boring into his shoulders, but he doesn't want to recognize them yet. He struggles with the stubborn locks on his suitcases and presses his knee into the leather cases. He knows that all he has to do is straighten up, turn around, and look at an arm waving at him over the crowd. And he would be transported into a perfect moment of his childhood. His passport, ticket, and bag with his wallet, planner, pen, and cigarettes, fall from his hands. The overheated air of the airport makes him sweat. He should take off his coat. This would, however, only impede his movements. This gives him plenty of time to listen to the wail of lamentations of the Azorean immigrants. The next moment is one of guilt: Nuno registers internally the scene of his social difference relative to that of the people of his land and his country being received there. The summary apprehension of bottles of wine unleashes timid, offended protests. The immigrants are again very old and tired beings, and he sees in their faces the insomnia of this life voyage. "I am in London and Toronto at the same time," he thinks. Frenetic officials move in from invisible offices, forming a human ring around the perplexed people who now have the enormous and humiliating challenge of holding the hands of crying children, opening suitcases locked and wrapped in nylon bands. The police poke around in those miserable precious belongings with repugnance, like aseptic angels, deaf to the protests. They toss the rolled up clothing to one side. To another, they throw the torn packages, the contraband, the Azorean foods that can't be allowed into the country. In the midst of the baggage appear bell jars, images of saints, wall clocks, music boxes. He is again in London and Toronto, because the same British police, or children of the British, hold their nose with their fingers, disgusted at the cod, the invisible bacteria, and the filthy detritus of that new human condition that invades the country of plastic and cellophane, the country where everyone says sorry in the supermarkets, the pedestrian walks, and even in churches. They don't speak English. This is why, when the police also decide to confiscate the pocketknives with whalebone handles, he hears someone raise their voice and protest:

"Hey, sir! Please let me keep my little knife. So much fuss for nothing!"

Nuno is torn between his humiliation as an Azorean man and tenderness for those poor people who come here to be happy and who will be squeezed dry by their sweetness. He always knew that poverty is noisy. But it touches him to hear at such close range the cries of the children, the laments of the women with big breasts who dress in mourning, the murmuring of that wandering, displaced people, singing the songs of their poets...

Jorge barely catches a glimpse of him as Nuno exits the customs area and walks to the waiting room. He is waving over the crowd. At his side, Teresa is blushing: she hardly remembers Nuno and seems to be embarrassed by the surprise of her big belly from her third pregnancy. Nuno then notices his sister-in-law's beauty, her big, sweet black eyes, the apple blush of her round cheeks. He had imagined her exactly like this, as much for her beauty as her modesty. He does not know his nieces. But when he squats down to embrace and kiss them, he recognizes the familiar smell, the strong shape of the mouth, the same blue eyes as Jorge. He hugs his brother for a long time and surrenders completely to the strength and energy of the muscular arms. He thinks: all of this is a lie, I never had brothers like this, tall, strong as boxers — and their smiles were never as broad or their eyes, shoulders, and arms as determined and impetuous. But embracing him again, he thinks that only this way can it be true. He absolutely needs to get used to it, to get back into the habit of being someone's brother, and to stop resisting this strange evidence of still being, himself, the son of a dead man and a dying woman. In a third embrace, the head of his sister-in-law joins that of Jorge and the bodies of two little girls, and that's when he hears Teresa overcome her shyness and murmur into his ear:

"If it's a boy, he'll be named Mark. Do you like the name? We had thought of asking you to be his godfather . . ."

5

The cities are unique, and they are twin cities in the way they resemble and differ from each other, for example, in their purposely rounded names. One has to say them slowly, weighing each syllable, and that's what happens to him now: To-ron-to. Just a name, that at first the jetlagged mind makes sense of, still confused.

Sitting on the upper floor of Jorge's house, he looks at the city as if he were contemplating a drop of oil moving in space and undulating on water. The specters of its octopus tentacles stretch from the center to the periphery. It's a female city, in body and in name, like all the others that he has been taken to live in. Seen or just admired from the heights of a house, it's just that.

Is the Toronto night flat? The nocturnal walls line up along the uncertain profiles of the buildings and the mushroom of the great Tower is concave in its stone flanges. It's a supposedly obscene phallic symbol in the heart of downtown: erect and triumphant amidst the illuminated rust of the metal landscape. It assumes the form of a lighted apple, after being bitten by a woman. It is a stationary serpent, without function, with its solitary head lifted high and the ashamed head coiled discreetly over the enormous cement platform.

Where is the center of the World? In Vancouver, Mama sleeps her sickly slumber, and an orange moon hovers in the cloudy emptiness of that crèche of lights, so high that the sky is like a house without a roof or dome in the middle of an immense, still ocean. Toronto's buildings sparkle, raise neon arms holding signs. The baleful night is drunk; only the traffic of limousines and the sound of trams on the tracks make it real. Toronto is in the center of the World, between the Atlantic and the Pacific. What flows in the vastness of the landscapes, the great highways walled in by towering steel barriers, seems to lag behind in a darkening evening, like a mournful symphony.

Everything multiplies: the intermittent neon lights, the letters that drip from the colored lights, the heavy cold. In Portugal the wind doesn't bite like this, nor does an embolus of static clouds blacken the grass and reduce the trees to larvae. The Portuguese cold has another volume and trajectory, it is more luminous and starry than this. Above all, it's not subterranean, or windswept, and it's vertical. He had heard that Toronto was a hollow city, with dug out foundations, so it could ignore winter. Jorge had taken him to see some of these underground streets, modern catacombs with transparent domes over which flowed a sky with leaden clouds.

Progress is easy: it's already been achieved; it's in the soul of the people. Is the Portuguese district in downtown Toronto the same as in Europe — the squat houses, the now deserted markets, the baroque design of the rustic stores? Jorge had said there are about two hundred thousand Portuguese in Toronto; it's about half the Asian population. You can see the Asian Canadians concentrated on their errands, smiling, always delicate in their transactions. They are educated people with an agile stride, unmistakable Asiatic eyes, and a perpetual, if sad, smile. Yet, Jorge told him, here nobody knows anything about anybody. There is order — a vast and sufficient order for this country of strangers.

On the Pacific coast, Mama sleeps her sickly sleep, early in the Vancouver night. Sometimes in the middle of her nightmares, in the agony of last days, she rings a small bell, calling mutely for help. Flor, in whose house she has decided to die, always comes quickly to her aid. She brings her the succor of a nocturnal goddess. She puts her back to bed, changes the positions of a complex arrangement of pillows and listens without blinking to her sad complaints. Then she goes back to her room, crawls into bed very carefully so as not to wake up her husband, and starts to sob. For four months her nights have been filled with those tears. Jorge, who had already visited twice, says that now Flor has cold eyes and purple lips and the slow thinking of someone who can't sleep. He thinks she runs the risk of going crazy.

"A sacred puzzle," thinks Nuno again, about this family. Where every piece has a weight and a time different from all of his. He composed it with effort, emotionless. He couldn't sleep, jetlagged and unable to adjust to Toronto time. Worse yet, he was here among people who were like strangers, from whom he had been separated all these years. "My body tells me it's time to get up and eat breakfast. The best of Marta is hearing her call me. To lie down next to her, help her get dressed, eat at her table, make a surprise visit to the clinic and invite her to coffee. And the worst of her is the routine of it all."

The sound of Niagara Falls still plays in his mind, the enigmatic thunder of those waters that form the border with Canada. Jorge had showed him all of this with passion, and done it with the euphoria of ownership. He had taken him to see the Nautilus, which was waiting for summer in the waters of Ontario in dry dock. Nuno also visited the woodworking factories, with machines that didn't resemble in the least the ancient and humble woodworking tools of his father. And there was the land, and the three-story house with a garden and an outdoor grill, and the drumbeat of a continuous dream: to get rich, sell everything, and return to Portugal for good. Jorge had declared all of this with the spirit of victorious possession. Because on that side of the earth, even the gods were different. There was the God Land, father of other lesser divinities. But the greatest of them went by the supreme name of My. Nuno understood this because everywhere he heard the immigrants in Toronto say My house, My money, My family, My car — and it wasn't hard to believe in the existence of a goddess named Happiness.

6

After its imponderable droning navigation of the clouds — limbo, pendulum, or Charon's ferry — the Air Canada plane suddenly points its curved snout toward the ground and rapidly loses altitude. It's as if it jumped out of the snow crowns of the Rocky Mountains, leaving behind the skeins of clouds, the crosswinds, and the rain that had pummeled the plane during three hours of flight. Nuno knows that he has once again been transported from one world to the next. He knows it from the balloon of light that surrounds the aircraft and makes him squint in the brightness. It's also another climate zone. He brought it in his body, different than the one that the sun makes sparkle at his feet on contact with the snow. What strikes him even before sighting the luminous detail of the landscape, is that it's very like the sky over Lisbon — a vertical sky, very high, under which the capital of its country, the white city of Alain Tanner, gains the incandescence of marble. After, when Vancouver is etched, clearly and languidly in the illusion of its colors, he knows that Lisbon is winning his chromatic bet over this new city and many he had known until then.

A blue halo hovers over Vancouver, a sign of the innocence and age of vegetation paradises. It becomes clear to him that it's a city without gods or memories, because there isn't a single monument of historical import. The buildings are like obelisks without a past; the intact towers are just geometrical solids where tinted glass, vinyl, and synthetic tiles predominate. But there is in all of this an almost prodigious equilibrium: the colors complete the forms, and the forms seem like objects that are inseparable from their colors. In Nuno's opinion, Lisbon's gardens don't stand up to Vancouver's: the profuse trees of great height, the flower beds, and very flat grass, the bamboo and metal fountains and the miniature streams. But how can he describe Vancouver now, since so much time has passed and his spirit is so far from that landscape?

"If you can't reconstitute its geography," Nuno confides to his double, "you suppose that you dreamed it. You lived the happiness, the dream, and the colors of Vancouver."

The blue of Vancouver, writes Rui Zinho, comes from its cold, clear air, and the clouds that crown the luminous, almost phosphorescent massive heads of the Rocky Mountains, and the Pacific Ocean, which has an oily sheen, in part magnificent and in part vulgar, different from the Atlantic; each ocean claims something different from those who come to experience them. The blue also comes from the small boats tied up in the marinas, the very black, wet asphalt, and finally the dull buildings whose square forms break out into the humid sun of the Pacific. Vancouver could be a violet-colored crèche, because its lights are like candles that tremble in the fog at nightfall. Rui Zinho had seen the same halo hover over the skies of Leningrad and Boston, and also over the city of orchids, Amsterdam, and he remembers reading about it in descriptions of Smyrna, Istanbul, and Beirut. However, Vancouver is the most magnificent city of all, impossible to live in, dream, or describe. Vancouver is at least as oblique, concrete, and sparse as the city of Funchal. The immense amphitheater of the Rocky Mountains functions like a windscreen, and for this reason the air is immobile, the trees are blue, blue as the clouds, the houses, and the boats. The only difference between the Atlantic and the Pacific resides in the strangeness of this harmony that no writer can ever capture.

    Rui Zinho has his fingers resting on the photos and he moves them around in front of him, hoping to recover the enigma of the landscape that Nuno's spirit still confuses with death and longing. The photos are just the cards of another game. They weren't taken with the intention of shooting a film, or even under the angle of vision of his writing. For Nuno, they represent only the shadow and not the memory of that time. He is in them with sad eyes, next to the ephemeral presence of his brothers and sisters. In the background, the blue of the snow-capped Rocky Mountains dissipates in the high flight of the lost clouds, those goddess-brides who don't have a lover or a destination. In other photos, Nuno has tired eyes. He is holding hands with his sisters, an arm over one of his sisters-in-law, or he is shoulder to shoulder with those three brothers who give enigmatic and incredulous smiles. Vancouver was subtracted from the rest of the pictures: there are details of the interiors of the houses of Luís, Amélia, Flor, and Linda Maria. The others are close-ups of people sitting around tables set with heaping platters, china, monogrammed napkins, innumerable glasses, and tasteless silverware. He sat at these tables to hear the interminable confessions of his sisters, and all the family gossip, and the chronicle of dead marriages, the news of a time that hadn't been and never would be his. Since he was there for a short visit, he had not had time to get into much detail. The only purpose of this trip was to allow the members of the family to absolve each other. With the nieces and nephews, it was different. He sat for hours with them on the plush carpets, talking with them in Portuguese and in English, or in both languages at the same time, and he had always been able to draw out long, tender laughter. The worst of the Vancouver days, thought Nuno, was sitting next to Mama's side, during entire mornings; everything was said and there was nothing to say. He had limited himself to listening to her sighs, and adjusting her pillows and helping her to change position, still afraid even to look at her face and understand he was in the presence of a human vegetable. Mama already had dead eyes, staring at the infinite, and premature old age concentrated itself around her flaccid neck. Sitting at her feet, he was incapable of saying the right thing; everything was said and still he couldn't tell her anything about himself. He wasn't even capable of coming up with the words a son should say: I'm so sorry Mama, it hurts to be here and not have the empathy to smile at you, a simple magic trip or a hope sufficiently strong to cheat death. As for me, my intestines give me trouble. Mama sighs, she always has a sigh fading on her blue lips, but I open my mouth to yawn and there is a continuous convulsion inside my stomach. The undefined problem of my presence, here next to her death, is having eight hours of time difference between these days of dying and Lisbon time. It's no use crying; I still haven't been able to invert the cycle of rest and activity of my guts. As for the rest, I continue to think that one can't, nobody can do anything for anybody, Mama.

So that Vancouver, Rui Zinho writes later, is not worth a simple flutter of the imagination. His hands freeze and he sinks into the unease of not being able to capture an essential feeling from Nuno's spirit. All of this needs a great poem: the image of the sounds, the color of the smells, the weight of the perplexed tears. And lacking is the music of nature that comes from the fruit trees, the rivers, the stamens of smiling flowers, the feathers, and the wings of the doves and herons of the Azores. Only this way can Vancouver fly again in his writing, be consumed by it or remain under the moon of a last and final symphony.

7

The first bags start to appear on the carousel, and then they go around in a circle to the clanking of casters, axels, and machines whose rumblings are confused with the robotic voices constantly announcing the arrivals and departures of flights. They roll by sleepy eyes, in reach of the passengers arriving from Toronto. They are as exhausted as Nuno and they don't talk; they limit themselves to saying sorry when they inadvertently touch someone's arm, or to stammer excuse me when they reach for the bags and their packages of sporting goods. Then Jorge's arm grabs him by the shoulders and pulls him toward him, in an embarrassed embrace that Nuno returns without energy.

"Close your eyes and turn around slowly," he orders. "Now open them and see if you recognize who's out there to meet us."

He doesn't point in any particular direction. It's up to him to discover the people and recognize the faces. Nuno looks beyond the glass doors and immediately sights the presence of his tribe. It's a small crowd that peers at him, waves, and then starts to smile awkwardly. He recognizes immediately the heads, eyes and mouths, and even the expressions of emotion and expressive traits of the family. He loses interest in the baggage. He by-passes the booths of the travel agencies, the money exchanges, the billboards that advertise, with a sweet smile, the services of rental car agencies, the vending machines with newspapers, tobacco, and chocolates, and then he's on the other side of the world. When he's in front of the still distant faces, he leaves behind the Portuguese time of Lisbon, the certainty of belonging just to himself, only to the dreams of his books, his life with Marta and the children. It's like riding a strange horse through the night. He needs to adjust his feet in the saddle and squeeze his trembling knees against the body of this unknown animal. After, when the movement of approximation becomes reciprocal and inevitable, Nuno starts to live in the interstice of these two worlds. Now, it's as if he were crossing the last bridge and finding his way through the fog of those times that are crossing and will fuse into a third reality.

All he has to do is deduce the identity of his two brothers by their likeness and the memory of their pictures. When it comes down to it, they all look a little like him. Even so, there isn't a perfect and immediate correspondence. The sporadic photos hadn't captured the anxious expression of the eyes, or the pendulum motion of the bodies that now walk in his direction. He recognizes, however, the wrinkles on their faces, the specific sadness and, better yet, the way they smile, lifting their thick eyebrows a little and with a discreet quiver from their nostrils. Everything obvious in those faces are the irreverent hair, straight and voluminous, the blue eyes of Linda and Mário (just like his and Jorge's), and the sad brown eyes of Amélia and Luís. Neither Domingas nor Zélia, who lives in Boston, are there, and neither is Flor, who certainly remains at her post, in the house where Mama has decided to die.

Nuno confronts other evidence: a few years ago he had met some of those siblings. Amélia and her husband had lived close to Lisbon, after their return from Africa. He had received them in Lisbon on their arrival from Angola. They had the look of the victims who carried decolonization on their backs. He had seen them disembark in Lisbon, bewildered, with hunched shoulders, and heard them curse the country that had betrayed them; the country gave itself the luxury of delivering the great Africa of the whites to a subhuman species that didn't deserve a proper burial. A few months later, he saw them off at the airport when they were taking a plane for Toronto. And now, seeing them again, he finds it strange to see Amélia's boyish haircut, without the great mane she had before. The absence of glasses, substituted by contact lenses, make her eyes avid, euphoric. The suddenly sharpened face of his sister, her extreme paleness, and her swollen stomach confirm her old ugliness but accentuate her decline. By his account she must have doubled her age from jealousy and her bad moods. But a discreet aging, protuberant and unkempt, starts to give her the look of a premature grandmother . . .

As for Domingas and Zélia, he had visited them recently in Boston, when he had gone to Rhode Island to participate in a literary conference. He had, in fact, hosted them in Lisbon, in the time of our revolutionary zeal, when it was still required to take American sisters to the bullfights in Campo Pequeno, to the Sanctuary of Fátima, or on a tour of the neighborhoods of traditional houses that bordered on the barricades set up by Popular Guards of the Revolution. Bearded civilians with fierce eyes searched the car. They smelled their perfume, their scarves, and the folded dollars in the bottom of their hand luggage, and they muttered under their breath about the CIA, the Mafia, and other dangerous reactionary agents. Nuno tried in vain to explain the unexplainable to them. He winked a complicit eye in the direction of the street revolutionary; he recognized him as a professor at the Faculty of Letters of Lisbon, one of those who still practiced the occult science of literary semiotics. To this day he swears that he has never felt as ridiculous; the professor opened his myopic eyes wide when he saw the card that identified him as a member of the Portuguese Association of Writers, under the pseudonym Rui Zinho. Two desolate arms opened to embrace his body, his spirit, and the recognition that this was the author of those precious small books. His Royal Highness knew Rui Zinho perfectly, but he did not expect him to be so young. But the comrade understood and wouldn't take it badly; he was watching zealously over the security of the people and the defense of the revolution. Nuno had stopped calling himself Nuno Miguel Moniz Botelho, and he now met half the world under the pseudonym that gave him safe conduct on the dangerous streets of his own country.

As for his remaining siblings, he could only imagine the gap from childhood to adolescence, when he had lost them; he found them again in the first decline of middle age, married, boring taxpayers, as the poet has written, confusing happiness with the art of living as naturalized Canadian citizens.

Luís can only be that human whale, who suddenly reminds him of Bud Spence of the *Insolent Cowboy*, only he is a Bud with prodigiously white, compact hair, and without the beard or bovine bonhomie of the actor's light brown eyes. He didn't know the woman Luís had married, but he imagined her with impetuous lips, a sharp chin, and a mocking smile that the family had mentioned in their gossipy letters to Lisbon. He also relied on the childhoods of Linda, Luís, Flor, and even Amélia to recognize their children, who carried the traces of family features. The mysterious in-laws of the photos were almost all strangers. He had lost them forever on the immemorial roadways, in early childhood in Rozário, on school benches, on the paths that led to the pastures and corn fields. There were, however, others who came before his tribe, and certainly they were Azoreans, including the parents and siblings of the in-laws, the friends, neighbors from long ago, and many other curious immigrants for whom the most important thing in the world was to continue to see the planes arriving from destinations that brought Portuguese voices.

The women lead the tribe; they do it with their characteristic courage, with timid smiles, and also with the first tears showing through their laughter. Nuno feels enveloped by their embraces and he returns their kisses and caresses on their hair. For a moment, his face touches theirs, and that is when the tears flow and perhaps mingle, in this emotional and fleeting contact. But he is not sure he started to cry. He crouches down to kiss his nieces and nephews; the faces bury into his shoulders and they end up hiding behind their mothers, so he can only manage a brief pinch on a fleeting cheek or on a round little nose that tries to escape the hands of the man they are told to address as Uncle Nuno . . .

Before hugging his youngest brother, he studies his age with astonishment. He suddenly remembers the frightened, beardless boy to whom he had taught the first words of English. He feels that he can perfectly well ask him his name and not recognize the metamorphosis of his body, his face, and his personality. He had left him still a child in the Azores, and now encountered him as a stocky, wary, and taciturn man. As soon as Jorge arrives with the bags, it's obvious that his thinness stands out in contrast to the strong torsos, visible muscles, and height of his three brothers. Even his nieces and nephews, who are introduced with their English names — Cindy, Steven, Mark, Joanne, Melanie, Bob, Susan, Billy — maintain this disproportion with his own children.

At the end of this interminable family liturgy, and after recognizing all the people who had come from or simply been born during his childhood, Nuno is led to the airport parking lot. There the family begins to argue over him. Joe, Amélia's husband, insists that Nuno ride in his big red car; sitting at the wheel, his smallness transforms him into a puppet and his little head seems even tinier over his birdlike shoulders. Linda opposes this idea tenaciously, in which she is boisterously supported by her husband. Luís does not consent, making it clear that he deserves the first minutes after almost twenty years of separation from his brother. Nuno decides, smiling, for Mário's car; eighteen years ago that silent boy with a face as small as a mouse's had learned his first English verbs from him. Besides this, he remembered the years of holidays from the seminary, when Mário was still crawling and he would turn his tiny face away from him when he arrived on the Island, before coming to his lap, and then later, that summer with Marta on Rozário, a few months before his arrival in Canada. His father had decided to free him from the war, as he had already done with Jorge; Africa was too far away from the Azores, he wasn't going to sacrifice the sweat or the blood of those sons to the stupidities of Lisbon, and as for duty to country, Luís's service was enough!

The cortege of big cars follows him euphorically through the Sunday streets of a blue city, on whose corners appear men and women carrying children and walking dogs in the park. He doesn't see Vancouver. He remembers leaning back on the front seat, next to Mário, and twisting around to respond to Linda and Amélia's many questions. They had decided to accompany him on this unbelieving journey toward inevitable death and absolution.

He feels himself taken in the direction of new neighborhoods that are far from the center and downtown, on the periphery of the city, where now the houses are surrounded by gardens: mansions with grass around them, a few cedars, boxwood hedges, and gardens with indecipherable flowers. He has the vague sensation of crossing a scrupulously clean city, with parks that have no statues; a city with the smell of that mystical sea that they call the Pacific — and there are tiny boats tied up to the distant piers, secular trees that bend over the streetlights, yachts and other vessels that bob up and down in the repose of the marinas, people who are not in a hurry in the taxis, and cars that never honk. Since it's Sunday, the big supermarkets look closed, public transportation is nonexistent or it glides by empty. The churches of the city don't have bells, and there is no sign of cathedrals. Perhaps other carillons vibrate in the air and with a nostalgia for Sundays. And it happens that the cars circle the low walls of the cemeteries; they are flat fields, with manicured grass and full of happy trees. Nuno takes it in and thinks that these are places that are indistinguishable from the green and blue world of the living. When Linda points in an uncertain direction so that he will know where Papa is buried, it occurs to him that perhaps a Canadian death is exactly that: a place without crosses and flowers on the graves, a simple feeling of the dead who live in a second time and a second eternity.

8

He doesn't notice right away if she is crying or if she is just smiling at him wanly and without great awareness. Her head is drooping over the shoulders of a body that is sitting at the top of the stairs of a Canadian house. It is somewhat twisted, leaning on one of the arms of a velvet throne, next to a fireplace that is not lit. For an instant, the face is blind and clouded, since it is contracted into a grimace. She is just an emotional mother who seems to sense his presence. Perhaps she smells her child. She is surely crying and smiling at the same time, because that's what mothers do after difficult childbirths.

Nuno is suspended for a moment, trying to decipher the unexpected reality of that face, and a chill runs through him. So is he face to face with his Dead One? Where he had always found an ineffable beauty, he encounters an abstract gaze, as remote as an echo. His mother's blue eyes burn behind happy tears, consumed, clouded by a feverish joy. He sees that her neck has lost flesh almost to the bone and that the folds of flesh betray an age that is beyond old age and ruin. Death is also in her mouth, and it appears slack and concave, pulling down the corners of her lips. When the voice speaks, it is just deploring the latest of her suffering. It mixes, however, with the opposite of pain. Before rendering accounts of her ailments, mother momentarily tries to forget her ills. She reaches out her trembling arms to him. Nuno envelops her shoulders, rests his face on hers and feels her body tremble under the weight of the first sobs. He knows that he won't be able to cry, because he has repressed this instinct his whole life. When he disengages from her embrace, he feels relief. In this precise moment, he understands that he has spent almost his entire life feeling the need to cry but containing his tears. He had forced himself countless times to swallow down his tears, mixing them with bread and fish, always on the other side of something he didn't understand. With the years, he had even lost the notion and need for those tears. It had not even occurred to him that it would be possible to come from so far away, to be taken to her presence, to embrace her, to receive the cries and pain of his mother and still remain an orphan, without the memory of her tenderness. His blood had become different from hers. His body didn't obey any other impulse except to return the emptiness of that physical and emotional estrangement. Since he had left Lisbon, that perplexity had become stronger by the hour, knowing that his love for his mother had another name. He loved her with the longing of not having had her in his life. He had to love her always for that reason — with despair and without hope. And for this reason he could swear that he liked her more than all of the others, because he worshipped her from a distance and in his imagination: beautiful, ageless, and out of time. He hears her now, and her hoarse voice has no resemblance to anything he remembers.

"Oh, son of my soul! And you came from so far, spent so much money, crossing endless seas and lands to see me in this state . . ."

Immediately Nuno hears the silent crying of his brothers and sister-in-law behind him. As for his nieces and nephews, they limit themselves to staring at him, not understanding why people are crying and not smiling, to celebrate the arrival of that unknown uncle who is different from all the others. The surprise of this difference is in his physical and social elegance, the way he speaks Portuguese, not with the Azorean accent but with the round, velvety syllables of Lisbon, and how he attempts almost supernatural English. Nuno had been announced as the family prophet: the vindication, the redemption of the ignorance and darkness of his parents' lives through his conquest of knowledge.

He can't overcome his skepticism or participate in the weeping of his family. When his mother decides to stop the kisses and caresses, Nuno is just a tired man. He still has the buzz of the airplane engines in his ears, and he carries the discomfort of hours of flight. He is weighed down by the time difference, the disconnection of the worlds that he was forced to cross.

"You are so thin, so worn!" stammers his mother, drying her tears on a Kleenex. "They say you work too much, that you sleep little. And you must be exhausted from the trip."

Nuno nods his head no, wanting to tell her he is not tired at all. He just lives fast. And since he has always been thin, he has the look of an unprotected man. "I have been the only master of my bones, Mama," he thinks. But it would be crazy to venture into those incomprehensible metaphors. For now, he just intends to return the same anxious smile to his mother. He doesn't want her to feel guilty of anything. He came to see her. He has come to her presence to absolve her of sins that have no pardon.

"Tell me, mother, how are you feeling? Tell me what they did to you. You are so sad and without courage. Have you suffered a lot?"

Then she lets her head fall to her chest, in resignation, and her mouth twists into another burst of tears. The sobbing becomes stronger now. Between sobs that shake her shoulders, she tells him of her terrible pain, her anxiety and cold sweats. She alludes to a fear of death. And as for her bones, she compares the pain to nettle stings.

"If you have to suffer so much to die, my son, then death is sad! If I only knew what awaits me at the bottom of that dark grave. The only consolation I have is that I will return to your father's side. I dream of him every night; he is always looking at me, wordlessly, sitting in a dark room. He doesn't speak but I sense that he is waiting for me."

Without knowing it, Nuno's mother touches on one of Rui Zinho's greatest sensibilities. In his little books, death was just dark and infinite. The difference was that she held on to the hope of going through a tunnel, to making the crossing by boat along the rivers of Gil Vicente, certain that God would be there with open arms to welcome her. Death, in Rui Zinho's narratives, was obsessively religious and cold as a dying mother. Now he is kneeling in front of her and thinking, as always, that death is perhaps the only problem Man has. He examines each one of her wrinkles, the greenish tinge of her cheeks, the febrile eyes, the head as fragile as yarn fluff, and he knows he won't be able to shed a single tear in front of her. His damned eyes are certainly disappointing the tragic impulses of his brothers and in-laws. Everyone had hoped that he had come to cling to her, to rock her, and to lament her condition at length. But it happens that the spirit of that death was coming up against a small misunderstanding: he had not come here to do anything. If they thought Nuno had come to soothe those howling choirs or to silence the bells that were beginning to toll for Mama, it was because they had all lost their senses. In truth, he had come out of an absurd excess of zeal, just to drag along the memory of that primitive mother, who had perhaps been beautiful and full of light in her heart, but never in her countenance. And he had not come to redeem himself from anything. That Dead One already lay in an agony that preceded the present hour. One can save the dead from a real death, it's true, but not from the death that comes from within, that has no body, time, voice, or place where one can or should remain in reverence . . .

9

I wake up with the first blade of light that pierces the slats of the blinds and illuminates objects that are suddenly unfamiliar to me. There is a glass shade that reveals a naked baby Jesus. There are the eyes of the same saints that disturb my sleep wherever I am. The Crucified One is there, and the bust of the Holy Christ of Miracles, and finally the open doors of a closet. On the other side of the room, piled against the wall of this wooden house that groans and snaps its noisy bones, the toys of my nieces and nephews are scattered around. A little bear with a pink nose smiles at me mischievously, with its paws in the air. Dented trucks with broken wheels and a tricycle with its horn squeezed between the remains of two toy boats and airplanes with broken wings and other miniatures imitate the still serious world of adults. I feel a shiver of tenderness. I have two children. They are, at this very moment, sitting on the other side of the globe. The most important thing in life is to know that no distance means being far from the smiles and existence of my children. They live inside me.

I see my clothing on the hangers. My shaving kit and books have been arranged by Flor on the vinyl table, behind the lamp on the night table. My suitcases are piled one on top of the other at the foot of the bed. I hear voices on the floor below. I turn on the light. I see my passport, plane ticket, the passport case with my documents and dollars, and a pad of lined paper. I will write long letters to Marta, ending them with funny stories that she'll read happily to the children.

My first act (I register it now on these pages) is to reach for my watch. I had taken care to change it to Vancouver time yesterday. It's three minutes to eight in the morning. My body tells me that it's four in the afternoon, I could be taking a nap, listening to Mozart, and reading the afternoon papers of Lisbon.

Or I can just sink into misery and dive deeply into the vice of being a man centered in his world. The time difference between Vancouver and Lisbon should matter little to me now. The perplexity resides in all the countless years, that invisible clock that separates me from the present and past of my Canadian family. My body refuses to live a single page of that novel. And my protest comes from my guts: they tell me that this is not me. Clocks lie. The ones here are from another place. They have no reason to be on Lisbon time.

I am aware of my restless sleep the night before, the false night of Vancouver. My brain reconstructs the times it thought it heard the little bell, the moaning and discomfort of my Dead One being taken care of by Flor. It remembers voices and hoarse phrases. Mama had peed in an enamel basin. She told Flor her legs had gone to sleep and her ears were ringing. Flor's voice rose and she told her coldly that all of that was normal; the doctor had warned her of the side effects of her medicines. A part of me says that I should have heard this with open eyes, sounding the darkness of the room. The other part of me refuses this notion; your family is something else, boy. You might have to invent it to make it real, or dream it so that you keep your memories of her. It had been important to be a son, to love a house, to respond when your name was called. Now, boy, just stick to opening your eyes, looking at the walls of a strange house, and listening in the dark. You don't even have Marta to help you get through another night of insomnia.

He feels a diffuse, remote, possibly inoffensive headache. Nuno? I'll also record it in this useless diary. Marta was always the only fairy of your sleep. Her fingers massaged your hairy body, you felt her breathing in your ear; that was perhaps the most profound truth of their love. "My dear, tender, and great love," you think. Do you remember? Your thigh between Marta's legs, feeling the stirring of a sleeping sex. What's the most important thing about marriage? Not to hate the smell, the repose, and presence of that other body. To caress her sex and breasts, to kiss her neck and shoulders, and to know that your body fits completely into the embrace and hands of a sleeping woman. No pain is moral, or even intelligent, in the face of the Pain of this Canadian mother.

Brothers and sisters, in-laws and nieces and nephews, indifferent to the silence of that Pain, stayed until three in the morning. The children fell asleep on the couches, on the carpeted floor or on the laps of his sisters. The television was on, giving continuous news of the provincial elections of British

Columbia. The others insisted that I drink beer with them, and they used their fingers to twist off the caps and wipe off the foam. They swigged it down, with their eyes closed, as if a mortal thirst was burning all the passion of their childhood. Horrified, feeling displaced in time, I heard from all of their mouths the story of a time that they were resurrecting. Luís recalled in luminous detail Papa's mighty death, his desperate agony, the begging for forgiveness in his empty eyes. Flor, in her comings and goings to Mama's room when she rang the bell or murmured a simple request, took advantage of the intervals to reconstruct the last four months of this morbid Pain. In her opinion, Mama's life is just a flower wilting in the cloudy water of a vase. Every day a petal falls off and the question is in knowing how many petals are left on the corolla, the decrepit flower of Mama's life. By her accounts, she can't last more than a month; she is like a Sybil who has the intuitive science that can predict Mama's progressive decline. Amélia brings up a practical fact, from her experience as a nurse: it's obvious we have to start thinking of dividing up the house, the lands, and the money — "especially," she adds, "since Nuno is here and will soon return to Lisbon, and you know how difficult the matter of inheritance can be."

"Inheritance? But what inheritance, sister?" Jorge exclaimed, standing up and then bending over so that they were face to face. "Nobody is going to talk about inheritance now. I can get a plane in half an hour to go back to Toronto."

At two in the morning (ten Lisbon time) it was my turn to tell them about myself, what had happened to me during all of those years of absence, the names of my children and their ages, what happened and didn't, my marriage to Marta. It was a type of allegory that was always missing the moral lesson or the explanation of the beginning and end of the family. I thought that perhaps we were just blaming each other. Heroes at the cusp of old age? No! "Just athletes who have already said their goodbyes to their happy full stadiums," I thought. The sisters even remembered the old stars that can only drop tears over the dead flowers of the big, lonely houses. Blaming ourselves, cursing our childhoods, but possessed by the passion of the eternal dream that we give the word *childhood*. All of us were heroes. Some because today they have big cars, two-story houses with gardens and a barbecue grill, and a country where you don't have to conjugate the future tenses of verbs; others because they have done well, they won the great race in which they had to run barefoot and now they can laugh about that badly told story that was worse when they actually had to live it. I gave them an account of some of my achievements, although without much detail. Not out of modesty, understand. But because I didn't know what kind of accomplishments these strangers would find most meaningful: whether the fact that I had been a barefoot boy on the Island, like them, and now showed up as the mysterious little professor of the family, or if there is virtue in the detail that life had taken me halfway around the world, running in front of and behind books they haven't read and would never read ...

"Now," I think, "they will start to show me off. They will eat me, force me to live like they do."

They had decided everything before my arrival in Vancouver. They would take me around from house to house, they would sit me down at their enormous square tables, I will drink the bitter wine of Alberta or Quebec, or the apple juice of their little secret lives. We will start by going to Victoria on Vancouver Island to wait for Domingas and Zélia, who are coming through Seattle. I will learn later that going to Victoria is as wonderful as a return to the beginning of the creation of the World, like a voyage to the past and the memory of the Greek Islands of Homer. Mário will say that it's just an island full of Canadian widows who come to warm their blood and bones, and to look at the festive ships that cross seas, traverse the cold, and dock at the supernatural piers of the Pacific. For me, however, the route from Vancouver to Victoria is traversed by the magnificent blue ferry boats that silently circle almost deserted islands. There are the majestic houses on the edge of pine forests, and other eternal trees whose branches scrape against the hulls of the boats, and bays as round as shells, and clouds suspended in the wake of a wind that has passed by. It will always be impossible for me to stop thinking of the waters and landscapes that lead to Ithaca. I think about it, during the crossing of this type of isthmus, knowing now that I was never anywhere else except on the boats that go from Vancouver to Victoria. If I could live on the tiny islands of the Pacific, I would certainly write books as prophetic as the immortal transparency of the ever-present, timeless wind.

Voices fill the house, coming from below as if rising from the foundations. They say good morning to the children and good day to the adults. I hear Jorge addressing my Dead One, asking for her blessing and inquiring about her health.

"Oh son, I'm getting along. My suffering is in the hands of God our Savior!"

Enter Luís, his wife, and two children. The sound of a ping-pong ball echoes from the basement. I can distinguish Mário's voice, insisting with one of the children to learn how to say in Portuguese, "your blessing, Uncle!" When I hear an attempt at this half phrase that gets caught on the child's tongue, I hear him ask if he has seen Uncle Nuno. Is he still sleeping? Does he like him?

"I think he's still sleeping upstairs."

I open the door of the bedroom and walk out to the hall. The same crowd as on the evening before, my lost tribe, looks at me up and down and seems once again to feel awkward in my presence. For a moment they are silent. The smiles are timid. My Dead One is once again sitting at the top of the stairs, with her body bent over on one of the arms of the sofa. She receives me with the same half smile and asks if I slept well and if I am more rested. I know that it's the duty of Azorean sons to ask for the blessing of breathing corpses, but I know that my voice will be as strange to me as on the day that an olive-skinned little priest from a southern parish pointed a malicious finger at my head, called me to the altar, and ordered me to read to the faithful a letter of the apostle Paul to the Corinthians. Just a few years had passed since my expulsion from the seminary and Marta had insisted adamantly that I attend a baptism mass. "You were always brilliant at Latin pronunciation," she said sarcastically.

Mama is surprised at my approaching mouth when I lean over to kiss her. She reluctantly returns the kiss. The sisters look at me, close their eyes, and keep their body at a distance from my arms. In truth nobody ever kissed each other during our childhood. Everyone is here but we are still on the Island. They brought it along, intact, inside themselves. Just like I did, but for different reasons, they gave it a different name — but they persist in the time of obsessive pilgrimages and processions, in the modesty of the most sacred nakedness, in the vice of talking badly about the neighbors. They meet to eat lupine beans and peanuts and to drink dark beer, to be far away from their wives. In spite of being unemployed, they continue to drive around in their long grey cars. Sad, enigmatic, they fake the pride of living in Vancouver. They dream of the cows, the lands, and the horses of the Azores, and they make plans for beautiful houses along the road that links the town of Nordeste to Ponta Delgada. In the meanwhile, it's more important to be Lewis in Canada than Luís in the Azores, or George instead of Jorge, or Joe and not José, or William, Frank, or John. Of the women, only Amélia adopted the name Mary when she became a naturalized Canadian citizen. The others kept their old names: it was a coincidence that Linda could be Linda anywhere in the world. Flor didn't want to be Flower, and Domingas always thought that her name contained an indefinable and divine religious significance . . .

10

I contemplate the enormous houses of Vancouver soulfully (from my soul, just from my soul). I enter each one of them early in the dun-colored Pacific mornings, still turbid in a kind of nocturnal gray that seems to hover over its leaden coloring. They are mornings of shadow, with very high clouds announcing the rain from a distance. I climb flights of stairs that lead to porches with wicker swings suspended from their hooks. I know right away that these houses are even higher inside; they rise above memory and time. There were little Chinese chimes that ring when the doors moved. Not now. I hear carillons vibrating over the calm of my few days in Vancouver.

I am startled by the beginning of Marta's absence in my life. It happened when I noticed the details of the double glass doors: cold that doesn't enter the houses but stays suspended between the two doors. "One of them," I think, "will close over the distance from her — from her wisdom and presence, the voice and body of Marta. The other will open to the strangeness and misfortune of these happy houses, where neither she nor any other woman, will ever celebrate my presence."

I don't know why these children who hide and spy on me from behind doors are smiling at me. Nor will I know what prompted these women, and not mine, to rise early from their beds. They don't tell me. But I know that they woke up at dawn and started their days quickly. They went to the bottom of their china cabinets and placed their beloved silver on the big square tables. After polishing the furniture, they placed plastic flowers in porcelain vases and went to dress, do their hair, and try out smiles in front of mirrors. And since the air is full of sweet aromas — of sugar, almonds, candied fruits, and apple liquor — I suppose they have beaten the egg whites, mixing eggs with flour and baking the golden cakes that steam under the little towels with monograms on their corners. I also guess at a discreet but persistent perfume of invisible flowers, coming from the gardens or the air freshener sprays. When I enter and start to look around the houses, the gestures of these women become perverse, circular, as if the light could come out of their arms and only this way illuminate the corners of the house with white and blue. I sense that this, and not anything else, is the source of their pride. A fleeting pride in their smiles but as perennial as the laurel leaves. It's all in the pleasure with which they hear me praise the spacious light, colors, and spirit of each one of the houses. Only then can I understand what they want me to tell them with those smiles; they had eaten the bread of tears, scrubbed basements and stairs, swept all the domestic garbage of other houses in Toronto and Vancouver. And they served, during the first years, under the disdain of Canadian ladies. Today they can finally smile, lift their chests, open the doors of their homes, and tell me that for them the dark time of white slavery has passed and will never return. Then the look of the men seems to light up with the same pride. They all came from my childhood. They crossed the cold of bright snows, the humiliation of the first Canadian bosses, the barbaric laughter of strangers. But now they can cross their arms over their chests, look down at me and think that they have some advantage over the golden time of Lisbon and the useless knowledge of a little family professor.

Even so, I don't lose the courage to refer to the small virtue of poor countries. I know they don't understand. They don't accept the praise of poverty and they can never comprehend the second dignity of that destiny. If they ask me why I like my country so much, I answer that I always have a reason. I always liked my country even when it was scorned. I will love it even in its nakedness, its vices, and its light. I will be Portuguese in my principles and in my soul, and with the blood of someone who carries inside him a verse, the smell of the sea, the fruit of his land.

Thus I notice that my brothers and sisters have spent all these years living with the challenge of my existence. It would be ridiculous to tell them about my tiny apartment in Lisbon. All I have to do is listen to the sound of the cues hitting the snooker balls, or the rackets on the ping-pong tables, or the sophisticated stereophonic sound machines sending me from afar the music of the saga of immigrants, and especially the big, long, luxurious cars that come and go from the garages under the vigilance of electronic security systems. My civilization is still beyond all of this. It lives in the time of refrigerators and television at the dinner hour. It has little to do with the luxury of machines and time is spent hurriedly consulting wristwatches or inquiring about the Lisbon bus schedules. For them, I am nothing more than a little man from that blue country, whose music doesn't come from machines but from voices and sounds, happy to have the right to a month of holidays each year, to ninety days of maternity leave and a Christmas bonus that has to be paid by December 15 . . .

Their conversation ceases to interest me. A tired sigh reminds me that I miss my children and my modest happiness with Marta. I was tired, sad, but again touched by a perhaps absurd longing for her love. In my previous travels, it always happened that this frisson of nostalgia came at the beginning, while crossing the thresholds of strange houses or hotel rooms. Now, my marriage with Marta crosses the first dilemmas of the conjugal game. The habit of being married to her addicted me to the game. It repressed in both of us the need to invent our existence from day to day. But when I hear the tenderness in her voice when she calls long distance, or reread the passionate letters that she sends me, I can't resist the ardor of the woman who has been able to give a voice to the silences and cry out from the desert of her own loneliness. What bewitches me about her is the spell she casts on me, her mysterious power as a priestess. I love her at the edges but not at the center of our destiny together, because I know that Marta's existence comes from the light. Her hands explain objects, not my complicity with them. It's impossible to describe how she makes a flower arrangement; it comes from her liturgical grandeur. It's impossible to say how those hands are adept at the ritual of making a bed, setting the table, serving me with the exact helpings for my frugal appetite. She is elegant in her way of separating the laundry, changing sheets, and smoothing the bedspreads! She does all of this with fairy fingers, without noticing that I am watching her and happy to be her man and to belong to the invisible expression of her life. Besides this, there is an almost stormy force in her nudity. The way she brushes her hair while she is completely naked, or the way she sleeps, curled up into an egg of slumber, will always be infinitely superior to any of my actions. In her, work is mixed with her style; she loves flowers on Saturday morning, the refinement of crystal miniatures, the cult of tiny earrings, and the rose-colored pearls of her necklaces.

For this very reason, Marta can't be exposed to the tasteless display of baskets full of artificial flowers that greet me in Vancouver. She can't be a part of plastic fruits or useless trays that are just a decoration on sideboards. In Marta's house the plants are round and leafy, a vegetal green that leans toward the light of Sunday afternoons. Her smile can't be in the innumerable pictures that smile at me from the depths of those heavy frames, forgotten among knickknacks. Here what impress me most is the excessive spaces of the houses, not the things that are supposed to fill them: the walls lined by incredible tapestries, the paintings by mediocre Azorean painters, the obsessive foliage of Chinese bamboo. On my sisters' walls the roses are not only frivolous but they have the contorted look of their tears. Not even the mirrors cast clear reflections of the indirect lighting or the golden fixtures on the doors. None of them reflect, even fleetingly, the magnificent smile of the woman I love.

These are light, proud houses, without a doubt. But they are too deep for my strangeness. I go into gardens that descend down slopes covered by artificial turf. I look out at the sky and the Pacific Ocean through the vegetation of these ancient trees, but it's as if I am seeing imaginary moons. Moons that tell me, from across the planet, that I am irremediably lost in the darkness of this family, and lost from my home and the presence of the woman I love.

11

Domingas Maria is the name of the sadness that has suddenly been changed into shadow and crosses the wrinkles on her face. You see it through the very thick lenses of the glasses with brown frames. It is a frozen, almost languid sadness, a fatigue that observes me, even before it starts to confide in me. Mary Amélia, on the contrary, shows it in the sharp features and prominent bones of her face. It bursts out in her nervous laugh. As for Linda Maria, she forced the sadness to descend to the bottom of her body; I see it in her swollen belly, in that perpetual imaginary pregnancy that reminds me of my mother's bulging body. I can even sense it in what she'll never tell me. Her face, which was the most beautiful of all of ours in childhood, has spread in the cheekbones. Hers is an oblique sadness that laughs, deceivingly happily and impetuously, but that cries silently. Zélia, the youngest of my sisters, displays the sadness in the difference of her blue eyes that in her childhood were as bright as marbles. Now, as I face them, I see that they are lusterless, washed out, and perplexed. Mary's sadness is full of resignation and disillusionment. Her short, wiry hair is as gray as Lewis's, and her eyebrows are as thick as his.

I am unable to see the beauty that all of our faces once had. What confronts me is a kind of ugliness that begins to hint at an old age in the smiles, the voice that has given up on life, and the terrible fate of unhappiness. The family gynoecium has degenerated in these lonely females, who fell into long-awaited marriages and then transferred all their love to their innocent offspring. Isn't that what's happening to me?

My nieces and nephews are the children of men and women who use false names, come from a country of strange fables, and slowly give up on believing in the time they were given to live. In Flor's dark fuzz over her upper lip, more than from the purple circles under her eyes, I see that happiness no longer is useful to the harmony of her marriage. I don't believe a single word that she utters in praise of her husband. Certainly she does it out of rivalry with her sisters, and in obedience to the sacred sacrament of marriage. She does it out of a religious sense of the indissoluble bond of the union of the flesh. I notice this in her cautious voice, the way she turns away her eyes and seems ashamed. So it's inevitable that I'm the one to call her bluff. This can't be love, sister, going to bed dead-tired, waking up every time your mother rings the bell for you, and dealing with a man who gropes for you, undresses you, and fucks you in the dark. He mounts you like a mare, grinds his teeth, rides you, comes, and demands that you be ready to sate his lust. It can't be love if he insults you under his breath so that no one can know about your small, secret hatred. You open your legs for him; you don't want to look at his face. You almost hate his breath on your neck. You only belong to him this way, as a dead woman. You perpetuate the illusion of passion, of having been a bride, the wife and joy of your husband.

"Is there a difference between being a wife and simply the mate of a man?" Zélia asks, blushing and making a great effort not to cry.

Zélia loved her husband and married against the will of the family. Lewis had never forgiven her from having run away from home. "She was just a girl, Nuno, but she shamed Papa and Mama," he would say later.

"She had started to menstruate," said Lewis, "and she was proud of her little sheep tits, and she gave it to the first one who came on to her."

Nuno also looks at her with the same disdain that still infuriates Lewis and makes his mouth curl. But this has nothing to do with Nuno. The sea tone of her eyes has turned gray. It mixes with tears and betrays the pain of a family that pretends to have made peace with her. She can't stand the rejection, even when it comes from Mama's sweet talk and silences. She knows perfectly well that Mama will die carrying the pain of the disappointment in her and that all the others will never let it go. Nuno suddenly feels detached from the moral code of this family. He will tell her this at the first opportunity, when he is alone with Zélia. In the meantime, he limits himself to feeling badly about her tortured look and empty hands. He knows perfectly well that the sickness of that body lies in the soft belly, the pummeled guts, and the inconceivable thickness of a male member. That's what the poor Portuguese women had told him who had not had nuptial ceremonies, or honeymoons, and whose bodies survive with destroyed loins. It becomes obvious that the marriage of this girl with gray eyes is summed up in an immense, perhaps unsustainable urge to scream. She is living the terror of that first, eternal night of being a married woman.

"No marriage can survive with a little man like mine," says Mary, both mockingly and enraged.

She brought him along with her to Canada, when he was blind with hate, from a rosy city in Angola. He was opposed to the move, knowing he'd never like the cold or the distance between Canada and his happy nostalgia for his Africa. Here he always missed having a black woman to slap around. He doesn't have a perverse white woman, or several, on whom he can spend all the money he earns. Most of all, says Mary, he doesn't have the old servants, the idols and heroes of Luanda. Coming to Canada with him was to accept the resentment, the debts of small, useless luxuries, the endless delusions of grandeur. "I put up with him as if he were a nasty neighbor, I tell him yes and maybe — but I won't continue to deprive myself of everything, and to keep my mouth shut with a smile on my face. I'm especially not in the mood to believe in his promises to adapt. One of these days, when he least expects it, I'll stop financing his whims, demands, and spending sprees with my overtime pay. I'll stop payment on all the checks, open the door, and pawn him off to the first buyer — there once was a little whiny man from Angola, Portuguese through and through, who came here with me from Angola and never wanted to be happy, as I am, in this blessed country called Canada."

"As for me," says Domingas, wrinkling her face again into its innumerable lines, "he can keep drinking until his liver bursts or he chokes on his vomit. But if he hits me again, I'll grab the kids and our clothes, I'll leave him a note on the dresser, fill the fridge with dark beer, and get on with my life.

And the stories go on. He listens to her for hours, and then the shadow passes and takes the shape of her face. Sometimes, silent tears fall with deep sighs. Nuno doesn't know a better personification of sadness, he doesn't know if it's because the woman is his sister, or because of the brown glasses or the wrinkles that distort her mouth.

He also notices that Domingas's children live in the shadow of this sadness. Sometimes they lie down on the floor and they start screaming for no reason and try to get her attention. The older girl shows the lack of affection of someone who lost their place in the cradle. She comes to Nuno and buries her head on his chest. She sits quietly, her eyes closed, on that ephemeral throne that her uncle offers her. For a moment she thinks it would be wonderful to have a father like this, in the image and likeness of this uncle-god from Lisbon in whose arms she pretends to sleep. Nuno allows himself to be moved and discovers in himself an unexpected foreshadowing of aging. Never until then had he admitted that the time had come that placed him at the top of an axis. This axis turned inside him and began to mean that he wasn't as young as he thought. He will always remember this inner moment when he changed age and lost the illusion of youth. He is already at the moment when one must get to the moral of the stories. He has to extract a moral lesson from the family allegory, and summarize it. He does it thinking that he and his brothers and sisters continue to struggle with the only problem of their lives. All of them are resentful of the inexplicable absence of the comfort of a mother's lap. This curse is in their blood, like a poison that is spreading to the fourth generation. First were the grandparents in the Azores who didn't know how to give affection and for this reason they didn't teach the parents the elementary science of the nurturing that was owed to the children. The grandparents, he thinks, certainly didn't get it from their parents. Papa and Mama lost their way, they forgot the virtue of opening their arms, bending down, lifting up from the floor, and allowing their growing children to sit on their knees for a long time. They didn't know how to study the lonely eyes, or the diffuse fatigue, or the imploring pain of this never satiated passion. So it doesn't surprise him that they all unconsciously follow the same path. You can share everything, either bread or the host, the wine or the honey, riches or poverty — but not the bottomless misery nor the muddy water of that abandoned childhood.

He, like everyone else, has a parable to tell. This time, however, he doesn't have to invent anything. Siblings, in-laws, nieces and nephews will know from him whom Nuno is talking about, now that they are all around him and seem anxious. "The only moment of tenderness I experienced in my childhood," he says ... The others open their eyes wide and lean forward a little, because they know Nuno is about to talk about himself and for everyone. "The only moment of tenderness of my childhood," he repeats, "was when father was lying on his back on a mat of dried sisal. He had his head on Mama's lap (the lap that should have belonged to us but was just for him). Mama had crossed her legs, she stretched her skirt down until it covered her knees. In between the pillows of her very white thighs you could see her pubic mound hidden inside her cotton panties. What was Mama doing? She was slowly picking the nits and lice from the head that Papa had placed on her lap. She pinched each strand of hair between her fingers and the lice burst with a crack between the nails of her thumbs. Then Papa's hands started to travel up her legs. They squeezed the folds of flesh and progressed greedily toward her groin — and I saw his saurian fingers approach the pouch that was to me always so mysterious. His fingers were as nervous as the legs of spiders when they crawl up a wall before they venture into the light. Mama continued (I think to this day she still does it) to pick the nits and the lice. Papa, delighted, fondled her. I saw it: at a certain point he inserted one finger, and then all the fingers of his hand, into the opening of that body that for me was always the center of an enigma. I saw sweetness hesitate between an invisible smile and peaceful pleasure, similar to the peace of sleep and malice, on her face. I saw in Papa's fingers tension and entreaty, desire and repose, pardon and guilt — and all the fire of passion that sweeps through any man possessing his woman. This was love in the best expression of their tenderness. To this day, if they ask me to define my concept of tenderness, I think of a man lying on his back and whose hands tremble in the search of a veil of black algae ..."

12

"Countless times," says George, "in Toronto, in the damned freezing Toronto mornings — I started to cry like a child. Me and my men had put on several pairs of pants, flannel underwear, layers of socks, leather gloves, and jackets lined with sheepskin. Some of us had even rigged helmets that went down to our shoulders, like the ones that Houston astronauts wear, to protect us from the polar wind that in Toronto has the weight of a bear and that howls like bitches in heat. High up on the scaffolds of those houses under construction or on top of buildings that broke through the clouds, the automatic nail gun would be covered with flakes of snow and would stop working. Our fingers, cramped from the cold, couldn't hold the hammer, the screwdrivers, the planes, or a miserable wood board. That's when I learned how the cold can burn. There is a strange fire, made of steel and Bunsen and that perforates our bones and seems to splinter them. There is no pain like it, or any worse kind of suffering, and that's why we weren't ashamed to cry.

"You could see Toronto in the far distance, squatting on the plain, and I remember thinking that the city was chattering its teeth and shivering, just like us, under the sky illuminated by ice crystals. Our bones were being crucified and we cried with rage, a proud immigrant rage. The damned tears of our pride froze in the hairs of our beard, on our eyelashes, and in the hairs of our noses. Our eyebrows, white with snow, turned us into a new species of old men, with white algae hanging from our sideburns and ears. With our mouths in a death grimace we were just immigrants from mild climates there to construct houses in the Toronto suburbs. But these were houses for people far superior to us, who demanded them ready on time and perfect, built on the edge of lakes. At the beginning of summer, we looked at them from a distance, seeing the boats arrive, the fishing rods, and the men in caps with the Canada Dry logos on the visors. So we wouldn't die we hurriedly descended every half hour to sit by the fire that was threatening to go out on the ground. When the fire started to crackle again in the wood chips, we wanted just to open our mouths wide, sip it with the brandy or coffee scalding in the plastic thermoses. We wanted to eat the fire, like they do in the circus, to be sure that we still had the instinct to live.

"But a man always showed up. Seeing us around the fire warming our hands and opening our mouths to eat the fire, he hurriedly got out of his shiny Chevrolet, waving furiously in the wind — and the breath of a drunk horse threatened us with an incomprehensible English and the most sophisticated of all Canadian whips:

'It's always the same, George! Every time I come here, George, I never see you working. What's going on? I'm sorry, but I don't like this, George!'"

"I came here to Vancouver," Lewis says, "because they told me that here there is everything to do. Toronto had come to the end of its growth. All the possible houses were already built on the shores of Lake Ontario. The sea of Vancouver attracted the fat blond women running away from the continental cold. Once they got here they bought villas with a view of the port. If there wasn't one for sale they moved on to the direction of Victoria, where the sea is even warmer and where gardens are abundant, the greenhouses and pigeons that old people like so much. They came full of imagination, pink as crabs, and took out permits, designed their homes, opened spaces for the garden, and remodeled the little wood houses into accordions that opened and closed, according to the season, either for outdoor barbecues or indoor fireplaces.

"I worked for all of those old people, one by one. They were greedy, stingy, and mean. Ordered around by little women with wrinkled noses and authoritarian chins, I planted roses and climbing vines, painted ceilings, made houses for the ugliest dogs in the word, invented dovecotes, solariums, and porches, I cemented garden walls that led to outdoor ovens and sauna huts. I always said Yes, Mr. Simpson Yes, Yes, Yes, Mister Whoever — and for what? When all the old people of Vancouver finished the dumps where they were going to die, they started to tell me: 'I'm sorry, Lewis! I don't have any more work for you. I don't need you anymore Lewis!'

"That's how I lost my job, went away, and applied for work to companies. Many of the foundations of the new neighborhoods of Vancouver I dug with my ears ringing with the noise of excavating machines. Then the accidents happened, the hospitals, the insurance, and one fine day they told me that I was disabled and couldn't do construction work anymore. Then I went to the buildings downtown, collected welfare checks, and lived from my wife's work as a cleaning lady. Making houses for people who were going to die, hearing I was fired, getting drunk from the disappointment of never having been more than a bum — those were my last years in Vancouver. While my wife has stairs to scrub and can clean the toilets of old people who pee on the floor, and wash baskets of clothes, we carry on with living here, little by little. Who knows if I won't go back to Toronto to live near George . . ."

James, Linda's husband, needs all morning to explain the process of chimney construction. He lists the materials, the risks, the secrets, and the prices. Almost morbidly, he narrates the story of clients and suppliers. His twisted smile hints at a pious irony about the competitors who lost business because of his skills as an artisan. As an aside, with his elbows on the table where the remains of breakfast still lie — the jams and the pancakes, the orange juice and eggs that were left over from my lack of appetite, the bacon, honey rolls, toast, and fruit salad — Linda approves this irony with the most malicious of smiles. Nobody in Vancouver builds better chimneys and at prices that can't be beat, than her man. She doesn't say it, even though she thinks it, because the arch in her eyebrows indicates a wrinkle of applause that is even more expressive than her smile.

"They got rich from heating," I deduce. "They tell me in other words, but it was because of fireplaces that they constructed the magnificent, almost majestic house where I now find myself."

I look outside; the trees extend horizontal branches over the grass. The girls play under the leafy canopies of those trees, and there is a blue coloration in the green that goes from the garden to the woods in the back of the house. If I could see the ocean, if I could hear it from here, this would be my dream house. I listen to the silence. It almost pants. For a moment I think I am being sheltered by the old poplars of the Azores. I know that it's the same Azorean silence because I always experienced it that way, between a gust that shakes the branches or vibrates in the depths of the soil, coming out of the tree roots, or from inside their trunks. My life was always separated from this silence that only exists inside houses placed in the middle of gardens, if possible with an arc of sea in sight and with its birds — herons, rock pigeons, or nocturnal Cory's shearwaters. It would be good if there were also red flamingos, swans, peacocks with wide rainbow colored fans, or big black turkeys with the necks of alcoholics. At least life could give me back the trees, the dovecotes, the walls that once surrounded the house of my childhood!

13

My father's grave starts where a number engraved in the surface of the stone emerges a handbreadth out of the grass. The stone was truncated at an oblique angle and the number contrasted in white against the black marble. Linda's finger points to the middle of a kind of golf course perpendicular to the most somber of the cedars that surround the Vancouver cemetery. Nuno doesn't see the box shrubs or the cypresses. He is surprised that you don't have to go through walls or go around tombs with inscriptions like in Portuguese cemeteries. He doesn't see the busts of angels or niches with images, portraits, and candles. The bronze tombstones, soldered to the ground, don't have phrases or epitaphs. Discreet, melancholy little crosses poke out between the tufts of clover that are now starting to flower. The moss is purple, a mourning, Lenten purple.

As they all walk in the direction of Papa's gravesite, going from the periphery to the center, the grass becomes thicker. It is humid. The tops of the cedars were trimmed into faceted pyramids, without apexes. They remind one of the obelisks from distant countries, possibly from the memories of the wrought iron street lamps that illuminate great moonlit parks.

"The civilization of the dead is really different here," thinks Nuno, taken along by the family cortege. "Nobody offers them flowers or messages of remembrance."

You see a part of Vancouver. Lewis extends his Bud Spencer arm over it to point out and curse the marinas, the ports, the railroad stations, and especially the white palaces that he calls *bulldinghys* and in which he identifies a city that will always be unknown to him. None of the others pay any attention to the landscape. Nuno sees the curved torsos in front of him, and has the illusion that he hears sighs and sobs, and it's then that he is filled with affliction. He can't see them, but he guesses at the turmoil inside these suddenly convulsed faces. They have the advantage of having seen it all: the illness, the complaints, the cries of pain, the agony, and the death of Papa. Not he. He had limited himself to reading about it in a telegram, and he wanted to think it was a happy death. Above all, it was a death desired by a man who had so long suffered the tortures of cancer.

"Even so," he thinks, "I should at least feel something. I need two big tears to disfigure my face a little. Otherwise, what will become of me?"

In a little while, sobs begin to shake the shoulders of his sisters. They stop talking. They enter the last enclosure of the cemetery. The garden of the dead is a temple made of passion, but without the architecture or altars that normally identify temples. Nuno now notices their embarrassment. The first to start to cry knows that she will bring along the tears of all the others, because no woman resists the votive call of tears. What surprises him is that it's his sister-in-law Mónica who breaks out crying. The family will never forgive Mónica the quarrels, fierce intrigues, and insults. Papa had died with the bitterness of having been thrown out of her house with Lewis's tacit complicity. Nobody had in fact alluded to the worst of all the family paradoxes: since Lewis was such a corpulent man, with an almost unmeasured muscular strength, he was always hiding behind the moods and caprices of his wife. But not even this kept Mónica from showing up at her father-in-law's funeral to begin a magnificent crying jag. She had done it with singing energy, sprinkled by the oratory of the mourners, and that was her reconciliation with the dead man.

So that, hearing her resume the recitation of that new canticle, followed immediately by the chorus of wails from his sisters, Nuno decided to put aside his scruples and to limit himself to observing the absurd spectacle of those orphans. The eyes of Lewis, George, Mário, James, and Joe were just red around the edges, seeming swollen and feverish. Ahead, Mary blew her nose frenetically on a silk handkerchief with a black border. Domingas sobbed inconsolably. Zélia, desperate, pursed her lips, and Flor struggled to control her trembling chin. As for Nuno, it suddenly occurred to him that perhaps he could squat on the ground to get closer to the earth where his old man was lying. He put his fingers on the bronze of the headstone, which now seemed as translucent as smoked glass, and he read the dates. He learned the years of his birth and death, and the days and months that had gone by in between and in the middle of which had played out the existence and distance of the one who had given him his name and changed the order and function of his surnames. Through this bronze glass, he can only imagine him fleshless, an almost vegetal green color like in an old photograph. His hands perhaps rest on his stomach, reduced not to bones but to shadows. And the bones of this dead man, who possibly still moves in the search of complete and definitive immobility, shake inside Nuno. They merge, sink, founder, going against the voices and in the direction of the silence. Pain is thus a lost cloud and comes from inside out. For an instant he feels it prick him, in some organ still not localized in his body. Then it's as if it had turned into a blind blade. A blade that inserts itself softly between skin and muscle or between childhood and the wound that bubbles up into his eyes, his suffering, bruised eyes, gazing on the flower of evil, but tearless.

14

I learned it from her, from the indescribable slack in her muscles and the disillusion in her eyes. My Dead One will have a hard time surviving this last, only phase of the Moon. I knew it the exact moment when her blue finger let my hand go, traced a bird scratch behind the iron grate, and gave me a signal of despair. She had called me, she said, because even though she was in my presence, she had suddenly been filled with an anxious longing. She didn't know how to explain it any other way, she said. She suspected only that we were living on the same side, on the side of solitude that hurts and seems to lie.

She had called me with the fatality of this somber gesture, one that vacillated between the extreme fatigue of being alive and the acronychal lucidity of the dying. I ran up the stairs, knelt at her feet, wanting to give her my hands and thus hear the breath of the woman who had always been the great enigma of my life. Then, as if her reality was being returned to me through a cracked mirror, I saw in her eyes the perfect, absurd, and certainly enigmatic evidence of death.

Flor told me she only cried under the effect of sedatives. When it was time for her morphine, her head moved, it stopped being peaceful or resigned, and her eyes looked through the blinds for Mary's arrival. On these occasions her mouth lost some of its sallowness and it smiled. It was as if a match had been lit in front of her mouth, just to illuminate her humid smile. This spark of happiness flickered, hesitated, and only afterward remained fixed on her face. The wings of her nostrils trembled with a discreet, almost anxious nervousness, and her ears were trained to the smallest sound from outside. Suddenly, without anyone hearing the doorbell, Mama straightened up, smiled at us from above, and announced in a voice that hardly could contain its euphoria that Mary was arriving. In a continuous motion, a car stopped near the garden wall, a door slammed, the sound of keys jangled from the street, and Mary started to walk to the gates. She always walked quickly, professionally, the hem of her uniform under her overcoat. She helped the Dead One to her room, closed the door, and administered the dose of morphine and left. It occurred to me to think that the supernatural hearing of the dead had started to work in Mama's spirit. In truth she had entered into a limbo of melancholy. She was suspended there and knew she wasn't allowed to return. That's why she was resigned, religious, and cold. She was renouncing the world of those who can feed themselves and live from profane passions. As in the liturgy, just waiting for her angel, everything had become ritualized for her. And this angel announced itself in Mary's fairy hands but not in her body or eyes. It surely traveled in the pocket of her uniform. None of us suspected, however, that the work of this angel consisted in separating the pain from the Great Pain.

In Flor's house, on my last night in Vancouver, the great rectangular table is set again. Here we will have the Last Supper of the family. It takes up the whole living room, from the fireplace to the eternally closed windows to keep out the spring cold that still comes in from the Pacific. The linen cloth, embroidered in a vivid indigo backstitch drapes over the table extensions until it touches the carpet. The overturned glasses, the napkin holders, the design of the dinner plates, and the wooden handles of the silverware have a certain funereal air to them. Looking at all of this I am repelled. I prefer the drink cart because of a sudden thirst. The other cart with sweets and fruit salad seduces me because of the sugar and the liquors.

When someone announces the arrival of the first men, Flor comes out of the kitchen, hears the doorbell, and presses the electric button. Then she returns to those who are arriving the enigmatic smile of mortal hostesses. And she carries with her the aromas of the kitchen, from the sweet taste of the spices to the smell of the stews. Sitting on the floor in front of my Dead One, I contemplate the lightness and ease of the other women. In the determination of their footsteps there is again the wonderful dizziness of bees, with their flowered aprons, their voices that cross the house to call the children, the way one of them checks the stuffed turkey and is of the opinion that it has to stay in the oven. One of them comes by with a tray in her hand. They offer beer to the men and ask if I'd like to serve myself. Another asks Lewis to open the wine and Mário to go to the basement to get a folding table so the children can eat first and then play when the adults sit down.

"Eight days in Vancouver, brother-in-law!" Mónica says to me, exactly in the same tone as she had that morning when I saw tears in the corner of her eyes, when I got ready to leave her house and spend the day at Mary's. I know that this time has been and always will be our greatest achievement. Worse is the ephemeral nature, the strangeness and fluidity of these days in Vancouver, when on the last night the Dead One lifted her blue finger and demanded I come to her side. She wanted to warn me at length of the gravity and contingency of her life. She had not understood why I had spent the days coming and going, taken by others and to others, lost from house to house, without having kept the promise of sitting at her feet, listening to her sighs, and contemplating the illusion of the infinite. She would never get used to the idea of saying good-bye. She had resigned herself to having to die for each one of us, except for me. With me it wasn't just about opening her arms to greet the next morning, to kiss me a lot and with all her tears, to caress my hair for a long time. It was always useless to think it would be enough for her to rest her face on mine and to say, amidst sobs: "Good-bye, my son, until eternity," and then lie to herself: I died for Nuno, I just have to do it again for the other eight children who are left. She wanted another pardon, and to become as eternal in me as the house, the land, the sea, and the moons of my childhood — and this pardon without tears or lies only I, and not she, could give.

She knew, she told me, that my previous existence was still tangled, deep as an anchor, in the shadows of resentment and shame. "It's true," she said, "I lost forever the chance to send you a kiss on your birthdays. I forgot everything about you: I didn't sent you a wedding present, a set of diapers, or baby clothes or winter pajamas for each of your children; nor did it ever occur to me that Marta would like a piece of antique china, a wall clock, a pair of earrings, Azorean embroideries, or a satin bedspread for your bed in Lisbon. At Christmas, but just since I've been living in Canada, I started to notice the real absence, but not the imaginary existence of my life. Maybe it was too late. However, I was prompted to pick up a pen and write your address in a painstaking, very round handwriting on envelopes addressed to you in Lisbon. I learned to put inside these envelopes a kind of saint's card with sad archangels, sleepy creatures who hid behind little bells and on whose reverse side was printed a silly Biblical verse. Under it the same imperative phrase followed: Have a very Merry Christmas and a Happy New Year!

"As for my children," she said, "it was hard to admit that I refused to baptize them," just as she never got used to the idea that I got married to Marta just in a civil ceremony, without priests or altars, just in front of a gray man who turned us into two equivocal lovers. She never had grandchildren, or a daughter-in-law, or even a son of her flesh in Lisbon. During many, perhaps all of those years, she had harbored the idea of being the mother of eight children and one more. The eight had never shamed her in front of God and men: they went to the Mass of the Resurrection, took communion on the night of the Baby's birth, confessed the eve before their wedding, respected the priests, the Lenten fast, and the bells of the Faithful Dead. This other son in Lisbon was a kind of lost patrimony. Whispered news, murmurs, signs of success that nobody could ever explain to her — just this had connected her from far away to the small and misunderstood part of my life. In the Azores, when Papa was still alive and was cursing me with a deaf, angry voice so no one could hear him, she had learned to lower her voice before saying my name. At home, in fact, everyone stopped asking about Nuno; they preferred to designate me as *The One in Lisbon*, because that was the logic, the only thing that could be said about the difference and evil of my destiny.

"Now, Nuno, I am looking at you, I can take our hands, see you again for the first time in my life and tell myself that it's impossible to have been so mistaken about you. It's impossible that I didn't love you desperately and that you weren't the most desired and loved of my children. You, more than the others, had the merit of never having thought of, or ever mentioned the subject of an inheritance. You didn't ask for our help with your wedding or to borrow money, and it never occurred to me that I should berate you, distinguish you from the others, and force you to make peace with them. Everything was excessively right, without protest or jealousy, and for this very reason we started slowly to forget you. I don't even know who is sitting on the floor in front of me now, that part of you listens to me in silence, seems to believe me, to see me alive — or on the contrary you pretend to hear an invisible voice and pretend to believe you are keeping watch over a dead voice . . ."

In truth, mother, I don't know, I can't hear you. I can't even remember the fatigue or the beginning of this surrender which is already assaulting the blue gray of your rat eyes. I suppose that Mama can only sense my presence with the instinct of a mole, by the pores of your skin and not the contact with the silent and ashamed hands. I don't know a big enough word to console this remorse; a single sentence continues to repeat itself, to cloud my memory and spirit of those who lived the anguish of that definitive night in Vancouver:

"I can't, Mama. No one can do anything for anybody!"

I said it or I just thought it; I didn't see the face look up with surprise at hearing that statement. Even if that could have happened, it wasn't the sound of it that made her tears rise and blur her eyes. It was perhaps just an inevitable sentence. I saw it better in the eyes of the women looking at me from the kitchen, wondering or suspecting the reasons why the Dead One had decided to call me to her presence. In Lewis's and George's hands I saw it too, and in Zélia's and Linda's silence, and above in that family daisy that was being plucked of its poisonous petals.

"That's not right, Nuno!" insists Linda Maria, placing herself like a sentinel at my back. "So many years without seeing each other, you came from so far, and you only give us eight days of your life in Vancouver!"

I can't hear a single word of this family delirium. I limit myself to sounding the intense mystery of my Dead One. It's been more than two hours since Mary injected her with the little angel of clarity. You see it in her sleepy fish eyes, the line that separates the physical suffering from the other Pain, from which she hides in a protest against life's betrayals. According to her words, the suffering of cancer was like an acidic, corrosive bite; the poisonous mushrooms, the foam in the depths of her guts. Worse than that, the whistle of damnation was in the very color of her blood. When Mama is under the effect of the drug, she can't define the suffering. She limits herself to recognize inside herself the achievements of a much bigger time that belongs just to her. The lesson of the dead already coexisted with her resemblance to a drowning person, the way suddenly she sinks and then fights against the current and takes a deep breath. The only, very important detail of being alive is to keep recovering one's human condition this way, even if provisionally. She wanted to tell me that she had simply gotten distracted by the passage of life, without ever having discovered the secret of the machine that produces the time of the living. If she had stayed in the Azores, as Papa always wanted to, it wouldn't be so hard to die. In the islands there isn't this idea of absolute separation. More than here, it seems like the spell of the bird facing the serpent, or the mysticism of the man who opens his eyes, walks into the sea, and discovers the jellyfish, the corals, and all the flora of a second incomprehensible happiness...

15

Then it all happened suddenly, perhaps too fast. My Dead One unbuttoned the cuff of her blouse, took out the envelope, opened it, and communicated her decision to me. She did it with the complicity of all of them, with the paradox of hiding and showing me a treasure. When she opened her hands and held out the precious sepia-colored papers, I didn't need to guess at the depth of her intentions. In the course of those eight days in Vancouver, I learned then, my brothers and sisters had opened up the process of inheritance. They had divided with me the moral goods, the cursed memory, and the spoils of their astuteness. Now Mama opened the envelopes, broke the wax of an invisible seal and would finally satisfy their curiosity about this hidden testament, without doubt surmised but not revealed. She would then unfold the map before furnishing the key or the code for this treasure, and then all of us would rush into the arguments and disputes of this gold rush. Mama had listened from a distance, we knew now, to each one of our remarks about the division of goods. She knew about the projects and designs that each child would have on her belongings. What else could she do except resign herself and accept this premature death that the voices of her children cross like a prophecy?

The expectant tension burns in my shoulders, and manifests itself in useless, nervous gestures and the silence of those who seem not to be listening; they hear the voice of their own guilty consciences. An instant later, Mama's face stops looking serious, it becomes perplexed and from it is projected an almost laughing sentiment:

"I decided to be the one to divide my belongings. I will start with the money: three thousand dollars to each child, and may it be for what you enjoy."

She doesn't accept my protests. She's driven by an almost ironic despair, knowing that I too am divided between modesty and an obvious greed for the money that will reimburse my travel expenses to Vancouver. She knows as well that I never before had expressed a desire for it, and as such my name had never been included on the list of covetous heirs. But she insists. Then she starts to cry. She begs me to take it and to do it for the salvation of her soul, for the health of my children, and for the love of Marta. And according to her, there is no need for thanks; this money doesn't pay back the discomfort of the planes, the lost days, and the presents I had brought for everyone — the little gold chain for her, the ties, earrings, and neck scarves for brothers, sisters, and in-laws, and the T-shirts for the children. I understand that Mama wants to return my devotion. I had come here like a pilgrim in search of grace. I gave her my repentance. And she decided to bestow me with the grace of these devout three thousand dollars.

"Don't feel the least bit of remorse about this, son. At the end of the day, I am only giving what doesn't belong to me anymore. I have bought my gravesite and my coffin. I have enough left for the funeral expenses, the medicines, the dark dress, and even the flowers that will cover me..."

She says this without bitterness now. Because fatigue is overtaking the energy needed to express her feelings. She doesn't need strength to cry, but she needs it to express indignation, an angry word, or a simple caustic sentence. I see a mist of tears and not a sob in those still eyes, the moment that her hands start to take the chain from her neck and prepare to return it to me:

"Nobody better than Marta deserves it. While you see it on her body, Nuno, that will mean I'm still alive in the heart of my son."

I shivered at the thought of the morbid idea of mixing life with death, and death with life, in the body and spirit of the woman I love. I wanted to tell Mama that the fusion of those realities was completely impossible in my relationship with Marta. Where the mortal cycle began there could not be another cycle of passion. The women of my life had never existed on the same plane, not even in parallel spaces, but in contiguous solutions, in the extension of my obsessions. And if I had ever been "unfaithful" to Marta, this only had meant a return to the beginning of my passion for her. To betray just to betray just happened with frivolous women who in Lisbon waved to me from the other side of the street, old schoolmates from high school, especially those who had the illusion of insinuating themselves into the imaginary of the luminous women that had inspired a few of my love stories.

I wanted to tell her all of this, but I didn't have in me an image, an essential rhetoric. The sensation persisted that speaking was the most useless and least intelligent of my actions. I looked around, hoping to capture this ill-defined sentiment from the others, and that's when I noticed I was in the presence of new accomplices. The red eyes of the sisters smiled at me through their tears. My brothers returned a mute, almost happy approval from afar. My Dead One continued to blow her nose into the little silk handkerchief bordered in a stripe of mourning black, into which the ashes of these tears were scattered. For the first time in those days, I felt the need to run away, to dash to the bathroom and release my need to cry. Understanding this, Flor approached, took my hand and invited me to follow her to the other side of the room. Mama took advantage of this to say good-bye, asking them to take her to her room. She would doubtless spend the entire night awake, waiting for me to come in at five in the morning, to embrace her and to tell her this was not good-bye forever but just a return to life.

Flor leads me to the others, who become rigid, suddenly mysterious, and they don't know how to give me the next surprise. With difficulty, Mary speaks for all of them. She starts by saying that George gave them the idea to contribute. But she gives up the explanation and suddenly, like in a circus act, lifts up a cloth; underneath there is a chair full of packages, where there are boxes of toys, the protruding forms of bundles and pieces of clothing.

"A dress for Marta, a pair of skates," she enumerates, "a radio with ear plugs, pants, shirts, and hats for the boys."

She takes a breath and pauses. She looks at the others out of the corners of her eyes, a thin smile reveals a row of teeth, and it gives her an almost oblique mischievousness and then rises to reveal her gums.

"For you a special present. And it can't be shared with anyone," she adds.

She says this with that suspect, even enigmatic smile, with a mocking tone — the same look that spreads to the lips of the others. When the lid of a box pops open, I know right away it's a typewriter. A shiver of annoyance cracks my jaw bones. I can feel this contraction, and I know they'll interpret it as the effect of the surprise. They don't suspect that a simple typewriter can represent a curse to a man who will worry and start to get old in writing the cursed dictionary of his books. It is more than a censored present. It brings the venom that feeds from distance, the definitive separation from his destiny.

"We thought this might help you write our family story," explains Linda Maria. And the strange thing is that Rui Zinho becomes a prisoner, as if hypnotized, by this sentence. Years later, Linda's voice appears over the sound of the keys. At night he writes his *Song of a Friend*, full of panic, suffering because of life and his writing; no one will ever write a worse book!

I pick up the packages and take them to my room. I throw them on the bed. The women had been ironing and folding my clothes. The suitcases received these miserable new treasures and became heavy. I would think that they could contain the disorder of this world that would have to be invented again and placed on the sidelines of life so that it would also become real.

I fled and closed myself in the bathroom. The first mirror returned a frightened look, on a face that was slowly becoming deformed. I saw that my lips were trembling and my teeth were rattling. And I saw the tears. And then the tears flowed, the mask of the pain of being alive and stepping on so many remains. I sat on the edge of the bathtub, just to escape the disapproval of the mirror, and I stopped being ashamed of my cries. I blew into the toilet paper with force, thinking that this way everything would calm down inside me. If this were the case I would rinse my eyes with water, wash my hands, and return smiling, thankful, almost happy, to the others. However, the more I wiped my eyes, the more irrepressible the crying became, deep from a troubled, former time. I tried in vain to throw up the pancakes, the scrambled eggs, the juices and toast of all the Vancouver breakfasts. I was full of food, but famished for the only moral food that had not been left over from the plenty of the banquets and parties that had been planned and given in my honor. I would always be an unworthy guest and an intruder. My guts continued to protest the time difference, the inversion of night and day. I just wanted the last, long night of wakefulness to come, next to the room where for the second time my Dead One was dying. She had already died a first time, an absent and fictitious death by extinction, like the light that fades in the twilight of the invisible and unrecoverable. It had been a luminous object, it's true. But it had gone underground, it had gotten lost, consumed in this submersed world, and finally had gone out. It had stopped being her, and had simply become my Dead One.

The next day, at five in the morning I present myself to a once again strange house, never known before, where everyone is still asleep. I wait for Flor's arrival, who must be getting up now, and the arrival of those who will take me to the airport — again in their beautiful, big, magnificent shiny cars. When they arrive, I know we are all late and that we have to hurry, sinking into the discreet dawn of a tranquil city and to race to the airport that is still half asleep. For nothing in this world did I want to miss the plane that will take me to Toronto and then to Montreal and then to Lisbon. I embrace Flor, who returns a sob to me, and I kiss her several times on her two cheeks. I then follow the bags to the cars; they are carried by Lewis, George, and James. When I am at the threshold of the door that leads to Flor's garden, she calls me with a distressed gesture and points up to the room of my Dead One. She says it in a whisper so the one upstairs can't hear:

"But aren't you going to say good-bye to Mama?"

I turn back to Flor, take her face in my two hands, and make her look at me. More than ever, I need her to understand.

"It's not worth waking her, sister," I say in as persuasive and calm voice as I can. "She is still sleeping. And you should never disturb anyone who just lives for sleep, don't you think?"

She said yes, and though bathed in a new gush of tears, through them there seemed to glow a last, lucid smile of gratitude. I turned to follow the bags. When the cars shifted into gear and pointed in the direction of Vancouver, Flor went to the garden and waved at me. Truthfully, I didn't know how long it would be until I again saw this sister who was now smiling at me and suddenly disappeared from my life when the car turned the first corner. About Mama, what shall I say? That nobody can do anything for anybody. Or that you can't kill a dead person or revive a living one. And that her death is no longer in her, but in me, with me and inside me.

"And besides this," I thought then, "There is still the story of the Hanged Man, by Gil Vicente. The Devil comes and asks, with that ironic slyness that becomes funny in the mouth of cuckolds, if the promises of Paradise had served as consolation:

"With the noose around my neck / preaching does no good," I answer him. "And the one who must hang / is annoyed by the sermon . . ."

"Who knows," I say, looking ahead and always and only ahead, "if those wouldn't be Mama's exact last words?"

Looking ahead, I saw white, blue, and yellow lights pass by, that remained lit over the colors of an unknown city. "It was just a city where there was no memory of obelisks, of the great bells and small temples," I said.

BOOK FOUR

The Other Version of Marta

1 · A Blank Page

Don't think, my love, that you left me old, bitter, and looking to the end. If you want to know, you haven't poisoned my happiness either. Your departure left me intact, still able to savor the taste of fruit. With you I learned that living is to follow the course of the rivers, to believe in the craziness of the voyage, and to discover that even poetry can exist in strange boats. I was consumed, my love, that's true. And I was definitely tired, and placed suddenly on the threshold of the age beyond jealousy. But I wasn't tired of everything, unlike many women who have been hurt by their men. You know, I still have the seventh life of the spotted cat with gray eyes that is always reborn in front of the fire. Restored to my own time, a time that now belongs to me, I'm ready as a bride who feels a second promised flight of passion. I will embrace my passion.

I am in the moment, I tell you, when I can once again sit on the floor, spread everything around me, and feel my own world with my fingers. I'm like someone who experiments on the keyboard and remembers through them the sound of ancient grand pianos. These, and not others, are the dreams that I have left. Where you raised walls of boredom and turned yourself into your stones, my presence was always the voice that was forbidden to speak. This is why coming here means that now I belong to myself. You don't understand? One could read the night in the incredible, incorrigible disorder of your papers. The feminine night that supposedly belonged to me and that I was to experience with you never came. If I opened the door, you'd frown at the soft sound of my footsteps. If the boys came to say good-night, you'd kiss them distractedly, lifted your face but didn't even move your eyes from your manuscripts. Successive drafts, full of doubts, I know, about the nocturnal birds that would later fly from your hands. You looked at yourself, and you were the bones, the skeletons, and the feathers of the terns, pigeons, and Cory's shearwaters. I saw you get older with each book, twisted and stubborn, and it hurt me to see the small shadows that started to pinch the face that I had loved so much in my youth. I imagined that you had chosen to die with a pen in your hand when your eyes grew cold. You were stooped over by the weight of your dreams, not of reality. And you ran the risk of just inventing the infinite. Your thin neck had in fact lost the last shred of pride. As much as I didn't want to believe it, I was witness to your earthly damnation, knowing that writers end up extinguishing themselves in the very light they think they create. With the years, they grow a big, cumbersome belly like that of sedentary oxen. Then their hair starts to fall out slowly, like yours did. And finally you grow a hump on your always hunched shoulders that's only good for crossing deserts . . .

If you could hear me now, my love, from this lonely side, this unbearably lonely side of you, you will certainly not believe the silence that my sadness has become. You couldn't even imagine how a woman can feel free, and still be touched by things that can have no other existence, and have no meaning if distant and out of your life. I feel like the morning bell of your restless sleep. I am certain that I will not feel the wind or the hand of another man. I am just sitting in my Lisbon night, love. From your time of ashes, the precious notion of that desert, I am left with the mirage of cacti and palm trees. And the church across the way continues to seem menacing in the cypress trees. And the old box shrub brings back the memory of predictable and relentless bad winters. In the years that your books took away my happiness at being yours forever, the world started to become a little billiard ball that your hands played with absentmindedly. You started to squeeze it in your eager fingers, and I lost the innocence of that glorious apple. I stopped being your tree, because my body, besides having never been the root and explanation of that tree, didn't fit anymore into our common destiny. I lost myself quickly, love, no longer mirrored in your falsely superior face. I was sunk, submersed in the whirlpool of your dissipation.

I learned early, for nothing, to put up with the commitments of your little literary fame. You called me from cities without names, I think from Barcelona and Madrid, because it was hot or there had been some last-minute delay with your return. In Rome, it was raining. And that sad event in the life of a writer, the rain, obliged you to confess your longing for the boys, the comfort of our home, and the beef with mushroom sauce with friends on Saturdays at our table, which I had laid. You never took me on any of those mysterious trips to book fairs. On this side of your secretiveness, I dared to ask what the *bateaux-mouches* of the Seine were like when you rode them, the domes of Leningrad, the jazz orchestras of Boston, the marinas of Toronto and Vancouver ... In Portugal, you left me to be exhibited like a circus bear in all the provincial fairs. I saw you leave alone to meet the smug, almost masculine women in the Faculties of Letters. One noticed your almost childish pride in being read, examined, and venerated by the superior critical intelligence of your country. From afar, I watched and imagined the twisted meanderings, the broken angles, the vices, the insidious audiences that the mellifluous editors of your trade prepared and sold the day before, with much zeal, profit, and no scruples. Focused, very serious, but spineless, you were then a happy man and available for the frivolity of those who declaimed your genius. And you were always so venerated because of your hypocritically humble speeches! The publishers had changed you into a snowball like the others, the ones who had learned with you to appear modest and smooth. They also changed you into the chalice of the adolescents running away from home, drugged, and sometimes daring to kiss you on the mouth in front of me. Your victory backfired into the order of our house, and changed it into the symphony of the very morose, failed women of your books. While I, love, continued to believe that only with you was it possible to have the solitude of second honeymoons, the honey of our solitary moons, and the laborious anguish of the writing of each new novel ...

The trench between my only existence and the others you were able to invent, or not, caved in before us, like a trapdoor. And since I lost your signal and the knowledge of how you had changed, love, the darkness of permanent nights also failed, and that is what my life turned into. I always observed it in the characters you gave false names to and that in fact were nothing more than fragments of yourself. You multiplied yourself even in the gray men who appear and reappear in your books. I also multiplied myself in the disappointment of your betrayed and wailing little women, who are less than grand, and who get old, use up their courage, and then become as sterile as bees out of their time. They have bird names, plant names that are perhaps too exotic for my taste, names of people who are happily unknown — but the body, the silences, the triangular gestures of these feminine monsters derive from the only one who is partitioned, and hidden, in the many poor women in your books.

Today I am again the same person who at that time asked about what had happened to the talent and the deep passions that were promised to me in marriage. I am the same as when the critics started to applaud the foreign influences on your work or the alchemy of your originality. I am the same, calm person as when legions of new readers flocked to you. I prided myself that your face, the face that belonged to me, appeared in the display windows, the catalogs, the first page of the literary supplements, in the brief article about your successes, the pallor of those stars that illuminate the balance sheet at the end of each year. I knew it was unreal to the others, who addressed you with a pseudonym, while at home we weren't impressed that you were that man, and we could call you to the table by your other name.

Do you remember love, that you started to write with poetry?

I never knew what early part of you was being revealed or hidden, or what precise forms the contours of your madness had taken to invent novels and to prolong the luck of repeating the success of the previous book. Your little portable literature, liturgical and edible, so useful and necessary to others, stole my nights, Sunday mornings in bed, the boys' trips to the zoo, the dull evenings in front of the television — during which many times I tried in vain to hope to be able to talk to you about me, my troubles. I wanted to share with you the successes and failures of my medical practice, to tell you about the useless details of my day. You would get bored quickly, hearing my first outburst. In your opinion, the lesser world of women didn't go beyond hormonal problems, petty intrigues, and long conversations about unimportant things. You didn't know, you never knew, that I was talking to you just to be able to hear you, I just needed to feel we were in love. I needed this verbal loving as much as the hands and lips that later made love to me in the dark and in silence. You approached me to pull me to you, you helped yourself to my body, always very tense, and then you criticized me for not being interested in sex. Because of the petty blindness of your writing until late in the night, you always came in late, woke me from my first sleep, and demanded from my sleeping body the simple surrender to your hurry to be a man . . .

And what I need so much, love — I said to you, as if I were asking pardon for that kind of spiritual frigidity — is that you talk to me. Tell me, like you did before, that I am sweet and that I have inside me sugar that you crave . . .

I lost the intelligent and not yet distracted understanding of the time when Literature had not given you the wings of genius. Our marriage turned into something serious, with a time for everything, like in the convents, ruled by the invisible pendulum of clocks. When I had my period, your distance from me became even more pronounced. My flows excused you from the twice weekly engagement with my body and you turned your back on my insomnia, depression, and headaches. Your preoccupation was in the duty to blank sheets of paper, where I saw the pattern of the growing vulnerability of your ascent. You launched into the writing of each new book as if this were the only and last opportunity to stay alive, by flying even higher. In my opinion, as I followed the anguish and growing rigor of your writing, you continued to feed yourself as much from me as your eternal childhood. When you used up the whole tortured autobiography of that childhood, your spirit hovered on the edge of the infinite, it howled in the direction of spiritual death, and I concluded that nothing in you was consistent now. You would begin to repeat yourself. You would become temperamental, cynical, and sarcastic. You would try to diminish the success of other writers, because the jealousy of that disrespect satisfied the despair of your empty space.

I knew, of course, of this challenge to your enemies. I also knew about the conspirators who in the shadows would place bets on your approaching literary demise. For them it was inevitable that you become irrelevant; you had crossed your bit of sky, attained the twilight of popular writers. Then you answered all those vultures that your masterpiece was yet to be written. You would write it even if you had to slit your wrists and take it with you to the grave . . .

I could never understand why writers get upset and become so involved in the anxiety of betting everything on the writing of their next novel. I could never abide that vortex, the spiral of fear of failure, the possibility of becoming a street name, the bad luck of dying and not becoming as eternal as the stone of the little statues in a corner of a church garden. Nor can I fathom the delirium that possesses writers, all of them, to pretend to be modest, to act out the hypocrisy of morality, and to always want to seem to be misunderstood. They tout their progressive ideologies; they are street revolutionaries, while at home they are demanding and all-powerful tyrants. They don't have humility. They don't have the aesthetic sense that would make them deplore the stone monsters that others turn them into. Worse still, they aren't aware how unhygienic it is to be the target of pigeon shit, pollution, and the sullen insults of passers-by. I don't know how they can stand the traffic that goes up and down, continuously, from morning until night . . .

You changed into a strangely distant man, ever more depressed, but still in love with the idea of becoming a stone statue. You were a man who was detouring his life for an obsession, an oasis without people, water, or even the trees of those poets who like to admire the birds perched on the branches. You became aseptic, judgmental, irreverent, and lunatic. I would tire of the violence of your manic highs and lows. When I was present at your successes, I discovered that you also had a sense of humor — in your caustic remarks, in the poisonous little way you swiped at the politicians. My wifely competence was being pushed to invent new drug cocktails so you could sleep. I took care of you with strong sedatives and became good at diagnosing your crises.

Why did I get tired of your anniversary presents? I got tired of them because they weren't love gifts or expressions of gratitude, but payments for the drugs, for my role as the family carrier pigeon. In the beginning, when I met you and saved you and gave you my passion, your love for me was unselfish and it celebrated my feminine virtues. With the years, it became demanding. You began to complain about my attention and acts of adoration. You criticized my attention to the children, the motherly love that the boys needed; you were jealous of them, you acted like you were their age and size, and also began to cry for the sun that shines inside a family home. And afterward, love, I could not forgive you for closing yourself in your study, turning into the centaur of the house and demanding, with loud shouts to the frightened, dumbfounded boys, the silence, respect, and cultish fawning for your renascent talent. Closed in your corner for hours on end, I waited in vain for your metamorphosis. I always imagined you were growing a horn, a bull's tail, a hairy hide, and that your limbs would soon transform into four legs with hooves as dangerous as those of a horse when it's being castrated . . .

It always seemed ridiculous to me that you would exchange the growing years of the boys and my presence for the elegant and eloquent verbiage that you would run to deliver to the impatient publishers of your trade. Stupid readers gathered in crowds, eager for the first editions. They would go home because it became worthwhile to go home, eat it, shit it out, and then return to their original state of stupidity — because you were just being consumed, you became part of their garbage. At Christmas, they confused you with the crèches, and you were December, the cold, the forked serpent that makes a circle with its body, bites its tail, and always stupidly poisons itself. And then there were the poor women who fantasized about the magic of your hands on a beloved body. Those poor women envied my marriage to you, the nights in a bed as big and empty as ours. Woe to them, who were jealous of the passions aroused by your words, composed on a music sheet; they would transform into the symphonic world of the music of your imagination. There was never anybody with as much ability as you to make music from words and turn long prose paragraphs into a symphony. But this took the toll of making you silent with me, drained from your poetry, suspended from a hook of silence, and hanging over the pond, like a fish, to serve as bait for the stupid fish that were and always would be, your readers.

Your nocturnal boat was filled with books given to you by other writers, adding to the disorder of your papers, the continuous beating of your typewriter, the newspapers with your photo, and the always voluminous and repetitive mail. You received passionate declarations, appeals for help, the well-informed greed of a few foreign literary agents, and a world full of people who were still strangers to me when I was still yours and you didn't belong to the others or their stupid passions! Besides, there was your implicit disapproval of my ignorance of things to do with Literature. Your trophy wife, at times introduced by you to erudite circles, a woman of timid, tranquil, and silent beauty, had the horrible defect of not being up to date with the names and titles of other serious writers and their publications. I had the little luck of not being intelligent like the literary critics, of not knowing how to assess the value of the first reading of your still confidential manuscripts, and this is why I hadn't learned to practice along with you treachery, blackmail, and the anxiety for absolution. The old trophy wife, who you adored for the flower of her smile, the light of her very big eyes, the waves of her beautiful hair and who you lost as she sank little by little into misery. Put into the same boat at the beginning of its only voyage, she sank with you, in the first publishing failure and then the second. By the third book at the end of this sea voyage, she got off and sank into the cushions of the sofa in front of the television that you scorned as a barbaric thing, the entertainment of the poor and ignorant whose lives are not illuminated by the awareness of books, world news, and made-up dreams that are always believed. Even when it was you who appeared on the screen that lit up the night of the poor, useless creatures that seek in television as the mirror of their daily frustrations . . .

You, love, started to change and not admit that you were getting old in the shadows and at the sidelines of those who gave you love and could have saved you. You were too distracted to see the smiles of those who waited for you at dinner, to go out with you, to take the sun and enjoy the miracles of spring. You came in late, annoyed, fatigued by your own state of decline; you asked me what time it was and it was always late. You deigned to give us the supreme benevolence of partaking in the roast tenderloin, the beef of bulls that didn't deserve to die or bellow from the dignity of writing, the baked fish, and the fruits of the season, the desserts that were whipped and leavened by my shameful hands. You were, by then, unaware of everything; you didn't see that the boys were growing up and becoming mute and rebellious. And you didn't look in my eyes, or stroke me as before, with your nervous clammy fingers.

"What's going on with you, love?" I asked while I washed the dishes, threw out the garbage, which was also the garbage of our lives. "What's going on with you, you are quiet, you don't have an appetite, and you have such terrible headaches? What's happened to your old presence, the bouquets of roses you used to bring to seduce my soul, and to anticipate the body you would possess?" Absurd questions that didn't get answered, because the hours in this house had stopped being mine and were just yours. The day started for me when you arrived and ended in exhaustion, when the dawn wrapped my body in the incredible cold that came from within it and chilled the covers and the walls of the bedroom and reminded me that winter was perhaps the only and last season of my years. Then you came to our bed, quickly got under the sheets, and how cold your body was avoiding mine, love! My solitude as a married woman told me that my life with you was this eternal winter. That's why I opened my eyes in the dark and witnessed your insomnia and started to talk to myself:

"I got married to live in this boring, conventional house. I married an opaque bishop: he comes home, tosses around restlessly in the sheets, and seems to suffer from the complete exhaustion of the forced labor of insomnia. My life isn't good or bad, but better this than to be found dead next to a bishop with insomnia!"

Do you remember, love, the first night when your wine breath made me cry? I discovered by chance that you had started to drink while you were writing; this was the last phase of desperation. I called this desperation, the need to get drunk to achieve nirvana, the absurd ecstasy of writing. If you had discovered this well of panic earlier, you would certainly have started to use hashish, cocaine, or the elixirs to which Baudelaire helped himself. While imagining the *Flowers of Evil,* "Get Drunk," "Death of the Poor," "A Martyr," "Destruction," "Dancing Serpent," *Que j'aime voir, chère indolente, De ton corps si beau, Comme une étoffe vacillante Miroiter la peau! Sur ta chevelure profonde Aux âcres parfums, Mer odorante et vagabond Aux flots bleus et bruns, Comme un navire qui s'éveille Au vent du matin, Mon âme rêveuse appareille Pour un ciel lointain.* I wanted to have intervened earlier to prevent the progressive destruction of your liver, because from that time it became clear that death would be a corolla of round petals opening and multiplying in your hepatic cells. Besides this you started to have bad breath, do you remember? But my love for you still wondered about the causes and motives that could be driving you to drink alone and to kill yourself quietly on the nights when the work of writing books was just an absurd obsession. It was obvious when you had writer's block because your restless eye stared at shadows and shapes and didn't recognize them. Not only didn't you hear the boys, but you didn't listen to me. The mere thought of having to put up with visits from my friends enraged you. Why? Just because. You were bored to death, you told me, without the will to live, with booze hidden in your bookshelf, doubling the volume, number, and violence of drugs to help you sleep. You had lost sight of the angel of sleep, or at least you had frightened it so that it kept far away from you; it's like shooting in the air and scattering the pigeons, the cattle, or the horses. If you hit a bird or an angel that had strayed from the rest, it would just be a bird or an angel stuck in the mud, wounded on the wing, and without the memory of ever having been able to fly. All of this because of the autumn and the twilight of your success, and also because the world was giving you back an unknown reality. Your spirit commanded, even with slack reins, an automatic nervous system, domesticated by habits; it saw that you wanted to die and didn't want to die. It knew a few of the processes of death, but didn't find the courage of heroes or the lucid madness of those who exchange misery for the liberation of suicide. You, a coward? To this day, I can't say it.

I had stopped being a trophy wife for the simple reason that you, if you looked at me, started to suffer; you wanted to ask me for help but you immediately thought that it would be ridiculous to ask help from such a fragile being who was already absent from you. I played the role of the mother-lover to be able to take charge of your distress. And you know, love? I started to forgive you not just your liquor breath, your sweat, your unshaven face, the copious madness of your red eyes, your wilted, bitten lips — but to forgive forever the despair of your premature ejaculations. Our love didn't make the bed squeak with the long and longitudinal energy of before. I didn't know anymore how to shout with pleasure and from that other supreme happiness of being a woman and being a snake and also being able to bite my tail and poison myself. Our love was hurried and divided, and had forgotten how to meet in the exact place where the paths of a joined life should cross. You always had a book in your hands, you never got the formula right, and you had made irreversible and impossible-to-cancel commitments to others. And you suffered, suffered, suffered from this undefined and complex condition, that makes you go silent when you are with others and can't confide in them, and you can't even rest your head on anyone's shoulders. You stopped, in the end, taking any interest in practical matters. And here I was in the role of the fairy of your tales. I bought your clothes, but you hated my practical taste, my mediocrity in looking at the displays and always being up to date with fashion and what was in season. I chose the furniture and the knickknacks for the house. But you tripped on the buffet, the tables, the brackets, and the candelabras — and you never realized that the furniture was new, that knickknacks were the substitute for my aesthetic sense. After months and months of things being in their places, you suddenly opened your eyes and looked at them in terror and asked me:

"Who put that monstrous cane rack in the hall, Martinha?"

Of course you were a stingy man! You got mad at me for making useless purchases, you were opposed to changing the carpets, and you sneered at my miniature boxes, ducks, and porcelain dolls. When taxes were due, you bellowed around the house, apoplectic, because it was inconceivable that art and the spirit, and the art of the spirit, would be cannibalized by the State!

You wore new shirts, but you didn't know if they were new or ironed. You wore pants that changed fabric with the seasons, but you didn't notice if they were too tight or if they needed to be altered. You were about to become crude and tasteless, refusing to wear a tie, refusing to wear suits, dressing yourself, when I wasn't around, in the incredible colors of green slacks with yellow shirts, not combing your hair or shaving. When the boys peeped through the door, they would see a kind of Antero de Quental painted by Columbano Bordalo Pinheiro, and they would run to me, in a panic:

"Papa looks so ugly, so ugly, Mama, that he looks like the Big Bad Wolf!"

Then I wanted to tell them that their father was just a Portuguese intellectual, imagine I had known them to be more or less this way, disheveled, badly dressed, and pretending to be ugly because just ugliness was intellectual. Horrified at the bad literature of the soap operas, hating soccer, and laughing like hyenas at the singers who always rhymed "embrace" with an amorous, sloppy, and sleepy "face."

You spent the first half of your life not noticing the little and big things happening around you, love. And you even stopped understanding that my body didn't want yours out of habit but because it was vital to me. In your opinion, I was frivolous because I just cared about furniture and mirrors, didn't read books or newspapers, and screamed at the day maid. And you alluded to my hysteria, my nerves, and my illnesses, how I had gained weight and was losing my waistline, with thickened knees and thin wrists. You laughed at my ass and my bitten nails, you pretended to lament the suffering of my ovaries, and I believe you even began to be ashamed of me because you stopped listening to me and loving me, because there were no more orchids on our wedding anniversary, ordinary dates, and public book signings.

And so it happened that my relationship with you became a reciprocal examination of your and my existence. I limited myself to studying you in books, not reading them, to discover where the husband who had been promised to me was, and who was lost. Calling you husband, love, was an excess, even a mistake. Medicine had become incompatible with Literature. Just like us.

You, it's almost certain that one of these days, will take your seventh breath; you will come from far away, from the place you are, and will explore again the golden domes. You will become a minor god, made of stone, and you will earn your bust. You will leave a body of work that the boys will inherit without pleasure, like a glass of bile that their faceless father forced them to drink their whole lives — while I, love, finding myself so alone, on the other side of the street where someone walks by under your gaze, will continue with my head down but not destroyed, to practice Medicine. I will hear for the rest of my life, the whistling of your lungs; I will always be the other woman and all the women who will save you. And I know your next novel will be about me, like all the others. Now you have one more reason to write it; you got lost and you'll try to find me. You will want to say that you still love me and that you will come back here to ask my forgiveness. And because your stupid readers demand it, you will give this novel the happy ending of our only hypothetical reconciliation . . .

The worst, love, the worst of all is that this whole story, after the ending, always has a moral. My disadvantage is knowing that in your turf you will always be the only winner. It will be a simple exercise of style to convince the readers that I never had the talent to be worthy of you. I presume you will accuse me again of being the bad lover who didn't know how to drink the holy water of your destiny. The one who won't deserve a tear, a single line written with passion, or a simple smile. They won't say that you had the past of a dog. They also won't give me the small benefit of the doubt about you. See here, since you are so inhumane, cynical, and lacking scruples, you always appeared in the eyes of the public as the innocent one, with the shameless, smiling face of a good person, love . . .

2 · The Ashes

Many, many times, before you arrived to consume and ruin my life, I had seen them: stuck in the mud with their keels tipped toward the docks and as decrepit as the ruins that now disturb, afflict, and sadden the house from which you are absent. They were the boats: stopped in the mist, lost even from the ancient memories of this river. Perhaps it's a little absurd to look at them from here and to think that they had been seafaring ships. They certainly had a name and a destination, and not the tomblike aspect of a time that is dying now in the oblique position of their hulls.

To me, who sees them mute and useless again, unlike the time that you took me to see them up close and to explain their reality, they are like the old shipwrecked galleons of long ago. Brought to us, as you used to say, just so the poets and the singers would still have a little of the old illusion of the sea.

The time is of water, ropes, crazy swans, in a soft slide of silence and fish that die in the tall reeds. The Portugal where I was born is now a forty-five-year-old country. It lives far from the sea, suspended from the birds, cloudy with the wine that in vain tries to explain or inspire us with the fate of those boats. It is really difficult to place them exactly in the slow flow and the geography of the Tejo River. Alamada, the moorish municipality on the other side of the estuary, is too far away to be worth the trip, and so far from my habits as the common people who bring with them the mornings of the South. Between Cacilhas and the Colunas Docks, crisscrossing the patina that oils and seems to give a metallic sheen to the river, there are always people wrapped in the mist. I am familiar with the intense traffic of those skiffs; they make the sleepy crossing in the morning between dreams and life. In the late afternoon when they return, they are dead again. Not exactly people, you understand? But they are people seated in their boats, sleeping the eternal, only night that they will never revive. Just like me and you, they belong to time. However they don't know they are living in the last century of boats.

I don't want to refer to those crowds, love, or to the difficult, concave existence of the small boats that will always go back and forth to Cacilhas. You know that I am just talking about our love that is covered by the same stone suckerfish, similar to the boats that I discovered sunk in the rocky waters of the mouth of the Tejo. Seen from a distance, where at the time I looked at them without interest, they were nameless, pensive packet boats. I never could discover why they continued to remain in the same places, anchored in the dead waters of the Tejo. However, when you took me to see them up close, and my life was not yet poisoned by you, and the yellow houses along the boardwalk seemed too corroded by the humidity — the hulls were leaning toward the cement docks. They were boats that had given up, useless boats. The rust of the cranes and the hoists flaked away in the wind. And in the naked torsos of the stevedores there was still the roughness and natural loyalty of people of the sea, love.

I could associate all of this to Sunday afternoons when we gave each other frantic kisses before separating. At that time there were names written in big letters along the length of the hulls. They reminded me of dead heroes and their patriotic martyrdom. And now, love, you are dying, I am dying, and we are meeting the same absurd fate as the boats. I am possessed by the vain illusion that you will perhaps come from the South, where the shade and the names of the boats come from. You will come surrounded by people shrouded in fog, or on one of the supernatural ships that once brought you from the Azores to consume and ruin my life. I belong to the ranks of hopeless women who shade their eyes with their hands and spend a long time looking out over the sea, in the hopes of glimpsing from afar the profile, the color of a shirt, the mariner's cap of my man. I am also daughter and granddaughter of the women of Alcácer Quibir, love; I have become accustomed to the distance and absence of my man. But I became religious to the point of believing in his resurrection. For me, the sea of Lisbon is what is beyond its landscape, a city crystallized in a mirror that reflects the scenery, the stupid arrogance, and the return of the old boats.

Before it wasn't certain that the world was hanging from the boats and the African anguish of our birds. Since, however, they flew over us on Sunday afternoons and landed on the masts of the boats, I believed and still believe in the illusion of those voyages. After all, you told me, they were never seaworthy. They made their silent crossings, perfectly still in our Portuguese time. You were nineteen, like many others, like all the Portuguese boys then. We read the terror of that age on the low walls of Lisbon. The night writers of Lisbon used the blue ink of angels. They left inscriptions, phrases full of hate, panic, and fear, and I thought I recognized your handwriting on many of them. It's impossible, in fact, not to remember or hear the echo of those nightly protests, DOWN WITH THE COLONIAL WAR! I hear it all over again, because I remember that you looked at the walls, took a deep breath, lowered your eyes, and I swear that a spiritual dog barked inside you. I squeezed your clammy hands, frightened, with a presentment of your death, projecting myself into your anguish. Did Guinea hurt you in the pit of your stomach? Even today do all the names of our common past hurt you? I've had my quota of acid reflux and African ulcers. I spent years, at your side, wanting to talk to you about the poor boys that doubled over in front of me, green faced, to vomit up the curdled milk and rusty rice of the diets I prescribed for them. Back then, Africa started in each one of us, in the unknown madness of Vietnam and Cambodia, in the misery of the people of Biafra. It was a time of waiting without hope. We had never been so close to war, all of us with our feet buried in the explosive mud, men and women alike, because the war was a threat to you. Pale with fear, wanting to flee, but stunned like the bird captured by the serpent that won't take long to swallow it, you stayed with me. Bird of the serpent, love, who in the best of our years fed itself from the shadows of other lives. You were a man from a different country than mine. I learned this from your day voice, your clairvoyance, present but with your back turned on the political moment in Lisbon.

As you know, my father was in Africa, an unbeliever going about his little dark business. You, who never met him, hated in him the general ideas of colonials who live in their straw huts, under big straw hats, fucking and enslaving their black women. You hated everything from a distance: the money, the complicity, and father's spelling mistakes. You could see him at the counter of his store and imagined that he had a pencil stuck behind his ear; he would have a big belly and the fierce smile of toothless colonists. It was in part because of father that you and the boys your age played the roulette of the time. So that when he was murdered on August 7, 1974, you sighed with relief. You wouldn't be obliged to receive him in our house. You wouldn't have to make peace with him or a truce in a second war of jealousy. Because you, love, never forgave him for opposing my marriage to you. He said so clearly, remember? Father had decreed, in one of his letters, that his favorite daughter would not ever get married to "an enemy who was collaborating with Mozambique." You returned the kindness, making me write to him that you also were not disposed to have a "bush pig" for a father-in-law. Mine was then a blood war, between the father of my mestizo siblings and the man who filled my blood with passion. And for this reason your triumph was to learn that a son of the Mozambique revolution picked up a big knife, crawled around the village, and stuck it in father's stomach. In addition to forbidding me to wear mourning, you wanted to convince me that he had always been useless — a human parasite. You even convinced me that he was responsible for Mother's premature death, do you remember?

You didn't know and never would how much I loved his dark eyes with their thick lashes, the grand weight of his hands, and the memory of the sweet names he gave me, calling me princess, and sending me big, mysterious birthday presents. You don't know how much I loved the stubbornness of that African exile, taken on and suffered just for me. And how he so tenderly harbored ambitions for my future? And his pride in knowing that I was studying medicine and would, one day, kiss his thick hands and thank him for the years, the sacrifices, the humiliations and only victory of a life that had no other purpose? I made up my mind because of you, love, because you made me believe in the petty poverty and Biblical greatness of your world. I followed you just so I wouldn't feel guilty or couldn't be accused by you or the others who thought like you, of the battalions shipping out from the Maritime Pier of Alcântara; so I wouldn't have to lower my eyes every time you read me the list of the dead in combat; so I wouldn't hear that one or the other of your friends had been put in jail, was being tortured, and that it wouldn't be long before they took you — always and just because of me. My old, absent, silent, and tender father: when you still were taking care of me, on the other side of the world in which the consciousness of your Africa was growing in me, everything was simple, and it wasn't necessary to hear the evidence, the hell of being just the shadow of my man. Punctually, full of that good cheer that my heart remembered from my childhood, you took responsibility for all the details of my existence: the monthly payments to the university, like in the past you had paid my nanny, boarding school, and holidays in the provinces. You bought me very expensive, thick books that always came from abroad and were in English. There were countless parties, new dresses, Christmas and birthday presents. From afar, from the convulsive Africa of coffee plantations, you sent me a discreet but firm pride in my grades in anatomy and immunology. Every time I sent you letters from here, full of kisses, explanations, and plans for study trips, you hurried to increase my allowance. I had never needed until then to know about a country trapped between clenched teeth, the silence of the Forte de Caxias, with prisoners who were exotic to me, sleepwalking with purple eyelids, as my husband told me then. It wasn't even disturbing to know that Portugal was the most backward country in Europe, the stirrup of the last modern empire and land of people who, like you, made spelling mistakes. Now, if I could look at you and see you beyond the walls that separate me from your death, I would just tell you that your love was my only science, and that it was also the art and music of my life. I would tell you much more, as you can imagine. I'd tell you about the times when I wanted to ask you to forgive me and to become just yours again. But I'd tell you that I would prefer a thousand times the spelling errors of your letters, the silence of your life, to the millions of words, the sheets of music, the symphony of prose that my ex-husband produced to paint a golden veneer on my life, to lie to me, and to make me grow old before my time.

The supposition of the other courage, love, before you came along to teach it to me, was as deep in you as an underground city that sinks into the sea and disappears. The literature of other writers was generally boring, pretentious, and eccentric — until you explained the hidden meaning, the dignity of silence, and the good name of your many mentors in this difficult and sometimes superior art. As for the rest, everything in you clamored against the God of the nuns from the university residence hall, the apples in the cheeks of the priest at Sunday Mass and communion, and above all the milk pudding, the fruit cake, and the fruit of our magnificent desserts.

I don't know love, after all these years, how I appeared in your life — just with the charm of a smile, brown eyes, and the peach complexion of my face where you finally seemed to have discovered the oval shape of your world. I had never had any memory of you, the way you looked like a shipwrecked sailor who was too thin for my taste, and the methodical blue of your eyes. I saw them staring at me, and I remember beginning to decipher from afar your confused shyness, the fragility of your body, and the light of your first passion. In you, I think there was an unexpected interior disorder, and an undetermined uncertainty, and the sureness of great solitude. It occurred to me that you had been introduced to me in the middle of the party and you kept insistently asking me my name. Unlike most people, you didn't tell me it was an immense pleasure to meet me. You didn't say it, love, because you had started to live me and desire me. You were dumbstruck and disarmed. It was just the look of a tormented man, who expressed in silence his gratitude for my existence, as close to poetry as it can be to dreams, to the promise and salvation of men who still didn't understand women's courage. I knew that you were promised to me from the first day of your life, as much as I feared the dogs when I left the university cafeteria, the news of our time without news, and the forbidden gardens of Lisbon nights. That wasn't the only fascination that attracted me to you. I could see you were a sweet, quiet little man, plagued by the terrible hemlock of a poisoned God that had been dying inside you for a long time. And I possessed a little distracted God, who visited on Sunday mornings, in whose pallor none of my surgery professors had diagnosed a twisted bowel or a malignant tumor, while you tried to pose in your difficult death. Expelled from the cloisters of the seminary, as you told me right away, where not even the footsteps had been different than God's silence. You brought with you the interminable sustenance of Gregorian chants, the fear of the longest dormitories in the world, and the curse of evangelical scripture.

 I was also moved by your poverty, you know? You had a single checked jacket, your shirt was frayed at the wrists, and your thin body seemed to rattle around in your bell-bottom trousers revealing the trajectory of your Azorean childhood. Without being beautiful, you had nothing in common with ugliness or with the dirty look of the poor people that my father whipped when they would come in bands to beg or ask for loans. Poor, sad, but directing those fearless blue eyes at everything that my father would never accept being taken from me. So that reconciled and uncertain, divided between the imploring sadness of your mouth and father's objections, it was inevitable for me to choose the love of your famished eyes . . .

Lisbon, at that time when dreams were possible and the world seemed vast, gave me the advantage of not being afraid of anything. The nights of parties, when you weren't there yet, were a contagion of lights, the pleasure of being alive, and the joy of being desired. The sounds of rhumba, Cape Verdean blues, and coladeras made the music of Saturday nights and New Year's Eve excessive, even though my life fit into a single word made of nighttime seductions and small transgressions. The night you showed up, future doctors made fun of you, knowing that my birthright was separate from your Azorean poverty. They laughed politely, all of them very beautiful people, the distinguished mulattoes with mustaches from Lumumba, who sought me out to oblige me to shake my hips in their cold, rented gymnasiums. Then they held me delicately in their muscular arms, asked me to excuse them for their smelly sweat, not realizing that their real aggression was in pressing their big sex organs into my stomach. On the other side of the room, you continued to explain the boats to me, to tell me that the mulattoes came from there with their scholarships, to the party with loud music and the undefined race of enormous phalluses. While the future doctors covered me with their sweat, and the music made me dizzy and deaf, and the cold of that month of January took over my body in another way, the fear of those perforating sex organs drew me to the purity of your fragility. You didn't even know how to dance; you didn't have the dark violence of alcohol to offer me. You were lucid, tender, and fragile in the midst of that craziness, and I understood that everything about you announced the fatalism, the risk and tenuous adventure of your poetry.

And now, love, that the years have gone by and we are separated, how do we explain the distance and the world that is stopped again at the threshold of those days of dancing the rhumba in any gymnasium, now that my life has turned into yours and become filled with the terrible mess of your dreams? I hear your voice in mine. I keep the warmth of your breath in my breath, since I am lost in you — while you certainly are being reborn from other ashes, you receive the accolades of your ridiculous success, and ignore the fact that I exist. I have moved completely into the twilight of your stories. I even copy your style and write myself into them, the same way that one day you decided to abandon your students, to trust in my income from my medical practice and dedicate yourself to writing novels. Not because it was easy or even utopian to believe in the power and success of those books, understand; but because you promised me the great dream that I had not experienced, poetry and the ineffable tenderness of your existence with me. You promised me the only truth of love, not the strange swindle of a writer's career. And you promised me the other kind of serenity as well: reciprocal growth, the tree of plenty, and a second life in the life of our sons. Not this, love. Not the final destruction of knowledge, home, and the way ahead...

3 · Trial by Fire

I began to be all yours, love, with the immense joy of giving you my hand, smiling at you up and down, and walking, beautiful and secure, at your side — little and innocent again as the time when I still had braids and was taken to see the ocean of my childhood. I was yours, love, even in the way my fingers sweated and I trembled all over from happiness, held prisoner by the strength of your long, nervous fingers. I loved your big hands, you know, because I thought then that love was just that, contemplating your blue veins and believing that your blood, the generous wine of first passion, had been promised to me from the beginning of time. You yourself told me, many times, that love is always primitive. Man begs Woman to give him back the water, the door to a home, and even the memory of the body in which he was created. And it happens that you became a very tall boy with fine bones, in whose fragility I always recognized your wish that I become your mother. From the long course of our years together, what I'm left with is the idea of putting you on my lap; I would caress your hair for a long time, give you my breast to suckle, so that you would feed yourself from me. And the possession of my body gave you your old dream. You always were like an angel, you know? Your porous aspect, the almost invisible lightness. When you lost that vegetal look, you became somewhat transparent, with your raven-like face, and you ended up becoming a horrible bird. Only then did I understand that I had fallen into the fraud of your second marriage.

True love occurred, however, on Sunday afternoons, when you would wait for me at the door of the university residence. You smiled at me from a distance, opening your thin arms to me, and I was suspended in the brief but infinite moment of your embrace. My body wrapped itself around yours, and you lifted me into the air over your head, and I thought that a single axis would always connect the point where my life began to fuse with yours. Then you stepped back a little, after putting me back on the ground, right in front of your eyes and in your shadow; you started to observe and inventory the beauty of the one you adored. You were fascinated, crazed by passion, not just for the big smile that lit up my face, but also because my curly hazel hair and my brown eyes made sense of the best and the worst of your existence. Above all, that imploring and frightened look offered me a silent gratitude. It thanked me for the fact that I had made myself as beautiful, on those Sunday mornings, as the first dawn. Beautiful, important, and unique, just like the fairy that had come from far away to give order, meaning, and a ray of light to your life. You even guessed that I would spend this morning and all future Sunday mornings of my life making myself beautiful just for you, without ever suspecting how deeply I wanted to impress you. I wanted you to be my captive, proud of my presence. I wanted you committed to the religious sentiment of that love liturgy on my Sundays. I never told you how important it was for me to consult other women in love about the colors I should wear, to hear them discuss the arrangement of my hair, the colors of blush for my cheeks, the way I applied lipstick to accentuate my lips that you would bite until they were pale — it was very important and almost a matter of life and death for me. Our mouths pressed together greedily, love, because it was Sunday in a park across the street; on the other side soldiers whistled inside the stone guard houses, gesturing as if they were masturbating. They grunted like pigs behind the walls, do you remember? Horrible and lonely, filled with lust, hate, and sadness, and with the kind of jealousy that only happens to locked up males. You would get very angry, love; you threw stones at them, chased them away, and gave them the finger. When dogs mounted stray bitches and impregnated them at the gates of the barracks, a strange excitement went through the cold bodies of the soldiers. If I asked you to calm down, to control yourself, because they were just soldiers with orders for guard duty on Sundays in the Portuguese garrisons back then, you didn't want to have anything to do with those men. They were there at the command of sergeants of the country, guarding zealously over the tranquil Sundays of the bishops, but under the threat of an Africa at war. You however, just wanted them to disappear from your life; they could beat off in there, in the guardhouses, or just unload against the walls like they did at the seminary.

You were already confusing politics with jealousy. You took years laboring under the illusion that political ideology had something to do with the little passions, spats, and social jealousies of your ascent in the world of Literature. Later, after many years, you experienced the small glory of literary fame. The political leaders began to notice you and invite you to their official receptions. You met the ministers that you had hated before. You entered the elite sphere of delegations of writers to their always-metaphysical conferences. It was obvious to me that only power seduced you, because you started to lose your convictions and grow soft. I lost my respect for you, love. I lost all my respect, my little love, seeing how those forms of betrayal prostituted you in the elegant salons. Every time I saw you participate in the banquets and ceremonies celebrating literary glory, my world diminished next to yours. You drank whiskey, ate caviar, feeling very important. And you still had the nerve to talk to me about your proletarian revolution!

Along with your big hands, I loved your undefined sadness. Women give their passion to mysterious, timid men. They are moved also by the clear dreams, extreme thinness, and the clouds that hang over the pathetic nature of that shyness. And if you want to know, all of this went along with the superior melancholy of your blue eyes. Their sweetness was honest. Your intelligence was sensitive. Afterward, I also discovered that your sense of humor didn't go beyond a simple prank. And your jealous fits and sulking prolonged your adolescence. Loving you meant saying sorry so that you'd give me a kiss on the mouth or caress my neck. And being married, I was always aware, meant that your passion was reduced to sexual foreplay. Married, we were afraid of Virginia Woolf: years and years and years, love, pretending to fight, insulting each other in the intimacy of our waning feelings. We argued in the dark of our room, with low voices so the boys wouldn't hear us, because we had the illusion of shedding a little light over the useless detail of our knowledge of each other. I said, I just wanted to tell you that I'm a different woman than the one you imagined. I wanted to know what had happened to the man from our previous existence, the man who had promised to love and honor me. Because, since I was your virgin, I didn't understand why you started to avoid me, and to not pay attention, and to become distracted with the very sound of my voice. You answered me with twisted accusations, deaf with anger: that I didn't understand you anymore, and that I wasn't supportive of you. You accused me of breaking my commitment to your art. If I corrected you to say that writing wasn't an art but a way of defending an ethics of protest against petty passions, you snorted with rage. I never thought I could tolerate so many intelligent insults. Your literary rhetoric turned entirely against me, full of unfamiliar words, with sentences as interminable as the night trains that go by and are just empty cars or illuminated tombs. I understood that it was possible that the only product of this marriage was a grammar, a dictionary of shame and cowardice. Suddenly I would start to cry, offended and embittered. I could see my tears upset you because your eyes would stare into the dark and your spirit gave in. Then your body would roll in my direction and your big arms would wrap around me and pull me to you. You begged me to forgive you. That you were just a man faced with the fatality of having gotten on the wrong side of life, of his wife and children, just that. And you begged me to love you intensely. The cruel game gave us back to each other, turning into an act of furious fornication. You practiced with me the marriage of a blind mole, guided by my sex organs. You helped yourself to me because the pleasure of coupling with my body masked the decadence of our other conjugal games and because it made you feel virile. There was a table, a shared bathroom, and a long hallway that led to the saddest object in the house: our bed. It was too large and very flat. During sex, you'd put your hand over my mouth, feeling that you had secured my complicity once again. If I wanted to talk to you about the women who are not important in the life of a man, of the unbearable loneliness of marriage, you'd glue your mouth to mine, run your hands over my thighs, and stick your big sex into my stomach, not allowing me to tell you how and why it was sad to see my personality die. What happened to your humanity, love? I asked myself, while the thrusts of your buttocks accelerated on top of me. It happened that your humanity was stuck in an inkwell, in the titles of books. Stunned, not understanding, I had started to experience the darkness and distance of two men. The one with the small books and the other one: a small, ill-tempered man, tense with anguish, who had the bad luck of living with me and his sons!

I loved your clear, rigorous ideas at the time that you described an unknown country to me, along with a future and the altar. Our passion grew even during a week of separation, fueled by the anxiety of daily phone calls to the university dorm. It strengthened during visiting hours, when we were forbidden to leave, in that room where there were always people from the provinces, under the vigilant eye of the nun at the reception desk and the enormous windows closed to the garden.

I was yours, love, in the dark of the movie theaters, when I put up a superior, obstinate resistance to your hands. You fondled my knees and my thighs, you groped for my breasts in the dark, and you wanted my fingers to touch the smooth tip of your scepter. I anticipated its fire and it was starting to burn in my face but I resisted, dying of shame, curiosity, and fear, just because I was on the brink of a great precipice and I was starting to enter the flesh of my man, little by little. Part of me said that virtue is virginal and that only virginity makes a woman powerful and desirable. The other part urged me to give my body and to feel the pleasure and mysteries of this man.

During our first year of courtship, I divided myself between the perversity and innocence of well-brought-up girls who refuse to give a man the second half of the apple. After the movies, the Sunday afternoons started to slip away. You took me to an empty bench, under the great trees. To the sound of soccer calls, on this side of the box shrubs or behind the cedars, horrible men spit or accosted us with obscene whistles. My idea of romance was to be in those gardens hungrily kissing my man and sensing that boys wearing sunglasses loved me too, masturbating to the sound of shouts from the soccer stadium. In the lake in front of us, dying fish swam in the rushes, struggling like us with the eternal and urgent call of life and love. And there were the swans, remember? They were rigid animals, as serene as that ebbing time. Everything was so beautiful, love, so beautiful and harmonious, that even today I have a hard time believing how it was possible to have seen the water become muddy, the bottom and surface of that lake, the fish, and the smugness of the swans that passed by, blotting out, witnessing our passion. I can't bear this deceit, love. I don't want to think that I have to get over you and move on, that you will be so far away from me. Here I am in tears, in the night as our boys are sleeping and are getting used to the notion of having been born just from me, out of the love I had for you. From where I am, I can decipher every signal of their distress. They are in slumber, these boys who are becoming men and look like you, but they sleep with empty eyes and with their bodies curled up in a corner of their bunks. They are cold. They will feel cold for the rest of their lives because you don't come to tuck their clothing around their necks the way you used to, and perhaps because this winter has no cure or remedy without the weight, shadow, and bones of your hands. For many years I got used to seeing you go into the boys' room before coming to bed, listening to their breathing in the dark, to pat them, give them a playful kiss on the ear — understanding that this was very important to you. Both were made in the image of their father, they slept peacefully, but they were living a happy childhood very different from yours. How will it be now for them to dream, to be at home and in the world and not be able to explain your absence?

As for me, I look at the fatigue in my eyes, in the bottom of glasses of whiskey, in the false transparency of glass and all liquids, and above all in the art of curing others' ills, while I am still suffering from the sickness that comes from you.

Are you being called by the sea? Nobody can stop my man from running; he is once again barefoot on his island. He took with him the time and the wind and the boats and the ideas he has of them. The curious thing was, love, to see how this little political animal came into my life — a man I could never have met in my homeland! I got used to having a little dog at my feet that barked at the regime. I rubbed its back, talked to it softly, and watched it calm down. My hand soothed its revolt, its fear and jealousy of the courage of others. Because the others were always your friends, and they had been arrested. They suffered torture, night interrogations, and the judgment of high tribunals. And they gnashed their teeth, went to exile or jail; they were your and also my hunted heroes. When they finally let them go, I saw you run to them, searching for the strange detail of every one of their experiences. You listened to them in a trance and came running home. You called me to the study and started to describe the horrors of a silent, dark country. In a trance, driven by jealousy of your political heroes, you imagined revolutions, coups, summary executions, a great popular fury capable of sucking the bones and the eyes of the regime . . . The worst is that when you spent your melodious hatred, you developed a huge appetite: you ate and drank to the courage of the martyrs and their myths, you quickly dulled the conscience of your free, safe body — and something very nostalgic beat deep in the stomach of my little dog. Do you know what, love? Nobody ever came to our door at dawn to drag you out of bed, violate my intimacy, and take you to Caxias. With the passing of the years, you had the misfortune not to have to demand your freedom. You had the bad luck of looking at the river in front of your eyes, sitting on the banks, without ever once having been taken to the delta of the courage that sometimes meant death, exile, or stopped time beyond the walls and the guard towers of the Peniche or Caxias forts. Yours was a good conscience that was at the same time disturbed by its apparent tranquility. Your poems and articles were obviously banned by the censors. You signed all the protests against the regime. You participated in protests against the colonial war — but never were any of your books taken off the market and nobody remembered to arrest you. It's not even certain that our phone had been tapped, while you cursed and sent death threats to the dictatorship. And never did any miserable undercover policeman come around the corner, climb up to the third floor of our building, or walk around the neighborhood spying on the comrades who came around to attend your little political meetings. I don't know, I never knew, how to explain the origin or the purpose of the strange masochism of my political animal. At the time you were of military age, your time to desert never came. You swore that you would dodge the draft if you suffered the small indignity of having to fight in Guinea. I watched you leave at night to attend the political rallies, to distribute the yellow leaflets of the resistance, to become the sleepwalker who levitated in the deafness of the martyrs of the Capela do Rato. Under your orders, I received bearded revolutionaries in our house, in whose eyes I always detected a boyish panic. They came, left, and you lost all the bets that they would be arrested or shot crossing the border to Spain.

The day you were going to leave for Mafra, I went to say good-bye to you at the Rossio station, I cried pitifully on your shoulder and felt sorry for your recruit's shaved head. I remember you repeating the word *exile*, seeing you say it with clenched teeth — but since our life transformed into a succession of weekend leaves from the garrison, I quickly lost hope of living a life of exile with you. I would have loved to join you in Paris or Stockholm, to be your secret passion during many years and then return with you holding hands on the morning of the Carnation Revolution. My life was never applauded by any crowd, the kind that on April 26, 1974, raised the fingers of victory over fascism in Portugal and in their hands they held carnations, hatred, dreams that they came to workshop in the exiles of their martyred country. You limited yourself to thanking me for my existence, the joys of my body during sex, and this during a very long and always safe time. My little political animal was never ever arrested, contrary to my fears and your expectations. You weren't mobilized to Africa nor did you desert the army. You were just a lucid man, because of the simple, stupid need to remain lucid!

The morning of the revolution, you said good-bye quickly and ran to the Baixa to see the bald, cold, astonished soldiers who were greeted with loud cheers for the revolution by the hysterical crowd. In the Largo do Carmo you witnessed in ecstasy the surrender of the dictators. I don't know if you denounced "suspicious elements" to the troops, if you followed informants of the secret police along the streets, or if you went to the Forte de Caxias to embrace the freed prisoners. They told me that you were a success in the first liberation rallies. You went to Santa Apolónia and to the airport to greet smiling exiles, who were pink cheeked, healthy, and with their fingers spread in a big V for victory. You deserved, I saw, the focus of TV cameras, and you gave a memorable testimony, even thought it was a little confused, about the Great Night of the Forty-Eight Years. I lost track of you during the following days and nights; I thought my man had finally been elected and transformed into the hero of the popular cause. You started to come home just to take a shower and change clothes; if I asked you how things were going in the decision centers or the places shown on television, you just told me that the country was changing. How was the country changing? Where was it going? You never answered me.

You failed, I think now, at each one of the basic principles of that change, love. When you attempted to jump over the ditch of mediocrity, your feet gave out on you, you fell flat into the theoretical, demagogical sludge and in the mud of your remorse at not having been either a martyr of the dictatorship or a hero of the revolution. In the end, no one knew who you were. You stood on tiptoe at the door of the political parties, waiting for someone to invite you in, to see if you could be useful and necessary to the democracy. Your comrades didn't want you on the inside of things. The octopi extended their arms, grabbed you by the waist in the street demonstrations, and that's where your bravado and immoderate revolutionary conscience remained!

And to think that I'd have to read all about it later, in each of your small, hurried, and vehement books! What still remains are the golden, victorious lies of your novels, as you know. In them you exalted all women for me and me for all Portuguese women, exactly like the time when you gave me your hand and took me to see and learn about the second truth of the ships berthed in the Alcântara. They say you sang the song of Woman. You restored their luminous and primitive grandeur, just as was reported by a cunning critic who later came to our house for dinner and spent the evening studying me myopically through his sensual eyeglasses. But here in this and all the houses we lived in, you were always rough with me; you became a brutish man, letting yourself ferment in the egotism of comfortable armchairs and long mornings in bed.

You never lifted a finger to clean up after yourself, even when you had put things out of place. When I was sick, you couldn't even make toast: you never knew where the bread, the butter, the honey, or even my favorite packets of tea were kept. And there is no memory of you in the objects that surround me now. There never was, not even your fingerprints. But there still is the air that was breathed in and out by your lungs. There are the forms and echoes of your words. Your shadow. Stopped time. And a copy of each one of your books, in whose inscriptions I have now come to learn that you would be mine for better or worse, in sickness and in health, until death did us part . . .

And what about the other, worst, and only falsehood of your books, love? All of them were precisely committed to the poor, it's true — but here, inside our house, you only drank expensive wines, you soaked yourself in the whiskey that I brought home, poured from the bottles that my grateful patients brought me on Sunday mornings because I had saved them from dying. Literary people have a sublime gift for talk when they have a glass in their hand and words cloud their fleshy lips. The literati and the writers' apprentices belong to the priestly caste, those who preach sermons with their little morals to others. I've seen them pass through my house in the course of these twenty years, attending my dinners, and I witnessed their greed, their bad manners, and their disdain for me and my silence. They were "your" literary people, love — fools promoted to intellectuals. The saviors of humanity who came to our house and filled their bellies while they talked badly of people like me, who didn't read Sartre or Marx, weren't on top of the Latin American "boom," and were unaware of the furious triumphs of Portuguese fiction!

As for you, you would wrinkle your nose at the lack of variety, the frugality, or the improvisation of my meals, and you'd threaten me with getting take-out from the corner restaurant. And I was so silly: I believed that you'd get out of my life and leave me alone. The revolution threatened all Portuguese women with divorce. It was in fashion to destroy marriage and to abandon those very sad women who had been destroyed, drowned in the swamp of love, and who can't make it to the water's surface. I thought myself that without you, the days and nights of this house would consign me to a widowhood similar to what you gave to the solitary women in your novels. I have, like them, the pale shadow, the empty lap. But I don't have the famished body or mouth or the empty eyes and poverty of those dependent widows. I conserve intact my art of being alive, love. Without doubt, I will live new passions, and experience strange challenges and charms. And I'll always return to the day that you came, took me by the hand, kissed it, and asked me to sit down and look deep into your eyes. You just needed my consent, you said. You had decided to leave your teaching job. You wanted to give expression to everything that was exploding inside you, and live just from writing and for writing your books. In addition to the innumerable projects that you carried around in your head, it would finally be possible to live from Literature in Portugal. I went along with you to the inside of that dream, as you know. I let it poison me. Without suspecting, on the same day I said yes and made a point of telling you that I believed in your talent, you would make the jump, run away from me, become famous, and be successful in countries different from mine, and that you would stop belonging to me. You would also become a kind of vain and temperamental dinosaur. And you would move into the night, on your continuous travels without me, for what you stopped calling "my work" and started to designate as "my life." Your life in exchange for mine?

Now, in my place of quiet, I imagine that I've been returned to the threshold of myself. My face is lifted, waiting for the morning. But will it be a morning return that is glorious, blue, and alive, as primitive and final as the one when nothing was dead in our passion and the world of our marriage?

4 · *A Bed in the Center of the World*

Our honeymoon, from our wedding night on, was to see you open your eyes wide and watch how you contemplated my nakedness. Trembling with amazement, you were in ecstasy, and you didn't know how to be grateful for the presence of a Woman in your life.

It was the time of precious, austere virgins, the time when virginity represented the best prize in the bride's trousseau, and heralded happy marriages. For this reason, I never talked to you about my disappointment in your excessive, ex-seminarian timidity. It had become clear to me that I was going to wed a lapsed little priest, who was still very religious about sex and who hadn't even committed the perversion of reaching out a hand to fondle my breasts in the confessional. You never knew how important it would have been for me to resist the malice and despair of your puberty. I always waited for something to exit the core of your body like a kind of energy field, an earthquake that would threaten to kill the modesty of my virginity. If you had known how to force me to go to bed with you, our complicity and the transgressive moment of our gift to each other would have been different. I would have moved in a more intelligent way to the inside of your world. So I became resigned to the encroachment of your hands in the movies, on stairwells when we sheltered ourselves from the rain, in elevators, and on public garden benches. I resisted you, love, just as I did the sly advances of the chief of clinical services who insisted on showing me the secrets of the X-ray rooms, and I blushed in front of you the same way that I did at the entreaties, the courteous compliments, or the crude passes of the residents who took me to tea at Toxinas in Santa Maria. Our love didn't experience the madness of making me yours in a room borrowed from a friend, one of those independent rooms, with a door to a stairway, and whose interior order would be monitored by the ear of any Lisbon widow — possibly even the miserly old woman who rented you a cubicle without a window and loaned you small amounts of money with interest. Instead of this you became a punctual and servile little rat. You would wait for me in the hospital atrium and sighed with relief when no resident showed up with me; I was always more beautiful than ever, and my little rat sent me a worried but happy smile from afar. Then I got a quick kiss on my tired lips, and left with you walking hand in hand. Then loving was to sit at your side in the car, listening to the continuous praise of my beauty and being in the center of a trance that had no end in your adoration. You were not just in love. I felt you getting sick from me, possessed by a strange coitus of love that made it platonic, almost a mystical adoration of my body. This is why I wasn't surprised on the afternoon when you looked me in the eyes, emotional and nervous, and proposed marriage. It was pouring rain, you were going to be released from the army, you had by a miracle escaped the war in Guinea, and you were full of projects for the future. You'd return to your old mediocre job, start up your studies again, and you needed me desperately . . .

Besides being a time of virgins, it was an age of fatigue without glory. The Beatles and hippies were wandering around the world, far away from Portugal. Here the flowers wilted in our hair. Out there, deaf disturbances occurred slowly, there were days when hope was forbidden. They sang songs that said "make love, not war" but you continued to recite verses about hunted lovers, deserters, nameless exiles, and little soldiers that came back in a pine box. You explained the Vietnams, the Biafras, the Israeli–Arab crises, the Mays of 1968 and everything in fact that bothered and seduced you. A man named Guevara had become your new Christ Martyr, the Americans were horrible in the bombed swamps and rice fields, the Russians were crushing a peaceful rebellion in Czechoslovakia. I never knew why you told me those things, if in fact on our wedding night I was your virgin-mother and I listened to you cry as you embraced my nakedness. You told me to make me an accomplice, as if to criticize my distracted way of living without this commitment to the world and to the hell that others lived in. In truth, I limited myself to listening to the memory of your resentments. You cried as you embraced me because nobody in your family had bothered to send a telegram to wish us happiness. Even for no reason, all of them had become angry with you and your distance, with the exception of me. Your sister Amélia would leave soon for Angola, dazzled by the richness of that primitive continent where in the end nothing happened; our troops were leaving on a mission to pacify and reestablish order; Portugal was defending western civilization in Africa, and we couldn't call war that mistake of armed incursion where infinitely less people died than on the Portuguese roads. Not a single miserable wedding present came from the Azores, an embroidered towel, an envelope with money, a set of cups or a coffee service for the rented rooms in the dark house where we would start our marriage cursed by a life that was ignored by two estranged families. For the first time, father had decided to punish me with a stubborn silence about my union with you. Against his will I wouldn't marry a prince. I was going to live with a little man who promised me only the dreams of books, political intelligence, and above all the bad taste of calling him a colonial, slaver, a redneck, and a fascist. As for your side, they had become distracted from the small detail of your Lisbon existence, used to thinking that it was a mere act of fate that had made them lose your trail. They started to migrate to Canada, taken by your father to escape the army and the war, or called by their sisters who had married the "Americans" of the Azores. Forgotten from your reality, they limited themselves to writing you letters that were incomprehensible to me and that alluded to triumph and tears. The worst of these letters, love, was that I was omitted from them; they didn't even ask about me, if I by chance was happy with you, or if my life was good or bad, or on the contrary, was it just the life you wanted . . .

Our wedding pictures and the reception with our twelve guests still show me a tense, irrelevant young boy, with salient veins on his forehead, ready to burst, and with shaking hands. In one of the photos you lift a glass; you don't know how to smile, and you can see your hand wavering in this gesture of raising the cup, as if it were your first mass. In another, you are dancing with me, falling over your feet, and the body bent over the bride is unexpectedly bony and thin. In a third, there are the few friends from this time in Lisbon: two ex-seminarians with beardless smiles, a boy of military age who had already been deployed to Mozambique, three ridiculous writers who were poorly dressed, perhaps being profane and ironic at this ceremony, since they spent the afternoon talking badly about all the writers in the country. It wasn't hard to figure out what they were laughing about or their sibylline way of already predicting the despotism of marriage. Our generation could have invented divorce and forgotten about the evils of the dictatorship and the colonial war. But it barely lost the right to be loved and understood by the next generations. It lost at least the moral right of revolutions. It didn't dignify the country, the morning of the carnations, and the liberation of April 25; today we live carping about lost opportunities, biting on the failure to make our own future. And this was predictable in the negligence and levity that we all present in our wedding photos. The little Portugal of that generation is now at the end of the 1980s, we will soon enter a new decade and a new century; it still has to join an imaginary Europe that just belongs to others. It left Africa and Asia, where it washed its hands like Pilate and resigned itself to being ruled by the outrageous intelligence of the yuppies. Between the prejudice and nostalgia of people like you and me, love, there is a country that doesn't exist; the one that has to be invented by resentful writers, lazy politicians, and presidents who are a kind of blotting paper for two reformed generations — the divorced and the children of divorced parents.

    My life with you was to teach you how to celebrate Christmas and to return to you, one by one, all the symbols of a family. I taught you how to celebrate Mother's Day, and your, my, and our children's birthdays. In a certain sense, it was up to me to tell you when you should be happy or sad, to be yourself or condescend to others — in the same house where you became distracted from everything and ran the risk of forgetting you were my husband and my lover, father of two sons, and the hero of a cause that nobody ever understood. I educated you, I made you my firstborn, and I sometimes got you to stop being the good-savage of Literature and capable of talking of everyday things. After all, the Earth continued to revolve around an axis, books were not the center of the universe, and your philosophical culture didn't go beyond a simple footnote to the life that I so much wanted to live with you. It irritated me immensely that you didn't even know how to hide your boredom when my friends visited; they weren't cultured but they were alive. I hated it when you wouldn't stop to chat with the neighbors as you came into the building. You turned me into your permanent cause for disapproval, always wanting to force me to become an intellectual, being psychosomatic and temperamental, always in suspense over the continuous tragedy of an everyday country, a country of the daily news, as conventional as the ceremonies of June 10. I ask you where the heroes are. The heroes are now grumpy old men who accompany the president to cities in the provinces and then receive the medal of freedom. What responsibility do I have for these dark ancestors from our time?

I started by making you a man and letting go of the romantic idea of living with a clever boy, who only cared about the tedium of working in badly paid jobs, an irresistible literary inclination, and a naïve vocation for politics. Of course you were going to change the world, as any visionary had to do. You told me this in 1969 and 1973, during the campaigns of the Democratic Opposition. You told me this the day that you came home and the dictator had died, the day you showed up with a bruise from a police club on your neck, and especially on April 25, 1974. The world was always changing, from the time you fought it in your first opinion pieces that the censors' blue pencil or the editor in chief returned because they were provocative, lacking talent, or not as sibylline or subtle as the censors' intelligence demanded. You were about to alter your poems, the first novel that the political police never even got around to banning — and later, every one of your novels, especially the one in which everybody except me became the caricature of a timeless, mythological country . . .

Making a man of you was to encourage you to take up your studies again; I wasn't going to allow you to become an easy adversary, the kind that shield themselves with heroes and end up not even deserving the moniker of martyrs, but of stupid victims of their own blindness. I insisted you go to the Liceu Camões and to excel in your studies in Literature. I went myself to register you for the entrance exam to the university, certain that only in this way would I be able to immerse you in the vortex of books. In fact, my little obedient, sensitive man won all of my bets. I did it all for myself, ever since the wedding night, when after crying about everything and everybody, you fell asleep exhausted on my shoulder, dreamt of the dazzling nudity of your virgin, and started to feed on me.

We spent the day in bed eating cookies and sweets from the wedding reception and cooing at each other like doves — finally we were married and grateful. You made love to me innumerable times. In the bathtub you played with me like a clown, squirting me on my back and shoulders with the shower head at full strength. You soaped me up, rubbed my shoulders, and insisted on drying me with a light towel, as soft as the tenderness of your hands. You were studying in me an anatomy that had been always unknown to you. As virgin as I was, you examined my breasts, buttocks, and thighs. You wanted to see what a vagina looked like inside, the geography of my conch shell, as you always called it, where you inserted your red member. After the careful examination that had started to excite me, you took me, pressing your full weight on me with your thin, muscular arms. And putting me on the bed, you initiated with me the great feast of the body. Only a poet would tell me the lovely things, the words and images that are written but no one dares speak. Something very luminous burst forth from you and allowed me to receive your erect animal into my conch shell without pain. Just a slight shiver told me that the end of my virginity had come. A kind of sob in my groin, after the pulsing of your member, the explosion of your orgasm, the heat of an acid toxin, and the force of your passion on that glorious day. Six consecutive times, I received the earthquake of that energy. By the seventh orgasm I was unbearably sore, almost destroyed, but at the same time happy and exhausted. And in the following days, I lived between dream and reality. Our fever had no end, nor did the strength of your member. Music and art filled your tender, intelligent passion. It had been worth staying a virgin all those years, to be finally married wisely. I had bet on your world and felt that I would never regret having exchanged the Good of others for the Bad that would come from you. I just didn't know, love, that both coexisted in your duplicity like a double poison, coming from the wings of an angel and the horns of a devil. My first lover told me that, the one I used as revenge for your cheating on me with your silly women. Certainly my future lovers will tell me this. We went on hurting each other, whether up close or from a distance, yesterday and today, in the time of hate and betrayal . . .

5 · *The Discussion and the Light*

"You want to know what your worst trait is, Marta, do you really want to know what turned me off? It's your sense of superiority, the way you never stopped sniffing at your lunatic, suspect, and inferior little man. I don't know why I wanted to settle into your life, becoming a domesticated bovine, just to vegetate in the pasture of your idleness. You couldn't understand that the world was always a drama in my head. I felt it pulsate and move around me. But you didn't want to notice the difference between the cold blood of lizards and the energy that expands a man's veins and burns his skin, nerves, and bones."

"Understand how, if we were running side by side and didn't know where or why we had to run, you'd be taken by the obsession of a competition that demanded the certainty, the proof, that you were better than me: wise, intelligent, sensitive in the extreme, with a feminine, adolescent sensitivity. You ran backward in the years that you spent eight hours a day at work: you took the subway, then the bus to the University City, and got lost in night classes, in the interminable seminars in linguistics and literary semiotics. You came back tired, with circles under your eyes; on a daily basis you rose to my level. You got a degree, you were erudite and useful. After the many weekends that you forgot about me and the boys, and disappeared with your classmates in study groups, you came home half drunk. You showed off, flaunted your university diploma, and I started to hate you. I was going to start a second race. And it would force me to run with you at my side, without knowing the goal or where it would lead us . . ."

"You hated me for it, Marta. My diploma struck a deathblow to the magic of your stethoscope, and the way you policed my body and belittled my life. I didn't want to be a mediocre man protected by you. You couldn't stand it that I started to diagnose my dreams, not by the sword of the angel surgeon that was taking care of me like a fragile object that seemed to depend on the drugs it dispensed."

"That's why you started to accuse me of laziness, of being a woman riding on the fame of her husband. I could see this the moment when I was not yet at the fringes of your life; you reduced me to a stagnant, acquired appendage. Medicine was never my philosophy, nor even my art of staying alive. When I became a doctor, as you know, I parked myself in the station of end of semester visits. I traveled in the periphery of your world. I did my hurried shifts in the halls of the Santa Maria Hospital, my clinic hours and paid my dues to earn my little medical degree — I did it for you, to deserve you in those straight-laced little places and so that you would lack nothing. At the end of every month I'd come home with my bag of money. I'd see you smile, your mood improved, and I knew that was a good reason for you to be happy and stay married to me."

"With you yes. Not with the mundanity or tyranny of your money: the extravagances that enraged me, the generosity of being considered an inferior, badly dressed, diminished by the salary of a public servant who boiled with rage at our abundance. We pretended to live not from my monthly defeat but from your rigorous social climbing and the complacency of two astonished children to whom it was never possible to explain the inexplicable."

"People of your ideology, Nuno, all those people of Literature and the Arts, hate money. In the hand of others, it's a cursed, unjust animal, the vice of all vices and crime of all crimes. When they have it, they lock it in a safe called remorse; they lose the dignity of poverty and become mortally offended when someone starts to see them as middle-class citizens. That happened to you. When you rose up in the world and became a money machine, you made a point of ending our ritual of eating out on Sundays with my earnings. You stopped enjoying our country drives and couldn't stand our walks in the garden. I took the boys out to play; it was like walking dogs. That was when you stopped being faithful to me, when you still called me twice a day to say nice things to me and to swear that you were guided by my star."

"Faithful, Marta, and in love and happy, but under the club of your powerful, astute hand. I wanted to stop being your caged bird, looking at the world sideways through the bars of your cage. Your love couldn't be that punctual, charitable birdseed, a necessary poison that filled the belly but not the spirit of someone who had been born a dove. You wanted me to be locked up, domesticated, so that I would offer you grateful, reverent love, with distracted caresses, and bitter lemons. You could lock in a dove, force it to coexist with other birds, small luxuries, a regular schedule, and harmony yellowed by jealousy — just so you could pride yourself on being loved, obeyed, and always so maternal toward me?"

"Let me say it another way, love; my little different, diligent professor was about to become initiated into the witchcraft of teaching and books. Literature would not take long to absorb his passion, the fascination of the one who had learned to navigate the waters of divine, unfathomable literary creation. I put up without judging the days of that little dutiful professor who set out to be different from my neglect. But when you started to slip between my fingers, to be the wise eel and to consider me to be dumb and frivolous, you became contradictory. Hadn't you taught me that writers were polished and tolerant? Well, here they were in front of me. Aside from being ugly and badly dressed, they put each other down, and reduced critics who were considered to be intelligent to the category of idiots. Most people, in their opinion, were hard to swallow. They were brainless, clumsy people with no talent. And these Literature types, love, taught you to criticize my ignorance, my laziness in not reading a book or in-depth articles in miserable political journals. To that part of you, love, I wanted to say that it wasn't important to understand the Iran–Iraq war or the Palestinian conflict to be a person and to deserve being treated in an intelligent way. It was never clear to me that perestroika or apartheid were as important to my love for you as smiling at you and the pleasure of taking you to my bed . . ."

"The bourgeoisie forgets so quickly, Marta! They do it for convenience and a desire for security. And also for self-defense. You became an amnesiac bourgeois about everything related to my past. You never remembered anything: how I had been poor and barefoot on my Island, how I had grown up in the politics of Lisbon. I had the right to my memories. One day, after we had been married for many years, I saw clearly that you didn't know me. It was when you averted your eyes from the television, called me, and had the innocence to ask me who was de Gaulle and what happened in May of '68."

"Then you became terribly irritated with me as if I had offended you. You got coarse and crude, shouting you didn't have the patience to deal with a stupid little girl who didn't know anything: Salazar, and Caetano, the colonial war and April 25th, the Secret Police and the Censorship. All that was missing was for me to be chewing gum, smiling idiotically at the cameras, and wagging a sensual finger to say 'hi.' My kept man started to look down at me; he wouldn't bother to explain what had so profoundly poisoned 'his' generation."

"I had gotten married to a shop girl or a dull seamstress. I had a hard time coming to grips with the fact that a doctor was capable of lowering herself to the level of housewives reading magazines about movie stars and society idols living in big restored houses, who had the bad luck of being rich, frivolous, and even more ignorant than you are."

"The only bad thing I ever wished for you, Nuno, was that you would marry one of those furious, butt ugly, and snotty intellectuals with square glasses and hysterical nerves. You deserved to die of boredom next to a sterile woman in love with opera. A woman who would spend her time listening to Bach and Beethoven with the volume turned up, startling the visitors and neighbors who carefully watched the intimacy of two sad, erudite crows. You were missing your luxurious, boring woman who was rooting for you and who shared your problems. When the journalists buzzed around you, you looked like an angry bear, not wanting to go outside so that you wouldn't see people laugh in your face. You pushed me far away so you wouldn't have to share the vicissitudes of your books with me. When I said 'your business' you interrupted me with an irritated gesture and corrected me immediately: 'my life, please.' And naïve as I was, I continued to invite people to dinner who might have been intelligent but who didn't ever deserve my hospitality. They would call at the last minute to say they weren't coming; something had come up and they were sorry. I had spent the afternoon in the kitchen, I had outdone myself with the cod in cream sauce, the desserts, I had bought flowers and whiskey, I had dressed and put on perfume — but these Literature people had no respect for anyone. The times they came on time, the evenings made me sleepy, a tiredness as profound as the tedium of your silky conversations — and then the intellectuals would leave drunk, always garrulous, and they never again asked about me. It wasn't enough to hate them, love. I wanted them all to be cuckolded, to get tumors in their guts, and terrible warts on their noses. How could I be available and attentive, to venerate and celebrate the talent and triumph of your books? Instead of this, I had stopped belonging, as you said, to 'your' generation. I had not inherited the tedium of Sunday afternoons with you, I didn't need pills to sleep, and I didn't depend for my happiness on translations, sales, reviews, and the whole metaphysics of your career as a novelist. We lived back to back in different hallways and in different sleep cycles . . ."

"You started sleeping on your stomach, wrapped up in a blanket and with your head covered by the pillow. With this fanatical way of sleeping it was obvious you had given up being a tangible part of my life. You turned your attention to our children. You made them your life rings and lost yourself in their care, devouring them with bloodsucking kisses."

"And do you think I would have stayed with you if it had not been for the children?"

"I loved them because they fed my laziness. For years, it was my job to help them with their studies. I explained photosynthesis to Diogo, direct and indirect discourse, the passive and active voice, the kinds of rocks, the laws of physics and economic systems. To Francisco, who was as lazy and weak-willed as you, I yelled at him about the concepts of the greatest and lowest common denominator, equations and square roots. And why did I do this? Because their mother was never available, or she had forgotten everything, or she just didn't feel like dealing with it."

"If I told you that each one of us should be themselves and live according to their vocation, you'd unleash another wave of fury. You told me to my face that those were just excuses. You screamed at me with hatred because you were no longer part of my happiness. We had again started to compete with each other. The best of you called for me, wanted my appearance at the moments your star shone in the cloudy firmament of Literature. You liked to exhibit my beauty, so others would envy you for owning and possessing me. The other part of you resisted this temptation and suggested that I stay home, afraid I'd open my mouth and destroy your literary elegance. No one in fact would forgive a writer married to a housewife who complained about how boring the speeches were."

"I took many years, Marta, to overcome my fascination for your beauty, from the time when you were more than a name, a house, and a habit of mine. The day I looked at you one last time, I was surprised that everything was extinct: my love and your physical beauty. You had gained weight suddenly, without my noticing. Your stomach was swollen and there was no light in your still sweet eyes. The lines around your mouth announced the beginning of old age. Your neck had been taken over by wrinkles that turned red from a simple twitch of your nervous system. You would grow an immense goiter. Your smile had become intentional, offensive, and acid as a prune. You weren't ruined yet, but you were ugly. It was becoming a cynical ugliness, cold and invertebrate like the laziness that had taken over your way of conjugating the verb 'to exist.'"

"You're right: that's when you took the bit in your teeth and never stopped running alone and trying to hurt me. My ruined body had stopped interesting you. Yours still had a disciplined, mature elegance. Your gray hair went well with the brittleness of your bones and made you seductive, perhaps even as irresistible as your sure ascent into Literature. I also knew that you used the pretext of the first signs of my aging to become volatile. You didn't lack frustrated little women. They were the same ones who got divorced in your books and that I recognized by their smell and their jealousy. I saw the shape of their mouths on the lipstick stains on your shirts. I sensed their presence on nights when you came in late, with tedium on your lips, the way your guilty eyes avoided mine and how you yelled at me to stop bothering you with petty nonsense. I had been your favorite lover and was now reduced to the role of the rejected woman who burns, sighs, and waits in vain through the night with eyes open in the dark."

"I still loved you and yet another side of me wanted to take permanent revenge on you. I was going to hate you Marta, just because with you Love was not eternal."

"You were going to hurt me to death. You should say that you were going to kill me, or kill in me what was left of my way of being different from you and your cruelty. You were going to hurt me with your strange presence: you not only couldn't love me but you didn't make love to me anymore. I didn't like giving you my hand. Even that started to seem ridiculous: all my fingers had been violated in an invisible way."

"It was an indifferent insult that came from the cold of your soul, but that passed through your whole body."

"I couldn't give myself to a man who gave me divided attention. I had readied myself to hate you. I was thirsty for revenge."

"And you were blind as a mole."

"Worse, I wanted to be a snake and inject you with my venom."

"We made one mistake after the other, and lost all notion of restraint. I erred in my pride, in denying that I should turn back and ask you to forgive me. I wanted to promise you flowers again, if possible the flowers of Goodness, and to free myself from the shadows, from the hate that hurts, from the little and who knows, useless, regrets."

"We met at the wrong time, Nuno."

"When I decided to pursue you, you were already a woman who had been irreversibly hurt. Sometimes I remember how cold our voices were when we humiliated each other. How we tried to cover things up so our children wouldn't notice, and couldn't do it. Even in the silence of our bedroom, their eyes were lit up in the dark, spying on us. When our voices hurled curses at each other, their mouths would twist into sobs. That's what I was afraid of Marta, the pain of our children, and if only for them I would have given it another try."

"That can't be true. You know perfectly well that everything fell apart when you found out about the 'other' reason. That's the only thing a Portuguese man can't forgive his wife."

"Absolutely. The thing is that you didn't exactly choose 'him' but because I persisted in carrying on with the affairs that made you jealous."

"Even so, I would have forgiven you all the women. I would have forgotten the bad things that came from you. For our children, understand. I would say to myself, and repeated it until I believed it, that I had never heard any one of your insults. That I had never been vexed, offended, wounded to the core by the voices I heard on the phone and that hung up right away, laughing at my face. I would start again at your side, like on the night I was your virgin. I would live again the other nights when I celebrated harmful nuptials made of promises and hopes, and passions that would be eternal again and would last for life and death. What an intense love Nuno, wouldn't have been ours, if we could have thought about the lonely, shocked eyes of our sons. And what a great and memorable pardon, love, if you hadn't known that a divorced man was offering me flowers, smiling at me with humility very different from yours, and begging me to take pity on him."

Unlike you, this other man was dying for me. If I had wanted to pursue him or even kill him, he would have let himself die for me. I knew his sighs and supplications. I loved him for that sweet death that was coming from you and your absence from my life.

Now in the same house that still travels through time in front of a church the spirit of that man still hovers. He has some endearing qualities, like you do. He tells me I'm beautiful. And that I would have been perfect if I didn't carry the curse of your memory.

I love hearing him list my merits: he says that, in addition to being a wonderful mother, I am the greatest and brightest of all women.

When we are both on duty at the Clinic, he invites me to have coffee two and three times in the same afternoon. If we have lunch together in the little restaurant across the street, and where you stopped coming a long time ago, he always whispers in my ear.

I really like it when someone whispers in my ear, did you know?

He says that I'm amazing at my profession, in my home, and in the kitchen. And contrary to what you might think, I am not for him a fat lover or a body that has to roll itself into a ball to sleep: I am also his goddess. That's what I most adore in him; I am a goddess held by his strong hands and the murmuring of a mouth that falls asleep near my ear.

This, Nuno, I'm sure you would never forgive. Aside from having turned you into a monster, it's true that I have stopped being old, bitter, and turned in the direction of the doors that only open to the infinite. Even so, don't wonder that I repeat it: you didn't completely poison my happiness. You consumed me, love, that's true. And I am definitely tired, and suddenly over the threshold of the age of jealousy. But I am not exhausted. As I told you, I still have the seventh life of the little spotted cat with gray eyes that is reborn next to the fire. I am once again in my own time, in a time that belongs to me. I'm ready like the bride who feels a second, promised dove of passion alight on her head.

Well, I will take my dove back, love.

BOOK FIVE

The Invisible Return

1

THE COWS ARE PERFECTLY
IN PLACE IN THE FOG ON THE
CREST OF THE ISLAND; FROM THE ROAD,
YOU CAN HARDLY SEE THE ROUND STAINS OF
THEIR BACKS, OPENING LIKE A SMILE OF FLOWERS.

You can see the blunt horns pointed against the wind, embedded on the surface of these spheres of fog. And the very big eyes, running because of the mist, send a sad cheer from afar that is characteristic of animals that only exist to exist, knowing they will die soon. Dispersed among the cows, dogs, sheep, and goats wander — and seen from this distance, they won't be bigger than the flies that during the rainy season of his time there bit the galls of the steers and made the beasts impatient when they stood at the doors of the houses. Even the cowhands, with their wool caps and boots muddied up to their knees, seemed to float among them, wrapped in the fog. They have the absent, sweet, and perhaps fatal look of those animals. Their disinterested footsteps, unhurried, lift their bodies and place them at the level of the wind, not to move them or make them go from place to place. In the morning and the afternoon, on days multiplied by the years, the destination of the clover would lead them there through the wet trail that was so shiny it looked like steel — making impossible the task of cutting down the brambles and ginger lilies with the scythes, the small hoes, and plows that in the old days had blades as shiny as a mirror held to the sun.

But the exceptional difference of everything was that in a still recent past, and even though they had long been extinct, the volcanoes were still the land that trembled in the basement of the houses, in the invisible axis of the lofts, the chests of drawers, and the beds. And the beams that held up these childhood homes creaked in an almost grouchy way. Because in the nights that still roared above the sea, an ancient sleep sealed the eyelashes of children with lead. An evil wind shook him, full of distant whistles and howls, and this wind carried with it the scent of fig trees and sugar cane, a smell of the Atlantic, of shells, salt, and clouds of frightened Atlantic Cory's shearwaters fleeing the coast. You couldn't escape to the yards, where the cattle, in a panic, bellowed in the barns, threatening to break loose. The eternally stupid chickens, their crests swollen with blood, became hysterical in a delirium of goo. And in the streets the dogs were like sea lions barking at the epicenter of the earthquake until Papa ordered them to be quiet. They only obeyed Papa's voice. But not just them. The land, the house, and the cursed wind also stopped moving — and then the night became a silent empty tunnel that put out all the sobbing. Soon after, Mama would come around, always very pregnant, a crazy female, and she would start to pray to a saint whose name it was a sin to invoke in vain. It was a being without a name and a face. But they said he was the patron of sleep, of peace, of the baptismal smile of God, and the Father of parents, godparents, and even priests. And that was happiness.

Even though it was hard for him from that side of the road to reconcile the sight of the mountains with the landscape of that tumultuous sea of snakes and haystacks distant from the coast, the great memory of the Island still was clear and euphoric in front of his eyes. He had admitted from the first moment that the long hand of time had changed many of the old things in his absence, but not the residual way that some endured, becoming part of the landscape. With the exception of the forests and the coastal promontories and the stone superimposed on the walls dividing the land, the whole Island was changed into a misty landscape of clove and rye, in the middle of which emerged, as the wind blew, the shapes of cows and horses at pasture. Dogs with reddish backs and standing on their hind legs perfectly sculptured in the cold sheltered themselves near the dunes, and Rui Zinho thought that they were the exact same animals from long ago, with their narrow haunches and immobile snouts. As for the goats and the sheep, they reminded him of winged, possibly mechanical creatures, riding the swift clouds. An unmistakable supernatural mist, coiling up from the dead craters, came down from the highlands. It navigated through the fissure of the valleys that were like ships or great wrecked galleons, and filled the early afternoons with an ammonia-like smell.

But in the places where in the old days corollas of clouds had hovered over the highest mountains, there were still the mountains — very high, perpetual, and twisted like stone dogs sitting in water. And where before the wind had been, and the sea was oblique, and the boats passed with inclined keels, full of happy people in tears going to America — there were still the wind cars, the boats, and flocks of very white gulls planing around the masts. Laden with rain, the same clouds that twenty-five years ago rolled from north to south in search of other seas where the fickle wind would take them. And since they never crossed the mountains, they had opted, finally, to remain in that low sky. They confused themselves with gods that sleep and breathe and are always in a state of levitation.

There was still the same oblique deficit of water around the earth. Just as when he was a boy, the volcanoes were still extinct. The fog was obsessive. And the very air, coming from the bottom of the craters, became a vegetal mud, as amphibian as the pasture grasses. And between this eternally white sea and the passing wind, in the places where before there had existed lands surrounded by walls or sheltered by the reeds and fields of corn and beets, vineyards, and orchards — he saw that the wind and the sea continued to coexist, but not the corn or the beets. Also gone from the landscape were the orchards, the vineyards, the haystacks, and the manure beaten by the hoe.

The Island, no longer the place he remembered, seemed to him to be full of exceptions. The blossoms of the hydrangeas would never be as blue. The green poplars had never changed color, he thought, because autumn didn't come there. There was just the sick torpor of the humidity that idled in the crypts of incense and poplars, giving him back the memory of the timid world of long ago. In his childhood it rained for ninety-nine consecutive days. The walls of the house became covered with a slime of lichen that bloomed into nests of mildew. And Grand Mama's porous bones seemed to crackle with rheumatism.

In the known past of the writer Rui Zinho, all these facts flew around in the ether of fantasy. He had never known how to explain why humidity increased the weight of the grass, the tabuga stalks, and the sweet potato plants. It wasn't clear why he had traveled so far propagating the myth of the whales. However, deep down, he had just been an Island boy. His adult body had revived the impossible poetry and the memories and passions of the boy who had left there one day only to become lost and consumed by the world.

"Dissolved," he thought, "as voluble as a salt bird. Or like a ship of birds disappearing in this sky of eternal clouds and rain . . ."

When the cowhands stopped to look at the twisting and somewhat tortuous progress of the passenger bus, watching it slide off the road, as always happened, on the tight curves of the coast, one could see that the faces were bronzed by the salt in the acid air that also corroded their bones and teeth. In spite of being consumed in the fire of a new way of life, they were the same as they were in his childhood. They had not even aged; their faces had just changed.

Sitting next to the window, he tried to personify in himself the dream of this return to Rozário. It didn't and would never have the importance of the myth of the return to the perfect origin of Man. It was just a possibly definitive return after twenty-five years of absence. It wasn't a resurrection. He had left from a ship dock. He was back in a sublimated, nonexistent world. Mentally he enumerates: the pumpkins and melons, corn and beets, the wheat fields and the rows of beans and lupines. There were also the plantations with their dark soil. The mothers of fruits: plums and guavas. He noted everything that had changed. He was no more than a man suspended, as if hanging between two different landscapes. And in the great delta of this difference survive just the habits and the names. There were immutable forms: the pointed body of the birds, the powder of yellow chalk that the sun spread on the seaside roads, the fearsome night of the trees. The experience of childhood told him that the acacias and the cedars thrived in the stream banks because there the humus was fertile and had the color of coal ash. In the old days, those trees cried when they were being killed by handsaws and then were dragged to the flatlands by yoked oxen that moved the harvest with their tongues hanging out. Threads of glue dripping from their open mouths spun foamy webs, pockets of exhaustion that exploded with the contact with the sun.

"Many, many times," he thought "I was the yoked ox, the pack mule, and the dog barking after the cows. And I was the party balloon, and the bird, I was the offense and the punishment, and the felled tree, and then a bird again . . ."

At this point the bus approached the sloping lowlands of Rozário. Sitting in the same seat as twenty-five years ago, in the same coach that made daily runs between Ponta Delgada and Nordeste, in the morning and sometimes at night. Squeezed between the Bakelite and the hips of an unknown maternal body, on whose lap the newest little angel was sleeping. He put up with the quick glances of the old women. It was a careful stare through deep, tearing eyes. They had been observing him during the entire trip. But the cedar faces of the old women, in the few moments that Rui Zinho had the courage to return their gaze, crumpled up even more and evaded the encounter and the recognition.

"Old women are alike everywhere in the world," he thought.

He had met women like them in several countries, at the doors of churches, on garden benches, picking through the garbage containers in Lisbon; they were standing, almost blind, in the streets of London and Amsterdam. They were lying down on the shelves of people in the stations of the Paris Metro. In Zagorsk, at the doors of the ancient sanctuaries of the czars and the emirs, the same old women were there. They spoke in a strange way, their hands outstretched, and they had the religious stubbornness of forbidden women. In Vancouver, Boston, and Toronto, many of them had given up being old. They skittered like rats under the shadows of the neon lights, the showcases of sex shops, and sleepy men, swaying next to the old ladies, the paradox of lost generations. Like all the old women of the world, they wore mourning and they were not in mourning. They were bent over like owls, and their bodies had nocturnal arms, shoulders, and bones. Just the eyes, blowing like embers in the depths of the darkness, had lit up to observe him during the trip.

A few sleepy men, swaying next to the old ladies, would sometimes half open their red eyes, seeming to criticize the indiscretion that fixed the lips of the old ladies to the sides of their mouths. They all had graying and unshaven beards and their hats were pulled down over their eyes. From the way they looked at him, they must have been casting on the stranger all of the experience of their suspicions. Perhaps it was an American who was unusually thin, a mid-level official on a trip to the provinces, or certainly someone studying to be a priest, because he had forgotten to look at the world without shyness. The discreet elegance of that middle-aged man, his smooth hands, the city skin of his face made the old men think that he could possibly be a man from that place, however he would be a wandering man full of the vain and obscure afflictions suffered by all who wander far from their people.

He doesn't remember any of the faces. But judging from the way they looked at him, he deduced that they must be people from his childhood. What stuck in his memory of that time were their gestures, the rough leather shoes, the hats black with rust and the eight-day-old beards that preceded Sunday mass and the tub bath in the middle of the kitchen.

He knew what he had done returning to Rozário, but he didn't know how much time he would spend seeking forgetfulness of his suffering. Life had changed in a perhaps definitive way, emptied of the presence and love of those who had been able to explain it until then. However he hadn't come to remake himself. Elephants would wander when they gave up, having lost the trail of the females and the young and the memory of the landscapes and the rivers. At forty-six, he might not have the age or the reason of the elephants, but he is not free to fall into the well of surrender. After so much time, it was also certain that almost everyone had decided to move far away from Rozário. This is why he didn't have illusions about who might have stayed behind. Returning just happened to him, in this downcast and grim way, like the owls that like the dark craters of tree trunks, abandoned mills, and houses in ruins. The others, if they returned, exhibited the dazzling wealth of Canadian dollars, gold teeth that studded their civilized smiles from the State of Massachusetts, and the health of the pensions of the Province of Ontario. They also brought a dignity that was different from his because they brought objects invented to have no function on the Island, they spoke with a caustic American accent saying *shut up* and *sonofagun* and drank *biah* instead of the black beer of the Azores.

He understood in fact that he was a man without a generation on the Island. The boys of his time had been taken by the Americans and by distant cities — big, frightening metropolises that devoured shiploads of happy people with tears in their voices, the memory of their dead, the white and always begging letters of the living who remained on the Island. They would have produced hybrid children who also began to procreate — and so the warm sun of his eyes, the heat of corn in his blood, the nectar of the bees on the Island were things of the past. Perhaps they were birds, with names of other birds, the voices that Rui Zinho thought he heard. From the Canadian correspondence exchanged with his older cousins, he had memorized a paragraph that confirmed the distance, the precocious and final disconnect between his life and the life of the entire family: *I know you are my uncle, but I can't remember your face. I haven't seen you for a long time, and nobody here knows anything about your life . . .*

The old people remained unchanged, the ageless cowhands, the goats and cows standing in the fog. And also the luminous rain, the wet sun from long ago, and the pallor of the concave stars that had then formed constellations in that darkened sky, that was so low that it seemed to inhibit our breathing. He was very young when he had picked up and headed to Lisbon. And it was dark. The cries of Mama and his older brothers and sisters crossed time and made that farewell perpetual. The time of growing up had passed. The years of study. The first jobs, the passion for books. And a great love that had failed. Everything had passed, consumed by his hunger. And now he happened to return, without glory or riches, just tired, and wanting to revisit the places, the gates rusted by the rain, the fallen walls of the properties of the Canadian new rich, in sum the nothingness of a life of many lost battles, dreamed but never won. The small and always decrepit bridge over the Salga creek — and suddenly, ironically, the vision of the great bridge over the Tejo, in Lisbon. And following up the Tejo to the city of Lisbon, the silent shipwreck next to Marta, the only one to whom he had belonged completely in a whole life of women. He remembered with pain her wounded voice, with pain, the bright smile that countless times she had given him and been hurt, and the lost notion of her lost body. A dog that suffers, he thought, is just a dog that suffers. It barks silently, twists its snout to the wind, and nobody will hear him. Marta isn't present. The time of metaphysical dogs is passed. And it's no use to bark at the waves of the sea that is so distant from the seas of Lisbon . . .

The bus went around the last patch of woods, before going over the bridge of the Salga creek. On this side there was a kind of ditch with beeches and ginger lilies, and banks of ferns, great old acacias whose roots sank into the mud to the sound of water. Around those places, besides the legends about the existence of hooded phantoms, sorcerers, and the horned little man they had given the name of the Devil, José-Maria had conquered the body and the spirit of Maria-Água, before deciding to take off with her around the world. However, the thought, this story, isn't part of the mythological catalogue of the province. It was just a fantasy of his, and it dated after his childhood: he had archived it in a half dozen pages in one of his favorite books. In a little while, after the vehicle had made it up to the heights of Caminho Novo, he could finally see Rozário — it was certainly languid and rusty with its run-down houses, eroded by the humidity. The only interesting thing, he thought, will be to confront reality with fiction. To see, for example, if the houses and streets coincide with the descriptions that he had given them in his books. If in the middle of this last ramp of almost a kilometer long, the ironsmith's shop is still there on the flank of the road to the Feteiras lands — or if this erroneous geography exists only in the pages of a novel. If in the memory of places and their old names, before arriving at the square with the milk stand, there was still the house where supposedly the administrator Cadete had been hanged, on an invented night of his childhood. And since the bus stop, in the old days, was right in front of that imagined house, he suddenly had the hope of hearing the braying of those suffering from worms and other intestinal disorders — as before he had heard them cry and moan, imploring the mercy or miracle of his big hands as a horse gelder.

Nothing was true, and everything, however, had possibly happened during his absence. The writer Rui Zinho had given up on Literature and his anxious opinion pieces in the Lisbon papers — since this entire universe of conjecture and fantasy didn't protect the failed philosopher from a litigious, stupid divorce, or from the letting go of imaginary worlds. He was astonished that his dream of living from his madness had vanished. He had lost his boys, his house, the heavily sleeping woman who suffered from insomnia. Then he had lost himself in the lesser women who come along when men are lonely; they were generally women who laughed a lot. When they were intimate, they touched him just to believe they existed. The myth mongers would believe that writers make love more eruditely, without the ludicrous pumping of their buttocks, or the gross words and especially that dog bark when they finish. The project of a forever postponed suicide had stopped becoming his last hope, because death was difficult, it demanded another kind of courage and was known to be cold. When he sought it, it turned out to be as stupid as the stone that statues of writers are made of. That's why he lost a motive for everything. Since he didn't even feel tiredness, rest was superfluous. He came here because he had given up. His father had died of prostate cancer in Canada; his mother had died of lymphatic cancer, also in Canada; his brothers and sisters could die one day of cancer, because they were in Canada. And because of the cancer and the absence of all of them, the only thing waiting for him was a deserted house, inherited from those two cancers, abandoned for years and with closed doors and windows — without bottles of whisky, dishes, or books. He didn't intend to be buried in it, but he came to take shelter in its walls. He was forty-six; he had published a dozen books. And even so, in middle age, he felt the approach of a long twilight, the vague disease of being alive without the others, and not even being able to point to a single friend. Without peers and family, who could be waiting for him, if he had never been close to anyone? His old aunts? The already misshapen women cousins, married and with children, or the male cousins who had gone to police school? He had never believed in the good will of his aunts. If anything could still seduce him, it was just the impulse of that other primordial call: this birthplace, the carillon of the mornings on the sea, so different from the hell of Lisbon. It had been always and just there, not any other place. He carried in his ear the strong hoofbeats of the mares. The cries of the animals. The groaning of the wine presses in summer evenings. The smell of dust, hot manure, and the wheat beard. The corn, the grapes. The breathing of the black nights. The velvet of the fig trees laden with figs bitten by the birds. The whisper of the doves that took flight very early and then rested like the birds, slowly and softly over the happiness of the children. The stench of the dung and the earth, on the eve of the sowing. The stumbling of the drunks at the shop doors: they drank cachaça, started fights for no reason, and winter was always in their alienated voices. The sun of Sunday mass. The sulphur of the air poisoned by dead whales. The passing of boats lying low in the water full of happy people in tears, headed to the America of their dreams — before America had taken all the others. The Atlantic deafness of Father Governo in his phosphorescent bones, now in repose in the Largo cemetery. The eternity of a man of fourteen generations that he had given a biblical name: he was called João Lázaro, he had been a beggar, he had cured the parasites with a look, he had died and been resuscitated, transfigured and eternal, to announce to all of us another time: progress and knowledge, the practical science of the people — and finally he had been taken by the marines. The light irony of Father Ângelo, the New Priest, regarding the deicides of his books. The incomparable silence of silence. The hurt. The desert of the sea with water and the desert of the water without the sea. The unbearable weight of Papa's hands that many, excessive, times beat him senseless and who had died of cancer in Canada — and a certain time, in Lisbon, that had made him cry as never before, on the day that for the first and only time he had seen him cry, as he said, saying good-bye forever:

"Son, my son! Forgive your father. Forgive me for everything, son, because you won't see me again!"

2

"THE WORST OF HOUSES," HE THINKS, "ARE YOUR OWN HOUSES." NOT BECAUSE THEY ARE SMALL, DIRT POOR, OR EVEN OBVIOUS IN THEIR EMBARRASSMENT AT BEING SMALL,

but it's the silence, the way they become a living tomb. Seen from the street, they stand out in your memory, as if from their depths shine not just the eyes but the bones of their inhabitants. The vision of those basalt walls, even though they were what he expected, deliver to him the silent nakedness of those bodies that lie there and live out their time. They are sitting men with rigid necks, old women with trembling mouths, and sometimes children who seem to have been buried alive with their grandparents.

"The worst thing about these houses," thinks Rui Zinho as he steps back from the half opened windows, "is they are empty of the people who left. They are so empty that you can hear a death drum in the footsteps that echo in them..."

Although they are still standing, they seem like solid ruins; they are small, immemorial temples crossed by the experience of voices that still talk and slip through the time that resists the age of the houses. They are, however, boxed ruins, still venerating the presence of the primitive owners. Some of the doors and windows were carved by his father. And this fact became acutely present in the spirit of the writer Rui Zinho. In truth, nothing there belonged to him, with the exception of his parents' house. But if one day Rozário had been flooded or razed by an earthquake, his father's life would still have its share in the shipwreck. Different from things that rest in museums, these creations of his father remained alive in their function, without being dislocated by time.

However, the real difference between the houses of today and the ones from his childhood were not obvious. This had happened separately, without reciprocal knowledge, to him and the homes. The first time he looked at them he had the immediate sensation that an old and diffuse equilibrium had been upset. He had left very young, when they had seemed majestic, proud as temples that forbade his presence. Now, in addition to being squat and dark, they seem hollow, stripped of everything he imagined existed inside them.

He doesn't know how to describe them. He experiences it. Rising two meters from the ground, they stand in gutters covered with tufts of grass and nettles, with the eaves a few centimeters from his head. If he wanted to, he could hang from the black roof tiles and soar over the second reality of these sad houses. He could be the hero of his own childhood, and he would become this with the madness of one who no longer fears the disapproval and punishment of the dead.

In this precise moment, doves with open wings, light and fiery, cross the muggy early afternoon sunlight. He follows them with his eyes. He sees them disappear in the distance in their phosphorescent flocks. They alight on abandoned lands, over the trees of young forests, and possibly over the sea that is the immense blue destination of the white doves. And once again thrown into the bowline of the air, they return to the center coming from south to north. Now they circle the little clouds lost in space, clouds that seem to be bowed by wind carts of which they are the wheels, the rims, and the axel heads. Then they fly over the new houses of the immigrants who have returned, houses with American ideas and shapes: the wrap-around porches, the low walls surrounding them to iron gates that open up to big interior spaces. America is in some of their plastic flowers, the round windows, in the bell jars that hang and clang in the wind, and especially in the striped flags with a blue square of immense stars.

"They are the same doves," he thinks. "They are as old as my absence: twenty-five years or the ephemeral lifetime of birds, their hollow bones, their withered feathers. But not the time of these American houses."

He had to admit that the existential poetry had dissipated. He was a man with a few memories but with few and tired emotions. The weight of life had filled his forty-six years with a new science, that of displacing his passions, ecstasy, and useless sentiments — those sweet clocks of his childhood.

Rua Direita was there. The surprise comes from the fact that it is deserted, with the walls from the old days at the back of the gardens. The stones support the roots of the same fig trees. The same cane fences divide and close in the same orchards, along the houses or behind them. It's strange that there are no children making noise, or dogs sniffing at the bitches, or roosters pecking at the insects in the ditches. With a suitcase in each hand, jacket over my shoulders, here I am walking home, to my childhood home.

"It's the worst moment of my life. I have the perfect awareness that I'm not dreaming. And I'm not alive or dead. I am just between everything and nothing of something that doesn't exist."

It must be siesta time; the muggy air had lowered the curtains, closed the wooden shutters of all the houses. The flies were big like winged dogs that had come to bark in his ear. He tries to look carefully at the houses, their locked, colorless gates, the same front doors. The difference was in the paving stones that now substituted the gravel roads from before. The horse and cow dung dried in the humid sun of the Northeast with a green swarm of flies in the center of piles that had been stepped on by their hooves. If a car came by, the wheels would make a squirting sound; the tire treads would be impressed in the golden mass. The rest were larvae, and the ostentatious, oblivious flies.

How could I have written books about all of this? How could I glorify flies, houses, dead people, women, men, and nonexistent priests, and then call them the books about my life?

In other times, when herds of wild steers that hadn't been castrated by gelder Cadete would come by, a convoy of combat cars made the foundations shake. There was the natural blindness of the calves, the shouts of the cowherds, and the shiny fat of the horses — and the hot smell of oxen that filled the feast days of childhood and the death of Rua Direita. It was still the time of the exceptional richness of animals.

There were no longer the men sitting against the walls of the Canto da Fonte, waiting for day work to fertilize land, prune vines, dig up the beets, the flax, or the wheat, or to hoe rows of corn. Their hand-rolled cigarettes didn't exist, or their unshaven beards. Or their bare feet, flat and thick as clay lids, or the tense faces that looked into the distance and smelled rain in the wind. There wasn't a mister Joãozinho do Canto, sitting on a kitchen stool, enjoying his American retirement and complaining of rheumatism. He clearly remembers his walrus torso bent over his cane, and his red face and wormy skin feigning the contentment and illusory happiness of sick rich people. The days of Mr. Joãozinho were long and boring next to the men who were waiting for the landowners. He absolutely needed their company, to be able to speak to them in a voice that mixed up Lisbon Portuguese, the flutes of the people of Algarvia, and a few American sounds: *tanquiu, sonababiche, foquiui, sharape*. His laughter rippled down him in short but vigorous cascades, and shook his double chin, revealing gold teeth on rosy gums. For hours and hours the men allowed him to repeat the incredible stories of the Land of America, which alluded to the odyssey of the construction of the railroads across the plains of the north — but they couldn't imagine either the tracks or the fiery cars they gave the name of trains. Fascinated, they heard the story of the cold, the dock work, the whips, and the iron fittings on the steers on the great American farms. To listen to him in silence, the children always were given caramel treats, chewing gum, and hard sugar candy in the form of lozenges that he liked to throw in the air to see who could catch them first.

There was, in the squabbles of these famished roosters, the greed and covetousness of people who had no sugar, or honey, or the bees swarming around a lily that might smile at them.

"It's really incredible that, in spite of the absence of the American walrus, nothing has changed here. Or perhaps the evil of change is in me..."

There were same stone front steps with two stairs that were broken or attached together by cement, the same yellow, white, or pink façades, all of them trimmed with blue or brown borders around the windows and doors. He had seen them in Alentejo, in Minho, in the northeast of Brazil, in the films of Glauber Rocha, or described in the books of Jorge Amado. The houses were covered with the same patina of rusty paints, looking melancholy in their old age; plaster debris was starting to curl up and down the siding and filling the gables with multitudes of mollusks; and the same fat gray worms left slime on the walls and moved to the corners with such amazing slowness that they reminded one of eternity. And the doors were stubbornly closed, the curtains dangling behind the shades, in the sacred and profane silence of the interior of each one of the houses...

He put his suitcases down and shifted his jacket to his other shoulder. He was in front of Rua Direita. At the top, the Padrão das Almas, raised over the Canto public fountain, continued to attest to the proven lack of talent for architecture. Father Governo had ordered it to be inlaid with a panel of tiles depicting the terrifying images of his sermons about Purgatory. The merciful arms of the angels opened in an invitation to pardon, over the bodies being toasted over the brassieres, and the eyes of the penitent were both supplicating and pensive. Sarcastic demons with two pointy horns, the Devils of Gil Vicente, stuck forks into the backs of the damned. The same legend of forty years ago, dating from this construction, continued to remind passers-by that they should pause and pray an Our Father and an Ave Maria for the saintly souls.

Two minutes from there, he had already caught sight of the house that belonged to him and his brothers and sisters. It was the incomparably unique house of his parents. It was longer than he had imagined: the big vertical red doors almost looked like palace gates. It embarrassed him to be the owner of this kind of rustic manor that seemed to come out of a novel by Júlio Dinis. At that precise moment he felt he had been recognized. Doors and windows opened behind him as he passed by the houses, and old women with teary eyes lifted their necks, peered at him, and let a name painstakingly escape their lips. Then half-naked children appeared, and very fat women whose youth was confused with the sadness of conjugal disappointments, since their mouths, in addition to being cold, drooped at the edges. From one instant to the next, there were multitudes of eyes and faces looking at him, and Rui Zinho thought he saw them communicating with each other. He even imagined that those hidden mouths were speculating inside and outside of the houses about a man who was known and unknown, about his look that was between discreet and distinguished but whose pallor seemed to contrast with the age and the strength of his blue eyes.

It had never happened, in fact, that at four thirty in the afternoon a man in a tie would walk by with a jacket on his shoulder and a suitcase in each hand. It had never happened that someone would walk to the house that had been abandoned and without an owner for so long — that was supposed to belong not to the living but to the disturbed spirits of their dead. And because nothing like this had ever occurred, it frightened them that a man had suddenly stopped in front of the wine-colored door with its opaque glass panes. They saw him put his bags down, straighten his aching back, search for a key in his jacket pocket, walk up the steps, and start to explore the secrets and mysteries of the house. Since he did it standing very straight and with a wrinkled brow, they thought it prudent not to confuse him with the dead but with those who had lived there in the silence of the living.

3

AT FIRST, THE SOUND OF THE LATCH SOUNDS LIKE CHAINS SLIDING IN THE SYSTEM OF MINUSCULE WHEELS, MOVING OR OSCILLATING IN THE RUSTY LOCK.

And since this bite seems to crush a strange body, one hears the sound of rusty bones breaking apart in splinters. He supposed that the dust of the filings had squirted out of that rusty chest. The eggs of crawling insects, spiderwebs, humidity, and granules of old steel made it difficult to turn the key.

It hadn't crossed his mind to go to the Azores to break down the door of a house that would belong to him one day, then had stopped being his, and would finally be returned to him as an inheritance. If necessary, he would force one of the windows, the most common form of invading the prohibited space of temples. He had other alternatives besides this: he could jump the back wall, make a path through the cane fence at the bottom of the garden, or even knock down, with the force of his shoulders, one of the barn gates. He didn't know if there were neighbors, or if they were the same ones, the ones in the house down the street where in the old days there had lived a tribe of grimy, noisy people as prolific as gypsies. In the time of the seminary, when he came home for the big holidays, Nuno was always introduced to the new sons-in-laws of the people down the street. The house bore the growing traffic of those sons-in-laws who were forever leaving for America. For every grandson that was born, the eyes of the old people filled with clouds, and it was almost sad to see how they would move into a corner to leave room at the table for them, or to go to the fireplace to fetch an ember for their cigarettes and not have the voice to shut up that unfortunate tribe.

This had to be done exclusively by him, without the knowledge of his neighbors. It was a personal challenge. He wanted to feel the effect of this encounter of the present with the past of the house. He wanted to feel deeply the sensation of limbo and memory, with the second childhood of the house. To be the owner of it now was sufficiently exceptional to merit this ceremony. He started by imagining the progressive possession of each of its objects. The flower boxes once full of vases of dwarf ferns and begonias had stopped being simply flower boxes. The family portraits, once hung on the whitewashed walls, over the brown border that matched the tile floors of the hallway, would no longer be family portraits but perhaps a plankton with webs of dead spiders and clumps of dead insects. The low, oppressive ceiling, made of cedar beams, that Papa had varnished during the remodeling of the house, were starting to rot. In the end Nuno's lawyer might have dropped his shoulders in resignation, not believing that this little professor from Lisbon would be up to repairing the damage and reconstructing the ruins of that temple without an owner. For Rui Zinho, however, the house was himself, but in the first person singular. He knew that one day he would come not to inhabit it, but to live in it. For the first time in his life he gave himself the reward of this postponed space, with its mystical sea from long ago, an ocean sky constantly being swept by the movement of the fairies in strange clouds, and the certainty that there, one couldn't worry about how time was passing. If the time and desire to create returned to him, he might be a happy writer. The divided assets after the divorce from Marta, and the honest punctuality of the publisher of his twelve books assured him the comfort of this first opportunity at leisure. Perhaps he could live this way indefinitely, feeding from himself and his submerged roots. He was feeling a relative state of grace, knowing that he was wanted. Every new book of his meant a kind of exhale in the breathing he did for others: the next would be the thirteenth. He wasn't connected to the readers by even a basic sense of respect: he knew them to be frivolous, cheap, and ritualistic. Readers as stupid as his could hardly be those of other writers.

When the door groaned under the impulse of his knee, just barely opening, the surprises started. There were not even the family portraits on the walls. Just stuck hinges, a last groaning of the iron fittings, and the almost total absence of light. There were no begonias or the bland smiles in photos. The tiles on the hall floor had been covered by a type of lichen, and weeds were poking through the cracks. Pushed by the force of his knee, the door groaned and its opaque glass tinkled onto the floor because the caulking had disintegrated. Then he was presented with the oppressive, tormented, and exceptional spectacle of a house that had been closed for a long time and consumed by neglect.

Instead of the window boxes and the portraits, in the place where he thought he would find those smiles and the varnished wood, he was faced with the unbearable chaos of a greenhouse of weeds, sludge, pockets of humidity, and hanging sheets. He quickly closed himself inside, to flee the first curious looks. Then, his body lurched, vacillating in the shadows, as if someone had stabbed him. It would be difficult to stand the sight of these ruins: the funereal flowers of the humidity, the scattering of the rats inside the roof beams, the smell of mildew, and the spots of mold that indicated the walls and furniture were rotting. In front of him, as if to mock him, swung shrouds of cobwebs, enchanted spiders, translucent and the color of tin, feeling the threat of his presence, moved their antennae and started to sidle away. From the deep cracks in the once perfectly stuccoed walls poked tufts of pale weeds. Other garlands of cobwebs hung from the chandeliers without lamps and the dirty electrical wires. The smell of rot, which he didn't remember, was unbearable.

He dragged his suitcases to the front room. The dust had buried the furniture completely — these were unknown to him — the mirrors and the big wall clock that had come into the family a half century ago and later, when he was absent. For a moment he was disappointed not to see the frames with certificates of marriage, the baptisms of his parents' first grandchildren, and the fat and open smiles of the latest brides in the family. He also didn't see the chests that had once displayed flower arrangements, embroideries, clay objects, and creations of his father that he had never explained. He didn't recognize a single of the relics that in his memory perhaps dated from the last visit to Rozário twenty-five years ago. That was the time when he was courting Marta, and both had come for the family blessing of their marriage, commemorated with glasses of passion fruit liquor, new wine, and cookies baked in Mama's wood oven. He had exhibited Marta like the most precious luxury object. She was the future mother of his children, and he had taken her to the Azores — he recognized this now — so she would be venerated by the family monarch and praised by his mother. He knew right away that his brothers had become fascinated with her presence and beauty. Her hazel eyes, with their mix of green and brown, her slender wrists and abundant hair that he adored made her a woman who was at once robust and fragile. It was enough for his younger brothers to fall in love with her. Her magnificent smile would always be, for each one of them, the exact model of the perfect way to smile, because it reminded him of nights of eternal nuptials, infinite pleasures, and an imperishable purpose for her nakedness. He knew now that the Marta of that time had been above all the image or illusion of his own triumph: through her, the family had learned that Nuno had not just found the right love but his independence and the strength of a destiny that didn't need the favors and protection of that house.

Instead of the things he had hoped to find there intact, he was presented with the solitude and disgrace of that diffuse memory, divided between reality and the ruins of the house. But looking at the glass ashtrays, he didn't know why he should believe in the desecration of that dead temple, whose walls were still standing, as dead as the stairs, the windows, and the mirrors. Stubbs of cigars and recent ashes filled the ashtrays, showing proof of that invasion. Astonished, he saw newspapers spread on the floor from the month before, yellowed papers containing drafts of texts, empty beer bottles, and brown wrapping paper. Some of his books were also there, with their spines cracked and their pages yellowed and dirty with ashes. The cardboard of the covers had been bent, and they were creased and smudged with fingerprints and ink. He opened them one by one. There was the unmistakable handwriting of his inscriptions to his parents and siblings, in invariably weak sentences that limited themselves to lamenting from far away the indeclinable sweetness and tenderness of this useless ritual. On the back cover of one of them was a photo of him in a studious pose. With a shiver he recognized its erratic and pretentious look, the ugliness of a frightened face and his false modesty and that of all the other writers of his country.

"They are certainly the worst books in the world," he thought, and he believed it sincerely. He had suspected it for the past twenty years. But only now, seeing that his parents and siblings had not wanted to take them with them to Canada, he was able to confess this. When all was said and done, he'd been read by thousands of anonymous people, had received the echoes of their absurd passions, but never the recognition of the people he wrote them for. And a writer who isn't read by a single person of his tribe will always be the worst and most useless of all writers in the world.

He picked up one of the crumpled pieces of paper from the floor and confronted a hurried handwriting that was attempting to express the political worries of the Opposition regarding the "insubordination" and the "despotism" of the Autonomous Government of the Azores. He also realized that this scribbled note was appealing to disengaged voters and misguided believers, calling for the dismissal and defeat of those who didn't have the morals or the talent to govern. He concluded that his childhood home had been used as the den for these mediocre, unnamed political nutcases! He clenched his teeth, feeling a surge of rage take hold of his muscles. When this happened, he felt himself levitate, and he lost his awareness of his body. It seemed that his anger emptied out his muscles, taking them by force, paralyzing him in the midst of an inner turmoil that was more moral than physical. Stupefied, trembling with rage, and suddenly stripped of mental energy, he was left without his usual strength. Other surprises, however, awaited him. In the room next to the living room, the big double bed showed signs of having been used. Just then the anger that had softened his muscles shook his body. He felt the unmistakable surge of his blood moving from inside to out, from his nerves to the pores of his skin. Because it was in this bed that he and Marta had celebrated their second honeymoon, that in spite of being extinct, had become eternal in both their hearts. They had made love to the sound of horse hooves leaving in the dawn for the pastures; to the sound of the Atlantic Cory's shearwaters that pierced the night of the lovers and whose cries startled Marta; to the piercing sound of the first roosters crowing in the morning, the tolling of the bells, the rustling of the fig trees in front of the house — so that he saw in all of this the dissolution of life in the origins and in the future of his man. He recalled losing him in the confrontation of this world that was so near and so private, thinking that he would never deserve even one of its memories. He forced himself to promise him the spirit of this little rustic world, certain that only in this way would Nuno belong to him for the rest of his life.

"Promise me you'll be mine forever, love. And that if you ever stop belonging to me the way you do now, you won't lose what we have right now. Promise?"

He promised her everything because Marta's body and her life force were both physical and at the same time almost supernatural. Her smell was like the waters in the streams, the humid scent of the grass, the roots of the yams and the leaves of the beech trees and ginger lilies. It wasn't even difficult to associate her breath with the perfume of the beeches and the laurels, the taste of peaches and guavas. But especially there was the mysterious smell of water that came from her body and the streams that had once crossed the forests and orchards — and this more than anything obliged him to confess to her:

"How can I forget you, love, if you are my childhood?"

Then Marta couldn't resist. She embraced him furiously, laughing and crying, biting the lips of her man and pressing the body of her boy to her breast and she said, "Nobody has ever said anything so beautiful to me. There isn't and will never be a woman happier than I."

So that the defilement of the bed was above all the defilement of the water of the streams and the fruits he had admired in the life and body of his wife. To give an outlet to his rage he went to the window and opened the wooden shades. The light spilled over the big bed, returned to him the vision of the faces that were spying on him from outside, dying with curiosity, faces that retreated in shame and then dispersed. He then opened the dresser drawers and the night tables and felt the dust billow up from them. He was beside himself, in a mood to drive out the crowd on the street. When he opened the armoire, his father's clothes fell at his feet, deboned, without the nature or the energy of that little iron man who had sworn he would return from Canada but succumbed to the invisible curse of cancer. His mother's light blouses and dresses also fell down, and a strong smell of moth balls spread out through the room. Nuno saw this sulphur cloud rise over the glass bell jar, with the baroque image of Christ Our Lord of Miracles, the oil lamps, and the music box of the Statue of Liberty. In the old days he'd wind it up and listen to the heroic melodies that would come out of it. Before discovering that this was the American national anthem, it seemed to him as sublime as the music bands that would come to Rozário to lighten the festivities, church fairs, and processions. But this had been in the time that the ugliest and most atrocious saints passed through the province, on their litters. Now his tenderness for these objects was very different. The rickety chairs seemed to be collapsing with fatigue in the corners of the room. The oil lamps on the night tables had no wicks; sad, useless, they were corroding along with everything else in the place.

In the kitchen he immediately recognized the long table where the family would take meals, which was shoved against the wall under the china cabinets. In another time they held great loaves of corn bread piled on trays. Now there were just big bowls, well-used tureens, and rusty cutlery. Long, low benches surrounded the table on the side of the back door. And from the wall, supported by slats, came the same poplar slab where the children sat. Next to it, was the baking table, where the clay bowls, the casseroles, and the round pots were stored. When Nuno opened the dusty curtain, the same panicked cockroaches scuttled away by the dozens — and their shells were the same as before, smooth and shiny as aluminum. The unbreathable smell of humidity rotting the air still hung over everything. So he opened the door to the yard. The light showed him the surprise of the small improvements to the house: the old wood stove had been replaced by an electric one, but it was crusted with rust. There was a refrigerator. The tiny heater had been covered by a rusty dust, streaked from top to bottom on one of its sides. Finally there was a big television covered by a calico cloth that was straining against its elastic bands.

He went out to the back and saw that the house had been enlarged on both sides of the kitchen. His father, on his return from his first stay in Canada, had brought with him the progress of mansions with bathrooms and two kitchens. The wood stove had received the benefits of science that had solved the problems of exhaust fumes. The primitive kitchen crossbeams were no longer in sight, because the house had been covered with suspended ceilings that were the product of lathe and varnish, imported from memory from the Canadian houses. Nuno's second discovery was the plumbing in the bathrooms. In Marta's time the toilet was a kind of bowl, unwieldy and deep as a trench, and over it was a thunderous flushing mechanism. There was no bathtub. Now instead of those primitive fixtures, there is modern plumbing, pink bathroom fixtures and sinks operated with a pedal, and a perfectly functional bathtub: two spigots that mix hot and cold water, an electric showerhead, porcelain shells for soap, and a bidet. In addition, the tiles were a discreet tone of lavender, and there were two racks for towels and washcloths. So the defilers of the temple had gotten there as well. The toilet had become a petri dish for larvae, and the acid smell of urine and cigarette ashes was recent. For a minute Nuno felt a kind of panic with the sensation of discovering the ghosts, the voices, and the putrefied bones of the house. He ran to the yard and looked for the shed where the water tank was located. It was filled with a rotten liquid that had been water but that now looked like a green soup; he calmed himself down with the realization that he could empty it, clean it, and bring in fresh water.

He went to the hall and tried the fuse box; immediately the electricity lit up the dust particles, the spiderwebs, and the stains on the wall. Then he discovered the gas cylinders between the wood piles under the storeroom. He couldn't escape a sensation of relief at these hard-won, late-civilizing additions to his childhood home. He suddenly got a burst of unexpected energy. He opened the security valve of the tank. Contrary to what he expected, the water surged into the obstructed pipes, overcame their resistance, and burst into the sink. In the bathroom he watched the dissolution of the waste and the worms, and he saw the clumps of dirt dissolve and the sandy stones disappear down the toilet. The weeds, born of the mold, the pollen, and airborne seeds, started to come apart, and they couldn't survive the torrents that Nuno's hand commanded from above, as if bombarding a weak enemy. If he had come back five years later, he thought, these weeds would be bushes, and they would be climbing the walls and pushing out of the roof tiles.

He climbed to the second floor on a narrow ladder, and this was done by Rui Zinho in memory of Nuno when he was twelve; he had come to Rozário on vacation and had worked the whole month of August on the house repairs, hoisting the joists, nailing the beams, and tiling the roof. There were two rooms divided by a partition. He had to climb down to avoid the bulge of a beam of tropical wood hewn with an ax and then smoothed with the plane and sandpaper. Beds of wrought iron, the same of childhood, jutted out in the narrow, chaotic cubicles filled with chests, improvised wardrobes, and dressers inherited from the grandparents. Everything had been covered with the bedspreads, sheets, and linen coverlets that Mama had produced on Aunt Olímpia's loom. When he bumped into one of the chests, he was face to face with Marta's eyes in a rusted frame. For a moment he had the illusion of meeting her again. The photo was of their wedding, in front of the door of the Conservatory, and Rui Zinho, better than Nuno, saw in it the passage of time, the effects of age and life, but not the sunset of the passion that still explained Nuno's fascination for Marta and hers for him. In the photo, he was still a timid young man of military age, with a shaved head, and his trembling hand was holding a white glove. Next to him, her arm in his, Marta's smile was a stark contrast to his insecurity. Her mouth was opened like an edible rose. She presented herself as wonderfully white and resolute, crowned like the goddess of fertility — and it's still like this that Rui Zinho projects her into Nuno's spirit. Magnificent, almost superior, she is looking mischievously at the fragility and the impossible shyness of her man. Nuno picks up the frame and tries to remove the photo from the white stains of mildew that stick it to the frame. Marta's face rips into two pieces; half of her smile remains stuck and the other peels off from her mutilated face. As for Nuno's body, it remains intact beside the destroyed relic. The one who had been his wife loses for the second time the beauty of her youth and her love.

"Look, paradise!" thinks Rui Zinho for Nuno, before seeing him tear the picture first vertically then horizontally. "What happened to our white moons, love?" says Nuno to himself. "What will become of you in his absence?" thinks Rui Zinho, substituting Marta's voice.

"Days and days," imagines Zinho, whom she answers from afar. "Days and nights, and more nights than days. I got distracted, I'm lost, love. I let my bird fly away, and now I don't know which sky guides it. Just that."

This and no other will be his angel, writes Rui Zinho; the good thing about angels is that they survive men who condemn themselves to be destroyed. Now it's about a wounded dog, his yowl is confused with the yelps of a man who can't stand looking at himself in the mirror. And it's always in front of a mirror that loneliness pits a man against himself.

He left in a hurry. He was starting to feel suffocated by the low ceiling, the beams, the forms of the great chests forgotten in the corners. He was especially disturbed by the presence of his mother in every object. Again in the yard he saw the afternoon lingering, as in the beginning, suspended by cloud castles. But the solitude of the house was not in this continuous natural time. Missing were the pregnant sows rooting in the chicken shit. And the mottled hens, the mare that would kick suddenly, the cows plagued by flies, the sad tame castrated steers who someone had deprived of the joy of females, the roosters, and the rats, and all the absences that suddenly explained or would never explain the primitive solitude of his childhood home.

Walking by the gate that separated the yard from the orchard, there was the corn bin, supported by six cement pillars. The dovecots were still there. But the biggest surprise was to see, over the grimy roof of the granary bin, the same proud doves from before. At first they seemed like stone birds, immobile, suspicious, as if they were sculptures. When he approached, they became frightened, opened their wings and flew away. What had made those birds stay for so many years, near an abandoned house? Rui Zinho will write what Nuno can't understand right now: the doves don't belong either to the memory or the houses of people. They live in time, they fly or are still in it, and they can't be subject to any place. There weren't any nests in their secret, arched shelters, reinforcing the idea that perhaps they were more imaginary than real. In a little while he saw them come back, land on the roofs around, and approach cautiously, as if taking the pulse of their own safety. Nuno experienced a sensation of great tenderness for those blue creatures, the color of certain fish, so beautiful and majestic, as if made of glass or porcelain.

"In a certain way," the thought, they are the spirit of the house. They live for it."

He walked around the granary, pushed away a branch of the old fig tree, and what he saw then made him turn white as a sheet. In fact the entire land of the vegetable garden, which extended to the cane hedge, was cultivated. He saw the onion bulbs, the cabbage, the bean stalks, and the parsley. On the opposite side, near the wall, were the flower beds, the picked pumpkins, and a pile of squash. He had already taken the decision to terminate the lawyer's services. During all these years he had paid his services and fees punctually, responded to his confusing, self-contradictory letters. He wasn't in the mood to forgive him these betrayals. He knew in fact that he didn't need to do much. All he had to do was take away his keys, cancel his powers of attorney, and retaliate with ruining his reputation — because there had never been in Rozário a worse affront than to suggest that someone was corrupt. Robbing one's neighbor or profaning his good name was always the most condemned of all sins and one that suggested the most severe penances. And that's what he'd do.

He went into the stables and climbed up to the loft in the barn. This was the last stronghold of the house, and Rui Zinho felt all the discomfort of the dark passage. Nuno stopped for an instant to examine his father's woodworking shop. For Rui Zinho that man was buried exactly in this place, in the dust of the tools, the cobwebs around them like shrouds, the adze, the planes, and the saw, in rust that was beginning to crumble the workbench. Nuno shivered, because he saw again his crowlike figure covered with wood dust. He wasn't a man who had been hanged or crucified, but he was the same taciturn figure, rough with the chisel and the puncturing irons, especially in the disorder of all these work tools. He tripped on the dark stairs that creaked, and he was afraid. In fact, he had tripped many times in the dark: his father was always present there, his voice extremely angry, the threat of the whip that was close at hand, the insults, and his great impatience for everything. So that he would run and palpate the darkness, feeling that persecuting presence nearby. At the top of the stairs he immediately saw Grand Mama Botelho's big bed, with the double straw mattress, the workmanship of the painted iron frame now a dirty white, and big pillows without pillowcases. To the side, leaning against the wall, a bulging chest had all its locks bent and the top was half open under the pressure of the blankets stored inside it. In the opposite corner was the ancient sewing machine of his mother; its formica coverings had come loose, and it was sad to pass his hands over the iron wheel and feel everything rough, grimy, and lifeless. Mama had arranged everything with the method and intention of someone who doesn't know how to separate themselves from them. Thus there were pictures of suffering saints on the rough walls, a rosary suspended from the neck of the Crucified Jesus of Nazareth King of the Jews, a religious calendar, a veil she wore to mass — and all of this attested to a temporary absence, not a good-bye for life and for death. Nuno knew she had left the house arranged for her return from Canada, with the illusion of being far and near everything, as they had told him in Lisbon. Contrary to his father, who always wanted to die and be buried on his land, she was fascinated at the chance to live in an immense country where the houses, the land, and the people were different. She liked Canada, she said, because it was the country of her children, of the plains, the *estoas, stores,* and the *safueis, safeways*; it was the prodigious country of Christmas industries, gardens with manicured grass and rose beds around the mansions: so that if an impulse of dreams of progress attracted her from so far away, it wasn't less true that it was hard for her to witness the pain with which her husband separated from his world. In Zinho's opinion, Nuno's mother belonged to the number of those creatures who were tormented by the longing for the future. If one day he could invent a fable about this mysterious woman, he would have to impute to her an existence divided between the love for her husband and a strange and perhaps enigmatic passion for the destiny of her children.

He had seen everything. He had gone through every corner and revived his own memory of the house. Now he had the sensation of having come not from the city of Lisbon but from all cities lost in time. He had not, however, entered this house nor was he back in the Azores: he had opened the family tomb, washed their bones, and was going to bury himself next to them. In truth he had stopped being alive from the moment he was kicked out of his house and Marta's and the boys' lives. Living like that, as if on the edge of a cliff, feeling his feet slip and his roots break, only happened to him in dreams. It was impossible that this would happen now, to him, Nuno, and was really his life. In Rui Zinho's books, this happened to others. The worst is that Nuno only now admitted that he was finally living one of the stories invented by his double. But his naïveté rested in thinking that Rui Zinho would always be just a pseudonym. That's when everything gets inverted: Zinho is the premonition of Nuno, his bad side, and Nuno is made to live twice, suffering in fiction and in life. Never had any book been so hard for Rui Zinho to write as this one. And it's a fact that writing and living in the first person is like dying in one dimension and not knowing what will follow.

4

AND HERE
THEY ARE, THE LAST
WOMEN OF THE FAMILY:
VERY OLD, WHITE, AND AT LEAST AS
NOXIOUS AS THEIR BLACK MOURNING GARB.

When they parade in front of him, the aunts first look like decrepit bodies, blond and too solemn in their distant posture. Nuno can't anticipate the first expression of criticism in their eyes. In fact, he thinks, this can't be the same nephew as the one from the other, so distant visits to the island. The nephew from that time announced months ahead the exact day when the boat would dock, bus timetable, the desire and longing for fresh fish and rice pudding. So that since they were in front of an almost stranger, they have a hard time accepting the fact that the first signs of old age are showing in his gray, sparse hair, the slump of his shoulders, and everything that contrasts with his elegance, his long, nervous hands and the rosy tone of his skin, which hardly disguises the pallor of his smile. They especially don't know how to decipher the strange serenity of those blue eyes, around which the first crow's feet are starting to show. Then there is still the mouth, which seems slackened by the shadows of his wrinkles. The aunts look at him in an astonished silence, before getting used to the almost haughty sadness of that crestfallen countenance.

Nuno stood up. He doesn't know yet if it's enough to bow in their direction or if he'll have to open his arms and press each of the short bodies to his chest. In the old days one would ask their blessing. It was the custom to kiss their hands and asked them to petition God to bless their nephews. He couldn't question the totemic value of this custom: in front of the group is the woman who had always directed the family circus, in moments of crisis, in carrying out cyclical traditions and rituals. It was the unmistakable Aunt Horácia who was now advancing with open arms her head tilted. She comes to press him to a breast as flat as a board; she has the bony thinness that makes her look like his father. Without resistance, he receives a trembling, almost weak embrace, but he considers it to be deathlike as much because of the smell as the cold of the black clothes. Besides this, he sees again in his aunt's silence the same absence of emotion that characterized his father's embraces. Her kisses, light and humid, came from a toothless mouth and suggest the cold blue of a corpse. During the infinite time of that embrace, the circus stands around, as if in formation, waiting for the disenchantment of masks or music that will make the sequins sparkle. The next moment, when her voice starts to chastise him and reduce him to soft scolding, and to remember her brother, all the others start to cry. Frightened, the children of these women seem dumbstruck. They try to hide their faces and defend themselves from his gaze, behind the skirts of their mothers and grandmothers. Nuno doesn't want to respond to these cries. He knows that they bring to him their role of official family mourners, but not the pain that had tormented his life. Besides this, his father had died almost ten years ago and his mother more than five; there wasn't a shadow of conviction in the pain of these sisters-in-laws, sisters, and nieces of his parents. If they did it for him, it would be even more insulting; nothing and no one was dead inside him. Even if it weren't so, none of those aunts would have any moral right over a single one of his sorrows. He had been very far away all these years, in a different and totally unknown existence. He had never belonged to the sentiments, the vices, the tender or austere gestures of those timid little aunts in mourning, and he didn't know anything about their lives for lack of news from them.

"Oh, my nephew," suddenly lamented Aunt Horácia, in front of the timidity and complacency of the others. "You are so thin, so wasted, my dear! What happened to you in that Lisbon life, Lord of my soul!"

In response to this volley, Nuno limits himself to opening his arms in a sign of truce. But her lightly bearded chin starts to tremble as if in a sudden onset of Parkinson's. Her wooden body seems to creak to the sound of this lament. Her oily, thinning hair falls like moribund eels over the bones of her shoulders. An inconceivable and almost immemorial old age has spread on that singed face a multitude of wrinkles, like a shroud. The tiny brown eyes shine behind invisible tears. The nose is pointed and impetuous. And her hands tremble so hard that her body obeys their oscillations. Nuno doesn't have any doubts: he is facing his ancestors. They are as remote as the wind that brought him here to their disinterred skeletons, the same wind that would take them back to their errant nests and to the places where death exists or is announced.

She wasn't and had never been his favorite aunt. She had the small detail of looking too much like his father. Her very smile was tyrannical. Like him she had beaten her children, acquiring lands with money tied up in a handkerchief or hidden deep in drawers. With her ambitions she had enslaved a man with a gauzelike body, asthmatic and abulic, who had the bad luck to marry her. Like his father, she had been involved in arguments her whole life, cut relations with almost all her brothers and sisters, and engaged in futile and inappropriate disputes over inheritances. In her old woman's taciturn satanic energy, there had always coexisted the matriarchal tyranny of conflicting land leases, trampling the fragility of that witless man, and punishing her daughters with harsh lessons. Besides, Nuno remembered her not at all feminine habit of biting her tongue. The memory of these discords crosses not only his childhood but a part of Rozário's recent history. Poor Uncle Jaime had learned to beg that devilish mare for pardon, modesty, and respect — and he had always done it barefoot, ragged, wearing a cotton jacket from year to year until it was ten years old, his pants up to his calves, and his felt hat that was so worn it had lost its color and made him look like a beggar. The misery of that man was given to the dresses of his daughters, the patent leather shoes of his sons, the gray shawls of his empress — beside the labor with the hoe, the rains that soaked him to the bone, and the sons that burned him under the brim of a straw hat. "Just like us, under the command and mood of Papa," he thinks.

The perfect contrast of this prosperous and impetuous woman could be seen in the inverted mirror of Aunt Sonia. Besides being skeletal, she had no will of her own, and she had gotten the reputation of being slow-witted. She mixed up her words, saying *sawim* instead of *swim*, she cursed a lot and mixed up peoples' names. In Nuno's opinion she had always been old and sick and starving, and she wandered from street to street hidden in her shawl, with the stumbling gait of a drunk and a blank stare. She was young but prematurely old when she married a dark, oblique man, burned from rust, hunger, and drink. Among the many bizarre jobs that Uncle Zacarias did, the ones of coal dealer and chimney sweep stood out. But since destiny had taken this man far away from everyone very early, Nuno wasn't really sure he existed. They said that American prostitutes covered his trail, while letters with dollars came less frequently, and for that reason Aunt Sonia got lost in the streets again, very old, fighting off the dogs and the boys with a rod. At that time, he remembers, it always seemed to be the lunch or dinner hours. She made up a weak excuse, a message without content and for nobody, and his father, even though he detested her, would order her:

"Sit down and have something to eat; maybe that will shut you up."

Tia Sonia would obey immediately; it was impressive to see her suck up the plates of roasted squash, lick the bottom of the bowls, burp, and become as chatty as an alcoholic, and then she stood up. She would assume the voice of the poverty she wasn't ashamed of to confess that she was hungry, and she left that hateful table that was never set for her and would say:

"Thanks be to God, I have been well fed. Now I'll leave. Zacarias might be returning from the big country America, and could come in the door any time."

Aunt Esperança hugs him next, without saying anything, as had happened during Nuno's childhood. Now he is especially impressed by the listless eyes that are so myopic that the lenses of her glasses look like the bottoms of bottles. He can't recall the frog in her voice, or the thunder and furious vitality of her womb: it dated from the remote time of her breaking relations with his parents. For this reason Nuno is surprised to find her here. But since their death had intervened, he accepts it as the justification and perhaps pardon of this presence.

Aunt Urânia and Aunt Mercés completed the family genealogy since the rest had died of unnamed illnesses and the youngest had immigrated a long time ago to Brazil. None of Papa's brothers were there, who had been involved in the middle of the disputes, the least obscure of which dated from the time the estate was divided. As for the rest, the wandering bachelor Uncle Sebastião, who was almost a dwarf, had become a pariah, as much for his decrepitude as for his laziness. Nuno had always known him by the sharp cough when he heard him return in the early hours of the morning from gambling in the taverns and from his infamous homosexual orgies. He still remembers the tiny teeth, black from lead, and the thick gums, pink as the pulp of a melon, besides the unforgettable bare feet that were flat as plates.

On his mother's side, there were numerous people absent, both from the living and from Rozário. The uncles had been taken by the great wave of immigration to Toronto, Vancouver, and Boston, following the eruption of Capelinhos volcano. Aunt Flórida had died of asphyxiation, victim of double pneumonia, if he was remembering correctly, or maybe it was cancer, as had happened to Grand Papa Botelho. The memory of these two deaths was as remote as the bright cloud of his early childhood. Left were Aunt Olímpia and Aunt América. Nuno discovers them in the timid smiles that peek out from behind the group. Both look a lot like Mama, now more than ever, and this moves him. Aunt América is almost as big as her strange name, however she is docile and peaceful. Her big boa constrictor arms encircle him and squeeze him hard. He feels like he's drowning in the mass of those breasts, in their pumpkin-like mounds, in the inconceivable volume of those breasts, and he remembers the wart on her round nose, the blue, mischievous eyes that laugh in the middle of a tragedy and seem to mock those with morbid temperaments. She had married late, almost in despair, the inventor Herculano, who had won all the bets with life. Taken by the fever of machines, he had discovered by intuition the secrets of clocks, engines, and other simple or complex mechanical devices. After learning about machines, he started to invent things: the threshing machine for wheat and beets, a rudimentary threshing machine operated by a crank, the plow with three tilting iron shafts, and the manual mill. Popular imagination also attributed to him the theories of solids, liquids, and gasses, the principles of compression, vacuum, and gravity, the study of the origin of fire, air, and water and the very chemical composition of the earth. Also according to the people, to him was also owed the invention of electricity, because of his Aeolian experiments, the design of the first generator, and the project of capturing the ineffable energy of the wind. But since the government didn't bother to answer him, he didn't register his patents, stopped inventing, and went back to his beloved watches. At the same time he started to draw caricatures. First he captured his wife's mischievous smile, even those she had never posed for him. Then he caricatured and drew the faces of priests, singers, politicians, and scientists of renown — and the walls of the hall of his house filled like the galleries of museums. Whoever visited him, as happened with Nuno on holidays from the seminary, he showed off his monsters, embellishing them with descriptive adjectives:

"Here we have the cuckold Salazar; there is the gangster Hitler, over there the despot Stalin. At the end, the great statesmen of our times: Kennedy, Churchill, de Gaulle, Tito, and Afonso Costa. The others, I know who they are, but I can't remember their names."

And finally here is Aunt Olímpia. She is the fattest, the most tormented by varicose veins and cardiac problems, but she is without doubt the treasure of all family tenderness. She went mad from eclampsia in her fifth childbirth, the only time that the perpetual smile of this tenderness was erased from her face. When Mama gave birth or was sick, she came to cook the chicken soup, boil up the milkwort tea, sweep the house, and make the beds. She knew, better than anyone, how to sweeten the disappointments of her nieces and nephews, visiting on Sundays, after mass, before going up to Burguete. Now the permanence of the smile is suddenly mixed with tears, and her eyes turn sea blue, almond-like and suffering. She embraces him with passion, as if those were not her hands but Mama's bones, and he knows that this body keeps for him a kind of intelligence comparable to maternal love and clarity.

"Rest, because I'll be here to take care of you, nephew," she says. And after taking his face in her hands, she studies him, pats his head, and adds: "You have a big wound in those eyes, son of my own soul."

"A great wound in those eyes," repeats Nuno. Possibly he has never heard anything wiser and more right about himself. A wound or a simple pain in his eyes, that's what could well define everything that is left of a man, his lost world, and a present time that still has to be invented. Just for this reason, it had been worthwhile to come back to that house in the Azores.

BOOK ZERO

Wise

Happiness

I can be here, facing the sea of the Azores and next to Marta and my sons, in the time when I am still happy in Lisbon, and I also peruse the fiction of it all: places, moons, the invention of every movement, or the pendulum that oscillates between fantasy and life. I can even be sitting from the beginning, as much on the first page of a book as on a crag on the tip of the Island. Facing North, which is where the damned winds come from and move the clouds, and also from where the illusion comes to me of never having followed anything but my own shadow.

That was my biggest mistake: to think I could live in the first person and at the same time be others, Nuno and Rui Zinho, the feminine plural of the five sisters I don't know if I met and also the gender and number of the vicissitudes of Luís, Jorge, and Mário. All, in truth, persist like a kaleidoscope of a single color. I love them equally — as I do this wide sea, the silence of my childhood home, and that which explains in me the fascination for the temples in this church of Rozário.

I love the Lisbon of many noises, the flat avenues on Sunday mornings, and the suburbs where I became a character of a daily life that never assumed a real dimension or even the fiction of a Portuguese destiny. In Lisbon, I limited myself to a discreet difference, to the second childhood that wouldn't be eternal or would ever contemplate this seascape anymore, with its cane hedges bordering hilly vineyards and lining roads that always went in the direction of the coastal rocks and mills moved by streams that come from the mountains. I listened to the impossible silences of the time of Lisbon: that of extinct birds, the permanence of everything in the Azorean landscape from where I was never absent or excluded. The sublime side of my happiness consists in fact in a kind of magic that brings me near to the gods and confers on me the power to invert the order, to opt to refuse the time that might not have happened in any place on Earth.

I also know that reality doesn't belong to the artifice or the accomplishment or the fantasy of books. Being here now means the end of this game. It might be that I was born of a night of love in my parents' bed. It could be that nobody has died and that old aunts are not the last women of the Island and the family. Papa and Mama smile at me again and prepare to receive me into their happy home. They kiss their grandsons, how big and beautiful they are! They embrace their daughter-in-law, who continues to be "perfect" and to have the virtue of explaining the happiness of their son. Then come my brothers and sisters: we were never and soon we will not be haggling about inheritances and shares. The house, the lands, and the orchards continue to belong to life, the village, and the balance of this space of sea that it is impossible to divide and see dissolve. There are still boats that pass along the coast, too far away to be real. They are bound for strange destinations that we don't have to follow: may those who can, dream of us, those who haven't loved the flowers, the laughter of the children, the wisdom of old people sitting at their doors, and the innumerous gods who here bless the wheat, the milk, the honey, and the fruits. Luís returns now with the cows, as I always suspected: he opens his enormous arms and wraps us all in the same circular embrace. In a little while, when he wins over their shyness, he will make my two sons laugh until they cry from the humor of family secrets. Some of the uncles and aunts will be almost as young as they are: Zélia and Mário, the youngest, will enjoy playing with Diogo and Francisco, and I'll sit contentedly by Marta's side, telling her how good it was we married young and that our love has after all been a fairy tale whose epilogue will always allude to the beauty and existence of these two princes.

There is no possible truth in this return to the Island: I was on it and on all the boats. I loved it with a smile and in a dream, and for its poets and singers. If I suffered from some form of absence, it was just a time of enchantment, sleep, and mistakes. Secretly I lived it during the years when I sighed for the green of the poplars and the fig trees and for the conch shells of the sea that will always seem white as innocence and childhood.

I loved it in a woman who nobody ever met: perhaps an eternal virgin, an unreal fish or a mermaid who gave me her hands, spread her hair on my face and talked to me continuously about books, angels, and the little boats that travel between Faial and Pico. There was never anything more beautiful in life than to travel with her, that woman who was as ineffable as a fairy, and to her song and cries at the sight of the nine islands of the Azores. Between two acts of love, the woman put her hands on my sweaty body and said Come fetch me and take me with you forever. I said that wasn't possible, and then the woman started to suffer and beg: Live with me right here, love, in the space that goes from one island to another, where we will always have a house on the sea, with a yard and a library, where you will call me as many names as occur to you: Moon, Water, Swan, and above all Marta. And I will always be the mysterious, unmistakable smell of the water and the streams of your childhood, the breath of the clover and the humid, superior smile of the salt.

But if I separate from her, the look of this woman becomes as distant and superior as that of the serpent. She will become desperate. She will lift her eyes to the mountain in front of her, and I will have to hear her curse me: you will cry so much, love, that not even I will be able to save you. I didn't know how to deserve her, because a passion like this passes or slips away in a minute and reaches eternity. You can experience it as a promise or a fiction, but never like the primordial journey or the perfect origin.

I came to rebuild a boat and mend the holes, the wounds from its wrecks: where I described great Canadian houses on the shores of the Pacific, I will slowly raise up new walls that will surround gardens of azaleas, hydrangeas, asters, and agapanthus. It will be an unbearably real house: with mirrors, pictures of blue landscapes, and vases of daisies and hyacinths. The faces will follow me with the gaze along the corridors, even if they are immobile and frozen in the portraits. The parents will be in the middle and they will become just the grandparents of my children.

Of course I won't do without the presence of the doves: they and not others are my ever-present myths. They have been with me ever since Papa observed them, with his hands on his hips and a protective smile, forbidding Mama to wring their necks and then to stew them secretly, mixing them with the chicks. They were blue doves. Beautiful, anxious, and light as angels.

And where I described the ruin and shadow of these walls, I will build windows that will open to the morning sun. On the street, as in the old days, copper-colored horses will pass by, herds of steer with sawed off horns, dogs with low snouts sniffing the stones, clouds of flies, and women shouting at their children. It will be perhaps irresistible to write it all again, in the silence that will follow me.

And I still have to laugh at myself.

I still have to think that all of this wasn't anything more than a laugh that cries or a sob that laughs — and literature!

LUMIAR, AUGUST 20, 1988